# Were-Squatch Love In Oakridge

(Accidental Were Series Book 1)

*Angela A Foster*

Were-Squatch Love In Oakridge (Accidental Were Series, Book 1)

**Dedication:** This book is dedicated to my family and friends; I couldn't do what I do without your support and to all the friends who are like family. And to my friends in the MCL, you have all been very supportive, Thank you ALL! And a special THANKS to my model on the front cover, Destiny Logan, you are my Carrie and to Lucy Lou Roberts, her companion and Mongo stand in (my son Dakota and his wife Lindsay Roberts' Dog, my grand-fur baby).

**Disclaimer:** This is a work of fiction. Names, characters, some businesses, some places and some locales, and incidents are either the products of the author's imagination or used in a fictitious manner. That being said, Oakridge, Oregon along with any other towns mentioned in this book are real and true places. All Native American tribes in Oregon that have been mentioned are also real and true as well as.
Now, any resemblance to actual persons, living or dead, or actual events is purely coincidental.

Cover design by Angela Foster,
Human Model used on Cover photo is Destiny Logan,
Dog Model used on Cover photo is Lucy Lou (Moose) Roberts
Editing by Tina Stam and June Wyland

# Chapter 1

The story I am about to tell you is rather unbelievable and you might think it's a crazy tale but let me reassure you that I am on the level. This in about me and my adventure that I was always went to have, so let me introduce myself and fill you in on my life and how it is about to change forever.

My name is Carrie Randolph and this is my story, I'm am whopping 5'3", 135lbs. and yes I am a curvy girl that looks good looks good in a dress but being a bit of a tomboy, I prefer jeans. I have a little muscle on me from all the work I do outside as well as a nice tan, which is from the sun as much as it is from my Native American heritage, the Molalla Indian tribe. I have medium length curly-wavy strawberry-red head of hair with a little bit of an Irish temper which you would think I would have pale skin and a lot of freckles but I don't, I got the best of my Grandparents on my Mother's side so I am always tan.

I was born here in Oakridge, Oregon where I grew up. I am an only child but I make it up with a very large personality. I went all the way through school here with my two best friends and then went to Reno, Nevada to take some classes at UNR by myself for 2 years and then finished in Eugene at the U of O with my degree in forestry management last year that took me another 4 years. I have always loved the woods, lakes and mountains around Oakridge so much that I wanted to have a job that allowed me to be in them as much as possible.

I live at the edge of town in a nice little house not far from the homestead that I grew up on. It is a smallish two-bedroom house with some land. The outside of my house is rather cool, it looks like a rustic log cabin and you can't even tell how old it is because I take care of it. The old wood burning fireplace that has been converted into a pellet burning stove fed from a side chute, one of my Dad's inventions. It heats the whole house in the winter and I have a solar powered heat pump that I use for keeping the whole house cool in the summer. I love my little house that butts up to my Grandparents forestland it has been in the family for generations, since before it was even called Oakridge.

My dog Mongo is my 85lb. dark chocolate brown almost black pitbull with a little bit of white fur running under his chin and down his chest and on the tips of his toes. He is my buddy, my baby, my best friend, my service dog and my partner when I am working and he loves his large fenced in backyard. On the other side of the back fence is where I grow a garden every year and that of course is surrounded by deer fencing so I actually get to eat what I grow.

Now about my family, my Mom mostly looks like an older version of me except she is a little taller at 5'5" and weighs maybe a whole 105 lbs. soaking wet and she is also more statuesque than I would ever hope to be. Her curly-wavy strawberry-red hair is cut short to her shoulders because she works a lot in the kitchen but her brown eyes have that look like she can see into your soul if you lie, believe me we did not lie to Mom. She is always on an eating healthy kick even though she makes pizza for a living! She makes the veggie or vegan pizzas that my Dad refuses to make because his heritage thinks it's blasphemy to make a pizza without cheese.

My Dad is a whopping 5'10" and has half Irish and half Italian heritage that he loves to brag about in his pizzeria. He has dark reddish-auburn hair with hazel eyes and a personality that everyone wants to get to know. My Dad is the kind of guy that would give you his shirt if you needed it and he makes great pizza too. They both stay in shape and go hiking, fishing and hunting together whenever they can. They also love to go wild mushroom picking for the freshest mushrooms you will ever get on a pizza and the best tasting if you ask Mom.

My Parents live pretty much in the middle of town not far from the pizza parlor or pizzeria depending on whom is saying it, they also have a small place on the homestead that they hardly ever use anymore. They own the Bigfoot Pizza Parlor on Hwy 58 which is the main street that goes through town. Everyone loves that the pizzas are in the shape of a huge foot, which was made on accident for the first time by the way. They were just supposed to be huge pizzas and that was all but Dad, James was making one of the really big pizzas when Mom, Janet swooped in for a kiss seeing if she could get one in before the pizza dough Dad had tossed in the air could come back down. It came down on both of them and the design of the pizza dough when Dad set it back on the counter was a perfect Bigfoot shaped pizza. Mom and Dad were covered in flour and laughing but the result was perfect for the restaurant.

Now that you know a little about me, here is how my story starts. When I woke up this morning it felt like any other day. It was a nice spring day here in Oakridge, Oregon. I have my dog Mongo by my side and I getting up to start getting ready for my job which is my dream job working for the Oakridge Forest Service for the last 3 years and I am so lucky to have. I have a wonderful family and great friends that are like family, but you know I still felt like something was missing. I just figured a man would come along when it was time so I wasn't rushing into finding one. My life is pretty good but you know what they say, every day is an adventure and today would prove to not be ANY exception to the rule.

First of all, the day started as it did any other day. I got up and went potty in the bathroom and then I let my dog out to potty while I put his food in his dish. Then I got dressed in my usual forestry service uniform of jeans and a t-shirt under my light long sleeved shirt with the forest service logo on the sleeve, Johnny doesn't make us wear the official uniform unless we have to work with the public. But Mongo had to get his breakfast before I could do anything else. When I returned to the kitchen Mongo was just finishing his breakfast as I started the coffee pot I looked in the fridge to see what I would be eating and most likely sharing with Mongo.

I made scrambled eggs and toast to go with my chocolate macadamia nut coffee with caramel macchiato creamer. My breakfast was great but when I was almost finished, Mongo of course got one of my slices of toast and about a quarter of my eggs which he ate very quickly. You would think he was starving all the time. Anyway, that's when the phone rang it was my friend Amanda Guffery.

"Hey lady, what's going on? Isn't it early for you to be calling me?" I asked my friend since grade school. She was not an early riser and didn't usually call until the evening after I get home to talk about her and my days.

"I had to call you and tell you what was going on in town last night!" She said in a rush, she was very excited. Not much happens in this town especially at night.

"What's going on?" I asked as she started speaking before I finished talking.

"There was a News crew in town. They were talking to people down at the bar and asking how they felt about that Animal Channel's show coming to Oakridge this weekend! I didn't even know they were coming and I guess a lot of others didn't either by the responses they got." She was talking so fast that I think she never went to bed is why she was calling so early.

"I haven't been told about any Animal Channel's show coming into town. Which one and why are they here?" I asked getting a little excited myself.

"It's that show about the Sasquatch hunting! They are here to do a Sasquatch hunt to see if they can catch one." She said as if I should know.

"Really? There haven't been any creditable sightings in years. Why are they coming now?" I asked her because I knew that she would not leave the bar until after she got all the facts. Amanda was a fill in reporter for a News channel in Eugene and she also had her own Blog as well. She was a really good reporter.

"The reporter said that someone had sent in some cell phone video of one walking down by Waldo Lake! Since Oakridge has a history of Sasquatch activity they decided to start here and see if they couldn't get a local to take them out. You really should call your boss and ask about it!" Amanda was so excited and I knew this would be on her Blog a.s.a.p. as well.

"Why don't you call your boss at your News station and ask if they got the same information and then let me know, I will call Johnny in just a minute." I said as Mongo started for the front door. When he goes to the door, you know someone in out there. "I got to go Mongo says there is someone at the door. Call me back with whatever you find out. Talk to you later. Bye." I had just put my phone back in my pocket on my way to look out the front door when there was a knock on the door.

"Mongo! Sit! Stay!" Mongo always does what he is told; he is a very good boy. I looked out the door to find a small group of people and what looked like my boss Johnny Case in his official forestry uniform and looking all official, so I opened the door.

"Carrie, glad we caught you before you left for the office. May we come in?" Johnny asked as the group followed him up onto my porch. Johnny was not only my boss at the forest service but a friend as well. Mongo knew him well and he was a very friendly guy. He looked like a younger version of John Candy from the Great Outdoors movie from the 1980's. He was 6' 2", I won't even guess on his weight but he was a big guy and not all of it was fat either that man was strong when he needed to be. His blonde hair and wise blue eyes fit perfectly with his age of only 45. Johnny walked through the door and patted Mongo on the head. "Good morning Mongo. There are guests with me today." Mongo licked his hand and then stood and stepped back so everyone could walk in. Mongo was a very smart boy and I not only took him everywhere with me but he also worked with me as well.

"Good morning Johnny and guests. My name is Carrie and this is Mongo. Please present your hands as you walk by him and follow Johnny into the living room. Mongo is not aggressive but needs to greet each of you. Once you make it into the living room please find a place and take a seat." I said as about 6 people filed in saying hello to me and then putting their hands down in front of Mongo as they went. Mongo sniffed each in turn and even gave a couple of licks.

I closed the front door and followed behind everyone into my living room, which normally is pretty good sized for Mongo and I but with seven other people it was a little bit tight. I walked past Mongo and he followed me into the middle of the room. Johnny stood by the fireplace and everyone else sat on the couch, the overstuffed recliner in the corner and two guys grabbed two of my kitchen chairs. I stopped in front of Johnny and looked around at everyone. Mongo sat at my feet just in front of me and looked at everyone, kind of like he was sizing them up or something.

"So, you are probably wondering why we are here so early. And I know you and Mongo weren't due in for a little while yet but pour guests really wanted to meet you and wanted to be here when I made my request to you." Johnny was always a straight to the point kind of guy, but it seemed like he was going to ask me something that he knew I would not want to do.

"I don't know if you have heard yet but this is the group from the Animal Channel's show Bigfoot Getters. They are here to see if they can catch a Bigfoot and they would like the forestry services help and you were the only one out of the whole office here that grew up in these woods and they would really like your help. Before you answer," Johnny said as he saw the look of bewilderment on my face at this point. "It would strictly be your choice if you should choose to do this and you would be getting hazard pay as well as the perks of being with the crew." Johnny was telling me when what seemed like the lead guy stood up to talk to me as well.

"Carrie," he put his hand out for me to shake, "My name is Terrance Smith, you can call me Terry. I am the lead Bigfoot hunter and the guy in charge of the making of our show 'Bigfoot Getters' on the Animal Channel. We would like you to help us film our show this weekend. There are a few spots around here that are close to Oakridge as well as a few others like Waldo Lake that we would like you to guide us in these areas so that we may not only see a Bigfoot but also capture this Bigfoot. We know that your boss Johnny here is paying you for your service but we would also like to add an incentive to you leading us on this expedition. We will be having a catering crew during the days we are her, also we will provide you with a camp trailer of your own as well as a bonus if we do in fact capture the Bigfoot we are after. Now I know you are a forestry employee and that you can refuse this job if you wish. But let me ask you one thing, wouldn't you be upset if someone on the crew were hurt because we didn't have the proper guide and wouldn't it be easier to help us rather than have to come looking for us if we get lost out there?" This guy, I swear barely took a breath the whole time he was speaking and Mongo didn't like the way the guy kept ahold of my hand the whole time he was talking. I don't think Johnny did either.

Terrance Smith looked a lot like he was more used to the woods than making a show of any kind. He was at least 6 feet tall and his hair and beard reminded me of a mountain man but it wasn't scruffy though. His hair and beard were both a light salt and pepper and the light wrinkles around his eyes would prove that he spent a lot of time outdoors. But he was a little on the muscular side so you know he is an outdoors guy. He was wearing jeans and a light blue long sleeved dress shirt along with his hiking boots which looked like they had seen better days. His fast talking and not letting go of my hand the while he talked showed me he was a passionate person and was used to getting what he wanted. But Mongo made a little growling sound, which made Terry drop my hand and look around like he didn't know where it had come from. I just smiled.

"Okay, so let me get this straight and sum up what is going on here. First you guys are the 'Bigfoot Getters' from Animal Channel and you are here to have me guide you to the areas in the mountains so that you can capture a Bigfoot. Johnny will not only pay me but pay me hazard pay as well as you guys providing me with a camp trailer and food while we are checking all these places out that you want to go? Have I got that right?" I asked as I pet Mongo on the head.

"Yes Ma'am that is right." Terry said as he took a step back to be closer to his group.

"And did Johnny tell you that Mongo and I are a package deal, he is my partner?" I asked and looked at Johnny as well.

"Yes Ma'am he did and we will provide for him as well." Terry sat down in the recliner once again.

"Okay then. Mongo, adventure?" I said as our code word that we were going into the mountains to find something. Once Mongo hears this he first makes his rounds of the house making sure all entry points are clear and then he grabs his go bag that is a small basic saddle bags that he wears with his gear. Mongo was on it and ran through the house after stiffing everyone once again before he left the room. Once he brought back his saddle bags I looked at the room, everyone had watched everything that Mongo had done and they looked amazed.

"I guess Mongo thinks it a good idea to go with you guys." I said as Terry jumped out of his seat again.

"That is amazing! Okay, well I should probably introduce you to the group." Each member stood up as Terry introduced me to them. First guy on Terry's left that sat in one of my kitchen chairs. He was somewhere around 6' but he could have been shorter. Basic blonde hair and blue eyes and looked like he was fresh out of college.

"This is Jerry Gordon; he is our cameraman and a really good howler." I shook his hand and he smiled at me and then sat back down with a "Ma'am". Then it was the next kitchen chair guy.

"This is Harry McKenzie." He was a tall Scottish fellow with auburn red curly, wavy hair, blue-green eyes and a crooked smile. He was wearing some very tight fitting wrangler jeans that hugged his muscular legs and a t-shirt with a Sasquatch shadow on it that also hugged his muscular chest and arms. He had a camo jacket folded over his arm that looked like it might have been from Cabela's.

"He is our trapper and firearms expert." Terry said as Harry shook my hand and gave me a very nice smile.

"Are you a tracker as well Mr. McKenzie?" I had to ask just to hear him talk again.

"Yes Ma'am I am? Are you?" He said in his Scottish brogue accent and winked at me and still holding my hand. That accent alone made me melt.

"Yes, I am." I said and just before he let go of my hand he said, "And call me Harry, Ma'am, if you please." He smiled and I knew he was flirting with me.  Wow and he was hot too, he reminded me of Sam Heughan who plays Jaime Frasier in a show called Outlander.  Damn this guy could be his twin.  It should make good small talk later.

"Only if you call me Carrie, Harry." I said and I actually giggled a little.

The introductions went on from there and I couldn't tell you who was who, there was a Jeremy Gunther, Alvin Sonders, Patrick Jacobs, Henry James and every one of them called ma Ma'am.  I'm only 27 years old, am I really a Ma'am?

"But I have one condition though." I said as my brain defogged.  "My friend Trina Mathews is a large animal veterinarian and she has worked at a couple of zoos with the larger primates, I would like it if she came along as well.  She can bunk with me and Mongo and she grew up around her as well.  You can get her job qualifications and experience from her and then make up your mind if you like.  But if we find a Bigfoot I know I would feel much better if we had her along just in case it gets hurt, or if anyone gets hurt really." Everyone in the Getters group looked at each other and then back at Terry who then looked at Johnny and I.

"If I can get her resume and check her out today then we are good to go.  Tonight is the night before the full moon and I would like to be out at least to the first spot tonight before dark.   So if you could give her a call and see if she is available then we should be good to go." Terry was actually looking very happy and excited at this point.  He looked a little younger with an actual smile on his face.

"I will call her right now.  Where do Mongo and I meet you guys once I have my things packed and ready to go?" I asked Terry as well as Johnny.

"Everyone will be at the forestry office when you get there." Johnny said as everyone started getting up and filing out to the door.  They all said goodbye to me and to Mongo as they went.  Harry made sure to stop and say good bye to Mongo and then he squatted down and petted

12

him on the head saying good bye to him as well, interesting, very interesting.

Johnny was the last to go so I walked with him to the door. He looked happy and yet he also looked like he wasn't sure of something.

"Johnny is everything okay?" I asked as we both stopped just before the door.

"Yah, I'm glad you're doing this because it gives more exposure to our mountains as well as to the forest service but I also am a little worried about sending you out there with people that we don't know. Do you really think that they will be able to catch a Sasquatch?" Johnny asked me looking very worried. He knew the history of my family here in Oakridge. We were one of the first families to settle here. With my family owning a large amount of land out on the outer edge of town, as well as the stories my grandfather has told about the Sasquatch on our land. My Grandparents aren't going to be too happy with me when they find out what I would be doing this weekend. But I am there to keep people safe too.

"Yah, just don't tell my folks or my Grandparents. I will tell them when it's all over. And I don't know if we will find a Bigfoot or a Sasquatch and I don't really know if I want them to. But I will guide them so no one gets hurt or lost. That's all I can do. Grandpa George and Grandma May will not be very happy with me about this one." I said thinking about it now. Grandpa George and Grandma May Hunter have been here for a long time. Grandpa George's family can be traced back to his Native American roots with the Molalla Indian Tribe and Grandma May has some Siletz Native American and all the Irish you can handle as well as the fiery temper to boot.

"Are you going to be okay with this?" Johnny asked yet again.

"If I wasn't then I wouldn't be going Johnny. You better catch up to the crew and watch over them. Mongo and I will be there shortly and I think I will probably swing by and pick up Trina on the way after I give her a call. She's been after me for years to get back out in the woods for a

Sasquatch trip, I guess she gets one now." I said and Johnny headed out the door.

All this talk about my Grandparents got me to thinking about them.  Grandma was a classic beauty, she only stood 5'4" tall with light brown eyes that would turn almost black when she was pissed and she had long strawberry hair that was always in a braid or a double braid Indian style is what she called it.  She loved to cook and bake and sew which she taught my Mom and her sisters and she also taught me some.  But you also knew she meant business when she yelled, because she didn't do that often she said that's what kept her so young.

Grandpa is the easy going guy unless you piss him off, then its look out he may be in his early 70's like Grandma but people think he is in his 50's.  He is still 6'4" tall his black hair always in two braids and his eyes the darkest shade of brown you can get, but they were filled with wisdom and he is the basic strong and athletic Indian that you see in the movies.  He once played a small part in a John Wayne movie when he was little.  It was filmed right her in Oregon.  He's the one that taught my mother her tracking skills which she then taught my Dad when they were dating and then they both taught me as well as Grandpa.  We were definitely mountain people; we could survive anything out there.  There are so many plants and animals that you can eat to survive as well as the many mushrooms or fungi.

And then I started thinking about my fiend so I pulled out my phone and started dialing Trina.  She always answers on the second ring.

"What up girl?  Did you hear the newest?"  She was ready for gossip.

"Yes and I have news.  Are you ready for a Sasquatch adventure?" I had to pull the phone away from my ear as she screamed her excitement.  I knew she would go for it.

I spent the next 20 minutes filling her in on what I had just gone through and what the deal was.  She was printing off her resume as well as sending it to Johnny at the office so that the Bigfoot Getters Terry could have it quicker. As well as packing her bags and grabbing her equipment that she might need to go with us. I was also packing and by the time we got off the phone I was ready to go and pick her up. I took Mongo out potty one more time and then we loaded up into my forest green Toyota 4runner and headed to pick up Trina on our way to the office.

## **Chapter 2**

    Trina didn't live that far from my house. And I knew she was excited to go once I pulled into her wrap around driveway and she was already standing outside and ready to go. She was never ready to go on time unless she was the one making the schedule, but this time she was at the back of the 4runner ready to throw her bags in before I even had the window down. She was dressed in her favorite wrangler jeans and a pink camo t-shirt with her usual black fuzzy hooded ski jacket. I guess she was ready for an adventure after all, it made me smile. Mongo and I stayed in the 4runner while she threw everything in and ran to the passenger door and jumped in with a huge smile on her face. Mongo ruffed at her no more that she sat down.

    "Hey Mongo buddy! Are you ready to go in the mountains?" she said as she rubbed his head and then scratched his chest, something he absolutely loves when she does it. She's one of the few people I would ever leave Mongo with if I had too, he loves her. Mongo got super excited and licked her hand and did his little ruff dance, but he never left his seat. It was a special dog car seat that was somewhat like a dog bed but he could sit in it and see out the window as well while wearing his seatbelt.

    "I think he's as excited as you are!" I had to yell a little to get over the noises both Mongo and Trina were making.

    "I bet he is. A chance to go into the mountains with the Animal Channel's show and in style too, this is going to be fun, camping, catering, the mountains and guys not from around here." Trina was saying as she put on her seatbelt.

    "Did you and Scott brake up again? Why didn't you tell me?" I asked as we pulled out of her driveway and headed to the office.

    "Sorry, I hadn't gotten a chance to tell you yet because it just happened last night. And it is the last time too. He was down at the bar when the News crew showed up to interview people and some young girl was hanging all over him on camera. He was so drunk he didn't even remember. My Mom called to tell me to watch the News and there he was. So I figure it must be fate that his door is now closed and new guys in town mean another door opens, right?" Trina was in a very chipper mood to have just broken up but he obviously had it coming, this wasn't the first time he had cheated on her and pretended to forget.

"Well, there were a few cute guys that I met out of the Animal Channel's crew. Like this guy Harry, OMG he was so hot. You know that show we watch, 'Outlander' on Starz? Well he looks just like Jamie Frasier. And he flirted with me in front of everyone. Can you believe that?" I said as we started to pull into the parking lot of the forest service office where I work.

"And did Mongo like him?" Trina asked as she looked around at all the vehicles in the lot.

"Yes he did. I was surprised that he didn't have a problem with anyone on the crew that I met. Not even the Lead guy that is also the producer I think, he was a little shady but Mongo had no problem." I turned off the motor and Mongo whined a little because he wanted out, he loves coming to work.

"Wow, well I guess that's good. Look at all the vehicles! The trailers, SUV's, trucks and the food trucks! How many people did you meet?" Trina and I saw so many people just running around doing things; it was hard to figure out exactly what their jobs were.

We left her bags and equipment in the 4 runner and took mongo into the office to see what needed to be done and to get Trina to Terry so that we could get the okay for her to go with us. Then we could get her bags and ours out before we left. I would be using a forestry service truck since this was official business.

Once we got inside Mongo did his usual rounds to everyone in the office and then came back to me before Trina and I went into Johnny's office where he and Terry were talking and looking at Johnny's computer screen. They both smiled as the three of us walked in the door.

"Trina Matthews, I'm Terry. Glad to meet you." Terry said smiling as he walked around the desk to meet Trina and extended out his hand to shake hands with her. Trina's smile was just as big as Terry's.

"Terry, it's nice to meet you." Trina said while they shook hands.

"So Johnny here was showing me your resume and I have to tell you that you are totally perfect for this job. I was a little hesitant when Carrie suggested you but looking at your resume and your schooling, I am tempted to hire you full time." Terry said still holding onto Trina's hand. I could swear Trina blushed.

"Thank you, Terry. Large animals are my passion, when I was younger I wanted to be Diane Fossey. I didn't want to live with them but I wanted to make sure they were taking care of them. My parents took me to the Portland zoo every summer." Trina said as they finally stopped shaking hands.

"Yes, I understand. And then you went to work at the Portland zoo for a short time. Why did you leave may I ask?" Terry was totally not even seeing anyone else in the room. Johnny and I just looked at each other and then back to them. The two of them walked over to the couch under the window and sat down while they talked some more.

"I was only filling in while the primate veterinarian was out for maternity leave. Best 3 months of my life." Trina said then she got this weird look on her face.

"If we catch a Sasquatch, what are you going to do with it?" Trina asked.

"Well, first I know we will take care while trying to catch one. And secondly, I just want to prove to the world that they do exist so their medical condition is very important to me and to my crew. Bigfoot must stay alive and be in the best health possible. That's why I am asking you, Trina, would you like to work for me? The job is yours if you want it." Terry was so very serious and Trina was too. You would think he was hiring her for the CIA or something.

"Yes, I would love to work for you Terry.  This is going to be so much fun!  Oh wait what is the pay and do I get to stay with Carrie and get all the perks she and Mongo get too?"   She was asking as they both stood up.  They both looked so excited.

"We can talk about the salary in private and should be included as well.  Would you like to go and get a cup of coffee with me at the catering truck?"  Terry asked, I think this guy just might be smitten with Trina.  Now I really want to know how old he is.

"I would love to."  Trina said as the two of them just walked out the office door.  Johnny jumped out of his chair, he and I walked to the door to watch the two of them walk down the hall and out the door to the parking lot.

"What just happened?"  I asked Johnny as we both started shaking out heads.

"I don't have a clue.  Wait, isn't she dating Scott still?"  He asked as he rubbed Mongo on the head.  Mongo I guess wanted to see what we were looking at as well.

"Nope, they broke up last night.   He was cheating on her with a young girl at the bar last night and the News crew interviewed them about the Animal Channel's show coming to town.  Whole town saw him."  I said as we went back into Johnny's office since Terry and Trina had already left.

"Okay, onto business then."  Johnny said as he sat in his chair and I sat in the chair in front of his desk.

"Okay, Mongo and my bags as well as Trina's are in my 4runner.  Are there any special instructions that I need for this and what vehicle am I taking?"  I just wanted to get this part done so that we had time to get on the road depending on where they wanted to start first.  There are only so many places we can take the campers and the catering trucks that are also known Sasquatch areas.

"Well, all I was told to tell you is to take them where you think they need to be.  They do have three locations that they really want to get to.

They are not accessible by vehicle and they have GPS coordinates and we have all the information her at the office as well. You get to take out the new SUV." Johnny was saying as he stood and motioned for me to follow him. We walked into the outer office where the main maps and the locked key cabinet were. He opened it and pulled out the keys to Big Ben, the brand new mint green 2019 DODGE RAM Big Horn Lone Star 4x4 CREWCAB marked with the Oregon Forestry Service on the doors as well as the roof. I got to play with Big Ben! This trip just got so much better!

    Just after I had placed my bags and equipment into Big Ben I received a phone call from Amanda, crap I was going to call her but forgot.

    "Hey Amanda, guess what?" was how I answered the phone.

    "I have no time for guesses; Johnny just called me and filled me in on what you guys are doing. At least he thought to call me. Now I can say guess what?" She said as she giggled a little.

    "I'm sorry; my morning has been a constant roll since I got your phone call this morning. Okay what?" I said as I started to turn toward the office so that I could talk to Terry and get Trina loaded up along with Mongo. And that's when I saw her. Amanda was standing in front of the office door in full camo gear and looking like some model that was super fashionable in her camo. This girl could have been a model, but she was the next best thing, a news reporter. My mouth dropped open and Mongo popped out of the truck and at my side, he was never very far from me.

    "What are you doing here and why are you dressed like that?" I said as I hung up my phone and slid it back into my pocket while walking toward her. Mongo ran up and licked her hand she held out to him.

    "Johnny and Terry both agreed that it would be a good idea if I went along to give the expedition a little more legitimacy for when we find the Sasquatch. I get to hang out with you and Trina and were in the mountains with some really cute guys too. Isn't this amazing?" Amanda said as she and I met in the middle of the parking lot.

"Wow that is amazing. Well there is safety in numbers and I guess this way we can make sure this isn't a hoax or anything. Have you met everyone yet?" I asked as we turned and headed for the office with Mongo leading the way.

"Yes, Johnny and Terry made sure to introduce me to everyone. The camera guy was pretty nice. And did you meet Harry? Talk about hot and who he looks like!"

"Yes I know like Jaime Frasier and he sounds like him too with that Scottish accent." I interrupted her to say. Glad I'm not the only one that thought so.

"So, I guess you will be bunking with Trina, Mongo and I as well in the same trailer?" I said as I opened the door for her.

"Yup, that is the plan. Where do I put my stuff? I have everything that I need and my boss said that I could film with my phone and Jerry said I could use whatever footage I needed from him. Did I tell you he was cute?" Amanda said as we turned the corner at the end of the hall and found the crew and Johnny in the breakroom around the lunch table talking. Good thing she shut up just before we were heard.

As we walked in I saw that there were a few extra people that I hadn't met yet. I assumed that they were the catering crew and the people that helped move the trailers and equipment around from place to place. Johnny and Terry both stood and had Amanda and I take their chairs so that they could talk to everyone before we left, Mongo sat next to me on the floor listening, I swear this dog understood everything that was being said.

"Okay everyone. We will be leaving from here in about 20 minutes. Make sure everything is packed and ready to go in that time. We will have three additions to the crew; ladies please stand up when I call your names. First we have Carrie Randolph; she is with the forest service and will be leading us to all the places we will be investigating." I stood and gave a small wave.

"You will listen to her without question! Next we have Trina Mathews and she is our large primate veterinarian and if there are any accidents or injuries of any kind you will go to her." Trina stood and gave a little wave; she had been sitting next to Terry before he stood to talk so she was now sitting next to Amanda.

"And last but not least we have Amanda Guffery, she is a reporter with a well-known news channel out of Eugene and she will be recording as much as she can, if she has questions please answer them to the best of your ability. Please welcome her as well." Amanda stood and did her little wave as well.

"That being said the ladies will be in their own trailer by themselves so of off limits to all but them, am I clear!" Terry was looking as each of the crew and then winked at Trina.

"Are there any questions before we get started?" he asked as everyone started to shuffle a little know they had things to get done before we could leave.

"Yes, I wanted to know what the driving arrangements are?" Harry said as he stood, asking Terry and then looking at me.

"Well, I would say we should ride the way we usually do but since we are being led by Carrie here I think that maybe you should ride with her and Trina should ride with me and of course Amanda can either ride with Carrie or she can ride with the Jerry in the camera suv. What do you think Carrie? Trina? Amanda?" He looked at each of us. I looked at the ladies and they both shrugged their shoulders so I guess that is the go ahead, that they would like to be with the crew instead of Mongo and me.

"I don't see why not. I do want to remind everyone that the cell phone service out in the mountains is going to be super spotty so if there is anything important you need to say or do then you might want to take this time and get it done. How does your crew communicate when in the field?" I asked Terry. A few of the guys pulled their phones out and did what they needed to do rather quickly; they must be used to this.

"Well we have special walkie talkies for short distances between the crew and then if there is an emergency then we do have two satellite phones. We also have a satellite GPS that is very accurate and can find anyplace around the world, it's that good. What do you use in the field?" Terry asked me as well as Johnny.

"Each of our vehicles has a CB radio as well as a Sat phone along with the same GPS you have. Of course each of our people has their personal cell phone, but as Carrie explained the service is spotty at best." Johnny replied while I just nodded my head as confirmation.

"Well then I believe we are set. Guys you all know what needs to be done before we can head out so please attend to that. Ladies, please follow me and we will see where you should put your things. Your personal things can be placed into the trailer you are staying in if you would like to do that right now." Terry said as we three ladies and Mongo followed him out to the parking lot with Johnny, Harry and Jerry following us, the rest of the crew flew out of the breakroom as fast as they could to get their stuff done.

Trina and Terry grabbed her bags out of my 4runner and Jerry was already carrying Amanda's things from the office to what I would assume was the camera equipment suv. And then there was Harry who was carrying a large duffle as well as a few other things in his very strong arms. And the smile on his face, even though I could tell he was trying not to look at me while he was scanning the parking lot at everyone to double check what they were doing and trying to hide his smile I think. It made me smile too.

I headed to Big Ben and opened the back door and said, "Load up!" Mongo jumped into the truck and went straight to his seat. I fastened him in as Harry opened the passenger door and climbed in. Big Ben was, well big. I had to literally climb into him because 5'3" is not that tall. Harry didn't climb in like I did but it was still a climb for him as well being over 6' tall. He grinned as he tossed his bag and equipment into the back cab with Mongo. Once I got his seatbelt on him he leaned over and sniffed Harry's bag and gave a "harrumph" noise.

"You either have a cat or a female dog." I said as I backed out of the truck so that I could climb into the driver's seat.

"A female dog, her name is Daisy. She is a bluenose-brindle pitbull, so she is mostly white with the brindle brown on her bottom and tail but her tail has a white tip." Harry said as he patted Mongo on the head. "Mongo you would like her she loves the woods too."

"So does she go on your Sasquatch hunting trips with you guys?" I asked as I started the truck.

"She does sometimes but my Mum wanted to have some time with her, she says she is her furry granddaughter and likes to have her with her. She just lives in Veneta so Daisy isn't very far away." He said as he put on his seatbelt.

"That's cool. Did you grow up around here?" I asked as I put on my seatbelt and tried to ask without it sounding like I needed information.

"No, I grew up in Scotland, then a few years ago I decided to move to the States and I've been doing this Bigfoot hunting for some time now. So my Mum and Da' wanted to be close to where I was working and in the states so they moved to Veneta. My Da' Bob, passed a couple years ago just after my 28th birthday and my Mum, Karen figures that I will never have kids since I am 30 now, so she has taken Daisy as her only furry grandchild. She likes to guilt me as much as she can. What about you? Did you grow up around here?" He asked, I could listen to his Scottish accent forever. It wasn't too thick but it was very much there and very much a turn on for me. I had to snap out of this and talk now, he was waiting for me to answer and I was just thinking about him, wow is he hot.

"I um, I grew up here in Oakridge, my family homesteaded here. My Mom's parents, my Grandparents own property on the outside of town, been in the family for generations, my house is in the front of their property. Grandpa is a full blooded Molalla Native American. Grandma is Irish with a hint of Siletz Native American and just so you know they hate Sasquatch hunters and will kill me when they hear that I am taking you guys out. And my parents own the Bigfoot Pizza Parlor in town, don't laugh." I said as he chuckled a little.

"My Dad's parents live in Salem, and they have Irish and German on their side of the family and we see them every so often, they prefer the city life to the country. I went to college in Reno Nevada as well as the University of Oregon in Eugene. And then I started working for the forestry service here in Oakridge ever since. And Mongo is my fur-baby, best friend and partner and my mother does the same with him as yours does with Daisy. Except Mongo won't stay there unless he has me with him. He doesn't leave my side most of the time, but when he does he loves to stay with Trina they are BFF's." I was saying just as Terry came up to my window so I rolled it down so we could talk.

"Hey guys. Everyone is ready, we will follow you. Harry you have our GPS programmed in for the first spot that is close, so we are camping in our trailers tonight. Carrie, I hope you are ready for an adventure of a lifetime!" Terry said as he jumped back out of my window. He had to stand on the sideboard just so that he would be able to talk to us.

"Okay, here we go!" I said and rolled the window back up. We were on our way. This should be fun; we had a convoy of SUV's, a food truck, camp trailers along with a huge cage trailer. We were taking them all Bigfoot/Sasquatch hunting. This was going to be an adventure all right; I just hope my Grandparents and Parents don't hear about this before I get back. They would track me down and drag me home or give the crew here a very loud talking to.

# Chapter 3

Once we left town headed to Waldo Lake which was our first stop to set up basecamp before the evenings hunting. We headed out of Oakridge on Hwy 58 out of Oakridge toward Waldo Lake road. Once we pulled into the Shadow Bay Campground I checked in with the camp host while everyone else waited at the side of the road for me to meet back up with them. I drove a little ways from the entrance to the camp hosts and found them at their camp trailer. I jumped out and left Mongo in the truck with Harry.

"Hey there Carrie, I didn't think you were coming back up this way until next week? Nice truck, Big Ben I believe?" Tory Lynne Larkham said as she came out of her camper with a smile on her face. She and her husband Don had been camp hosts her for the last 6 seasons. They are both retired and love it when I come up to check on them every 2 weeks. Tory Lynne is about 5' 5" with silver short hair and always has a smile on her face. She reminds me of what Mrs. Santa Clause would look like in the off season. Her hubby is around 6', maybe a little taller, he also has silver hair but his smile always makes you wonder if he is thinking something profound, he is more of an Albert Einstein with his matching mustache. They are both very fit from everything they do to help out around the campground; they assist campers with whatever they need. The couple always wears jeans and matching white t-shirts that say camp host on them in bright yellow. They are some of the friendliest people you could find.

"Hey Tory, no I'm not up here to check in with you guys I am here with a group that will be needing all of loop E. I know this early in the camping season. You probably don't have anyone in that loop because it so far out from everything else around here. Johnny gave me Big Ben for all this fun." I said as I nodded my head at Don when he came out as well.

"Morning Carrie, loop E doesn't have anyone on it. Is this a forest service thing? Will you need any help with getting them set up?" Don asked as he put on his usual OSU Beavers Cap knowing that I was U of O Duck. He just loved to pester me whenever he could.

"Yah its forest service stuff, so I have a paper here for you to put with your payments, Johnny sent it up with me." I said as I smile at Don, he knows I saw his cap now by the grin on his face.

"This group is a documentary crew.  Most of the people will stay at the camp site; others will be out and about with me mostly at night.  I just wanted to touch base with you guys because we will be using a few generators.  It may be noisy, so when people come in you might want to steer them clear from that area so they won't be disturbed by us."  Since it was early spring, more people will be coming out to the lakes or just plain camping after being cooped up in the cities.

"Well we will do just that Carrie, thanks for the heads up.  So who is the guy in Big Ben with you and Mongo?" Don asked with a smile on his face.

"That is Harry McKenzie; he's with the filming crew." I said as I turned and looked at Harry since Don was waving at him and Mongo.  Mongo put his paw on the window and woofed, Harry waved back as well.  Mongo was used to us coming to see Tory and Don as well.

"So how may are in this crew that you are with?"  Tory asked.

"I'm not sure.  My friends Trina and Amanda are with me as well as the Crew.  We will definitely fill up the whole loop.  You can come and see us tomorrow afternoon if you like, I am sure they won't mind." I said as Tory walked around her small wood pile and hugged me.

"We just might do that, not too many people around here yet." She said when we parted.

"Any of them play cards?"  Don asked as he hugged me too.

"Not sure but you can ask when you come and visit."  I said as I started to head back to the truck.

"Okay then see you later Carrie."  Tory said as I walked to the truck.  When I opened my door she said, "Nice to meet you Harry, bye Mongo."

"Bye Ma'am, Sir!" Harry said nodding his head at each of them and waved back before I closed my door so that we could get back to the crew.

Mongo woofed again, he was letting me know he didn't get his treat that he usually gets from Tory and Don.

"Sorry Mongo, you can have two next time." I said into the backseat.

We backed up and headed back to where the crew was waiting for us. When I turned around to get in front of the convoy they all jumped back into their vehicles and started to follow us down to loop E. It is literally a large loop but not so large that you couldn't walk between the camps. Everyone can still socialize without a problem. Being early spring means that the temperatures in the day will be light jacket weather. While during the night it will be a little cooler and you may need a heavier jacket to keep warm. While camping I am sure the crew will have at least one campfire and people socializing as well.

Once I pulled into loop E everyone followed me and started parking in spots as we went around. I stopped the truck in the last camp site and watched as everyone else seemed to know what they were doing as they parked, I was glad to see the flat trailer that held the very large generator for all the trailers along with the food truck to use for power. The trailer that was meant for us girls was pulled past Big Ben and then backed into the spot I was waiting at. Harry, Mongo and I jumped out of Big Ben the Forest Service truck that Johnny loaned to me for this fun adventure.

"I have to go and attend to my trailer and the things that need to be done to make camp. I will catch up with you in a little while." Harry said as he smiled and winked at me then he grabbed his bag and patted Mongo on the head and headed off to what I assume was his trailer that I am sure he shares with other crew members because there were only four trailers for everyone to sleep in plus the one they had set aside for us girls.

"Okay, see you later." I said as Trina and Amanda were headed toward Mongo and I. We decided to stay out of the way while the two guys set up our trailer.

Once they were done setting up our trailer, we took our stuff into the trailer with Mongo and his gear. The trailer was very spacious inside.

When you walk into the door the first thing you see is a couch that folds into a queen sized bed on your right, a table that makes into a double bed on your left. The couch is the living room area with a 32-inch TV on the wall so that you can lay in bed and watch, if you like. Next to the table is a nice sized kitchen in a tilt out with a tile floor and a backsplash both matching with the counter top and a double sink. A four burner stove with oven and lots of drawers and cupboards, along with a very nice sized fridge/freezer combo. Then you walk toward the back and there is a bathroom on the right with a full shower and tub, very fancy. Through a doorway is a large bedroom with a closet and queen sized bed complete with a nightstand and another 32-inch TV on the wall next to the door you walked in. Mongo jumped on the bed.

"Well I guess we know whose room this is, don't we Mongo?" Trina said as she was looking around. We all just laughed; the girls knew that Mongo had to sleep with me.

"If you guys are okay with it." I said as both Trina and Amanda walked out and back toward the living room area.

"It's good with us." Amanda said after she looked at Trina and she nodded her head.

"Cool, hey Mongo lets unpack." I said just as we had started to put our stuff away. It didn't take long for the three of us to sit at the table with Mongo resting on the couch and we started to talk about what was going on today as well as what to look forward to tonight when there was a knock on the door. I answered it because I was on the outside of the booth closest to the door to find Harry and Terry were at the bottom of the stairs.

"Who's ready for lunch?" Terry and Harry asked at the same time. They looked at each other and laughed. Trina, Amanda, Mongo and I walked with them to the food truck parked in the middle of all the camp sites. A huge campfire was going with chairs and tables set up all around it. We got to see exactly what the guys had been eating while on Bigfoot hunting trips.

We could smell food cooking as well as seeing everyone sitting and talking and enjoying all different kinds of food. Terry and Trina walked in front of Harry, Amanda and I when Jerry joined us as well just as we got up to the food truck to see what they had to offer. On the side of the truck was a menu and they had everything you could think of for a quick lunch. They had everything from hamburgers and hotdogs to chef salads and Fruit bowls. Then they also had small snack things that they set out for everyone to have in their pockets for in between meals, like granola bars and fresh fruit. They had an amazing spread.

"If there is something you would like and don't see it here all you have to do is ask. You will find some of these things like the fresh fruits, some cereal and milk in your trailer already stocked. We wanted to make sure you ladies were comfortable Johnny picked up Mango's dog food brand and placed it under the sink in your trailer along with food and water dishes for him too." Terry said smiling at the surprised look on my face.

"Thank you Terry, I guess you really thought of everything to make us and Mongo feel right at home. This is almost like going on a vacation." I said as I patted Mongo's head. He looked excited to smell all of the food.

"Well, we just want to make sure that you and your friends are all happy. A vacation for now and work comes tonight I am afraid. Let's all find something to eat and then we can find a table to sit and relax." Terry said as he turned to Trina waiting what she would like to order form the menu.

"Do you mind if I order something for Mongo as well?" I asked Terry even though his back was slightly turned and he was paying attention to Trina.

"I am sure you can order whatever the two of you would like Carrie. He is a little preoccupied at the moment, if you know what I mean?" Harry responded to my question instead.

"Okay good, I usually share my food with Mongo but he really loves a good fruit salad. It says it has apples, pineapple, watermelon, cantaloupe, bananas, peaches and strawberries, everything he loves and dogs can have.

Plus, I can steal some of them to." I said smiling as Mongo started to whimper a little at me and pushed his paw on my hip when I was describing the fruit.

"The fruit salad sounds good the way you describe it, I think I will have one also." Harry said as we got up to the side and ordered our food. I got a hamburger with the works and fries plus a fruit salad and Harry ordered the same. It didn't take them long to have our order, the fries took the longest and they we headed off to the table that Terry and Trina were sitting at. Amanda and Jerry weren't very far behind us, they both got chef salads, and everyone seems to grab water bottles which were among the different soda cans and energy drinks in the coolers set around the end of the food truck once you got through the line and then you grab your silverware and napkins.

This lunch smelled so good, my mouth was watering and I hadn't realized how hungry I was until I started eating. Mongo got a few fries to start off with and then I started giving him his fruit which he loved. He was such a good boy. I did get a little of his fruit and I got super full on the burger and fries, which Mongo got a little of those as well. This was a really great lunch and great company too.

It seemed like everyone was in the same frame of mind and once lunch was over and the garbage dealt with Terry, Harry and Jerry started to talk to the whole group, but mainly explaining what our roll in the evening hunt was going to be.

"As everyone knows Carrie is going to lead us and be there is case anything goes wrong. Trina is a large primate veterinarian and a trained medic as well. If anyone gets hurt at all you will go to her. Last but not least we have Amanda who has full access to everything and everyone during this expedition. She is here to validate everything as truthful and also news worthy. Any questions?" Terry asked and walked around the fire pit to make sure everyone had the chance to say something.

There were a lot of "No Sir's and Nope's" I am guessing everyone understood.

This is where I found out that Harry usually starts out in a different direction and is separate from the group during the hunt.

"So for those of you that are new here, once we get to the area we are hunting in I will go in another direction from everyone else. My job is to call the Bigfoot in and make sure that they are heading your way." Harry said to the group.

When Harry calls the Sasquatch in and that way the others have a chance to see and hear more. The crew has come to expect this from the evening hunts and this is nothing out of the ordinary for them.

"As the crew already knows the rest of us will be going in at one spot, the cage will obviously be left with the vehicles unless we find really good evidence that one is in the area. Then we will set the trap and see if we can catch a Sasquatch. Any questions?" Jerry finished the rest of this meeting with a smile.

No one had any questions so the group went off to start getting their gear ready. Everyone except for the food truck guys, they stayed behind to do the food prep which takes up most of their time. We will be traveling using as few vehicles as possible along with the cage truck of course. The ladies, Mongo and I went back to our trailer alone so that we could talk and get ready as well. Terry, Harry and Jerry headed off to do what they needed to be done saying they would catch up with us just before it was time to head out.

When we climbed into the trailer to grab our stuff you could feel the excitement. This was definitely going to be an adventure to say the least. I was just a little sad that I wouldn't be spending any time with Harry while we were in the woods. But I had a job to do and so did he at least I still had my Mongo.

It didn't take long and I had my gear and Mongos ready to go. I had stuffed some power bars and granola bars into my pack that I had picked up from the food truck since they tasted better than the ones I had brought. And it didn't take Trina and Amanda very long to get their gear together either. They each had a small backpack and then they had their smaller things in what looked like fanny packs but they carried in the front. I shouldn't laugh my backpack was a little bigger than theirs and Mongo's saddle bags weren't super small either.

"Are we ready to do this ladies?" I asked as Mongo gave a woof and we looked at the door.

"I would say I am ready, I have my small survival pack here and I also have my recording equipment and my phone ready." Amanda was saying as she grabbed her jacket. Being late May it was still going to get chilly at night. I was glad the ladies were used to the weather around here and were prepared.

"Yup, I have my first aid kit as well as my survival kit and I am also going to use my phone, you never know what I might see that you guys won't." Trina said as she put her jacket on and then her backpack.

"So I have my survival pack, first aid that I always carry along with the pistol that I don't want anyone else to know I am carrying. Just because we haven't had any bear trouble in years doesn't mean we won't run onto something in those woods that might give us some trouble. I just want to be prepared. And yes some of the crew are also carrying firearms and the forest service knows as well as fish and wildlife. Johnny made sure before we left that Terry had covered all the basses. Terry and Harry both also have the tranquilizer guns as well, just in case." I was saying as Trina got a small smile on her face.

"Well then I should tell you as well that I also have a tranquilizer gun and also the drug that counter reacts the tranquilizer as well." She said rather sheepishly.

"Good to know in case someone accidently gets tranquilized." I said laughing.

"That would just be our luck, wouldn't it? We get a Sasquatch and one of us accidently gets tranquilized and misses out on everything." I said as everyone started for the door that Mongo was so very intent on going out of.

I opened the door and Mongo stepped down then sat at the bottom of the stairs waiting for us. He was ready to have some fun but he was also all business when he puts on his saddle bags he knows it's time to work. We were ready to go and catch us a Sasquatch.

## **Chapter 4**

We left the campsite in three vehicles with the cage/trap trailer. It took almost an hour to get all the way to the spot in which they had wanted us to go to. This time the ladies rode to the spot with mongo and I, which I thought was a little weird but it worked out. I guess it was easier to cram guys into trucks without having to worry about us girls being smooched. We stopped when we were about 20 minutes from the GPS location to have a quick dinner of warm burritos and salads for those who wanted them. Mongo ate a small bowl of his food and half of my burrito because I was super nervous about tonight so my tummy wasn't too happy right now. Then we were back on the road headed to our location.

We arrived at the GPS coordinates and everyone piled out of the trucks being rather quiet, I didn't think that many guys could be that silent. We were parked at the end of a road and everything was set up. We were already to walk in just as it was starting to get dark. As luck would have it we had great signal for our handheld GPS and our phones as well. Jerry and Amanda started filming no more that we got out of the trucks. Terry and Harry said a few words to the camera before heading out. Harry also had his GPS, phone and a go pro camera strapped to his chest recording everything as we went in. Harry made sure to pat Mongo on the head and scratch behind his ears before he said good bye to me and headed to the right of where we were heading straight in to the woods.

As we were walking with Terry and I in the lead everyone was very quiet. Every so often we stopped so I could check the trail for any kind of animal sign. There were only the tracks of the usual, raccoon, deer and lots of birds, nothing too big or out of the ordinary so far. When I stopped to look around that's when Terry took the chance to talk to the cameras to explain what we were doing and what we had found so far. Boring stuff that I am sure will be edited to a smaller amount later.

We had been walking for more than half hour when Harry checked in using the walkie talkie.

"Terry, got some sign over hear and a few tree knocks. Have you found anything over there, over?" Harry sounded miles away.

"Nothing here but sign a few of deer and smaller animals. Which direction are the knocks coming from, over?" Terry said. Everyone circled around Terry to hear what was happening.

"Knocks are coming from your direction. Turn a little toward my location and you should hear them soon. I can see your tracker on the GPS, over." Harry sounds a little winded while he was talking this time. He was probably walking up or down an incline at the time.

"I'm heading your way, over." Terry said and the whole group of us turned toward his GPS signal and headed that way slowly listening to hear the tree knockers, I found out the knocks were a form of communication between Bigfoot.

"I'm heading into an area that my signal is getting weak. My go pro is starting to malfunction, over!" Harry said into the walkie talkie with some signal interference as well.

"Head back toward us then Harry, over!" Terry said into the walkie talkie.

"Okay, Over." You could hear Harry was walking through brush on his end of the conversation. He was really down into the little valley we were coming up on.

We didn't hear from him again for another half an hour. Terry was starting to get worried but that's when we started hearing the tree knocks finally. You could hear the thud, thud, thud and it echoed up to where we were. Harry's GPS signal said he was coming up on us and was a lot closer to us than the knocking was. And that's when we started hearing the grunting coming from the left of the group. Mongo got right in front of me and had his hair up. It took a lot to scare Mongo and the group all seemed to tense up. There was something in the woods and it wasn't happy we were there.

Terry got the great idea to start some howling to see if the thing grunting would respond. He let off an eerie sound that kind of whooped it started out low and then got loud then abruptly stopped. He did this a couple more times. Jerry as well as Amanda were both watching him with cameras recording everything. We heard nothing for a few minutes.

"Can I give it a go? I would like to try the female mating call of the ridgeback gorilla?" Trina asked Terry.

"Sure give it a try we've never had a female do a call before." He looked like he was really excited to hear her do it too. She started low and then went high and then even lower and ended on a really high whoop with a little grunt at the end that kind of made the hairs on my arms stand up.

That's when we heard a whoop and grunt from both sides of our group. They both sounded excited as you can imagine if they were looking for a female. I think Trina just opened a can of worms that I am not sure we wanted open. Then there was crashing through the brush on both sides, it really sounded like there were two Sasquatch in a hurry to catch the female that just rang the mating bell. The crew gathered around us ladies and Mongo was growling in in both directions and then he gave a bark first to the right of us then to the left of us. All noise stopped in the trees and underbrush. I hadn't realized that I had pulled my gun and was ready to use it if need be.

Terry pulled up his walkie talkie, "Harry, are you okay? Over." We waited a few long seconds and then Harry talked.

"I am just down the slope to your right. There was a burst of activity with whatever you guys just did. I think there are at least a couple Bigfoot out here. They are waiting to see what happens next. Since Mongo barked, they might think the female is protected and they aren't sure by what. I am going to sit here for a few minutes and see if any of them leave. Don't do anything else to attract them. We are not ready for this many of them tonight. Over." Harry sounded extremely winded and his voice was a little growly as well.

"Okay. Over" Terry said and then we all kind of just stood there for a while. I am not sure how much time went by but Mongo started to relax so I am thinking that he thought the danger was less now, but he didn't totally relax yet. That's when the rocks started hitting us. Not large rocks but they were still rocks.

One rock hit at Terry's feet, then another hit to the left of us and then another larger one hit toward our right. Then more and more small rocks and then the grunts started. Mongo growled a little then barked. The rocks stopped. Then we started hearing the tree knocking that was loud and very close. Whack, whack, whack! Then Mongo took two steps in front of me facing the right side of the group where most of the action was happening. He let off a woof, a growl and then a double bark. Then he turned to the left side of our group and did the same. One last rock was tossed at us then you could hear whatever they were, Bigfoot, Sasquatch, whatever leave heading down into the small valley below and they were not happy. They were making so much noise and they were actually grumbling like they were talking under their breath and pissed off because they couldn't have the female.

A few minutes later Harry came up the right side of us and he looked a little shaken up. I think we all were really. Mongo sat at my feet and looked up at me and smiled. He knew he was a good boy and kept his Momma safe. I bent down and kissed his forehead and he licked my chin. I gave him a little scratch behind the ears like he likes and then stood up. Everyone else starting with Trina and Amanda started to come up and give Mongo loves as well. Who knew what would have happened if Mongo hadn't been there with us. That was intense! Harry finally made it to the group.

"That was intense! What did you guys do?" Harry asked, a little out of breath. A few of the guys were still watching the trees and Jerry was still filming everything, which I am sure Amanda was as well.

"Well, I let Trina give a howl that was apparently a mating call." Terry said as Trina walked up beside him.

"Actually it was. I even messed it up a little bit as well. So what are we doing now?" Trina asked and everyone was shocked when Terry hugged her.

"We go back to camp and watch the footage!" Terry was so excited and then he let Trina go, he was blushing so bad we could see him in the light from the flashlights we were using.

"Everyone grab everything that we could. Henry, Patrick gets some gloves on and grab as many of the rocks that you can find that were thrown at us. That is evidence and we are keeping everything that we can have tested for finger prints or DNA." Terry was talking a little louder than he needed to but I think it was because he was so embarrassed. Henry and Patrick both gathered what they could still staying close together just in case they Sasquatch hadn't all gone away.

"Okay everyone we are staying together this time and going out in sets of two. Everyone pick a partner and stick with that person. Harry and Alvin will be at the end of the line and watching our backs as we head out. Carrie and I will lead the way back out. Trina and Amanda will follow right behind Carrie and I so they are protected and Jerry with Henry right behind the ladies. Everyone else file in between us. If there are any problems, we make a circle and the ladies and Mongo go in the middle. Any questions?" Terry said as we all started to rally into position to leave.

"Okay people it's a long walk let's get us out of here and back to camp safely." Harry said as he gave Mongo a pat on the head and a "Good boy Mongo" as he passed by me to make the end of the line. He then smiled and winked at me. I smiled and headed with Mongo to the head of the line with Terry so we could get the heck out of these woods. I guess I can say now that if I wasn't a believer before from all of Grandpa's stories I sure as hell was a believer now. I'm just lucky I didn't pee my pants, which we will have to make a stop at some point of the way out but not for a little while. I want to put as much distance between us and them as we can.

Everyone was lined up with their partner, Jerry still filming as well as Amanda and we were on our way out of these woods so we could get back to safety.

It took us almost three hours to get back to the trucks. We had no incidents and Harry and Alvin didn't see or hear anything following us. We had made a very exciting discovery tonight that was a very scary discovery as well. There must not be very many female Sasquatch in the area because they were really interested in the females in our group.

We loaded up in the trucks this time though they split us girls up into the three trucks. Harry rode back with me and Mongo along with Alvin. Terry took Trina, Henry and two others with him and Amanda rode with Jerry, Patrick and another guy. We had no problem getting back to camp. It was a little after 1 am when we got back and of course Terry and Amanda wanted to check out the footage right away to see what had been captured on film.

A TV and computer were set up in one of the larger trailers that had a lot more room in it for everyone to fit into comfortably. This way everyone could see all the raw footage. There we were in the first part of the footage was rather slow but when you go to the exciting stuff, you could see a lot more.

Jerry's camera was set up to see things in the dark so you could see the dark humanoid figures and you could see their eyes lighting up in the dark. It made my goose bumps get goose bumps! And the sounds, you could hear everything so much better, it was eerie as hell it was like we were back up there in the middle of it again.

We all counted at least five or six large males that we could see by their glowing yellow eyes. The way they acted so excited when Trina did her mating call. I truly don't know what would have happened if Mongo hadn't told them to back off. Would they have taken just us females and would they have hurt the guys with us to get to us? So little is really known about them, no one has ever caught one of them to learn from it. I've heard the stories about woman getting abducted by them. It's even in some of the Pacific Northwest Indian tribe's lore about how their young women were stolen, most didn't return and if they did they were not the same.

After watching everything that we had just lived through the whole crew was quiet. Everyone had the same look on their faces that I am sure was on my face as well. Then all of a sudden Terry jumped up out of his seat and yelled, "Hot Damn, do you know what this means people?" Everyone just about jumped a mile out of their chairs.

"Jeez, why did you have to scare the crap out of us all again!" Harry yelled back at Terry. I had my hand over my heart and was trying to catch my breath and I wasn't the only one either.

"Sorry everyone! I was just caught up in the excitement." Terry said as he sat back down next to Trina who looked white as a ghost.

"So what is the next plan of action Boss?" Jerry asked as he finished uploading all of the footage to a USB as well for back up later if needed.

"Well, I think that everyone should go to their trailers and try to get a good night's sleep, tomorrow we are getting everything prepared for a capture tomorrow night. We will have a long day ahead of us preparing everything, we can have a meeting with breakfast in the morning. Harry and I will walk the ladies back to their trailer. Everyone else get ready to turn in for the evening and who needs a wakeup call in the morning? It's now 2:15am and I will make sure everyone is up at 10am at the latest." Terry waited for an answer from anyone needing a wakeup call but no one said they did. I knew Mongo was mine which means that he was for Trina and Amanda as well.

A few minutes later Harry, Terry and Jerry walked us along with Mongo back to our trailer, which is on the outer most campsite of the loop. I am kind of rethinking where I parked now. The guys checked around the trailer and Mongo went potty before we all climbed inside. There didn't seem to be anything out of the ordinary. Mongo wanted to go back to our room no more than we walked in the door so I followed him back with Harry right behind me. Once we were in the room he closed the door and looked at me with a very concerned look on his face.

"I know it's your job to be with us out there but I am really concerned about you and my friend's safety. Terry and Jerry are too blinded by the excitement and with the fact that they actually caught something on file besides grunts and tree knocking." Then he moved closer to me and grabbed my upper arms and looked into my eyes. He looked like he wanted to tell me something but he just couldn't do it.

"I was pretty scared out there tonight Harry, I won't lie. And I think Trina and Amanda were too, but this is important. It's a once in a lifetime kind of thing, you should know you have been hunting them for years. And have you ever gotten such a response before?" I asked him, our faces were so close that I was staring into his eyes then I just had to look at his lips, those beautifully full lips that were just made for kissing a girl senseless.

"Yes." Was all he said then he kissed me. The heat was amazing the pressure was perfect it was as if our lips were made to be together. His hands wondered to my back and pulled me closer to him as I leaned into him as well. The passion was intense it was almost animal like. Then he stopped and we just looked at each other. Mongo was laying on the bed and he made a little noise I had never heard from him before. We both turned our heads and bodies to look at Mongo. But he just did his little smile thing he does and put his head down on the bed. That's when there was a knock on my door.

"Harry, um Terry and I are heading back to the trailer are you ready to go?" We broke apart putting a tiny bit of space between us when we heard the knock. Jerry sounded like he kind of knew what we were doing. How embarrassing, but so worth it.

"I'll be right with you Jerry!" Harry leaned in and kissed me again but it was a very fast touching of the lips and then he touched my cheek.

"I have wanted to do that from the moment I met you. I just want to keep you safe Carrie, I know we haven't known each other very long but I feel so connected to you and I was very scared out there tonight. Not for me or the crew but for you and the girls. I can't explain what I want to but just know that I will be there to protect you if you need me." Then he kissed my forehead and turned to go out the door. Then he whipped around and talked to Mongo, "You were a good boy tonight Mongo." Then he patted his head and left the room. I followed him out and the others were waiting by the door.

"About time, we really need to get to bed so we can be rested and ready for in the morning. We have a big day ahead of us. Good night Ladies'." He touched Trina's shoulder and rubbed it really quick and then turned and opened the door and started walking down the stairs. Jerry was next, "See you Ladies' in the morning." Jerry hugged Amanda and then followed Terry to the bottom of the stairs.

"Well I guess it's my turn now?" Harry winked at me smiling as he walked back to me and took me into his arms and kissed me senseless yet again. A girl could get used to this. I could hear the girls gasp in shock but we didn't care. Then he released my lips and said, "I will see you bright and early in the morning. If you have any problems you yell for me and I will come running. Good night." He gave me a quick peck and then let me go and headed out the door where the guys waited. I was a little in shock but I managed to come to my senses before Harry closed the door.

"Good night! See you in the morning!" Was all I could think to say, I was on cloud nine right now. Trina and Amanda were giggling like school girls once the door was shut.

"Wow what was that?" Trina asked as the two girls grabbed me, set me on the couch and sat on either side of me.

"Okay spill the details!" Trina said.

"He kissed me." I said still kind of shocked. I touched my lips and they were still warm from his kiss.

"You haven't known him that long, when did this happen?" Amanda was saying as she got up and walked to the fridge and grabbed us each a water bottle and handed them to us. I opened mine right away and must have drunk about half of it before I stopped.

"It just sort of happened. I was attracted to him the first time I met him, he said it was the same for him. I can see myself becoming addicted to his kisses. He talked about a connection between us and I have to say I felt it too and yes I felt it before we kissed. He is super easy to talk to and his voice, oh I could listen to him talk about anything." I know I was getting dreamy eyed but they seemed cozy with Terry and Jerry too.

"What about you two? Terry and Trina? Amanda and Jerry? What's going on there?" I know I was turning the tables on them because they were a little shocked looking when I made them face what they were doing as well. I could tell they liked the guys and I wasn't the only one that had a man interested in me in that we barely knew. My man was just a little more up front about it and I know it has to do with his Scottish blood that makes him more compulsive than other men.

"Well, I guess we should give you a break." Amanda said sitting down next to me again and hugging me.

"Yah, Terry has been great too. He has made it very clear that he is interested in me for more than just this one adventure. He just isn't as outgoing as Harry is about showing his emotions I guess." Trina said as she started hugging me too.

"Yah I got that from Jerry too. But it's only been," Amanda looked at her watch.

"Two days since we met them, I know we have had hours in the trucks together, all in all it's been really exciting, an adventure being with them. We should get to know them a little longer before we start talking to seriously right?"

"Yah tell that to the Scot! Talk about red-blooded; he has it bad for you Carrie if he is willing to show you affection so openly with his Boss around. Just be careful, and take some time with him." Trina was saying as Mongo came out to where we were sitting.

"Yah I know. You have to go potty again Mongo?" I asked him as he tried to climb up into my lap and lick my face. He was either jealous or really ready for bed.

"Okay Boy, let's go to bed then. We all better get to bed because apparently we have an exciting day tomorrow and then what will probably be a super fun evening!" I was trying for sarcastic but it didn't sound like it really to my ears.

"All righty then." Trina stood with me and hugged me and then Amanda did as well.

"Night guys." I said as Mongo led the way to the bedroom.

"Night Lady." Amanda said as she stretched then grabbed her overnight bag to get her night clothes out.

"Night." Trina was doing the same. I stopped off at the bathroom to potty and brush my teeth on my way to the bedroom. I changed quickly into my night shirt and sweat pants to stay warm and then I climbed into bed with Mongo hogging half of the bed already. I must have been super tired because I was out in no time.

## Chapter 5

I know I was out for the count because I didn't hear Mongo until he was growling and then started barking. Mongo did not do those things unless there was really something to bark at. I woke with a start from the barking and was trying to figure out where I was to start with. Then I heard Trina and Amanda in the front of the trailer. They came busting into the room where Mongo and I were and they seemed super scared.

"There is something throwing rocks on the top of the trailer!" Amanda was yelling as she was trying to get one leg into her jeans and while coming through the door. By this time, I had jumped out of the bed and was standing at the side when Trina dove on top of the bed with her pants in her hands.

"What the hell is going on out there?" Trina was yelling and then she rolled over the edge of the bed that Mongo was sleeping on because Mongo was headed for the trailer door and he was pissed.

"Mongo, NO!" I yelled before he got to the door. There was something out there and I wasn't opening the door. There was a loud thud on the roof, I grabbed my personal handgun that I took everywhere and not too many people can see it when I carry. It's a Remington RP9 Pistol, 9mm, 4.5", Black Polymer Grips, Black Finish, and it holds 18 Rounds. My Mom gave it to me when I moved to Reno; I was raised around guns all my life so I knew how to handle it and myself.

Mongo had backed up and met me coming out of the bedroom. We both stood in the kitchen area and we waited to hear what was going to happen next. The girls were getting dressed in the bedroom; I think Trina was grabbing one of my t-shirts to put on because she left hers on the floor in her rush to get back to me and Mongo. There was another bang on the roof, it was definitely rocks being tossed as us, which from what Grandpa said is something that Sasquatch's like to do when they are pissed at someone and want them gone. Well, I guess they were pissed that they didn't get the girl, huh?

"Mongo howl!" I gave Mongo the order and he let off one of his don't fuck with me howl that I loved to hear so much that I also started howling with him. I don't mean to brag but I have won coyote calling contests with my howling skills and I gave this one my all. Maybe we can scare them off thinking that there are more than one Mongo in here.

Mongo and I did this for a few minutes together, he was so happy with himself. He gave me his little pitbull smile and had his tongue hanging out the side of his mouth. He got me to howl with him and he was happy. We waited a few more minutes and didn't hear anything. Trina was on the walkie talkie that Harry had left for us in case we needed anything. She was upset but she was holding it together. All I heard was a very loud voice yelling they were on their way. We still didn't hear anymore rocks on the roof, and then the whole camp lit up. Someone had started the big generator and I guess someone had placed big flood lights around our camp while we were out in the woods earlier because you would think it was noon outside or something.

There was banging on the door and Harry and Terry were yelling to let them in. Mongo sat down next to the door while I opened it. Mongo tensed up and then relaxed as Harry was the first through the door with Terry hot on his heels.

"Carrie are you all right?" He was saying as he looked at the gun in my right hand and then grabbed me for a hug anyway.

"Yah we are all good. Something was throwing rocks on the roof of the trailer. Mongo let us know that something was wrong with his barking didn't scare them this time. He and I started howling and I think that might have scared them off. They followed us guys! They followed us down to the campground and there are a few other people here in the campground, not just us." I was saying as I pulled a little out of Harry's hold on me to face everyone else in the living room area. Terry had Trina in a bear hug that was anything but platonic and Amanda was just about to sit down when Jerry came running in through the open door and grabbed her as well.

"They could not have been following us. They would have had to cross over through the woods to be here by this time. There is no way they ran as fast as we were driving to be back to camp." Jerry was saying as he held Amanda and kissed her forehead. "Are you oaky?" he asked her and she just nodded and held him tighter.

"That's the only explanation, but how did they know where we were camping?" Terry asked no one in particular. Trina was still holding on to him and he didn't look like he was letting her go anytime soon.

"And how did they know which trailer the girls were in?" Jerry was wondering out loud.

"Scent most likely, they were asleep so it wouldn't have been their voices." Terry said. Everyone was in total shock that these Sasquatch were smart enough to meet us back at our campsite as well as know which trailer was the exact trailer that we girls were in.

"Well, think about it! They have eluded hunters for how many years without being caught and without leaving any DNA for people to find either. These sons of bitches are smarter than we thought." Terry was saying as he finally led Trina over to the couch so that they could both sit down.

"We have guys checking the whole camp to see if anything was damaged or if the Bigfoot are still around. Now that I know your safe I am going to check around this trailer and see if I can find anything." Harry said then he kissed my forehead and started for the door.

"Do you want us to go with you?" Jerry asked as Amanda held onto him tighter.

"No you guys stay here and keep the girls safe. Though, I have a feeling that Carrie and Mongo could have kept them all safe. Keep you pistol out Lass, I will be right back. I'll knock on the door and let you know it's me when I come back." He said as he stepped down.

"Double lock this door!" He said as he turned with his flashlight and walked toward the back of the trailer. I closed the door and double locked it. Then we waited.

48

We all about jumped out of our skins when the walkie talkie that Terry had blared to life when I think it was Alvin saying it was all clear and that they needed Terry to come and have a look at something.

"As soon as Harry gets back we will all head that way." Terry said to Alvin.

"Okay Boss." Then Alvin was silent. A few minutes later there was a knock on the door and Harry asked to be let in, so I opened the door and he climbed in to talk to us.

"Not much sign out there. They pretty much kept their distance from what I could see; I will know more when it gets lighter out. It's almost 4am now so not too much longer till it starts to get light out." Harry said as he grabbed me and hugged me to his side again.

"So Alvin checked in and said it was all clear but that there was something that we needed to see. I told him all of us would come and take a look, I don't want to leave the girls here alone, even if Carrie is packing heat. Do you really know how to use that thing?" Terry was asking me.

"Yes, I grew up hunting, fishing and trapping. My friends have a private gun range out on salmon creek road. We spent a lot of time out there, I love those tannerite targets." I was saying while smiling.

"Yah those were always fun." Amanda was saying as she seemed to find herself again and wasn't as scared anymore.

"Can we all just go and get this over with, please?" Trina asked Terry more that she was talking to us.

"Sure as soon as you ladies go and finish getting dressed we can head out there." Terry said and looked at all three of us. We definitely needed to put some real clothes on. I was still in my night shirt and sweatpants, good thing I put on the sweatpants. Mongo gave a woof that was his I have to go potty woof.

"Hang on buddy I will take you out when I get dressed." I said as I patted his head.

"I can take him out, and the guys can stand outside with me so you ladies can dress quicker instead of trying to dress in the bathroom or your bedroom all at the same time." Harry was saying as he confirmed with Terry and Jerry.

"Yah." Both Terry and Jerry said at the same time.

"Okay, it shouldn't take us too long to get dressed." I said then I patted Mongo on the head and said, "Harry will take you potty. Be quick." And then I headed toward the bedroom to dress leaving the girls out there to get dressed as well.

It didn't take us long to dress then we were out the door to find the guys and Mongo waiting just outside the door. I was the last one out the door, Trina went straight to Terry and he held out his hand for her to take as did Jerry with Amanda when she stepped off the last step. Mongo was at my side as I stepped down and closed the door to the trailer and so was Harry. Everyone was very quiet. The sun was coming up and things were getting lighter out. I have this habit of thinking things through in my head until I just have to blurt it out to get a different view from someone else and I was tired of thinking about what had happened.

"So, this has been bugging me." I started saying and everyone stopped and turned to listen to me.

"I know I am new to this Sasquatch hunting thing but I grew up with the Sasquatch stories from my Grandfather and he warned me about what you could encounter out there with a Sasquatch. He told me about the tree knocking, the rock throwing, the howling as well as the Sasquatch following people and messing with them. But he always made it sound as if these things were mostly night time things. Now why would these Sasquatch cross through, not follow us, to our camp and then throw rocks at just us girl's trailer just before it became light out? If they aren't really active during the day wouldn't that mean they wouldn't really travel during the day either?" Everyone seemed to really think about this and no one said anything for a few seconds.

"Maybe all the rules don't apply when they think they are going after a mate?  This was the first time that I know of in my research that a female has done a howl in the field.  Maybe that is our key to catching our first Bigfoot?"  Terry was saying.  Then there was a whistle from one of the crew over by one of the trailers, so we headed that way to see what was going on.

We passed by the food truck and you could tell that he cooks were already starting breakfast; you could smell the eggs and bacon and sausage cooking.  I didn't realize I was so hungry until I smelled the food.  Mongo bumped my leg and woofed.

"Yes, Buddy we will eat soon.  You earned a whole plate of eggs today."  I said as I rubbed his head.  That's my boy, always protecting me.

"He sure has.  I will personally make sure he has sausage too."  Harry said and then Mongo bumped his leg too.  Mongo is really taking a liking to Harry; I sure hope that is a good sign.

When we got closer to Harry's trailer we noticed a pile of stuff sitting by the door.   Once we got to it we noticed there were cedar bows piled up with some dead rabbits, some dead fish, berries wrapped in large leaves.  What was all this?

"Holy Shit!  Do you know what this is?"  Trina asked us as she walked around the pile looking at everything.  She was in total shock and I think I was catching her train of thought.

"They were trying to buy us!" I said in astonishment.

"Yes, they were paying the males to take the females because we were in a trailer alone, therefore unattached and available.  It is a classic primate thing to do, many of the gorilla and chimpanzee cultures do it.  Hell, the Native Americans did it as well as our own history in the Americas.  Men paid a dowry to a woman's family to be able to wed the woman of his choosing."  Trina was stuck in biologist mode for a minute there.

"Do you know what this means?"  Terry asked everyone and no one in particular.

"Yah it means they want our women!" Jerry said rather pissed.

"No, it means they are basically showing they have intelligence beyond what most people think they have. They could be early man that just refused to evolve!" Trina said with a shiver and rubbed her arms. It was chilly out here but I don't think it was from the cold.

"Well people this just got a whole lot more interesting than a simple hunt and capture, now we have to outsmart them as well." Terry said as he looked around at us all. By this time the whole crew was circled around us hearing what was being said while wondering about the presents that had been left by the Bigfoot who had decided that they wanted the females that were with them.

"Don't you worry ladies; the whole crew is here to make sure you stay safe. Those Bigfoot aren't getting any of you." We all turned, Alvin making us ladies a promise and all the rest of the crew were nodding their heads. That made all three of us feel a little safer knowing we were there first priority.

"Now before we go too far I want to make sure that you all know the risks involved here and I am not talking about the Bigfoot either. Once this gets out that we have not only encountered Bigfoot here but also have captured one. Then the Bigfoot Hunters will be coming out of the woodwork to cash in on what we have found." Terry was saying as he walked in a circle looking at everyone.

"My boss won't let that happen Terry!" I said as loud as I could without yelling because everyone started talking amongst themselves, names were being mentioned and stress levels were rising.

"Well the forests are open game to all those who want to go out there. I don't think your boss can stop them all. Let me tell you a lot of these guys are out to kill Bigfoot and not to capture him. We know a group that isn't far from here that we have had a few run in's with. They play hardball with real guns and ammo." Terry stopped to talk to me, making sure that we girls know the risks if this were to get out before we were ready to deal with it.

"Johnny has more people than you think and we can close parks and roads if need be.  There is no hunting to be done in certain areas anyway, which means they can't have their guns.  Who is this group and should we tell Johnny about them ahead of time?"  I wanted to make sure they knew that the forest service did not mean we were weak.

'They call themselves the Sweethome Mountain Men Bigfoot hunters.  The leaders are a couple of rednecks brothers named Jedidiah, Jed for short and Cletus Monroe.  Jed may be a redneck but he is a smooth talker who can get them into places not too many people get to go Bigfoot hunting.  Cletus is the trap maker he makes things to grab the Bigfoot.  Think bear trap from the 1800's with the huge sharp teeth but worse, the bloodier the better, and their three friends Billy Bob Brockman their Weapons specialist, then the Munster twins Tray "the tracker" and Ray "the mechanic" Jones.  The Jones twins are called the Munster twins because they look like an older version of Eddie Munster wearing black from head to toe including combat boots, have black dyed hair and are so light skinned that you would think they were vampires.  They do their hunting at night with real guns and just want to kill Bigfoot just for the bragging rights, not even for research.  They all grew up in Sweet Home, Oregon and have played in those woods as well as anywhere they can get into that has had sightings of Bigfoot.  They are bad news, the worst of the worst.  They almost shot Harry once when they came into an area we were already in.  They have no boundaries what so ever!   To answer your question, yes I have had a long talk with Johnny about who might come sniffing around when people in the Sasquatch/Bigfoot community find out we are here.  Even more so when they find out we have video proof of the Bigfoot in this area."  Terry was so upset about these guys.  I hope that Johnny was planning ahead for this.

"Okay so bad guys are coming, good to know."  Trina said as she went to comfort Terry who looked like he really needed it.

"Okay well let's move on to the more pleasant things shall we all?"  Terry said as he and Trina walked off a little way off to talk quietly.

## Chapter 6

Breakfast was first on the agenda since we had daylight and I don't think anyone was going to get anymore sleep tonight after what we went through. Mongo not only got a large helping of scrambled eggs all to himself and he also got six sausage links. Once everyone heard Harry recap what had happened to us ladies and how Mongo and my howling scared them off finally. It seemed like Mongo's plate got bacon as well as more eggs. He was definitely a happy guy. I knew I was going to be paying for that later because his egg farts were terrible. He usually only got a little bite of eggs to go with his dog food. Oh well he was pretty much a hero for both last night as well as this morning.

It seemed like after every meal there was a meeting, this morning was no exception. Terry gave a recap of everything so that the crew that stayed behind were also caught up on our full adventure last night long with everyone knowing the events that happened this morning in camp. When Terry was finished he and Harry gave assignments to everyone on the crew. Amanda wanted more camera availability so she and Jerry went to his trailer to adapt her small camera for this evening. I felt it was my duty to go and see Tori and Don to let them know what had all happened here. Who knew if these Sasquatch weren't living closer than we thought?

"Harry, Mongo and I are going to see Tori and Don to let them know what happened this morning so they can be on the lookout for anything strange." I said as I finally got Harry aside from the group.

"Are you taking anyone besides Mongo with you?" He asked.

"No Trina and Terry are talking about the cage as well as what the plan is for tonight, since she has more of an insight into the primate that they seem to be." I said as Mongo bumped my leg needing attention. I rubbed his head.

"Can you wait so that I can go with you?" He asked as a couple of the crew came up to ask what they should be doing.

"It's not that far away and Mongo and I can handle a short visit. They are friends of mine and I would like them to be updated a.s.a.p. If they have anything strange going on in rest of the campground then I am right her to handle too. I can handle myself plus I have Mongo." Mongo woofed and smiled at Harry then licked his hand before it made it to rub his head.

"Okay, make sure you have a walkie on.  I will be checking in on you every 30 minutes. Don't be too long, we still have to talk about tonight." Harry said as he leaned in and gave me a kiss. We both smiled and I turned tail with Mongo right at my side as we headed to Big Ben and climbed in. Damn he was hot.

It was a little after 9am so I figured Tori and Don would be up by now.  Mongo was a little more excited than usual when we pull up the road stopping in at their trailer. Once I turned off the engine Tori and Don were both out their door heading toward me with a worried look. Don was not in his usual playful mood, that's when I knew something was wrong. I barely got out of the truck by the time they go to me.

"Thanks goodness you are okay!" Tori said as she and Don ascended on me and hugged me. I had to let them go when Mongo jumped out of the truck past me and had his nose to the ground sniffing everywhere. He stopped and woofed.

"Okay guys what's going on?" I asked hoping that I didn't already know what had happened in the campground.

"We had at least three or four bears in camp last night.  Three families packed up in the middle of the night barely, stopping here to let us know they were leaving because of bears. They were all tent campers that felt it was unsafe." Don said as we walked closer to their trailer.

"Can we go inside for a minute so I can tell you guys a few things? Then we can go out to check on all the other campers that are left." I was trying to get them inside to talk about the Sasquatch just in case others were listening.

"Yah Carrie, come on in. We have coffee on and treats for Mongo. We've been up for a while now with everything that's happened." Tori said as she led the way, I tapped my leg and Mongo followed me inside as well.

Once inside we all sat at the table and Tori poured me a cup of coffee handing me the hazelnut creamer that she always had on hand for when I visited. Don grabbed Mongo a chicken jerky treat that they keep for campers dogs plus it was Mongo's favorite and handed it to him. Mongo took it but he was still full from breakfast he laid it in my lap and then laid down on the floor next to me.

"Is Mongo okay? I've never known him to turn down a jerky treat." Don said as he slid in next to Tori.

"He's okay; we just had a really big breakfast. I needed to talk privately with you guys in case anyone is close enough to hear us. This is something you can-not repeat until the episode airs but I felt that people in the campground might be in danger so I wanted to let you guys know." I was nervous about telling them knowing that people thought there were bears in the area last night but they probably were the Sasquatch, instead.

"Okay, Carrie spit it out. What's going on here?" Don asked as I took a sip of my coffee. Mongo got up and walked over to the water bowl that that Don and Tori kept for him and took a drink as well. Then he looked at the door and sniffed. He then turned around and came back to me. I hadn't realized that I was holding my breath as he was doing this. When I let my breath out I turned back to talk to Don and Tori to find them watching me.

"Carrie, you are white as a sheet. You are really scaring us." Tori said as she reached across the table and put her hand on mine.

"Okay, so you know the Animal Channel's crew that is up here filming?" I started with.

"Yes." They both said as once.

"Well they are called the Bigfoot Getters. Well we ran into some last night that somehow found out where we were camping and came in giving an offering to the guys. They threw rocks at our trailer to get us to come out. We think they were waiting to take us because they were looking for mates. You probably didn't have bear problems last night it was probably the Bigfoot trying to find new females because Mongo and I scared them away. Now we are trying to figure out a way to capture one that is the main reason they are out here in the first place!" I know that by the time I got to the end I was talking louder than I should have been. Also know at some point I had closed my eyes so when I stopped talking I finally took a breath and opened my eyes to see Don and Tori staring at me. I wasn't sure if they believed me or not but I had to make sure that they understood what was happening.

"Okay, well then. We had better get out there and make sure that all campers are accounted for since they are trying to find females for mating." Don said as he got up and grabbed his hat and jacket.

"So, you don't think I am crazy then?" I asked getting up and standing next to the table.

"No we don't. Over the years we have seen and heard many things in these woods while being the camp hosts last night was the first time anyone has left because of it. Someday you will have to tell us all the details because I can tell by your face that you left a few things out Carrie. We are glad you and your friends are okay and no one else was hurt." Tori was saying when she got up grabbing her jacket too.

"We haven't ever heard or seen things much during the day or this close to sun up at least. This time was different." Don was saying as Mongo went to the door, sniffed woofing to let us know it was clear.

"There was probably about five to seven of the Sasquatch that we encountered so that may make a difference." I said as we started out the door. Don stopped mid step on his way down and turning back to look at me.

"Why are there so many? We only would hear one or two at any time, seriously? Five to seven of them? Shit!" Don was not one to us profanity often but I had a feeling he would be using it more today.

The campground wasn't very big so we hopped into Tori and Don's little razor that could fit us all.  Then we started with the campsites that the people had left in the early this morning complaining about bears. Leaving in a hurry they had left a few things that Don put into the small trailer hooked up to the back of the razor for carrying firewood. A line that the people had had their dog on, was still hooked up in the middle of the 3 campsites was probably why the Sasquatch didn't get anyone there because they were afraid of the dog.  Which is why they didn't go any further with us, because they were scared of Mongo, at least that helps my theory.  In each of the campsites there were bigger rocks than you would normally find around the tents that tells me that they were probably thrown at the tents.

I helped Tori and Don collect and tag everything and they placed on each of the items so we knew what campsite they came from.  Harry buzzed me on the walkie doing my 30-minute check in.

"Yes Harry I am fine.  We are out checking now."  I said as a response.  I thought he was just going to talk not buzz me first to get my attention.

"Okay, I will check in 30.  Be careful."  He said as and then he was gone.

"That Harry a nice Fella?"  Tori asked me.

"Mongo and I seem to think so.  Maybe I will bring him by for a real introduction later on."  I said thinking that man could get me into trouble right now.  I had to stay focused.

"Sounds good."  Tori and Don both said at the same time.  They did that a lot.

Finishing up we headed into loop B.  There were only two trailers in this loop so we went door to door talking to the people, Don and Tori let me do all the talking.

The first trailer a Man and woman came to the door.  I introduced myself, "Morning folks, sorry to disturb you but I was just wonder if you had any issues last night?" They looked at each other and then looked back at me.

"Yes actually, we heard growling and grunting, then something was throwing rocks on the top of the trailer." The man said as the woman just shook her head.

"We thought it was bears! Something went through the garbage cans by the restrooms. We heard it grunting and then you could hear the cans being tossed." The woman said.

"We were leaving this morning anyways but we are glad that you checked in on us." The man said.

"If you are leaving early, Tori and Don can mark this down to send you a refund for any days that you have already paid for. Thank you for understanding." I said as Tori came up and wrote down what the lady was telling her. Don and I backed off a little waiting for Tori to get back to the razor. Mongo was normally would be sniffing everything he could right now was literally leaning on my leg to be close to me. So just to be safe I started scanning the trees all around us. Don saw what I was doing and did the same. By the time Tori came back to us we were ready to move on to the next trailer that was next to the bathrooms, which was perfect timing after all the tea I had drank this morning, I had to go. So I stopped at the bathrooms first. One of the three trash cans were there. Now mind you the cans are chained to a post with a really thick chain. Don went in search of the other two cans with Mongo while Tori and I went into the restroom to relieve ourselves. I was surprised that Mongo wanted to go with Don but he had a hunch I am thinking on where to find the trash cans. He knew that Tori and I were safe enough in a building.

We finished up and were washing our hands when a lady came in, startling us to a halt when she saw us.

"Oh goodness, you guys scared me!" She said as she held a hand over her heart.

"Sorry Ma'am, we were on our way over to see how your camp fared last night with all the noise." I said as we stood talking to her.

"Well, we didn't hear much except for the bears in the garbage cans. We were just getting ready to leave anyway. My husband has to get back to work by this evening so as soon as I go potty we are out of here." She said. She didn't sound all that scared at what had happened which was a good thing, right?

"Okay, well then we won't keep you. Have a great rest of your day." I said

"Bye." Tori said as the two of us walked out the doorway to find Mongo and Don standing next to the two missing trash cans that had definitely seen better days.

"The chain was intact but it would need a new padlock, I have extra's and I'll come back later to fix." Don said.

"So we ran into the lady from the other trailer and they did hear the bears in the cans but nothing else. They were heading out this morning anyway." I was telling him as we walked back to the razor.

"Yah I think they were supposed to leave this morning. I vaguely remember that." Don said as we all climbed into the razor.

"Okay well Loop D is the last camp site loop, there is only one trailer there. They do have 4 dogs with them and they are all men. I believe it's for a guy's weekend or bachelor party, not sure which. We will still check on them anyways. If your theory is correct then they would have been left alone." Tori was saying as we drove the little distance down to loop D.

There didn't seem to be anything out of the ordinary in loop D. The trash cans were fine and you could defiantly hear the dogs before you got to the trailer. They probably heard the razor so that's why they were barking. We pulled up in front of a huge trailer with massive tilt outs. There were two big Chevy trucks sitting next to it. Tori checked her paperwork and they were all paid up for three more days. The dogs inside sounded like hound dogs almost. Mongo was on alert and staying by my side as we all walked up to the trailer door. I knocked, then several somebodies started moving around in the trailer and then the dogs quieted down.  A man with a very grizzly look like he had stayed up all night and hadn't shaved or bathed in a week came to the door.

"Hello, I'm Carrie with the forest service. I'm here to ask if you or anyone with you had any problems with bears last night?" I was smiled and then he did too.  His hair was very dark brown and it almost looked like he had leaves and mud stuck in it.  They must have been hardcore drinking till they pass out kind of guys.

"Well Carrie, my name is Frank. We got so drunk last night that I doubt any of us heard anything." His smile gave me the willies. He was gruff but flirty, is that weird or what?

"Okay well for your safety can you make sure that no one is missing please?" I asked nicely I had to keep my public face on no matter what I was feeling personally.

"Yah, hang on just a minute. Some of us are not descent this early in the morning." He then closed the door.  The trailer rocked a little and he was talking to whoever else was in there.  Then the trailer really started rocking and the dogs were barking on and off which made Mongo a little antsy.  He was leaning up against my leg but I could feel that his body was tense as well.

When the door opened again I had to back up along with Tori and Don because 7 guys came out of this trailer, each one of them was in different stages of dress and cleanliness. Let me tell you, these guys smelled like they had been rolling in the mud and leaves and with just a hint of garbage. Every one of them was unshaven, unwashed and each one was smiling like a fool looking at me. They all were over 6' tall with the same shade of dark brown hair and light brown eyes that made me think of a jersey cow the ones with the pretty eyes and eyelashes.  They all wore sweat pants and t-shirts while others had nothing on their top half at all. They had to be cold?  What was this the backwoods bachelor show or something?

Frank came to the front of the pack and grabbed my hand to shake it.

"Sorry we are all a little messy. It's a guy's weekend and we didn't really plan on seeing a pretty woman out here in the woods Ma'am." He was saying when the next guy came up to shake my hand.

"My name is Gary, Ma'am. Sorry we didn't hear anything last night we were all dead to the world." No more than he finished speaking the next one grabbed my hand.

"My names Abel, Ma'am. Heard nothing last night except us. Do you live around here Ma'am?" He asked but before I could say anything the next one grabbed my hand out of Abel's.

"Names Zeek Ma'am. I thought I heard something last night but it was only Abel." And then another guy grabbed my hand from Zeek.

"I'm Kelly and I think I heard something but I would like to talk to you about it in private, Ma'am." He said and then winked at me. Before I could answer him the next guy decided to pick me up from under my armpits which he soon realized was a back choice when Mongo went off. He doesn't bite unless he has to defend me or himself. His barking snarl will make you think he was about to take your head off. The guy set me down and took one step back as Mongo walked with his back hairs up and a growl in his lips right in front of me sitting at my feet. Every one of the men took a step back.

"Sorry Ma'am, I get a little excited when meeting a pretty lady. My name is Jeffery." He said rather sheepishly.

Then the last guy who was the largest of the group pushed his way to the front of them all. He presented his hand for me to shake over the top of Mongo. Mongo made no moves so I extended my hand and he met me the rest of the way, "My name is Tom Johnson, these are my brothers. As you can see we don't meet very many women when we go camping. When we are camping we kind of let our wild sides out so to speak. Sorry for our unkempt appearances, normally we are very well behaved men." He said as he let my hand go looking down at Mongo.

"We are sorry to disturb you while you are vacationing here we had a bear scare in the campground last night. We just wanted to make sure that no one was hurt. The rest of the campers have all either decided to leave or were leaving anyway so I just wanted to apprize you of the situation so that if you guys wanted to leave then you would receive a refund for whatever nights you had left. Tori and Don here can take down what days you have left to send you a refund check in the mail." I said as Tori and Don came up behind my back. Why did I feel like these guys were sizing me up for something? They all had a wild gleam in their eyes that made me feel very uneasy. That of course is when my walkie went of making everyone jump.

"Carrie, its Harry how are you doing?" I excused myself to go and talk to Harry on the walkie. I didn't walk very far but Mongo was not leaving my side. Tori and Don took a few steps back from the brothers as well, I am sure they could feel something weird about these brothers too.

"Hi Harry, so we talked to most of the people in the campground and they heard bears and a couple trash cans got thrown along with some rocks, three sites of just tent campers left super early so I helped Don and Tori pack up the stuff they left behind. So far everyone has left or are preparing to leave; we are at the last site to check in loop D." I wasn't trying to put too much detail in, but I also wasn't in a hurry to get back to finish talking to the brothers either.

"Okay so when are you heading back?" Harry asked. I heard the brothers shuffling their feet and whispering to each other. They were a weird bunch that was starting to freak me out.

"Not much longer, I'll head back with Tori and Don to help unload the camper's belongings then I will head back to camp." Mongo was starting to get uneasy; I know he was feeling it from me.

"Okay good, we have a few things to fill you in on when you get back."

"Okay, check in 15." I said hoping that he would get the hint to check in with me in 15 minutes instead of 30 minutes like he had before. This way he would know I was not sure of this situation.

"Yup check in 15." He said. I sure hope he got the hint and not anyone else.

I walked back over to the group and acted as if nothing was bothering me. Mongo was not leaving me untouched either. He had to touch me so that he knew what I was thinking and feeling, he was a very intuitive dog.

"Okay, so where were we? Oh, yes. So if you gentlemen would like to leave early then Tori and Don will make sure that you are paid any days you have already paid for. Most people don't want to be around where there are bears while camping, but it is completely up to you and your brothers." I said with a smile on my face. I was not as close to the group as I was a bit ago, but I kept up my chin up because I was here on official business.

"Well, I have to tell you Carrie, I can call you Carrie, right?" Tom started so I gave him a nod that it was okay.

"We aren't scared of any bears. We only get to do this every so often because of our work schedules. So I don't think we will need to leave early. We can take care of ourselves you don't have to worry about us. If you do get concerned for our safety, you can come and check up on us again anytime." Tom had this aura of a man who got what he wanted. It was plain to see what he wanted was me. I wasn't having this, it was time to go!

"Okay then if you need anything just go to Tori and Don here and they will do whatever they can for you. They can contact me in case there is an emergency or if the bears come back. You can still leave anytime you like, I don't want you guys to think that you have to stay after I leave." I said as Tom came forward to shake my hand again. I shook his hand, when I went to turn to leave Mongo growled, so I turned around really quickly to find the brothers getting into a line again. They also wanted to shake my hand again.

So, I shook each of their hands again ending with Tom yet again. He was rather cocky if you ask me, because Mongo was literally sitting on my feet for each of the handshakes and Tom decided to kiss my hand.

"Until we meet again, Carrie." Tom said with a smirk on his face and then he winked at me. His wink did not do the same things to me that Harry's wink does that's for sure. Mongo growled and Tom stood back up again releasing my hand.

"Good-bye" was all I could think to say.

I turned again to walk away and all the brothers said "Good-Bye Carrie!"

Tori, Don and I turned and said "Good-Bye" yet again to them all. This was weird. The four of us couldn't get out of there fast enough. We headed back to Tori and Don's camp in the razor just as Harry called on the walkie again. He was waiting at their site for us to get back there. I was so happy; Tori and Don were a little more relaxed after hearing that.

## **Chapter 7**

No more that the Razor stopped, Mongo and I both jumped out and Harry picked me up and hugged me like he hadn't seen me in forever.

"You have me so worried!" Harry just before he gave me a huge knee shaking kiss that made me weak. Mongo was yipping and running in a circle around our legs bumping into us both. It made us stop kissing so that Harry could say hello and rub his head and face. Mongo was so happy to see him, it was like when I came home from somewhere without him.

"Well at least we get to meet you in the flesh this time." Don said holding out his hand for a handshake.

"Yah, she was in a hurry to get to business last time. Good to meet you!" Harry said and then he shook Tori's hand.

"Harry, this is Tori and Don. They have been camp hosts for many years along with being really good friends of mine and Mongo's."

"Let's step inside to warm up some coffee or would you rather have something else?" Tori asked as we all filed into the trailer. Harry sat next to me on the outside with Mongo on the floor beside him. Tori and Don had coffee but Harry and I went with some bottled water instead. Mongo drank rom his bowl when we came in.

"So we just had a very weird experience with the last group of campers that they aren't going to leave." I said. Harry had me explain everything from the beginning about the brothers in the camp trailer. He didn't look very happy to hear about them. He didn't look happy at all.

"Just whatever you do make sure that you stay away from them. I don't know if these guys are your run of the mill wackos. You know yourself that if Mango doesn't like them, then there is something wrong." Harry said and then Don said, "I concur with that. There was defiantly something off about those Johnson brothers."

"I just hope they stay away from all of us or decide to leave. They gave me the creeps and the way they were all drooling over you Carrie, I don't know how your skin didn't crawl." Tori said as she rubbed her arms as if she was cold.

"My skin did crawl but I do have bar tending experience so I know how to handle creepy guys. I tended bar when I was going to school in Reno as well as in Eugene. Believe me I have seen creepier, but not by much." I too got a cold chill from them too. Mongo got up and went to the trailer door and sniffed then woofed.

"I better take him out to go potty. I don't think he's gone since we got here the first time." I said as Harry stood and let me scoot out.

"I'll walk out with you. We should head back to camp so I can give you the details for tonight's expedition." Harry said as he kissed my forehead then turned me around.

"Okay. Well I guess I will see you guys later. You know how to contact me if you need too. Make sure not to go outside at night." Both Tori and Don stood and gave me a hug and shook Harry's hand again and we made our way out of the trailer.

Mongo sniffed around and then ran around the trailer and then back to me after stopping to pee. That's when I noticed that there wasn't a second vehicle. I turned to Harry.

"How did you get here if you didn't drive?" I asked him.

"Well you sounded upset so I thought you might be in trouble so I ran here. It didn't take me long." Harry said with a grin as we walked around to the passenger side of Big Ben.

"Wow you must really be in shape? I couldn't have run that far. Mango, load up!" Mongo was loaded and in his seat, I fastened his seatbelt and we waved good bye as we turned around heading back to our loop.

The camp was buzzing with activity and when we pulled in and parked next to my trailer Terry was at Harry's door. Harry rolled down his window and Terry was very excited to see us.

"Hey, was everything okay? Harry you took off out of here like a bat out a hell man!" Then he looked at me.

"Carrie did you have any trouble, what did you find out." He asked and I was going to let him know what I found but Harry cut me off.

"She is fine, most of the campground is now empty except for a trailer of men on a guy's trip who took a liking to Carrie and fell all over themselves to talk to her." Harry said putting a less creepy spin on what I told him.

"Okay good, good! Well we are almost ready setting everything up and so we will have another meeting after lunch to that everyone knows what is going to happen. So be ready, we will have lunch soon. Okay, got to go more to do. Bye Carrie!" Terry was wired; I guess we know why there were energy drinks in the coolers and who liked them. Then he was off, actually running toward the group over next to the cage.

"So, is he usually that wired?" I had to ask. Harry smiled at me and leaned over to kiss me. It was just a quick peck on the lips but it was nice.

"Yes, when he hasn't had much sleep and he has had way too many red bulls." Then his smile wasn't as big when he said, "I hope you don't mind me down playing the incident you had with the brothers. I take it very seriously, especially since they were hitting on my girl." He winked at me. "You are my girl aren't you?" He was fishing to see what I thought of us being together. I always thought it was us women that did that, but I haven't had too many relationships to compare it to.

"I think it sounds kind of good." I said leaning over to kiss him. This kiss was not just a peck on the lips. This kiss was a lip burning fire starting hormone revving kiss that I felt through my whole body. It was waking up not only my libido but I could swear I was getting tingle in certain places.

Just as things were getting a little too heavy for being in my truck in front of everyone someone knocked on my window. Harry and I both jumped at the sound and slowly moved apart. When I pulled back I took a glance at Harry's lap and had to smile, then I looked Harry in the eyes. He winked at me. I was not the only one affected by that kiss.

"We'll finish this later Lassie." His accent gets thicker when excited, good to know.

I fully turned myself around to see who was at my window knocking, which was a feat in itself. I hadn't realized how far I had climbed over to be almost on top of Harry. That's when I noticed that the windows were actually a little foggy, but Trina was smiling while knocking again at my window to get my attention, so I rolled down the window.

"So we girls need to talk and you should probably adjust your shirt before climbing out of the truck. You also have an audience over there." She said as I looked at my shirt to find it was yanked up over my bra. Then I saw that half of the crew was watching us so I yanked my shirt back down. Pretty sure I had changed at least three shades of red by this time. Then I heard a chuckle from Harry so I turned to look at him starting to get a little mad that he was laughing at me being seen by the crew. He was looking in the backseat where Mongo was, so I turned to see what he was looking at. Mongo had gotten out of his seatbelt and was lying on the floor with his paws over his ears. Something I had seen him do when he thought I was being too loud with something like the radio or the vacuum cleaner. He was shutting out the noise of Harry and me. This would lead me to believe that we must have been pretty loud to start with. How embarrassing!

"He doesn't like loud noise when he is relaxing so he covers his ears." Was all I could think to say. Harry caught my chin and kissed me quickly and then he said, "We will continue at a later date my dear. I have to go and I will see you at lunch while you and the ladies do what you need to do." Then Harry kissed me a peck again on the lips then my nose and then my forehead. My eyes closed and I was in a trance or something because when I opened my eyes again he was out the door and closing it. Since Harry was now gone I rolled up my window as Trina opened the back door to let Mongo out. Mongo ran over to a tree not far from our trailer door and started to pee. Then he ran around the whole trailer marking his turf which I would assume he had done earlier as well when Harry took him potty while I got dressed.

Then we went into the trailer where Amanda was waiting for us. Mongo gave her kisses and then ran to the back and climbed on the bed to take a nap. He knew we were safe here, for now.

For the next hour I was explaining my interesting encounters with the campers especially with the trailer of brothers, which Amanda and Trina both wanted in detail. I was surprised that I remembered each of their names really. I mean they each introduced themselves differently so that was probably why I remember them so well and Tom was definitely the oldest not sure how the order went from there except that Jeffery was definitely the youngest. Frank and Gary were definitely close enough to have been twins but they all were pretty much just carbon copies of each other. It was super weird and I was still having a hard time forgetting them and they way they treated me.

"I think that if you hadn't met Harry first then you might have taken the situation a little differently Carrie, they were just being nice and they were probably still hung over from last night's drinking." Trina was saying, not trying to be mean but trying to get me to see from their point of view, something she has always done.

"Maybe, hey I know! The next time I have to go and see these guys, if I do, then the two of you can go with me so that you can see for yourself what is like." I was trying not to be pissy but seriously they weren't there to feel the creepy vibe. "Besides Tori was there and they didn't even acknowledge her or Don the whole time I was there."

"Well they probably just figured you were the only single one, which you are, right?" Amanda was asking because Trina told her how she found Harry and I.

"I wouldn't call myself married, but Harry did ask me if I was his girl." I wasn't actually sure what that meant myself so I couldn't quite explain that to them.

"Anyway we are getting off topic here. If you have to go and see these brothers again I would be happy to go along just to see the dynamic between the brothers and I am sure that Amanda will go too. Right Amanda?" Trina was saying as she looked at her watch.

"Sure, I will go too. As long as they are not Sasquatch I am there, okay? We wanted to tell you what has been going on since you left but it's time for us to go and grab lunch before the meeting. Wait until you see what is happening tonight. It's the full moon tonight and they say that the Sasquatch are more active during that time." Amanda was saying as she went to stand. I am sure that mongo heard something about lunch because he jumped off the bed and ran to the front where we were standing. We grabbed our jackets and headed down the steps with Mongo in the lead. He ran around the trailer yet again and then came back to my side. I leaned down to rub his head and ears. He licked my hand so I kissed his head. We were going to eat and find out what the crew had been up to.

When we got closer to the lunch area we noticed that all the guys had already gotten their food and were sitting down. So we went to get ours. The girls went for salads since they are always watching their figures. I got a hamburger fully loaded with fries and a plain hamburger for mongo with a large fruit salad so that I could have more. Terry, Harry and Jerry sat at a table alone waiting for us to join them. They hadn't been there very long. Once I sat down I noticed that I had forgotten to grab something to drink.

"Did you forget your drink?" Harry asked me when he saw me looking around.

"Yah I forgot to grab Mongo a bowl too. I'll be right back." I said as I started to get up but he put a hand on my arm so I sat back down.

"I'll get them for you. You go ahead and start eating, I'll be right back." He kissed the top of my head as he got up heading to the food truck. He came back a few minutes later with two bottles of water and a paper bowl for Mongo's water. Oh, he was totally racking up the boyfriend points now. When I got Mongo's food plate and water bowl set up on the ground next to me. Mongo had been waiting so patiently to eat. I tell you what these burgers were so great, I don't know if it was because we were eating in the great outdoors or if they did something special with them. In could just be that I had great company next to me too. You know I have never been one of those girls that only ate salads in front of guys that I was dating because I didn't want them to see how I really ate. I am always just me, the greasy burgers and fries, jeans and t-shirt, hunting and fishing kind of girl. Take me as I am. Apparently that is something that Harry likes about me. I like that he can be just himself around me too. I have to keep reminding myself that we only met two days ago because I really do feel like we have known each other forever. I can be me and be relaxed around him. But there is one thing that even I won't do around a man this early in a relationship, I will not fart! At least not yet….

## Chapter 8

Once everyone was done eating the conversations around us came to an end then Terry stood and walked over to the campfire at the center of all the tables.

"First off I really want to thank everyone for being totally on task and getting everything done even on such little sleep from our incident early this morning. That being said, if anyone here does not feel safe and would like to leave, no questions asked. You will have a room at the Oakridge Lodge & Guest House and I will pay for that and whatever room service you want. That being said does anyone want to leave?" Terry asked and it was a unanimous shower of "No's", "No way's" and "Are you crazy?". Everyone was staying to be a part of what was going to happen tonight.

"Ladies' I know you live in Oakridge and all but I also want to make sure that you know you have the same offer is extended to you a well, especially because of what happened last night. If you do decide to stay I want you to know that every man here will protect you from whatever comes next. Am I right men!" Terry got another unanimous response from the men in the crew plus our guys as well. They weren't letting anything happen to us ladies. Which I know we are going to be in for one hell of a night, and it's the full moon. Grandpa warned me about the full moon and Sasquatch.

Trina and Amanda looked at each other then they looked at me, we were going to be in for one heck of a night.

"We are all in Terry!" Trina said with a wink to Terry.

"Thank you Sweetie!" Terry said right back to her. I knew something was going on with those two as well; I would have to find out details from both Trina and Amanda later, much later from the sounds of it.

Everything was set up around camp and Terry filled us ladies in on the plan once everyone else went off to double check all the equipment for the night of chaos that was about to unfold in our camp of all places. Terry said that he and Jerry had come up with the idea and Harry was very adamantly against it.

"I just think it puts the girls in way too much danger, Terry. Why can't we just take a recording of Trina doing the mating call instead of the girls being there?" Harry was very upset and had been holding me to his side ever since Terry started explaining what we were going to be doing tonight to catch a Bigfoot.

"You know yourself that recordings haven't really done any good in the past for hunting them. This is the first time we have had such a large amount of Bigfoot actually forget they were hiding from us. Just so they could get to a female which they thought was one of their own. Now Ladies' if you are not comfortable with this we can stop right now and get everything packed up and out of here before sundown. But we only have about an hour before that happens and I am pretty sure they will be back shortly after that, it is the night of the full moon, the most active time for Bigfoot!" Terry was getting pretty adamant himself.

"Calm down Terry, we already said we would do this. Can we go over the plan one more time though? I still don't understand where Carrie and I will be?" Trina was trying to calm Terry down. He had her pretty close to his side as well and she seemed to really enjoy being with him. Amanda and Jerry were leaning into each other right next to Harry and I and Jerry seemed to be a little less of a hands on guy from the looks of it but you could still tell that he and Amanda had some vibes between them. Now if we could only capture Bigfoot without anyone getting hurt or stolen.

So the plan was as follows; first everyone would be stationed around the camp with tranquilizer guns. Secondly, Amanda and Jerry are manning the cameras that are positioned all around the camp as well as in and out of the Bigfoot cage. Nothing would get past them without being seen or filmed. Thirdly, Trina, Mongo and I were going to put into a small caged area at the back of the larger Bigfoot cage as bait. This way the Bigfoot would go into the cage to get to us. Then we can go out the other without having any contact with the Bigfoot itself. Trina would to give her primate mating call every few minutes. Terry figured since the Bigfoot knew where the girls were at already that they probably hadn't went too far away.  This is why we are doing this in our camp instead of in the woods. Mongo was my incase anything goes wrong clause of this arrangement, anything goes wonky he and I would start howling to make the Bigfoot leave.  If they didn't leave then it was also the signal for Harry, Jerry and the crew with the tranquillizer guns to come a running.  Harry was being sent to the outer ring of the camp to listen and watch for them before they get to the cameras or tranquillizer guns ring giving us all had a heads up. Once the Bigfoot is in the cage it will be shot with the tranquillizers along with any other one that might follow.  Easy Peasey, Right?  Let's hope so, for our sake.

    Once the plan was explained us girls hugged and headed to where we were supposed to be.  The smaller cage was a little smaller than I thought but the three of us fit okay enough.  Mongo was at my feet and he didn't seem to care what was going on.  It was already turning dark when we got into the cage so it wouldn't be too long.  We were sitting on a some camp chairs because we didn't know how long this was going to take.  Our walkie talkie was quiet for only a few minutes, I figured Terry was waiting for it to get a little darker before Trina started.

    It felt like hours had gone by, it was super dark and silent.  No crickets chirping, no frogs croaking, nothing.  Then the walkie came to life with Terry's voice.

    "Okay everyone is finally in position.  Trina you can start at any time.  Remember to wait a few minutes in between.  Everyone stay off the walkie unless you have a sighting!  Go ahead Trina." Terry sounded nervous, I bet he wasn't as nervous as us bait though.

    Trina stood and placed her hands around her mouth and howled her primate mating call into the sky.  Then she sat back down while we waited a few minutes just listening.  We heard nothing, so she then stood and did her call again.  Nothing was out there, we heard nothing at all.  So we waited.

When Trina went to stand to do her call again for the third time, that's when we heard the howl in return. It made the hairs on my neck and arms stand on end. Mongo came alert and was looking though the cage and beyond. That's when we heard more howls chiming in, they were coming!

We are safe in this cage; I know we are. Terry said they modified it to be very strong so we could trust in that. But when you hear something howling in the distance and you know they are coming for you, well you start wondering how strong are these things and just how safe is the bait for this trap?

Mongo started growling and I patted him on the head.

"Not yet buddy. We have to get them into the cage, buddy." Mongo sat back down looking up at me with his sad eyes. I don't think he thought we were very safe either.

Trina grabbed my hand and we looked at each other when the grunting and howling got very close. It had only been maybe five minutes since the last howl. I guess they thought they were getting the girl tonight, huh. I really hope that they are disappointed in the end and not us.

"It's going to be okay. We are safe in here no matter what." I was telling Trina just as we heard the grunting growl from just beyond the open cage door. We both turned seeing three sets of glowing eyes that were staring straight at us. Mongo stood up and started to growl. I placed my other hand on his head again.

"No Mongo we want them to come in." Mongo sat on my feet just glaring at the eyes that were staring at us.

Trina didn't stand this time to do the howl but she took her hand from mine, surrounding her mouth to give a smaller version of the mating call. That's when all hell broke loose!

There were Bigfoot coming from all directions! The three sets of eyes we saw came charging out of the trees and straight into the cage just as another three came from the backside of the cage where we were. They were trying their hardest to get us out of it.  More of them howling and grunting and growling all around us. That's when we heard the shots; the guys with the tranquillizer guns were shooting the three inside the cage. Then they started shooting the ones outside the cage that were trying to get into where Trina, Mongo and I were.  No more than the ones hit the inside of the cage to get to us Mongo started barking and growling back at them. He almost bit one of them. Then I started howling like I had never howled before and then Mongo joined in with me.

      The Bigfoot inside the cage started getting slower and looking at us like we were crazy. We were just out of reach for them to touch us.  The Bigfoot that were attacking the part of the cage that Trina and I were in weren't giving up. I don't think they had been shot yet. They were definitely strong too; some of the bars were bending but not much.  That's when there was a howl that sounded like a Bigfoot crossed with a grizzly bear.  They all stopped.

      There was something out there that even these Bigfoot were afraid of? The ones in the cage were starting to slump a little.  The others that were trying to get into our end of the cage were giving up, along with the others that were coming around to the ones in the cage.  Where was everyone?  Why did the shooting stop?  Mongo and I started howling again and within seconds there was another howl not the same as the grizzly bear Bigfoot cross howl but very close to it.  This one made all the Bigfoot stop and look around like they weren't expecting something else to be out here.

      When a larger Bigfoot came out of the trees in front of the cage he looked pissed. He was the same color as all the other ones.  He actually hit a couple of them upside the head.  What a weird thing to do for a wild animal.  Then he made the others pull the Bigfoot out of the cage and leave while he walked into the cage all the way up to where Trina and I were. He didn't even give Mongo a second look as Mongo was growling and snapping at the extremely larger Bigfoot that was now staring me right in the eyes. I could see that there was intelligence in his eyes, not just an animal. His face didn't look as pissed off anymore; he looked like he was trying to read me, my facial expressions.  Then he put his hand up to the cage bars in between us and I looked at it then I looked at him again. He smiled; he actually smiled then took his hand away and leaned all the way to the bars with his forehead. I couldn't hear or see anything going on around me. I hadn't realized that I had stood up and walked close to the bars. I couldn't hear Trina yelling at me until she went to pull on my arm to pull me back toward her I heard something crack and go boom. I threw my hands up thinking that something was coming in from above us into the cage with us and then I felt it. The huge Bigfoot had grabbed my hand as they flew up to cover my head and bit the side of it. I was shocked to say the least. I felt the pain almost immediately and yet I was flabbergasted that he had bitten me. He let go right away, then I held my hand to my chest looking at him. I swear that bastard had a smile on his face.

Then he was gone. Something had grabbed ahold of him and pulled him out the open doors of the cage and into the trees. I started crying and Mongo was trying to climb into my lap to lick my face. I was sitting in the chair again. Trina was saying something in the walkie talkie, but I couldn't hear her. I was bitten by a Bigfoot and I think I am going into shock. Oh, shit! What if I get rabies, does Bigfoot carry rabies? Where the hell was everyone? What is that noise? It sounds like two grizzly bears fighting? Do I need to go investigate that? What am I doing in a cage? Why is Trina and Mongo running around me? Why does my head feel so light and full of air? Why am I so tired? I closed my eyes just to rest for a little bit. I wasn't needed anywhere, was I? Darkness that was what I found after my eyes shut and I heard nothing after that.

I woke up hearing people arguing about me. Mongo was laying on top of me and he was going back and forth between licking my face and growling. What the hell was going on? I slowly opened my eyes; I was laying on my bed in the trailer. My left hand was kind of stiff so I raised it up to take a look at it. It was wrapped in gauze and you could still see blood coming though the gauze. When did that happen? Mongo was on my chest with Trina and Amanda on either side of me. Every time they touched me he would growl, he never growled at them before.

"She's awake!" Trina yelled and I could hear sets of feet running back to the bedroom.

"Finally, Carrie please tell me you are alright!" Terry was asking, his face was white as a sheet and he was sweating very profusely.

"Well, my hand hurts like hell and so does my head. What happened?" I asked as Harry helped me sit up better. When Harry helped Mongo move off my chest Mongo didn't growl at all but he laid next to me.

"Well, you got bitten by a Bigfoot! I would have to say he was the boss of all the others because he had them pack off the ones that the tranquillizer darts hit but didn't affect them much. It only slowed them down a very small amount. Then he decided to take a bite of your hand. Why did you get so close to him Carrie? He was dangerous and you just stood there giving him your hand? What were you thinking?" Harry sounded more disappointed than I could believe.

"You made it sound like I volunteered to have him bite me! I was in my chair one minute. Then I was face to face with this big one with something exploding over my head and I covered my head with my hands then I felt the pain!" I was remembering some of what happened; it was all flashing back now.

"Where were you guys? Where were all the tranquillizer guns? Why didn't you guys have our back?" I was asking as I started crying. They never came to help us; they weren't there with us.

"Carrie, I am so sorry baby." Harry held me in his arms as I cried.

"I'm sorry Carrie; we didn't take into account that they would be more intelligent than we thought." Terry was saying as he and Trina stood to the side of the bed.

"They knew we had cameras and guys out there. They took out the cameras, the ones that stayed on the outskirts of the first group then knocked out all the guys with the guns. They waited to see where they were shooting from. They were smart about this; they knew we were setting a trap. They are definitely smarter than we could have ever thought!" Terry was saying hugging Trina even tighter.

"Trina, did you get hurt too? Did anyone else get hurt?" I asked through my tears. They hadn't abandoned us, they were taken down.

"No one else got hurt, or bitten either. I tried to pull you back into your seat Carrie I did! You wouldn't let me pull you away from him. Then another Bigfoot landed on top of our cage and you flung your hands up, that's when he bit you. I'm sorry I didn't try harder, Mongo even tried to back you up. He was barking and growling and tried to bite the Bigfoot the whole time you were standing there. We couldn't get your attention, so I radioed Terry." She was saying as tears started to fall down my face.

"It felt like I was under a spell or something? Do you know of anything like that happening before?" I asked Harry and Terry. Jerry came forward though the doorway looking very ashamed and sad.

"I've heard of it once, but I thought the person telling me was off their rocker so I didn't think anything of it. I'm sorry too Carrie. We should have been better prepared." Amanda walked over to him and put her arms around him.

"She knows you guys weren't to blame. But we need to get out of here. That other thing might come back thinking that the ladies are up for grabs since it got rid of the other Bigfoot." Terry was saying.

"What other bigfoot?" I asked not remembering another one.

"Just before you passed out another large Bigfoot, a reddish one came out of nowhere yanking the huge Bigfoot out though the doors of the cage and took him into the woods. You could hear it beating the crap out of the Big Bigfoot as well as the others." Trina said as she hugged Terry a little harder. She was still scared and I couldn't blame her. Bigger means stronger and the smaller ones almost got into our side of the cage.

"Yah, you could hear the others running through the woods like they had fire on their tails. I saw some of the fight before I finally made it back to you and pulled you, Trina and Mongo out of the cage. Trina bandaged up your hand but she thinks we should take you down to the hospital in town to have it checked out." Harry was saying as he looked at everyone else and they were nodding their heads.

"That about sums it up, what do you think the Hospital in Oakridge or River Bend?" Terry was asking me.

"Oakridge is fine. Can I get rabies from a Bigfoot bite? Do you know? What exactly are we telling the doctors when they ask what happened?" I was very curious to know.

"Well, we could tell him the truth but we still have no proof since they took out all the cameras. That might bring other hunters up here blowing our chance at trying to catch them again. Maybe say a bear bit you? That would be my best guess." Terry said as Trina crossed over to the side of the bed and took my hand in hers.

"Well the only problem with that is that it doesn't really look like a bear bite. More like a huge man bite, really. But I am only a primate expert what do I know?" Trina said as she giggled, trying to bring a lightness to the situation.

"Well I have never been attached by a bear before but I don't want anyone out here looking for a bear to kill either. On the other hand, no pun intended I don't want people out here looking for the Bigfoot either. I will talk to the doctor when we get there. Depending on which doctor it is I may have a friend on our side that we can leave it up to him. Is everyone okay with that?" I asked as I started to move a little. Harry gave me some room but Mongo wasn't letting me out of his sight.

"Okay it's up to you." Terry said as Trina grabbed his hand and led him out of the room but not before she could comment, "Fine with me too, say hi to Chuck for me." Then they were out of the bedroom and into the living room area where it sounded like Trina was packing.

"And who is Chuck?" Harry asked with a little growl.

"Chuck Stone is Trina's ex-husband, the guy before Scott Marjoram that she broke up with before coming up here. Gosh, it seems like that was

81

days ago. Anyway he is the head doctor in the emergency room most days. He will probably be the person I will get the most help from at the hospital." I said as I swung my legs over the edge of the bed making Harry stand up and move out of the way.

"Here let me help you get up." Harry tried to grab me by the upper part of my left arm to help me.

"I got it. It's only my hand I should be able to stand and walk around." I said a little on the snappy side.

"You are a hard headed woman. But I think you will need some help." He was saying as I started to sway, my head getting super light again. I had to sit back down again and almost landed on mongo who was trying to hold me up from behind as well.

"Has anyone checked in with Tori and Don or the campers that didn't leave since last night?" I asked just as I went down and darkness took over. I was out for the count.

## Chapter 9

All kinds of odd sounds are what brought me around. I knew I had passed out, something I have never done before. I always had a cast-iron stomach and nerves of steel but I know I passed out. The loud beeping of machines, along with someone snoring next to me. I was lying in a bed that wasn't my own. There was no Mongo next to me but someone was holding my hand. It was a small cold hand, which felt like my Mom's hand. People were talking and walking by where I was lying but they weren't doing it so loudly. I hear all of this then know what these things are before I even open my eyes. When I do the room is dark with my Mom sitting beside my bed holding my hand while sleeping with her head on the bed. I never knew my Mom even snored. Dad was sitting in a chair watching a western on the TV with headphones. He must have had it up loud because I could hear what they were saying word for word. People were walking past the window to my room, doctors, and nurses, and then I recognized some of the crew walking by. Then I saw movement to my right set back a little in my peripheral vision, it was Harry.

"I'm glad you're awake finally." He whispered but it wasn't a very low whisper.

"Where is everyone, was anyone else hurt?" I couldn't remember anything that we had talked about this morning after the Bigfoot fiasco.

"Everyone is fine; they have been fine for a week now." He said as he got closer to me and taking my other hand.

"A week, no we just had the run in with the Bigfoot last night, don't you remember?" I was confused and I'm not sure if it was me or him that had this wrong. Maybe he got hit on the head?

"Where are Mongo, Trina and Amanda? Did they get hurt?" I didn't see them in the room but it must be getting lighter outside because my room was getting lighter and easier for me to see.

"Mongo is with Amanda and Trina is here with Terry on a small couch a little farther down the hall in the waiting room. Your parents have been here every evening. Some of the crew have been here at all times." He was saying as he sat down in the chair on my right, scooting it up to the bed. The beeping was from the monitors on my left side that were really getting annoying.

"How do you feel? You look a little weird." He said as he put a hand on my forehead like he was checking my temperature or something.

"Hey Pumpkin, you are finally awake!" My Dad was rather loud so I winced a little at the volume of his voice which woke up Mom too.

"Don't let Harry fool you he hasn't left your side since you were checked in." Mom said as she sat up, she was awake and I hadn't noticed she had quit snoring because I was trying to block out sounds to focus on the fact that I had been asleep for a whole week.

My Dad moved in on mom's side leaning in to hug me as Mom also hugged me. We hug a lot in our family. It felt good to be held and loved.

"Now Harry you get on in here with us." My mom was saying and then Harry actually listened to her hugging me in a group hug with my parents! What has been happening since I fell asleep?

"We just wanted to let you know that we have spent time with your Harry here and we just adore him Carrie." Mom was saying as they all stood to give me a little room to breathe. Just then a nurse walked in and seeing that I was awake she turned on the overhead lights which kind of blinded me for a second. I guess sleeping all that time made my eyes a little more sensitive to light.

"Good you're awake; I will let Doctor Chuck know." And then she was gone. My Dad picked up the conversation from where we left off, I had a feeling the nurses had been in and out of my room a lot while I was sleeping.

"Yes, and Carrie he loves my pizza too." Dad was saying as he put his hand on Harry's shoulder. Harry just had this strange look on his face, but a happy one. I don't think he was used to having people like him right away and be affectionate, besides me and Mongo of course.

"How are you feeling dear?' My Mom asked as she sat on the bed and Dad took her chair.

"I feel a little strange, everything seems to be so loud and I am starving but I guess a week without food would do that to a girl. How is Mongo, Mom? We haven't been apart this long before." I was saying as I scooted up farther in the bed and Harry grabbed the pillows from behind my head to adjust them for me so I could sit more comfortably.

"Mongo is fine. We just have to worry about you right now. The doctor said there was no reason for you to pass out after being bitten. They ran some blood tests but found nothing out of the ordinary. The bite on your hand has practically healed with not much of a scab left the last time the nurse changed your bandage." Mom seemed a little less worried when I woke up. Harry was shuffling a little bit like he needed to go somewhere.

"Do you need to go? I know there was a lot to do with what happened to all of us. Did we get anything we could use?" I asked, Harry looked at me like he had been listening to someone else talking then tuned in to hear me.

"Sorry, I was thinking. No, I just thought you might like it if I told Trina and Terry that you were awake. No we didn't get anything useful from that night and yes your parents know everything so don't worry about talking in code." I turned looking at my parents and they nodded their heads.

"I had to tell them and doctor Chuck what happened so that they had all the information on how to best treat you when you came in." Harry was saying as he took my hand. He was seeing if I was angry with him for telling my parents.

"It's okay, I would have told them anyway. The doctor needed to know what was going on. And I am guessing I did not get rabies?" I asked with a giggle.

"No you do not have rabies. Doctor Chuck said you could go home once you woke up and ate. So let's get you some food, what would you like?" Mom was saying as they all laughed with me.

"I thought I heard laughing in here! I am so glad you are up and smiling again. You had us worried lady!" Trina said as she came in through the door heading straight for a hug from me. She was even crying which made me cry of course.

"Would you stop crying! You always do that, you cry then I cry and then you laugh at me for crying. Turd!" I said as she hugged me again. Then I noticed that Terry wasn't very far behind her.

"Come on in Terry! Would you like to hug too?" I asking trying to be funny but the man actually walked in around the end of the bed and Harry stepped back to that Terry could get in on the Trina hug with me. Now this was weird, right? I didn't die, did I?

"Hey guys? Did I die or something? Why is everyone so emotional right now?" I wasn't sure who would answer that question. Everyone just kind of looked at each other; Mom and Dad were just kind of standing back a little so that everyone could fit by my bed.

"No Honey, you didn't die. We all are very worried about you though. There has been a large group of people in the waiting room every day that you have been in here. Between the Bigfoot crew and all the people you work with, this hospital has been super full of just visitors. I was told to let you know that Johnny went back up to check on Tori and Don as well as the campers that were up there during the... Well during the time you guys had the issues with the Bigfoot. They have already been down here to check in on you since you have been asleep and the campers left the same morning you guys all did. The campground it closed for a little while and Tori and Don are camping out at your Grandparents property until then." Everyone was watching my Mom as she filled me in on what I had needed to know. Everyone either nodded their heads or smiled at me.

"Okay, so I would really like a cheeseburger and fries from Dari-Queen Dad. Would you please get me a deluxe cheeseburger meal, please Daddy!" I whinnied a little because I know what that does to my Dad.

"Yes, Love I will go and get that right away. Do you want anything to drink with it?" He asked as he hugged and kissed my Mom and then he leaned in and kissed my forehead.

"Oooh yah, chocolate milk shake please!" My tummy was rumbling now just talking about food.

"Carrie, I just don't understand how you can eat that stuff?" My Mom was saying as Trina chimed in.

"I know she has always eaten that stuff and she never gains weight, she just stays curvy. I wish I could do that." Trina pouted as she stood and walked to the end of the bed where Terry met her.

"We are going to head out and I will call Amanda to let her know you are fine, so she can tell Mongo, who by the way has been beside himself since you passed out." Trina said as she and Terry started to follow Dad out of the room.

"We will talk to you later; I will let the crew know you are good. Do you want visitors or should they head back to the trailers? Which are also on your Grandparents property, just so you know? Your Grandfather has been telling us some crazy Bigfoot stories. He even let us record him for some of them. We will all talk later, they are having a gathering later next weekend, Harry can tell you more. Bye!" Terry said as he pushed Trina out the door with a "Bye, Love you" from her and a wave.

"Wow, a lot has been happening while I was sleeping huh?" I asked as Harry sat back down in his chair. My Mom headed for the door as well, "I am going to use the restroom I'll be right back. That way you too can talk a little bit without me around." She winked at us heading toward the visiting area which is where there is a bathroom, I'm sure the crew is still sitting there.

"So we have some things to talk about." Harry started to say. I leaned forward and put my finger under his chin putting the lightest pressure there as he rose up I pulled him closer just with my finger to meet my lips for a much needed kiss. When his lips touched mine they kind of sparked which made us both jump then we went in for a full on the lips, him climbing into the bed with me kiss. This was what I wanted from the moment I saw him standing in my room. This man had some power over me that I could not explain. I know he felt it too.

So we sat like this for several minutes just enjoying kissing each other when there was a knock on my door. We stopped kissing and Harry turned with a little growl, it was so sweet. Then he stood at the side of my bed again as doctor Chuck came in.

"Well I would ask how you're feeling but I can see you are doing better. Awake with the pink in your cheeks would make me think you are ready to go home, huh?" Doctor Chuck was saying as he grabbed my chart off the door taking a look as to not embarrass me too much.

"I am definitely awake and starving. Dad went to get me some DQ. So what happened to me Doc?" I wanted to know but I also didn't.

"Well it looks like you had some kind of reaction to the bite," he wiggled his eyebrows, "the bite we won't talk about. We put you on antibiotics and let you sleep it off. Do you have any questions for me?" Chuck was always a funny guy. He stood at 5'5" with black hair, brown eyes and he always had a smile on his face. He had his serious side but he refused to make people worry unless they had to. He is like a brother to me, so much so that when I was living in Reno and my friend Jessica had some problems with a guy hurting her and stocking her later, Chuck came down with a bunch of his friends and helped me pack to come home to finish school here in Oregon. But he and Trina just weren't meant to be I guess.

"So I don't have rabies or anything from the bite. Does that mean I can go now or what?" I asked as he put my chart back. He then walked up to me and looked into my eyes with his little penlight and then had me open my mouth and say ahhhh. Then still without saying a word took my blood pressure, then he finally he says, "You are good to go!" then he turned and headed for the door.

"That's it? Not even a good-bye?" Harry asked as Chuck turned and waved as he went around the corner into the hallway.

"He doesn't ever say good-bye. He has this thing about not saying it to someone he cares about. So that good-bye isn't the last thing he said to them if they happen to die. He's been like that forever." I said as Harry went to the doorway to see Chuck at the nurse's station talking to the nurse that had been checking in on me earlier. Then he came walking back to me and sat in the chair.

"I guess we can either wait for your parents to get back or we can get you up, get dressed and get your things together?" Harry said but he didn't look like he was in too big of a hurry to do anything right now. And I wasn't going to let him help me get dressed. It was too soon for anything like that, kissing is great but we should stop right there for right now.

"I say I wait until Mom gets back so she can help me get dressed. By then Dad should be back. Did you have anything you needed to do?" Harry looked at me with a smile and then he kind of shook his head like he was clearing an image from his mind.

"Not really, you are my only priority right now. When your Mom comes back I will let the crew in the waiting room know that you are being released." He said as he got up and kissed me lightly on the lips, just enough to tease me. Then of course is when Mom walked back into the room.

"Damn, I thought I gave you guys enough time to kiss and talk before I came back." Mom kind of giggled as she walked in.

"Well, Doctor Chuck came in and let us know I can be released when I am ready. Can you help me get dressed please and gather my stuff,

Mom?" I said and Mom looked from me to Harry and I can't believe she said this, "Why don't you have Harry help you?" Harry and I both turned red and Harry excused himself to go and update the crew.

"Mom, how could you say that? We haven't known each other that long and we haven't even had sex yet!" I was so embarrassed I can't believe she said that, in front of him!

"Sorry, I just assumed that you guys had been together longer, you two seem to have a real connection of some kind. And I just assumed that since he refused to leave your side for very long at all that you too were connected, you know sexually. Damn, how long have you known him then?" Mom looked flabbergasted and that was not something that came easy to do to Mom.

"We have only known each other for 3 days when I got bit, so basically a week and three days. Since I was out for a week of it I don't think that it is time I can count toward a relationship?" Now I was confused. I climbed out of bed and was a little wobbly on my legs. Mom came to my side to help me.

"Well let's not think about those things right now. We just need to get you changed and get your stuff so we can take you home. Your truck and all of the things you took camping have been taken to your house. I called Amanda while I was walking and she wanted me to text her when you are leaving. She will meet us at your house with Mongo. Which leads me to another question, if you guys haven't done anything yet then were is Harry going to sleep? Because he said he wanted to stay and take care of you so that you could go back to your house to recover, so?" Mom left it hanging like that. Harry hadn't said anything to me about that yet. Maybe that was what he wanted to talk about when the doctor came in?

"Well, he hasn't talked to me about that yet, Mom. I guess we can talk about that on the way to my house." By this time my feet and legs were okay so I headed for the bathroom to relieve myself, I hadn't realized how much I had to go potty until I stood up. Mom was pulling my clothes out of the cupboard as I closed the bathroom door. That's when I heard Dad's voice talking to Mom. She told him everything that we had just talked about in like 5 seconds, even the part about Harry and me not having had sex yet but that she still knew we had a very serious connection. I was so embarrassed, now Dad knew too. I took a couple extra minutes in the bathroom to take a quick shower then I brushed my hair which had looked like a wildfire was unleashed on my head before my shower. I brushed my teeth even though I was going to be eating my burger and fries in a minute, my teeth had fur coats on. And Harry still kissed me after my hair and mouth were so terrible, wow, what a man. Mom passed me my clothes through the door because I wasn't coming out yet.

When all the embarrassing things had been said and I could hear that Harry came back to the room. Then I came out of hiding to find Harry with a table set up with my food from DQ along with food for him. I felt better after showering and to be in my own clothes and know that my hair and teeth were clean and presentable. I looked around but my parents weren't in the room anymore.

Harry saw me looking and said, "They left you in my hands. The crew has all left and your Mom has put all your stuff into a duffle bag that she brought you. I figured we would sit and eat and then get you discharged." He was saying as he smiled pulling out a chair for me, that accent gets me every time.

"Okay sounds good to me; I wasn't really looking forward to a lot of people anyway." I said as I sat in the chair and he helped push me in a little.

"So your Mom, she said I needed to talk to you. I'm sorry that I let them believe that we had known each other a lot longer than we had and I let them believe that we were together-together. I just couldn't leave your side, every time I thought I should I got this pain in the pit of my stomach and had to be by your side. Did your Mom tell you that I said I would watch over you when you got to go home? I planned on asking you but I just wanted time with you." Harry was kind of rambling on and on and I couldn't get a word in, he just kept asking me questions and I know he wanted to make sure that I understood his motives and though they weren't bad intentions in the least.

"Slow down Harry." I said as I put my hand on his that he had outstretched to me palm up.

"I understand, and I feel the same way. Yes, you can stay with Mongo and I but you will be sleeping on the couch not in my bed. You may have misled my parents into thinking we have already had sex but we haven't and I have to take this slow. I will not get into a short term relationship with someone that may not be around later. I know it is your job to be a Bigfoot hunter but I don't do one night stands or 1 week stands, I am not that kind of girl. I do appreciate you being here with me.

"I have no problem with either of those things Lass, I'm glad you are who you are that is kind of what has attracted me to you." He raised my hand to his lips and kissed it. Then he looked down at our DQ boxes and said, "We should probably eat before the fries get to much colder, your Dad had them in a pizza box heater that he had in his truck to keep them warmer longer."

"So we got delivery but not Pizza? That's funny! Leave it to Dad to find a better way to do something." Harry let go of my hand so we could start eating. My burger was heavenly and my Milk shake was gone in no time but my tummy felt so good to be full again. Once we are done eating, I get to go home. I can't wait to see my Mongo I bet he missed me too.

## Chapter 10

Harry had one of the crew trucks to take me home in. It only took a few minutes to get discharged and then we were out the door. I had to ride in a wheelchair to leave but it wasn't too bad. When we turned off on Fish Hatchery Road to my part of the property I could see in the not too far distance all the crew had trailers set up on my Grandparents property. It looked like Grandpa had the fancy port-a-pot's brought in for the crew to use. They had the food truck as well as the cage trailer and the whole crew.

"I also kind of forgot to mention that the whole crew was close by along with that your Grandparents want to have a little party for you when you are totally better. The whole crew, your parents and all of your friends are invited. They weren't very happy to hear that you were helping us, but when Terry and Trina went to talk to them with your Parents. They kind of took a liking to Terry then they met the crew and they have had many campfires that included talks of Bigfoot which I think your Grandfather has just been waiting to talk to people about. You can just tell, he even let them record him on a few of the stories he told. I am sure that he has told you the stories." He was nervous again.

"I have heard all the stories many times growing up. I'm glad the crew and my family have gotten on so well together. Hey Amanda's already here, I forgot to text her!" I was so excited; Mongo was running around in his yard trying to jump over the wooden fence.

"I texted her while you were signing paperwork." Harry said as he parked the truck next to mine in front of my small two car garage.

"Thank you Harry!" He was definitely a very good and handy man to have around.

"It's what a man does for a woman he Luvvvvv.... Likes." I really think Harry almost said Love! Wow, I think I will let that one go for now. He obviously didn't mean to slip and I am sure he wasn't ready to say it or else he would have, right?

I almost jumped out of the truck and Amanda let Mongo go through the gate to get to me and he jumped up for a hug. He is a tall dog when he stands on his hind legs and that was what he was doing, putting his arms on either side of my neck and licking my face like he hadn't seen me in a week.

"I know Buddy, I Love you too Mongo! Okay, okay! Time to get down now." Mongo dropped down and then started going in circles around my legs sniffing me up and down then he stopped at my hand that still had a bandage on and he licked it.

"Yes, my ouchy is getting better. How was he?" I asked Amanda who was smiling to see Mongo with me.

"Well he was beside himself; he stayed by the door ready to go to you or for you to show up. He did eat and sleep with me. But overall he was a very good boy." She said as she patted him on the head then gave me a hug.

"You scared us all you know? Don't do that again!" She kissed my cheek hugging me tighter. Then we walked into the house. I could tell that my Mom had been there, everything was cleaned and some things had been moved and reorganized, her calling card.

Harry brought in my duffle bag plus all the things from the hospital and placed them into my room. He placed his duffle at the end of the couch; all the while Mongo is going room to room stiffing everything. Something that I have come to expect because he does it every time we come home no matter how long we have been gone. Mongo made all the rounds and then he went to the backdoor and gave a woof. So I thought he wanted to go out into the backyard to play but when I got to the curtain and moved it aside to unlock the sliding door I noticed some mud on the window.

I went ahead and slid the door open and Mongo shot out of it like a rocket then turned and woofed at the mud on the door. He turned around and started at one end of the fence sniffing his way all the way around the fence until he was back to me. Then he ran back to the far end of the fence yet again and woofed at some mud that was on the top of the fence.

Harry looked interested in the mud that was on the door, I went out the door just to get a better look. It looked like a face print with a cupped hand print just above where the forehead would be. My mouth opened and my jaw dropped, Harry was cursing then Mongo started barking and running toward us then back to the fence.

Harry and I both walked to the fence where Mongo wanted us to see that something large had basically stepped over the fence and left not only mud on the top of the fence but a huge footprint on this side and I am sure we will find yet another on the other side. Harry jumped the fence with a little difficulty. He was over 6' tall, so whatever stepped over the fence had to be a lot taller.

"They followed me home?" I started to shake; I was in shock I think. Why weren't they following Trina she gave the first mating howl?

"Carrie, we don't know if it was them. There are only one set of tracks here. I will call Terry and the crew to have them come over and make casts of these prints. They also have some of the casts they made before we bugged out when you got bit. We will be able to tell if it was one of those. Stay calm, I am here and so is Mongo." Harry pulled out his phone and snapped photos of the prints then he called Terry. I didn't hear anything he had to say while he was on the phone. Mongo came up to me and grabbed my wrist like he does when he wants to lead me somewhere to lead me back to the house. We walked right in and I sat down on the couch, Harry came in a few minutes after we did.

"Terry and the crew are on their way over." He said as he sat down on the couch next to me, with Mongo at my feet with his face in my lap. Harry put his arm around me.

"Your shaking lass, are you okay?" He asked with real concern in his voice.

"Why are they following me Harry? Trina started the mating call, why aren't they after her?" I started crying and turned my face to the crook in Harry's neck. Mongo tried to climb higher into my lap but couldn't quite manage it.

"How do we know if they aren't after Trina too?" I asked in a panic.

"She has been either with Terry in his trailer or at the hospital with you. This will make the guys look around to see where the tracks started as well as if there are any tracks around their trailers. We will get to the bottom of this Carrie, I swear it to you!" Harry's Scottish accent was very prominent right now and he seemed very passionate about this. It made me feel better that he was here to protect me.

In no time at all the crew, Terry and Trina were there at my front door. Trina just walked in and everyone else followed her. Mongo never moved from where he was, he had gotten used to the crew and he loved Trina too. He was not leaving me for anything. Harry helped me walk back to my bedroom with Mongo to get me to lay down on the bed; I suddenly felt so drained and needed some rest. He kissed my forehead and said he was going to check on how everything was going on. Mongo was cuddling with me and I fell asleep.

The dreams I was having of running through the woods and there were so many others like me, I felt the freedom. I could feel the wind in my fur and the dampness of the ground under my bare feet. I slowed to a walk to smell of the wet earth all around me; it wafted into my nose as I walked through the brush. There were others like me, I could smell them too. I was chilly but also warm, it was confusing how much the smells made me feel at home, but I also know I don't belong here and the others are here to get me, aren't they?   Then I heard a voice talking to me.  It was a deep voice, a manly voice with an accent that made me smile.  Then something touched my lips and something else wet and warm slid up my cheek.  Was it the trees and brush I was walking though?  Then the warmth shifted and was behind me and in front of me, I could feel arms around me so I looked down and there was nothing there but a reddish fur coat, when did I get a fur coat?  Why was I wearing it in the woods at night?

  I opened my eyes to come face to face with Mongo; I closed my eyes just in time before he licked me right between the eyes.  That dog of mine!  Then I felt the arms around me tighten and someone was nuzzling and breathing in my hair.  I turned my head just a little and then I was kissed on the cheek.

  "You looked so comfortable I just had to join you Lass, were you having a good dream?   You sure were smiling and sounded like you were smelling something, was it flowers?  I didn't mean to wake you Darlin'." Harry asked as I realized it was him in my bed beside me.

  "I was having a very weird dream, a dream like I have never had before."  I was saying as my stomach took this opportune time to growl.

  "I guess I had slept for a while?   Where is everyone?"  I asked as Harry let me go and rolled off the bed from behind me.  I wanted to sit up and Mongo decided he needed to lay across me so I couldn't go anywhere.  I have a feeling he won't be leaving my side for a while again.

  "They took some castings along with some photos of the face marks and then Trina washed your windows so that it wouldn't bother you anymore to see them.  Your Grandfather came down on his quad and asked what was going on so Terry informed him of what we think happened, which then your Grandfather asked if the crew wouldn't mind pulling their trailers closer to your house to kind of circle the wagons so they did.  So everyone is within screaming distance now.  I hope that makes you feel better?"  Harry was looking at the expressions going across my face and I have to say that first I was upset that Grandfather would ask that of them.  Now I would say I am kind of glad that he loved me enough to make sure someone was watching out for me.

"Okay, I guess that makes sense. So is everyone in their trailers or what is happening now with everyone?" I was kind of confused I guess it was my brain still coming out of my dream world, right?

"Oh, well most of them are going over the evidence they collected, Trina had to go home to get some more clothes so Terry and Alvin went with her. I haven't heard a peep out of anyone since. I can tell by the growling of your stomach that you are hungry for dinner. Your Parents asked me to see if you would like me to take you to the Bigfoot Pizzeria for dinner. The gang is welcome too and we can text Terry to have them join us. I know the cooks will be happy to not have to cook tonight." Harry's cellphone buzzed in his pocket just as he finished asking me.

"Ya, that sounds good. Go ahead and answer that." I was saying as he looked at the screen and answered it right away.

"Hay, what's up?" Then Harry paused for the other person talking.

"Shit really? Okay so you already have them there?" Another pause while he waited but my interest was piqued in who it could be calling.

"Okay, you and the gang finish there then meet us at the Bigfoot Pizzeria; yes Carrie's folks own it. Yah, I will let the cooks know. Yes, I will tell her too. Okay, meet you there." Harry hung up the phone then sat on the side of the bed next to me. I knew this wasn't going to be good. Harry waited a couple seconds while he sent a text to the cooks about dinner, they texted back that they had a hunch and would meet us there. I have noticed that this crew can text really fast. Harry put his phone back in his pocket and looked at me. I knew he was going to tell me something bad.

"So you know when you asked why the Sasquatch were after you? You wanted to know if they were after Trina as well? Well when Terry and Trina got back to her place they found the same kind of prints on several of her windows as well as three different sets of Bigfoot prints. The crew is all over there right now collecting whatever they can find. Trina is a little shook up but Terry is with her now." Harry stopped talking because he saw that my face had turned white as a sheet. Trina only lived a mile from my house down at the end of Swank lane, I used to walk to her house during the summer when we were kids. I spent a lot of time at her house and she did at mine too. But the time we spent in the woods in between was always the most fun. And Amanda's house wasn't but a half mile to the west at the end of Park Lane. We had all the woods in between to play along with all the woods on my Grandparents property, that's why I love being a forestry agent the most.

"Carrie Lass? Are you okay? Do I need to call a doctor or your parents or something?" He took my hands in his and they were so warm, I could just snuggle up with him and forget everything.

"No, I'm okay Harry. I'm with you." I smiled and just saying that made me feel better. I had Harry and Mongo with me so I was going to find where someone put my pistol because it was going back into it holster just in case I need it. I can do that before we leave to get some pizza and see my Parents.

"I would like to go freshen up before we go to eat. Mongo let's go to the bathroom." I knew he was going with me even if I didn't ask so I figured I better ask up front. Harry got up and moved aside then offered me his hand to help me get out of bed. Mongo followed right on my heals. Once inside it only took me a few minutes and I even washed my face. When we walked out of the bathroom Harry stood up from sitting on the edge of the bed with his phone out.

"I texted your Mom that we were on our way and that the crew would meet us there. She's happy we are coming and will have a table reserved for us all." He said smiling.

"You look better already." Harry said as he crossed the floor and kissed my check.

"You do know that I'm not sick, right? That I won't break, I may be freaked out about this Bigfoot thing but I am not going to break." I said as I leaned forward giving him a kiss that I had been trying to share with him since we left the hospital. He put his arms around me so slowly and pulled me up to him as he intensified the kiss. His hand went into my hair and the passion was so intense I could feel it all the way through my body. I could swear my temperature was rising and getting out of control like a brush fire spreading downhill with the wind pushing it.  Because that is what I was right now, on fire!  My left arm was over his shoulder my right was under his arm to get the best hold on him to not let go.  When his hand started moving down my back and then around to touch my left breast Mongo gave a woof and that stopped us both.

Our heavy breathing could be heard in echoes in my bedroom.  It almost sounded like there were more people breathing than just us.  We both looked down at Mongo and he woofed again and started walking to the bedroom door.  Then he stopped and sat down again, just looking over his shoulder at us like he was saying, "Come on guys, food!"  I swear that is what he was saying with his eyes.

"Okay Mongo, Okay!  Well I guess we were saved by the dog?"  I giggled a little feeling a little more like myself again as I slowly pulled out of our entangled bodies.

"So maybe we should pick this back up later when we get back home?"  Harry asked wiggling his eyebrows.  He was so cute right now.

"We will see."  Was all I said as I turned around and headed to Mongo.  As we went down the hall I grabbed my coat and purse from the hanger by the door.  Then I grabbed Mongo's official Forestry Service halter and leash for public.  It helps with the whole health code thing while in restaurants.  I wouldn't want Mom and Dad to get into trouble for Mongo being in there.

After putting the halter and leash on Mongo I turned to find Harry right behind me putting his jacket on.  It wasn't dark yet but it definitely would be by the time we came home and it would be a little chillier too.  We walked out the door and Harry locked it behind us while Mongo took a pit stop before jumping into my truck.  He was so easy to put into his seat and when I went to get into the driver's seat Harry stopped me with a hug and a kiss.

"Do you think you can let me drive?  I know it's only a hand injury but it would make me feel better if I drove you around."  He was seriously racking up the good guy points.   How can I say no to this man?

"I guess so.  Do you know how to get there?"  I asked as he walked me around to the passenger door and opened it and helped me get inside.

"Yes, it's on Main Street.  We've passed by it a few times since we got here.  Do you need help with the seat belt, Lass?"  He asked but he was already helping me to put it on, I think it was just an excuse to touch me some more.  I smiled as he clicked it into place.

"Thank you Harry."  I took his face between my hands, bandage and all pulling him in for a kiss.  Not too long but not to short either, but just right.  He pulled away with a devil of a grin on his face then he backed up and closed my door.  He was back around and up into the driver's seat before it even registered that he was gone from my hands.  That man really has an effect on me, how was I going to keep myself from having sex with him in my house while doing all these things for me.  I really need to talk to the girls.  But right now I am so hungry and Mongo and I want pizza.

## Chapter 11

  Harry drove us to Bigfoot Pizzeria without any issues. When we pulled in we could see that most of the crew including Trina, Terry, Amanda and Jerry had just pulled in and parked so we would all be going in at one time, which is good. The crew waited for us all to gather before we went in. The place seemed to have its normal Sunday night crowd; you had a few small families and a child's birthday party in one of the private rooms on the far side of the room when you walk in. Mom and Dad had all their people working tonight it looked like. They employed quite a few Oakridge High school students and they are great bosses, I should know. Trina, Amanda and I all had summer jobs here for a few years.

  When we walked in Mom was right there to greet us all, Dad hardly ever leaves the kitchen when he is working. She gave me and the girl's hugs. Then she even hugged Harry, Terry and Jerry, so weird. But I was out of it for a week so I am sure they were all talking to each other since there wasn't really much else to do except watch me sleep or the T.V.

  Mom led us to one of the private rooms so that we could well, have our privacy and be able to talk openly about things that were going on now. Mom sat down at the table with us. She sat at the head of the table closest to the door. There were two tables in the room and everyone kind of split into smaller groups at the tables. Harry and I along with Trina, Terry, Amanda, Jerry and Alvin sat at the end with my Mom.

"Okay guys, my Dad said there was some stuff going on at Carrie's house, now spill." She said in her no nonsense way that she has.

"Well first off it didn't happen at just Carrie's house. These Sasquatch have been to all three of the girls houses here in town. All of them have the woods very close by and they were able to check out the houses while the girls weren't there of course. They have been with us or Carrie at the hospital. We gathered evidence at all three sights. Sorry we didn't have time to tell you before we got here Carrie." Terry was saying as Trina reached across the table, grabbed my hand and gave it a squeeze.

"It's okay Terry. I knew about Trina's place but I hadn't heard about Amanda's until now." I looked at Amanda and she didn't really seem to be fazed by it.

"Jerry and I thought we should check it out with a couple of the guys while they were at Trina's just to make sure. They had walked the same trail we had when we were kids from Trina's house down to mine. It was so eerie. They left foot prints and face prints on the windows just like at your places." Amanda was one tough cookie so I am sure she was holding her anger back at them violating our space. All of a sudden Amanda just popped off with, "Those Damn Dirty Apes!" Everyone in the room stopped talking turned to Amanda and we all started laughing at once. Leave it to her to break the stress in the room.

Mom was filled in on all the details of each of the houses along with the evidence that was picked up to be analyzed like crazy later. Amanda and Trina will be staying with Terry and Jerry in the trailers that are currently circling my house like the wagons circling against Indian raids, which is funny if you think about it. My Grandfather wanted them to do this at my house with me inside and he as well as we have a lot of Indian heritage in us. I had to laugh about that. Then everyone looked at me.

"Sorry did I just laugh out loud?" I asked while looking at everyone staring at me.

"So what was so funny?" Mom asked so I told them about what I had just thought about the circling of the wagons and our Indian heritage.

Everyone had a good laugh at that one too. Mongo even came out from under the table at my feet to give me a lick on the hand that was in my lap. I petted him on the head. I think everyone just needed to decompress after everything that had happened so far.

Mom left a few minutes later with our orders. She made sure to talk to Mongo to let him know that Grandpa, my Dad, would be making him his personal peanut butter and sweet potato pizza that he made special for service dogs that come into the pizzeria. They just love it.

Dinner was great as usual for Dad's pizza and the conversation was definitely animated to say the least. Everyone had a theory but it felt weird to think of the Bigfoot as anything but humanly, I mean they look like animals but there are definitely brains at work here not just instinct, right? So on the way home we stopped at Johnny's market for some supplies. Since I will have Harry staying inside the house with me and they had Mongo's favorite treats. Unfortunately, the whole crew decided to stop too. Which is good business for Johnny's but it really made the store packed while we were in there too. Most of the crew was grabbing snacks and things while the Food truck crew were getting some of the more perishable items that they had run out of. All in all, it didn't take as long as I thought it would, plus not too many of the regular town people came in while we were all in there either.

Once I had everything for my house on the belt at the register it became our turn Harry decided he was paying for everything, which I kind didn't mind but I had to at least act like I was good.

"Harry, really I can get this." I said putting my purse on the little tray next to the card reader.

"Nope I am staying at your place I pay for the snacks and things. No arguments please Lass." That accent gets me every time, I hope there is never a day that it doesn't affect me.

"But I also have Mongo's treats on there too." I said as they were scanned.

"I am invading his domain; I think I can get his treats so he is still my buddy." Harry said as he reached down and petted Mongo's head. Mongo was at my side and gave him a woof then licked his hand before he pulled it away. I really think Mongo knew what we were talking about all the time, pitbull's are a very smart breed of dog.

"Okay. Well, thank you." I said as I stepped down to where there was a high school kid bagging the groceries. Harry paid and then took the two bags of groceries from the kid instead of taking the cart so I put the cart back into the cart return. We could now go back to the house to relax.

As we walked out to my truck I noticed a truck that looked familiar parked at the side of the parking lot pretty close to the road. There were three guys sitting up front in a newer Ford extra cab truck. It was a dark brown with large tires and it had a fifth wheel hitch in the back of bed. The truck was facing away from us but he guys were looking in the side mirrors then they climbed out of the truck and headed our way toward the store entrance. I am guessing that Mongo noticed them too or he felt my body tense up or something, because he was extra clingy to my legs. He was watching them and I could tell he wasn't very trusting of these guys by his body language so I patted his neck running my hand down his side a couple times as they walked closer. The guys were all pretty tall, clean cut and kind of cute, it was more their aura of confidence that had me looking at them. All three of them were wearing jeans, nice clean t-shirts, cowboy boots and baseball caps. They were in their early to mid to late-20's and I had this déjà vu thing going on. By this time we had reached my 4runner and I rolled down the back window so Harry could put the grocery bags in side when the three guys stopped by us.

"Ma'am." They all said with thousand watt smiles on their faces, it was kind of weird. I didn't recognize them but they seemed so familiar to me. The oldest looked at my hand then nodded which made the other two guys look at my hand as well.

"Good day gentlemen." I said not wanting to be rude but not being overly friendly either.

"Yes Ma'am it is." The tallest and I am thinking the oldest of the three said then he touched his cap and winked at me, then lightly wacked the guy on his left on the chest.   They all looked at Harry while walking away toward the store still smiling.

"Do you know those guys?" Harry asked me because I couldn't stop watching them.

"I don't think so, but I just have the strangest déjà vu going on right now. I feel like I shouldn't turn my back on them too, which is totally weird." I said as Harry and Mongo walked me to the passenger side of the truck so Mongo and I could get inside.  Mongo got into his seat, Harry fastened him in for me so I didn't have to use my hand.

I was about to close my door when Trina and Amanda came up to stand beside me.

"Who were those guys?" Amanda asked me still looking toward the store entrance, which they should be inside by now.

"I'm not sure.  Do either of you recognize them?" I said as Trina pulled out her phone and texted something.

"Nope, but I just texted Alvin who is still in the store to see if he could get a picture of them so we can check them out." She said as she put her phone back into her pocket.

"Why did you guys get a bad vibe from them too?" I asked glad I wasn't the only one.

"No, I just wanted to know who the cocky guys were." Trina said as she giggled.  She then tapped Amanda on the arm.

"Terry and Jerry are waiting for us.  We are staying in the trailers at your place, so if you need us text us. Okay see you later." Amanda said as Trina grabbed her by the arm and they kind of giggled as they ran to the truck Terry was driving.

"Don't worry Carrie; I got a bad vibe from those guys too." Harry said as he climbed into the driver's seat and started the engine.

"Thanks, I thought it was just me.  I don't know about you but it was like a dangerous animal awareness thing that was making me watch them.  Like I thought they were going to attack me, is that weird or what?" I asked Harry as we pulled out of the parking lot headed for home.

"No that's not weird; I was getting the same vibe off of them as well. Why don't we just forget them and talk about something else?" Harry suggested as he patted my knee, which in turn made me forget what we were talking about and turned me thinking of what happened just before we left the house. I needed to talk about something else and think about something else now.

"How about we watch a movie when we get back to the house?" I needed to change the subject in my mind or I was in trouble.

"Sure what do you have in mind?" Harry asked concentrating on the road ahead but also it seemed like he was watching the rearview mirror a little more than before.

"I don't know I have quite a few for you to choose from, I like all kinds of movies. Is there a reason why you are transfixed on what is behind us?" I asked as I started to turn to see who was following us. It was only the crew truck that Terry was driving with the girls and Jerry in it. I didn't see anyone else back there.

"No, I was just being a safe driver. You know making sure that the people behind us aren't tail gating or anything." He just sort of laughed a little, but he wasn't fooling me. I started watching in the side mirror to see if I could see what he was looking at but all I saw was Terry's truck for the next few minutes. Then you could barely see there was another truck keeping its distance from Terry's truck. Maybe it was the rest of the crew?

I waited until we pulled into the driveway to say anything to Harry.

"Were you worried about the truck that was following Terry?" I asked as we sat in the truck for another minute or two. Terry pulled in driving around to the back of my part of the property to where his trailer was parked. Then we still sat there for another couple of minutes to see who was following Terry. Harry still hadn't answered me, it seemed like we were both holding our breath, waiting. A few seconds later a truck passed by my driveway and it looked just like the truck that those weird guys were in but there are so many of those trucks in this town is was hard to tell. You couldn't really see how many people were even in the truck.

"To answer your question, yes I was waiting to see who was following Terry's truck." Harry said on an exhale of breath that I also let out at the same time. I guess we were both holding our breath. Just then 2 more trucks also passed by my driveway. The last truck looked super familiar both were darker shades of blue almost black but I could see the colors.

"Harry, how is your memory?" I asked really quickly while I was trying to memorize the trucks plate.

"Pretty good, why?" I answered him right away.

"Oregon plate, CTY112, you got that?" I asked him and then I started to ruffle through the glove compartment to find a pen and paper not waiting to hear if he got it or not, he didn't say a word. Not finding one I pulled out my phone and started a text to Johnny.

'Need to know if this license plate was used at Waldo campground last weekend. Let me know ASAP. Oregon plate' I stopped and said to Harry, "Okay what was the plate number?"

"CTY112" he said and I typed it into the text and sent it.

"Thank you, I am not good at remembering numbers connected to letters but if you give me a service road number I can tell you exactly where it is and how long the road is also where is comes out and the road it's connected to." I said with a smile.

"I have a really good memory for all kind of things." Harry said just as my phone dinged for an incoming text.

'Yes it was the camp of all the drunken guys. Why? You aren't supposed to be working!' Johnny texted me, he is suck a big brother.

'Not working just saw the truck and thought it familiar, must have stuck in my brain when I checked on the drunken campers. Talk to you later.' I sent the text and then let Harry know, "I was right, it was a truck I have seen before. It was one of the trucks that were parked at the drunken guy's camp."

"That is strange. Maybe they live around here? There are a lot of people who go camping close to home, especially when it is a beautiful place to go." Harry said as he climbed out of the truck opening the back door to undue Mongo's seat belt to let him out.

"Yah it's probably just me being paranoid." I said as I opened the door and climbed out myself, Mongo met me in like two seconds. He must have run around the truck to be at my feet so fast.

"It's okay Mongo, go potty before we go into the house boy!" Mongo ran to the yard and did his thing then was back at my side before I even got to the front door. Harry was only two steps behind me that man was not only fast but very efficient it seems. He had undone Mongo and grabbed the two grocery bags from over the seat so he didn't have to roll down the window.

Just as Harry got to my side at the front door is when the other crew trucks pulled in and drove around the side of the house to the trailers waving as they went by. It seemed that two other crew trucks had gotten home even before us, so everyone was accounted for. Now it was time for movies, popcorn and maybe a little ice-cream too.

It didn't take me long to change into my comfy clothes. It didn't feel weird to change into sweat pants and an oversized t-shirt to watch movies with Harry at all. He had done the same thing! Mongo was ready to rest too, because once I sat on the couch he dragged his dog-bed over to lay on top of my feet and then he laid down in it. Harry popped popcorn in the microwave and grabbed me a glass of unsweetened ice tea as well as one for himself.

"I do have to warn you that my tea is rather unusual." I said as he sat next to me with the bowl of popcorn in his lap and he set his drink on the side table.

"What do you mean?" He asked as he took a sip of it and smiled.

"It's peach-black tea. I just love that it tastes like summer so I drink it whenever I can." I took a nice drink of it; it felt so good and tasty. Mom had brewed me a new pot when she knew I was coming home. She always thinks ahead for me.

"I can taste the peach, this is really good tea." Harry smiled and then took another longer drink of it, "It does taste like summer! Yum!" Harry set his drink back on the side table and got back up to pick a movie. I have a lot of movies in my living room, and by a lot I mean I could open my own DVD rental store but with movies on demand and downloads so easy, there just isn't a market for that anymore.

"How about……. Princess Bride? I haven't seen it in long time. It has swashbuckling, brain teasers as romance. What do you think?" Harry asked as he looked at the back of the DVD case.

"Sounds good to me, I haven't seen it for a while either. So what was your second choice?" I asked because I saw him hovering over another movie before he pulled out the Princess Bride. Harry kind of smirked then he pulled the other DVD out and showed it to me.

"Harry and the Henderson's?" We both started laughing so much that Mongo lifted his head and looked at both of us like we had lost our minds. I could just hear in my head what he was thinking, "Silly humans!" Which only made me laugh a little bit more.

Harry sat back on the couch after he put the movie in and he started the show and then handed me the remote. Huh, a man that relinquishes the remote to the woman, interesting.

We had so much fun watching the Princess Bride that we even watched Harry and the Henderson's right after that. When I finally made it to bed I was exhausted.

"Why don't you go ahead and get ready for bed and I will clean up and put things away." Harry said as he saw me yawn for like the hundredth time.

"Okay, thank you. I am pretty tired. You would think a week sleeping then my nap today that I would be all slept out, but I guess not." I said as I shrugged my shoulders.

"Come on Mongo, bedtime." Mongo jumped out of his bed, dragged it back to where he kept it then followed me back to our bedroom.

I changed into my actual night shirt and my men's night clothes pants and Mongo met me in bed ready to snuggle. I had just sat on the side of the bed when there was a knock on my doorframe, since I don't close my door.

"Harry, come on in." I said kind of nervous. Was he expecting to sleep in bed with me after the kiss we shared earlier? I haven't had a real relationship in a while so this was all new to me. Harry walked in and he looked a little nervous.

"I just wanted to say good night Lass; I had a great evening being with you. I was hoping that you would let me give you a good night kiss?" He said as he walked closer to me. I stood up and he pulled me into his arms. Then our lips slowly met making this was the sweet kiss, not the hot passionate one of earlier but this one was just as memorable. My arms wrapped around his neck and he bend down to me with his arms around my

110

back. Time stood still for me at least; his lips were strong yet loving and tender.  They say that you can tell if a man loves you by his kiss, but if that were really true how you would tell which kiss was the one?  There are so many kinds of kisses, or is it just Harry that has all those different kinds of kisses?  Nice!  We separated very slowly out of each other's arms; I swear I saw something flash in Harry's eyes.  They almost glowed, or that could have just been me.

"So I will be right there in the living room if you need me." He said as he slowly backed out of the room walking a little sideways which made me think that he might have had an issue in his pants so of course I looked and OMG yes he did!  There was a tent in his sweat pants that made me smile.  Then he saw what I was looking and smiling at, which only embarrassed me.

He put his hands on his hips and gave me a huge smile and then he winked at me and said, "Lass you make me feel like a Man!"  I know my face turned three shades of red and I actually giggled again.

Mongo razed his head off the bed where he was waiting for me and gave a woof, I swear in my head he actually said, "Come on guys! Bedtime!"  I looked at Mongo and he put his head back down again.  I know my eyes must have looked like saucers.  Harry came back into the room and put his hands on my upper arms.

"What's the matter Lass?  You look like you have seen a ghost!"  Harry really seemed flustered as well.

"No, no ghost.  I'm just hearing things that I really shouldn't hear.  Never mind, I think I am just super tired Harry.  I'll see you in the morning." I leaned in and kissed his cheek while he was looking at Mongo and then he let go of my arms.

"Ok Lass.  See you in the morning then."  He then walked out of the room and I turned off the light and crawled into bed with Mongo who moved letting me hold him to go to sleep like we always did.  I just needed sleep.  I will feel more like myself in the morning.

## Chapter 12

Have you ever been in a dream that was so vivid that you could feel everything, hear everything and even though you know you are dreaming? All the while in this dream you just feel like this should be your life? This was my dream; I was walking in the woods feeling the earth between my toes, smelling the earth, trees and bushes all around me. I could hear the animals in the bushes I could hear their little hearts beating when I passed by them. I saw a little bunny run out from under the bush that my leg brushed against. I didn't feel like chasing it, but I did feel warm and cozy. I rubbed my hands up and down my arms to find them fuzzy with fur. So I looked down at myself to see that I was totally covered in fur. Was I wearing a fur coat again? Why would I wear a fur coat into the woods? And my feet! They were freaking huge and hairy too. Why was I barefoot in the woods and where was Mongo? I didn't go to many places without him and the woods weren't one of them.

I could hear people talking so I headed in that direction. I didn't have far to walk when I smelled a campfire and the voices were even louder. I followed the smell and the voices now. I stopped at the edge of the trees in the bushes and low hanging branches from a cedar tree. I could see them now even though it was dark my vision was really good. There were four men sitting around a campfire just talking and laughing. I could hear what they were saying too. Wow, my hearing and sight were really good in this dream! But why would I dream about strangers? What they were talking about caught my attention.

"Did you hear about the Sasquatch sightings close to town?" The man in the blue baseball cap asked the others. Everyone got really quiet. Then the man in the U of O sweatshirt talked.

"Yah, they were seen in two different areas close by the Hunter family's land. Do you believe the Bigfoot stories that old man has been telling over the years?" He sounded scared to me.

"I think it's a bunch of crap, there ain't no such thing as Bigfoot or Sasquatch, at least not anymore. They were probably some Indian tribe that was like, super hairy so people feared them so they went into hiding from the rest of the world. But I think they all died out by now!" This man in the red checkered jacket sounded mad. They were talking about Grandpa Hunter's land, my Grandpa and his stories. U of O sweatshirt stood up and tossed his beer can on the ground next to his red cooler.

"I think you believe what you want to believe and I will believe what I want to believe. The Hunter's family has been here since the town was started, if you were going to see a Sasquatch anywhere it would be close to their land. They protect them out there in those woods. I've got to pee, I'll be right back." U of O sweatshirt walked off to the tree line not too far from where I stood. I stood super still so that I wasn't seen and I stayed quit listening to the others talk.

"Do you guys really think that there are Sasquatch out there on the Hunter Family land? I wonder if we could check it out sometime? Do you think the old man would let us go out there if we didn't take any guns with us?" This was the smaller man in the group he sat closer to the red jacket man; it could have been his son. Most of the men looked to be in there late 40's early 50's and this kid looked to be maybe 21.

"Nope! Mr. Hunter has a strict policy of not allowing anyone on his land except family. So that is why I am wondering why he has all those trailers around their granddaughter Carrie's house? I thought maybe they were family from out of town. Most of them have cameras on them at all times like they are doing a documentary or something of the town and they just happen to know the oldest family in Oakridge?" Blue baseball cap was saying as U of O sweatshirt came back out of the woods and sat back down in his chair.

"I don't want to bust up this part but we do have to work tomorrow. Mikey grab our cooler and I'll get the chairs. Hopefully your Mother isn't too upset when we get home." Red jacket was saying to the boy, Mikey.

"Yah it's getting late, George. Who's got the bucket of water to put out the fire this time?" Blue baseball cap man asked as he stood up as well.

"I'll just dump my cooler on it since I'm out of beer anyway. You guys go ahead and load up, I got it." U of O sweatshirt guy said as he then dumped his cooler of ice and water onto the campfire. I could hear the hissing and crackling of the fire being drowned then smell hit my nose and made me sneeze. It was only one sneeze and I didn't think it was all that loud. I stopped after it and waited to see if anyone heard me.

"What the hell was that?" U of O sweatshirt guy yelled and the others came back over to see what was happening.

"What's going on?" George asked with Mikey at his side.

"I don't know I thought I heard someone sneeze or something?" U of O sweatshirt guy said as he dropped his cooler into the back of his truck that looked like it was an older Chevy truck from the 1980's, rust and green made up the color scheme. George and Mikey had already loaded their stuff into their newer Chevy truck that was a very bright red color. Blue baseball cap had the small SUV, I think it was a forest green Rav4.

"Nah you are just hearing things. Your imagination is working overtime with all the Bigfoot's in the area!" Blue baseball cap said laughing. George and Mikey joined in on the laugh as well.

"Anyone have a flashlight so we can take a look?" U of O sweatshirt guy asked.

"Not worth the time, Man." Blue baseball cap man said as he walked back to his SUV and climbed inside.

"Nope we got to get home or my wife will skin me alive. Night Monty!" George said as he steered his son back toward their truck. They climbed in and started their engine, but hey seemed to be waiting for the U of O sweatshirt guy, Monty to get into his truck.

"Monty! Let it go! We got to get home and so do you!" George yelled out his window as Blue baseball cap guy pulled past his truck heading down the gravel road that their trucks were parked on. Why hadn't I noticed the road earlier?

"Fine, but I am telling you guys there is someone or something out there." U of O sweatshirt guy, Monty said as he threw his cooler in the back of his truck.

"Yah it might be a bear, dipshit! Let's go!" George hollered as Monty climbed into his rig and started the very noisy truck. Then he peeled out getting back onto the gravel road throwing rocks and debris in all directions behind him. He was pissed at George you could tell. One of the smaller rocks flew and hit me in the forehead can you believe that? It really smarted too. I rubbed the spot and I am really sure it is going to bruise at least. When I rubbed my head I also found that I was wearing a fur cap, no wonder I was warm.

By this time, I was feeling very tired and I just wanted to get home. I turned around and headed in the direction I came from; following what I can only guess was the smell of home because that is what I thought of as I walked. What a dream I am having, I can't wait to tell Harry about it nor should I? It might be the medication I was taking making me hallucinate or it could be something from the Bigfoot bite I got? I wonder if Harry knows anything about Bigfoot bites? I'm so tired I don't want to think, my mind goes blank, I am back to smelling the earth that is under my feet and the air that is so crisp and cold but I am warm.

The next morning, I awoke to find myself in the bathroom asleep on the toilet. I must have come in here to pee and just fell asleep. Would that be why I was dreaming of the earth and fresh air smells because of the clean bathroom with the air freshener that smells like the woods? I guess I was only dreaming after all. Too bad that would have been a great adventure wouldn't it have? At least I am less worried than I was before.

I have to shake my legs to wake them up because even they had fallen asleep while I sat on the thrown. How embarrassing was this? I finished peeing and by then my legs were pins and needles but awake enough to stand. I pulled up my pajama bottoms to find that my feet were muddy. Did I sleep walk last night, was that why my dream was so vivid? How did I get past Mongo and Harry both? This is what I was thinking when I started washing my hands and wet a washcloth to wash my feet off. Then I looked at myself in the mirror to find a little cut that had crusted blood and a bruise forming on my forehead.

"What the hell happened last night?" I asked myself and not expecting a response I dried my hands, washed my feet off and then opened the door to walk into my bedroom to find Mongo. Mongo was laying on my side of the bed on his back sound asleep and snoring. Wow, I guess I wasn't missed at all.

I grabbed my jeans and a t-shirt that had 'Save the Drama for your Mama' written in bold letters on it. Then I slipped on my slippers, I knew I wasn't going in to work for at least the rest of this week so I might as well be comfortable.

"Hey Mongo, you got to go potty?" I asked him and of course he flipped over and jumped off the bed heading out my bedroom doorway. Once we got to the end of the hall I saw that Harry wasn't on the couch sleeping in the living room. So I went to the back slider door to let Mongo out to go potty. When I opened the door I noticed there were some muddy small foot prints on the small patio just outside the door. They led into the house where they were then wiped, at least the bottoms, on my door rug. Mongo ran out and went potty by his favorite little bush at the back of the yard, not far from the muddied spot on the top of the fence from the

Bigfoot stepping over it sometime before I got home.  Then Mongo came running back because he knew once he went potty then it was breakfast time.

"I let him go potty earlier."  I jumped at Harry's voice coming from the kitchen.  I just about peed my pants, good thing I had just gone potty myself, huh?

"You scared me!"  I said holding my hands over my heart because it was about to jump out of my chest.

"Did you go outside earlier before I got up?"  Harry asked after a minute or two.

"I think was sleep walking last night, I haven't done that in a long time.  I had a very vivid dream about the woods.   I am hoping that I didn't really walk out there while I was sleeping.  How did I get out of the yard?"  I was kind of scared of the possibilities of what could have happened to me while I was out there.  I could have been taken by the very Bigfoot that was after me.  I could have run into a bear or cougar.

"Okay, well when Mongo came out and woke me up to let him go potty your bathroom door was closed with the light on.  So I just figured that you were also going potty.  Mongo was quick and back into bed before you came out so I just went back to bed.  I'm sorry I must have left the slider unlocked and you just walked out.  I'm not sure you made it out of the yard though unless you climbed the fence?  But your brain could have been telling you that the backyard was the woods you were walking in?  That's my best guess."  Harry said as he shrugged his shoulders.  He looked a little confused as I am sure I looked.

"I guess.  Do you know if the crew got all the cameras up that they planned on arranging around the house in case the Bigfoot comes back here?"  I asked as I took a look around the backyard fence.  I did in fact see a few cameras but they all seemed to be either facing away from the house to see what was coming or they were focused on the windows that had face prints, which did include the sliding door.

"As far as I know they did. We can go and see Jerry after breakfast so we can take a look and see how far you made it out of the yard if at all." Harry said as he turned back around walking back into the kitchen. That's when I noticed the smell of fresh coffee and what smelled like scrambled eggs cooking, Mongo and I both followed him.

"Yum smells good in here. By the way, would you happen to know why my sense of smell, hearing and sight would be getter a lot more acute since I returned from the hospital? Could it have something to do with the bite?" I know he must have some kind of knowledge about this stuff, he is a Bigfoot expert isn't he?

"Well, I guess it could have something to do with it. But I'm not really that sure." Harry said as he put toast in the toaster.

"I kind of thought since you were a Bigfoot expert you would know if this was a side effect from the bite? What about the medication they gave me. Could I have side effects like this from those?" I wasn't sure why but I put my hands together at that moment then I noticed that I was no longer wearing the gauze on my hand that was bitten. I didn't even notice that it was gone when I washed my hands in the bathroom. Harry saw me looking at my hand.

"Is everything okay? When did you take off your bandage?" He asked as I sat down at one of the barstools tucked under the island in the kitchen.

"I don't even remember taking it off. Look at my hand, there are no marks at all. No scars or scratches, nothing!" I know by the sound of my own voice in my head that I was starting to panic. Harry came around from the stove top and took my hands in his to try to calm me.

"It has been over a week since you were bitten and your Mother said you were a quick healer! Calm down Carrie, everything is fine. As soon as we eat we can either go see the camera footage or we can go see Doctor Chuck, okay?" He was trying very hard to calm me down and with him touching me it seemed to be helping. I could feel my heart slowing down. I hadn't noticed how fast it was beating until I stopped to focus my breathing. By this time Mongo wasn't acting like himself. He kept trying to get in between Harry and I. He was trying to calm me down but couldn't get to me with Harry in the way. That's when I heard Mongo in my head say, "Get out of the way man, she needs me!" My eyes went huge and I took my hands away from Harry to touch Mongo on the head. He stopped and looked into my eyes, "Carrie, calm. I must help you be calm."

"Holy shit!" I stood up and stepped back as the barstool feel to the floor. Harry went to pick it up when he said, "What's going on, what just happened?"

"Mongo sit!" I said and he did, right at my feet.

"Mongo I am calm." I said in a calm voice. Then I heard Mongo in my head again, "No you're not, you can't lie to me. Your body tells me you are scared. I must help you stay calm." It was Mongo looking at me, his lips weren't moving but I swear it was his voice in my head. I bent down and put both of my hands on either side of his face and looked into his eyes.

"I heard you." I whispered so that Harry wouldn't hear me. He had put the stool back and went to move the eggs off the burner while I was with Mongo crouched on the floor.

"Finally! I always talk and you never hear me!" Mongo was saying and I suddenly planted my butt on the floor in front of him. Mongo looked over at Harry and then back to me.

"I have always talked and sometimes I thought you heard me." Mongo's word phrasing was interesting kind of like a child's but very emotional.

"Should I tell Harry I can hear you too?" I asked Mongo in a whisper again.

"No!" Mongo tilted his head and looked just over my shoulder where I am guessing Harry was standing listening to us. I turned my head and yes he was there with a very big smile on his face.

"Is there something happening here that I need to know about?" Harry asked as he helped me get up. Mongo came around and sat on my feet in front of me.

"No but we should probably eat now because my tummy is rumbling." I said with a smile that I was hoping didn't make me look insane.

"Okay well everything is ready including Mango's food dish. Would you like me to make you plate for you?" Harry asked as he grabbed 2 plates out of the cupboard.

"Yes, please. And grab a small plate for Mongo; I always give him some eggs and a piece of toast to go with his dog food." I said as I sat back down at the barstool to eat at the island.

"I love it when I get eggs, toast is ok but eggs are so good." Mongo said in my head as he was eating his dog food very loudly.

"Okay, I think I made enough for all three of us then. Do you give him his before or after he is done with his food?" Harry asked as he set my plate in front of me and his plate next to me.

I usually wait until he is done.

"I could take it anytime; I will still eat my food too." Mongo said in my head as I smiled and then turned to Harry.

"I think we can just set it down there for him, he can eat it when he gets to it." I said with a smile. This being able to communicate with Mongo was going to come in very handy I think. Mongo and I always had a great relationship but now I think it will work even better because I knew he could kind of understand me before but now I think the communication is better both ways, like he can understand me better too.

No more than I finished that thought Mongo turned toward me and woofed, does that mean he can hear what I think too?

"No only when you are thinking of something to do with me is seems. Your eggs are better by the way, not enough milk in his scramble." Mongo said in my head. I must have looked like I was staring into space because Harry nudged me to make me look at him.

"Is everything really okay? I know your upset about sleepwalking last night but we can fix that. I can make sure you don't get out of the house by making sure to lock the doors too. I wouldn't want anything to happen to you. I kind of like you Lass." Harry said in his cute way. He was so supportive and ready with answers to help me make sure that last night doesn't happen again. Then a thought came into my head. What will I do when he isn't here? He will leave when the Bigfoot Getters leave, that's his job. And I can't ask him to give that up, no matter what I feel. But if he were to come up with the idea I sure wouldn't mind.

"I'm good now. I will feel better after we see exactly what I did do last night though. I was surprised that Mongo didn't wake me or you, something while I was sleep walking." I said as I looked over at Mongo who was now devouring his eggs and almost done.

"You don't wake sleep walking people! Besides Harry wouldn't wake up either." Mongo said in my head.

"It was probably a good thing he didn't wake you. Doctors say you shouldn't wake a sleep walker because it could cause seizures or something like that. Besides you were apparently very quiet because I didn't even hear you." Harry said as he took the last bite of his eggs too. He was smiling and had a great morning personality. I really like that. But this talking to both of them when Harry couldn't hear Mongo was very weird. I looked down at my plate and most of my food was gone as well. There was only a little bit of eggs and half a piece of toast, which is what I usually give to Mongo.

"Mongo do you want the rest of my breakfast?" I asked as I scooted my chair back and started leaning down with the plate. The plate didn't make it to the floor before Mongo was right there eating in all gone.

"I guess you were a hungry boy." I said as I took my plate and then grabbed Harry's and took them to the sink to rinse them before I placed them into the dishwasher.

"I was super hungry from following you all night. I am better now though. I need to go out and poop now." Mongo said in my head then he went to the sliding door woofing to be let out again. He knew I wouldn't talk to him in from of Harry.  So I would have to wait to find out what he meant, I had a very sinking feeling that he was my guardian angel while I was sleep walking last night.  I wonder how many times I had done that before and not known.

"A few that I know of."  Is what Mongo said in my head as he ran out the door to his pooping spot in the far right corner of the yard.  Come to think of it, Mongo has always been a strange dog.  He had never had real training but listens to all of my commands almost perfectly.  He only likes to do his business in the same spots so he doesn't make the yard messy.  He doesn't bark a lot unless it's something serious and he has never left my side unless he had too.  Now he basically tells me that I have sleep walked a few times besides last night.  Mongo and I will be having a conversation later.

"Okay, poop now.  Talk later."  Mongo was trying to poop and was getting upset I was still talking to him.  I closed the sliding door to give him privacy.

## Chapter 13

I took Mongo back to the bedroom with me while I changed into some jeans so I could put on my socks and shoes. I didn't really want to walk out to Jerry's trailer barefoot. Mongo hadn't said much to me since he came back in from going potty. I closed my bedroom door so I could not only dress privately but so that I could talk to Mongo too.

"When did this start with me being able to hear you? Because I don't remember you talking in my head until after I came back from the hospital." I said as I pulled my jeans out of my dresser drawer.

"I have been able to understand you forever! You just couldn't hear me till after you got bitten. Don't know why." Mongo was saying in my head while he laid in front of my closed bedroom door. He was acting as if he was guarding me and half listening for Harry.

"Okay so that would mean that the bite definitely has something to do with it. I can also hear, see and smell better than I ever have before which must also be a side effect. My hand is healed so maybe fast healing is part too? If that's all I get from that bite, I am happy." I said as I pulled off my sweatpants and then put on socks and then my jeans. I was sitting on the edge of the bed when Mongo got up and moved over next to me on the floor while he stared at the bedroom door.

"Harry, out there? I don't like to talk unless I have too around him. You respond to me and it makes you look crazy. He's there now." Mongo said just as there was a knock on the door.

"Carrie, are you about ready?" Harry asked as I finished tying my left shoe.

"Yup all ready to go. Come on Mongo, let's go see Amanda!" I said and Mongo started for the door as Harry opened it for me. Mongo ran past him toward the front door as I slid past Harry he caught my shoulders pulling me in for a quick kiss. We smiled at each other.

"You are looking good in those jeans, Lass." He said and then let me go. I leaned forward and gave him a quick kiss back.

"You don't look to bad in your jeans either." I turned and walked down the hall with him right behind me. I know he was checking out my butt, I could feel it. He did look good in his jeans; they contoured to his muscled legs as well as his nice package and butt. And I swear he has an endless supply of muscle t-shirts, his arms just pop in them. Yummy!

When we got to the camera trailer we knocked on the door and Amanda opened it for us. She and Jerry had been sleeping in here so that Terry and Trina could stay in the trailer that us girls had stayed in when we were camped out.

"Hey guys, you must be here to see who those guys were that I took the photo of yesterday?" Amanda said as she stepped back so we could climb inside. Mongo went first and running up to the trailer finding a doggy bed under the table to lie on. It seems he had spent some time in here. I just raised an eyebrow at him and Amanda saw me.

"He stayed with us in here while you were in the hospital. Harry bought that bed for him to stay on so he had something of his own." She said as she patted Harry on the back as he walked over to one of the chairs set up in front of the monitors. He was still going through footage from the cage fiasco we had. Wow that was over a week ago that it happened. The things you miss while you are sleeping....

"Well Mongo and I want to thank you, Harry. And thank you guys for taking care of him while I was in there. I'm sure glad I have friends I can rely on when I need them." I said after kissing Harry on the cheek then I hugged Amanda and patted Jerry on the shoulder.

"It's okay; you can always count on me. Oh the guys, you wanted to know who they were!" Amanda sat down at the table where her laptop was sitting open and brought up the photos and some information in another file.

"Actually we came in for another reason but now I'm curious about the guys." I said as I walked around to see over her shoulder at the photos that she had Alvin took in the store.

"So these are a couple of the Johnson brothers. They have a security company called 'Emerald City Security'; they cater to the high end celebrities and rock stars that come into Eugene to do concerts and shows at the Hult Center and the Mathew Knight Arena. There are seven brothers and I did some Facebook stocking to find out who is who. Tom is the oldest and the CEO of the company but still works in the field with all of his brothers. There is Frank, Gary, Abel, Zeek, Kelly and Jeffery." Amanda was saying their names as the faces of the drunken men camping flashed through my brain; I started shaking and took a seat on the other side of the table from her.

"Those are the drunken guys camping! The weird guys that were also camping at Waldo lake the weekend we were there investigating." I could hardly believe this, the same guys? They obviously remembered what I looked like but they must have shaved after their wild weekend of drinking.

"Seriously, these were the weird guys? I also saw these guys at the hospital while you were there too!" Amanda was saying as Harry got up walking over to see the photos on her laptop.

"That's the drunken guys with mud and scraggly hair? They sure did clean up, but why did they leave so fast from Waldo? Didn't you say they wouldn't leave even when you told them they would be reimbursed?" Harry asked as he leaned in having Amanda move to the next couple of photos. They don't look like drunks.

"Well, that is what Don and Tori told me about them. I saw for myself the way they looked to be in dirty clothes with mud, sticks and things in their hair when I talked to them. They didn't smell like booze but they sure were weird, and I mean weird. Those brothers treated me like I was the last woman on Earth or something. The way they were all falling over themselves to introduce themselves to me." I said rather defensively. I have seen drunken people in the woods before and I've met some really weird people in the woods doing shrooms too. These guys were by far the weirdest of the weird.

"According to the Facebook stocking I did. The guy that tried to talk to you at the market was Tom the oldest and CEO of Emerald City Security, I wonder what happened to them that they not only cut their trip short but also cleaned up? Why were they at the hospital when you were there? And why were they still in Oakridge? What is keeping them here? Shouldn't they be back in Eugene for their company or something?" Amanda was always the investigative reporter. She smelled a story here, maybe for later?

"Can we just forget about those guys please? I really don't think that they had anything to do with what is going on with the Bigfoot. Let's get to the thing we really came out her to see." Harry stood up and walked back to the chair he had just gotten out of.

"Miss Carrie here was sleep walking last night so we wanted to see how far she got out of the yard. Can you bring up that footage so we can see Jerry?" Harry asked as he turned to Jerry who of course Jerry was typing before Harry even finished talking. Jerry had the footage from the backyard cameras running with all angles on all the monitors. It was rather late when you saw me opening up the backdoor slider and walking out, I didn't even close it. Then a couple of seconds later you see Mongo walking out of the door looking like he was tip toeing like Scooby-Doo, it was funny. Then you see me just walk around the yard for a few minutes with Mongo sitting a little way away from me just watching what I am doing. Then I paused and turned to the back fence where the Bigfoot had stepped over before. Then I started walking to that spot. For few seconds I just stood there, then all the camera feeds went down and didn't come back on for two hours when I am standing back in the same spot as before, but now I am facing the house and panting. Mongo is asleep on the ground in front of me. Then he perks up following me as I walk back into the house this time closing the sliding door just after Mongo walks in after me. I must have had to go potty right after that because of me waking up on the toilet 30 minutes after I walked inside by the time on the camera stamp.

"What the hell happened that caused the cameras to go out for two hours?" Harry asked, he was rather upset. Now we will never know what happened for those two hours.

"Well, I don't think she ever left the backyard. She was there when the cameras went off and still there when they came back on. I don't think you have to worry." Jerry said as he skipped to some other cameras around the time of the backyard cameras went out. They were all working and they hadn't caught anything out of the ordinary. That's when I heard Mongo whimper so I looked in his direction.

"You did leave the yard but not as yourself. You were different." Mongo said in my head.

"I need to go to the restroom, so I think I will take Mongo back into the house." I leaned over to Harry and gave him a kiss on the cheek. Amanda looked at me funny but I leaned in giving her a hug and whispered, "Don't worry, I'm fine. It's probably just the medication the doctors gave me in the hospital that made me sleep walk." Amanda hugged me back.

"Maybe, but make sure the doors are locked for sure and maybe set something in front of the doors before you go to sleep tonight." Amanda said as Mongo and I stepped down out of the trailer and before we closed the door.

"I'll be in shortly Lass!" Harry said as I almost had the door shut.

"Okay!" I said and finished closing the door.

Mongo and I walked to the house without a word. I didn't want anyone to hear me talking to Mongo in any other way besides like you would talk to a dog. So I waited until we got into the house and Mongo and I went back to my bedroom to talk.

"Okay Mongo, what do you mean I was different?" I sat down on the side of the bed while Mongo sat at my feet. I was petting his head and rubbing his ears, something he loves that I do when I'm nervous.

"You were you but then you climbed over the fence and weren't you anymore. I couldn't get over to following you but I tried. Then I laid down to wait for you. I didn't hear you come back over the fence until you started breathing hard. That's when I knew you were back and you were you again. I was scared for you; you've never left me behind unless you had too." Mongo sounded so sad and lonely. I leaned down giving him a hug and a kiss on his forehead right between his eyes.

"I'm sorry Mongo; I didn't know what I was doing. I still don't know where I went but I do know I went somewhere for sure now. I dreamed about some men that I was watching in a clearing with a campfire, I was wearing a fur coat and cap while I was out there by myself. I couldn't figure out why I would have a fur cap and coat on in the woods, I still don't know why or where did it go when I came back over the fence?" I was talking to Mongo as well as myself just to try and make sense of all of this.

"I think I would like to take a bath now. It might help to relax me. Mongo would you like to lay by the tub in case I fall asleep in the tub?" I was getting up and walking across the bedroom to the bathroom when I heard a knock on my bedroom door which stopped me in my tracks. I turned to see Harry standing there with a sheepish smile.

"Hey, I just wanted to let you know I was back in the house. So you're taking a bath right now? Do you want me to get us some lunch for when you get out? The food truck in up and running, or I can make something here at your house?" Harry was being so nice to me; I hope he hadn't heard me talking to Mongo just now, how embarrassing!

"Whichever is easier for you? I'll take whatever you bring me. Can you grab a fruit salad for Mongo to go along with his dog food? Please and thank you." I walked over to where Harry was standing and I gave him a quick kiss on the lips.

"No problem." He said as he snaked his arms around my back deepening the kiss that made my toes curl! I could really loose myself in this man and I have a feeling that it will be sooner than I was expecting too.

When Harry finally loosened his hold on me and I slid down his body I could feel the tale tale signs that he was very interested in taking this further. My brain was foggy with lust at this point and I wasn't really thinking very clearly when he set me back down on my feet. I hadn't even realized that he had picked me up in the air to be totally held by him while we kissed. OMG! Okay Carrie calm down, calm down!

"I'm going to take a bath now to relax a little, not that I'm not relaxed now! I was just, yah, I'm going to take bath. You are getting food." My brain is mush and I am babbling like I am high or something. Maybe I am high, high on hormones that haven't been used in a very long time.

Harry's smile said he knew exactly what he had done to not only my body but to my mind as well. That naughty Scott!

"I will let you soak for a little while and then I will go get the food. Would you like me to serve you in the tub, my Lady?" Harry asked as he wiggled his eyebrows. I could picture that in my brain and had to shake my head to clear it out.

"No thank you, I don't really enjoy soggy food." I said trying to joke around so that this sex fog could leave my brain so I can go and take a bath. Harry just smiled at me even more.

"No problem I will catch you after your bath then. I will let you know when I come in with your food. Maybe we could watch another movie? And I also wanted to mention that Jerry, Amanda and some of the crew were planning on going down to Miss Mary's Pub after dinner tonight. If you like we could go shoot some pool?" He asked as he was turning to leave, but also waited to get my answer.

"Sure, Miss Mary is an old friend of the family. I haven't been there for a while, sounds good. Okay I am going to go run my bath to soak for a little while. Mongo will be with me so I don't fall asleep in the tub. Come Mongo." I saw as I walked to the bathroom yet again and I tapped my leg so Mongo jumped off the bed and followed me inside. I closed the door slowly as I saw Harry walk down the hall and heard him go out the sliding door; Mongo and I were alone again.

When my tub was full of warm water it didn't take me but a minute to climb in. Now I know why Mongo always turned his head or closed his eyes whenever I undressed or dressed, he was a good boy.

"Wow, I hadn't realized how long it has been since I shaved my legs. I guess they don't do that for you in the hospital, huh?" I was saying out loud even though I know that Mongo didn't really care about such things. I sank into the tub and decided not to shave just yet, I would wait until I was almost done, that way I wasn't sitting in my hair for too long. That always kind of grossed me out, but I do love to be silky smooth, especially if Harry and I get any closer really soon.

I soaked in the tub for about an hour and almost fell asleep it felt so good to be almost floating in warm water. It was easing every ache and pain I didn't even know I had. I found that my feet weren't any worse for the wear after my sleep walking adventure, wherever I might have gone. I had finally decided to get out of the tub, wrap myself in a warm towel and sat at the end of the tub to put my feet and half of my legs back into the tub so that I could shave them. The hair was a little thinker than I was used to. It seemed like it took forever but I finally managed to shave them nice and smooth. Then there was a knock on the door which startled me.

"Lass I hope you didn't fall asleep in there! I have yours and Mongo's lunch here, I have set it up at the table in the dining room." Harry said as he rapped on the door once again.

"Okay, I'm almost done in here. Can you close my bedroom door when you go out please? Mongo and I will be out there in a few minutes, thank you!" I said as I started to pull my legs over the side of the tub so I could dry them and that's when I noticed that both of my legs looked like I hadn't even shaved them.

"What the hell!" I said so loud that it sounded like Harry must have heard me as well because he came back to the bathroom door.

"Is everything okay in there?" Harry asked as he rapped on the door yet again.

"Yes! Everything is fine; I just need to shave my legs really quick! It shouldn't take me too long!" I was already lathering up the soap so that I could give them another shave. I was so sure that I had shaved them already, maybe my brain flaked out and I hadn't really done it? Am I going crazy? I could hear Harry leave and close my bedroom door.

"This better work this time!" I said as I shaved my legs in record time without cutting myself. When I was done I pulled first one leg out of the tub and dried it with another towel. Okay everything is going good so I then pulled out the second leg and started drying it with the same towel. Okay so the hair is still gone and I am silky smooth still. I gave a sigh of relief and stood up so that I could head out of the bathroom to get dressed and go eat with Harry, I only stood up for a few minutes when I got so light headed that I had to sit back down.

"You okay?" Mongo asked in my head as he got up and put his head in my lap for reassurance.

"I just got super light headed and had to sit back down for a minute. I'm okay Mongo." I rubbed his head and ears while I closed my eyes for a few second.

"I'm probably just hungry. Let's go into the bedroom so I can get dressed." Mongo led the way from the bathroom and he jumped up on the bed and laid down, waiting for me to get dressed. Since we would be going out later I decided to just put on jeans and my favorite pheasant blouse in a light blue. I usually tuck it into my jeans but for right now I left it untucked. I put on my soft socks and my tennis shoes that are comfy as well. Mongo lifted his head.

"Harry is outside the door and he's going to knock again." Mongo said in my head and just a second after Mongo said that there was a knock at the door.

"Hey Lass, your Granddad is here with your Mom. I told them to take a seat that I would check on you. How much longer before you come out?" He had just finished saying as I opened the door.

"Wow you look and smell nice Lass." Harry said as he smiled and held out his arm for me to take so we could walk down the hall into the dining room.

"You look so pale; I think you should eat while you visit." Harry said as he led me to a chair and I sat down. My Mom and Grandpa were sitting at the table with food in front of them.

"Sweetie, are you feeling okay?" Was that first thing out of my Mom's mouth? She was sitting in the chair on my right and Grandpa Hunter was sitting across from me. Harry took the chair to my left and sat down.

"I'm fine; I think I'm just hungry is all." That's when I noticed the nice huge juicy burger with the works sitting in front of me with a pile of French fries and they were still warm. Harry must have had them in the oven until he thought I would be out to eat. What a wonderfully thoughtful man.

Grandpa had a burger like mine but with less fries. My Mom the forever on a diet woman that she is, even though she owns a pizzeria was having a salad that was on the large side for her.

"I was just asking her about being so pale, is this something that happens when she doesn't eat on a schedule?" Harry was asking my Mom and Grandpa; I know he was concerned about me.

"No, I don't think that has ever happened before. But her body is out of whack with all the medications and the bite she received and all, so it probably has something to do with that." Mom was saying as Grandpa watched me eat. I took that hamburger and squished is a little so that it would fit into my mouth Scooby-doo style. That first big bite was heavenly, the flavors exploded in my mouth and I swear I was drooling while I was chewing. Then I took a few fries and put them into my mouth once I had swallowed the burger bite and they were also heavenly with the salty greasy goodness that they were.

"Wow, I guess you were hungry Lass." Harry said with astonishment. That's when I noticed that everyone at the table was watching me eat my burger. I was on my third bite before I came up for air, then I noticed that Harry had gotten me an iced tea to drink with my lunch. He sure was good at taking care of me, a girl could get used to this!

"Sorry," I said after taking a drink to clear my mouth.

"Don't be sorry girl, I have always told you that you were too skinny anyway. You eat whatever you want, you always work it off anyway it's in your blood. Grandpa said with a smile knowing that him saying that it really pissed off Mom. She just huffed a little and went to eating her salad. I heard Mongo whimper a little under the table next to my feet and then He set his head in my lap. I reached under the table and rubbed his head a little even though I shouldn't while I am eating.

"Oh, sorry Mongo I got your fruit salad right here." Harry said as he took the fruit and placed it next to Mongo's empty food dish; he must have eaten the dog food already.

"Thank you for doing all of this Harry." I said as I took another drink.

"Yes, thank you for taking such good care of my Granddaughter, Harry. This leads me to talking to you guys about something. I have already talked to the crew and to Terry as well as to your friends Carrie about having a huge BBQ and party to kind of celebrate all the scientific information you guys were able to obtain during the investigation into the Sasquatch in this area." Grandpa cleared his throat and went on to say, "I have also enjoyed have people to talk to about the Sasquatch stories that I have been handed down to me from my elders and family. It's been great fun telling these guys all about them. And I don't sound crazy to them because of what you have all been through in the last couple weeks." Grandpa was a little teary eyed when he raised his glass of iced tea and said, "To new friends and future family, may the Sasquatch never want to add you to their family." Grandpa said on a laugh. We all raised our glasses and toasted to that.

"So when do you want to have this BBQ thing?" I asked Grandpa when I set my glass down.

"I am thinking this weekend. I am trying to get your Cousin's band to come and play. You know you're Cousin Koda and his friends actually wrote a song about a Sasquatch incident they had up around Waldo Lake? I hope they sing it at the party." Grandpa just loved hearing my Cousin Koda's band 'Right Around the Cornerstone' play.

"Well your Aunt Maggie and Uncle Berry will be coming up from Harrisburg as well as your Aunt Nova and Uncle Adam, possibly. They wanted to see everyone and meet the 'Bigfoot Getters' along with watching Koda and the band, of course." Mom was saying between bites of her salad. My Aunt Maggie, short for Magpie is my Mom's little sister and she married Berry Forester who was from the Siletz Indian tribe. They all live in Harrisburg, Oregon.

"That's great; we haven't seen them for a while. I can't wait to see Cousin Koda, I wonder if he has changed much?" I said wondering out loud.

The last time I saw my Cousin Koda he had every bit the Native American good looks. The long silky black hair and beautiful brown eyes, the only difference was he could grow facial hair, he loved growing a goatee. He was very tall, around 6'4" maybe and slender but muscular. He had the most considerate and caring personality and his band was a great group of guys as well. Koda played guitar and sang most of the time but he could play any of the instruments.

There were three other guys in the band with him. Koda's little brother my other Cousin Caleb Forester, who is about 6' even and he plays guitar like Koda and he helps Koda write his songs as well as sang a few of them. Caleb was also Native American with his lighter brown hair but the brown eyes are more like Koda. Caleb isn't as slender as Koda but he is very muscular, he lifts weights for fun.

Christoff Beach, my other cousin is the base player that can really play. He is also Native American and has been Koda's best friend from basically birth. They looked so much alike that people think they are brothers. The only difference was that Christoff was about 2 inches shorter and he couldn't grow a goatee at all, plus his eyes were a lighter shade of brown. Christoff's Mom is my mom's other little sister Nova the spitting image of Aunt Maggie. Aunt Nova married Adam Beach, no not the actor but he is also a member of the Siletz Indian tribe. They live in Harrisburg too.

Then you have Jody Abrams played drums, a bit shorter that most of the band he was around 5'5" with a blonde hair do that made me think of Shaggy from Scooby-doo plus he also wore a goatee that was blonde but it went well with blue green eyes that always seemed to have a hint of mischief in them. He had a swimmers body but the guy loved to eat, I think that is the other reason they call him Shaggy sometimes. He came into Koda's life around 3rd grade; these guys were always up to something together. The whole band grew up in Harrisburg, Oregon where they play all kinds of festivals and a few bars in the area. They have played in Oregon, Washington and some in California and Nevada. They have their own U-Tube channel too; they have Facebook followers in the thousands.

You know that feeling you get when you think someone is watching you, well I was getting that right now. I hadn't realized I was inside my own head for so long that everyone at the table stopped to watch me eat. I wasn't sure if anyone had asked me a question or what. I had four sets of eyes watching me, including Mongo from the floor right next to me. I was now licking the grease and juices from my fingers when I noticed them. I stopped what I was doing.

"What? Is something wrong?" I asked.

"You were so focused on eating that you didn't say a word when people were talking to you. But every time you took a bite you grunted. It was so weird." My Mom said as she just stared at me.

"She's fine Janet, let the girl eat in peace. She was obviously starving." Grandpa said and he took his last sip of his tea. I looked around and it seemed that everyone else had finished their food also, so what was the problem? So I grunted while I ate, it was good and I was super hungry.

"Well, Janet we should get back up to the house to talk about the supplies needed." Grandpa said as he stood and took his garbage to the can and placed his glass in the sink. My Mom followed suit and did the same. They both gave me hugs and kisses as well as Mongo and Mom hugged Harry and Grandpa shook his hand. There was some unspoken thing going on between Grandpa and Harry. At least it seemed that way to me.

Then Mom and Grandpa left through the front door. Mom drove them back up to the big house as we called it. I just sat in my chair at the table and I felt so tired again. Harry cleaned up the table.

"Thank you for everything Harry. You have been super great and I have loved having you here." I said as I stood and pushed in my chair and walked into the kitchen where he was at the sink. Harry slowly turned around with a weird look on his face.

"Are you breaking up with me?" He asked in an are you joking but not joking way.

"What? No I was just thanking you for being a great guy. And I was thinking maybe we could sit and watch a movie or two before we go out later to Miss Mary's Pub. Break up with you? Do you think I am crazy?" I said as I walked up to him and put my hands on either side of his face pulling him down for a kiss. Once our lips met, the fire down deep inside of my very soul started.

## **Chapter 14**

Mongo laid across Harry's and my lap while we watched a couple movies. I know Harry had things he could probably be doing with the crew but I just wanted to spend time with him and since the doctor said I was to take it easy this is what I thought of to do. Our kiss in the kitchen earlier got interrupted by a very jealous Mongo, that's what I think anyway.

Harry got a text from Terry just as Amanda texted me to find out if we were ready to go to Miss Mary's Pub to play some pool. Harry and I looked at each other and then we both replied yes. He kind of knew what I was getting as well the same kind of text. So I woke up Mongo and went to get my jacket along with his service dog vest, yes he goes everywhere with me.

"Come on Mongo, were going to Miss Mary's." Mongo was happier that he was going with me. It never takes long to put on his vest, he wears it proudly. Once he has his on I put my jacket on with Harry's help, he is always such a gentleman.

"Do you have everything?" Harry asked me just before he opened the door.

"Yah, I have my small wallet in my back pocket and anything else that I might need is in my truck. Are you still wanting to drive or would you like me too instead?" I asked as we stepped out the door and I heard Harry lock it while we stood on the porch. Harry still had my keys from the last time he drove me around.

"If you don't mind I would like to drive, since you were light headed and all earlier, I wouldn't want to put any stress on you." Harry said as he placed his hand on my lower back as the three of us walked to the truck.

"Actually I would really enjoy you driving me again. I hadn't realized how late it was already. It's starting to get dark." Harry opened the backdoor for Mongo to jump in and then opened the passenger door for me. He waited until I was buckled then let me close the door then he walked around to fasten Mongo's seatbelt then climbed into the driver's seat. By this time there were three trucks waiting for us next to the road.

"It looks like the whole crew is going with us, Miss Mary will like that! She loves when new people come into the pub. She makes some of the best fish and chips, and I am hungry again by the way. In case you hadn't noticed I know all the good places to eat in this town." I said as Harry backed up the truck and we started to follow the last truck in the line.

"Yah, the whole crew wanted to go and I'm hungry too. The cooks needed a night off and everyone loves to play pool. Your Mom said there were eight pool tables at Miss Mary's, this should be a fun evening." Harry said as he took his hand off the wheel taking my hand in his. Then he put it to his lips and kissed my knuckles. I was just happy to be with him.

By the time we got to Miss Mary's Pub the parking lot was only half full on a Monday night. This was fine, that way we had the choice of how many tables we could use at the same time. The smells from all the yummy bar food when we walked in was amazing.

Miss Mary was behind the counter with her sister Miss Karen. Both women were in their late 60's but they had hearts like 20 something's. Mary and Karen are twins; they both have white hair and light blue eyes. They stand only about 5'3" if they aren't wearing their shit kicker boots, which they always wear. They are a little on the stout side but they can move when they need to break up a bar fight. Plus, Miss Mary is known for two things, her shotgun and her catch phrase, if you piss her off she says,

"Bite Me or Run for the door." Then she cocks her shotgun because she aims to use it.

Miss Karen is the quiet one until you piss Mary off, then you have pissed Karen off. Miss Karen doesn't have a catch phrase; she just yells for her hubby Big John. Nobody wants to mess with Big John; people have been put in the hospital by Big John. Big John is a 6'6" tall full blood Native American from the Sun'aq Tribe of Kodiak Alaska Indian tribe. Big John and Karen Martin and Miss Mary Mayfield, they will have your back if you need it. And they loved our family.

"Carrie, Amanda, Trina and Mongo, it's been a while since you guys have been in here to visit!" Miss Mary said no more than she saw us.

"Hello Miss Mary!" The three of us said as one. Something we have done since we were old enough to step up to the bar. In our small town we could come in here and play pool when we were younger but at 9pm all minors had to get out. The three of us have had some good times in here.

"Girls, have you seen the newest addition to the pub?" Miss Karen was always excited about something new she bought for the kids to do here in the pub.

"What's new, show us?" I said and both Miss Mary and Miss Karen looked at each other and then back at the crew as they filed into the pub.

"She can show you later. Are these all your friends?" Miss Mary asked.

"Yes, let me introduce you to the 'Bigfoot Getters'!" Amanda said with flare as she turned to showed everyone to the ladies. I hadn't realized there were so many of us. Amanda and Trina pointed to each of the crew introducing them as they walked by to a very long table in the back that was saved for big gatherings, which would accommodate us just fine. When they got to Terry and Jerry then they looked at me and I introduced the ladies to Harry.

Miss Mary and Miss Karen looked and each other and then did this giggle snort thing that they do, so weird. Really it's a little animal like sometimes. Then they looked at us with huge smiles on their faces and walked around the counter and stood in front of the full table of the crew. Miss Mary and Miss Karen both patted Mongo on the head as he sat at my feet.

"Well everyone, welcome to Miss Mary's Pub, Miss Mary that's me!" Mary said pointing to her chest with her thumb. "Since you are all here with my favorite girls and Mongo, the first beer is on the house! Please don't get drunk and don't cause any trouble! Our girls here can tell you that you do not want to do that, if you behave you might just get to meet Miss Karen's hubby, Big John on a good note instead of a bad one." Miss Mary was saying and then her sister chimed in.

"So on that note, relax, play pool and we will get started on any food orders you might have. Big John is making a fresh batch of deep fried catfish and chips which are the special this evening, any takers?" Miss Karen was always the nice happy one of the two.

"Guys, if you like fish and chips then you will love Big John's catfish. Trust me!" I said as I sat down next to Harry at the far end of the table. Everyone ordered the catfish and chips. Miss Karen was so happy. She took the orders back to Big John. Us girls know that when Big John starts the jukebox from the kitchen with his favorite song, Trace Adkins – 'Honky Tonk Badonkadonk'. He even sounds like Trace Adkins when he sings. To tell the truth it's one of our favorite songs to dance too as well.

I looked at Amanda then at Trina and they looked at each other then we nodded and headed toward the dance floor as Trace was singing to us, Mongo stayed at the table lying next to my chair but always watchful. We had fun dancing and singing along with the music. After a few minutes of this Harry, Terry and Jerry all joined us for the ending. I was just letting loose and having a great time. And Harry wasn't a bad dancer either; I think he just might have a little cowboy in him.

Once the song was finished we started walking back to the table, a little out of breath but feeling good. We all sat back down noticing that Miss Mary and Miss Karen had already delivered our drinks, knowing that we girls don't really drink alcohol they left us iced teas as usual. This was definitely sun brewed iced tea, Miss Karen brews in on the roof, just above their apartment on top of the pub.

Everyone was talking and a few of the crew had gone over to start playing pool on a couple of the open tables. That's when I heard voices that I remember from somewhere. I stiffened as I listened to them talk. It must have been noticeable because Mongo sat up and put his head in my lap. I pet his head while I listened. Then I started looking for the faces that went with the voices. I turned part way in my chair to see further into the sitting area. There at a table in the back were four men. A man wearing a blue baseball cap, a man in a red jacket with a smaller man that looked like him and a man wearing a U of O sweatshirt. Why do I know these guys? Who are they to me? I was really trying to rack my brain.

I must have been very obvious that something was wrong because Harry took my hand in his and made me focus on him.

"Lass, what is wrong?" He asked in a quiet voice.

"I know those guys over there but I am not sure from where?" I said and Mongo could tell there was something wrong too. He started a little whimper.

"Stay calm. I am here with you. Everything is okay." Mongo said in my head. Then he lifted his head and looked at the table in the back where the four men sat.

"I don't know them. I don't know their smell." Mongo said again in my head.

"I wasn't with you when I met them or I don't know them then?" I was saying to Mongo but making it look like I was talking to myself. I really hope Harry doesn't think I've gone crazy.

"Lass, you could have met them anywhere and not remember them. Maybe they were at the hospital and hadn't heard them until now?" Harry was really trying to calm me down and give me some very believable scenarios but that wasn't it. I know I have seen these men, not just heard them and if Mongo doesn't know their scent then I wasn't with Mongo when I met them.

That's when it hit me and my brain froze! They were in my very vivid dream last night. My sleep walking dream! The one that I was wearing a fur

141

coat and hat in. The one that I was walking through the woods alone in my big bare feet. OMG!!!! I think I sleep walked to wherever these men were and watched them from the woods thinking it was a dream! Mongo felt me go super stiff and so did Harry.

"Do we need to leave? Are you okay? I can take you home right now, no problem." Harry said as he squeezed my hand and kissed my knuckles. That's when I looked at him, he didn't look at me any differently, and he didn't think I was crazy but I am sure he thought I needed more rest.

"Carrie, it everything okay?" Amanda asked as she and Trina moved over to talk to me.

"Yah, I'm okay. I am just having a very bad case of Déjà vu is all." I was trying not to show how shocked and upset I was to finally understand that I had seen and heard these men in a sleepwalking adventure in the woods by myself last night!

"Listen we know you have been through a lot that past couple weeks or whatever, but you should just try to relax." Trina said as she tried to be the upbeat person that she is.

"Yah, everything is okay. It's all good." I was petting poor Mongo on the head so much that I was sure he was going to lose fur from me rubbing so much.

"I don't mind." Mongo said in my head yet again. Mongo hadn't talked to much to me this evening except when I was stressed; maybe that was a trigger for it? I don't even care about that right now. I was trying to decide if I should tell Harry about what I just found out or not. I really don't like keeping secrets from him.

After a few minutes of just sitting there listening to everyone talk and have fun, Mongo made a whimper.

"Need the potty, please." Mongo said in my head. I petted his head and turned to Harry.

"I have to take Mongo out to the potty. I know where to take him, you go ahead and stay here, I'll be right back." I said as I started to rise and placed my hand on Harry's arm.

"Are you sure you don't want me to go with you, I don't mind." Harry said as he watched me put my jacket back on.

"No, really I'm good and besides our food is coming out in a minute. It won't take long." I leaned over to give him a quick kiss before Mongo led me out the door. I could hear the others asking where I was going and Harry let them know that Mongo had to go potty.

I stepped outside in the cool evening air. The parking lot still didn't have too many vehicles in it but that was fine with me. I took out my cellphone turned on the light app so I could lead Mongo to the back of the building where we usually went. It was weird though, I could see better without the light than with it. We weren't out there very long when I thought I heard something in the bushes that surrounded the back of the building from the small amount of forest that was back there. When I looked I didn't see anything though. Mongo was quick to potty and he was ready to head back for food.

That's when I heard voices coming from the front of the building. When I got closer I noticed that it was the four guys from the table that I thought I knew from my dream. I was a forest service ranger, I could talk to them, and I wasn't a wimp.

"Hey guys? Can I talk to you for a minute please?" I asked as Mongo and I got closer to them. Mongo wasn't pulling me he was by my side and didn't seem bothered by them in the least.

"Sure Ma'am, do you need some help or something?" Red jacket campfire guy asked.

"Not exactly, I was wondering if any of you guys knew me?" I asked feeling kind of stupid after all.

"Yes, Ma'am we do. We have seen you all over town and in the woods. You're the Forest Service Ranger Carrie, right?" Red jacket campfire guy, George said and his son Mikey chimed in too.

"Yes, you helped me and a friend last summer when we got turned around on one of the back roads out by Odell Lake." Then the other two guys were nodding their heads in agreement.

"Why do you ask?" Campfire guy, Monty asked me.

"Well I have one more question and I it might sound weird." I said as they all walked closer to me.

"Okay, go ahead." Blue Baseball cap, I still don't know his name said as he leaned against his truck.

"And this may sound weird but, were you guys out by a campfire last night?" They all looked at each other and then back at me, almost like they thought they were in trouble for something. So I went on from there.

"Your name is George and your son is Mikey." I said pointing first at Red jacket campfire guy, George and then to his son.

"And you are Monty." I pointed to Marty.

"But I never heard your name." I said pointing to Blue Baseball cap guy last.

"It's Craig and I am sure you know that we were at a campfire last night or you wouldn't be asking. We weren't doing anything wrong and we put the fire out. If your Grandfather is upset, please let him know that we have always respected the land we just go there to get away and he had told my Father a few years back that it was okay as long as we didn't burn his woods down or leave a mess. We always clean up after ourselves and no one else knows where we go." Craig was saying as he stood up to talk. No longer leaning and relaxed against his truck.

"My Grandfather is not why I am asking, but thank you for respecting his wishes. I was sleep walking in the woods last night and it seems that when I thought I was dreaming about you guys around a campfire was actually me seeing you guys around a campfire. Please don't be offended or upset with me, I was not me while sleep walking." I said and they all seemed very interested in my explanation.

"Wow, I have slept walked before but to know that you were way out there in the woods by yourself that has to be scary as hell?" Craig was saying. I could see the understanding in his face as well as the others. They were no longer protecting themselves they were more worried about what might have happened to me.

"Wait a minute, I heard someone sneeze just before we left for the night. Was that you?" Monty asked me as he walked closer to me and Mongo. Mongo just sat there watching everyone.

"Yes, I remember sneezing and you guys looking into the brush to find who it was. I remember everything like a dream." I was saying as Mongo suddenly stood up and turned around toward the back of the building were the woods butted up. I remember hearing something rustling out there before but now you could really hear something. All of us turned to watch the bushes. The guy's kind of circled around me so they could see better, then we heard more noise at the front of the trucks parked across from Craig's truck. Then we heard growling and grunting noises. Mongo went ape-shit! He started growling and barking at the area in front of us then at the area in front of the truck. I knew that sound! The Bigfoot was here in town, in this very parking lot. The light from the overhead lamps was not the greatest but the light from the front of the pub was better.

"Gentlemen I think we should head inside!" I said as I pulled my pistol that I had hidden inside my jacket. I don't go anywhere without one.

"Head for the door, now!" Craig said as we all started backing toward the door of the pub. Then the door flew open and Harry came running out with some of the crew following him.

"Lass, I heard them! You guys get inside now!" Harry was yelling as the five different dark figures came out of the darkness and started to come into the light. Craig and the others stopped and I swear each of them went dead silent and stiff as a board when the Bigfoot came into the light. There were five Bigfoot in very close heights coming toward me, not even paying attention to anyone else, not even to Mongo who by this time was pulling on his leash barking and snarling so much that he was salivating and drool was flying! Harry was right behind me in a second that seemed like forever. The crew were grabbing the four guys that were paralyzed by fear and dragging them into the pub. Jerry and two other guys from the crew had their phones out, Amanda was hanging out the door of the pub with hers trying to get whatever footage she could.

He was holding my shoulders trying to pull on me but it seemed like my body wanted to move toward them. My brain wasn't working so well right now.

"Lass, tell Mongo to stop. He won't listen to me and we need to get you and him into the pub." Harry was saying calmly into my ear. Then I snapped into focus, Mongo and I were in danger.

"Mongo! Down! Mongo! Retreat!" Mongo looked at me like I had just told him he was a monkey or something.

"I must keep them away from you! They will take you if I don't stop them!" Mongo said in my head.

"Mongo come! Into the pub with the others! Please Mongo!" I yelled then I whispered so he knew what I felt. I was afraid for him as well as for me. Mongo gave a howl and I automatically chimed in with him. This made the Bigfoot stop in their tracks. It gave Harry, Mongo and I a chance to move quickly without turning our backs to them to get into the pub. As we got closer everyone taking video moved into the pub just before us, we were the last in the door. Harry closed the door and Big John was standing there waiting to close the security steel door to close as well. The Bigfoot was not getting in here tonight.

"Well I would say the preverbal cat is out of the bag now!" Terry said as people were all talking and I guess someone called the cops because they were at the front door pounding within minutes. I really hope that the Bigfoot were gone when the Police showed up.

"That would be an understatement." I said as we were all looking around at every single person in the pub was looking at their phones. Either posting what they had recorded or they were calling someone to tell them what they just witnessed. I hadn't realized that so many people came outside when the Bigfoot showed up. This could be really bad and I thought Bigfoot in the city would be bad?

Well us girls, Mongo and the crew ate our now a little on the cold side catfish for dinner while we waited out turn to talk to the Police as they make their way through to get everyone's statement about who or what was outside and what happened. In a small town most everyone knows at least someone you are related too and unfortunately I was related to the Sheriff himself. My Uncle Jared Randolph, my Dad's little brother who is only about five years older than me and my friends. We actually used to hang out with us every once in a while during the summer, until he got too grown up to hang with us. Trina always had a hugs crush on him too. He is an almost photo copy of my Dad only younger and more muscular with his dark brown almost black hair with brown eyes and he is about 6' tall too.

Uncle Jared got out to the Marines about five years ago and then he was working in Eugene as a deputy. So when the Sheriff job came open here in Oakridge he jumped on it without hesitation. Everyone in Oakridge loves him he is a super nice guy and we haven't had many problems here over the years. This was going to be one for the books though. I had just finished eating and gave Mongo a piece of my fish without breading when Uncle Jared came over and pulled up a chair next to me.

"So Little One, I am guessing that everything that has been reported here tonight is true? I talked to you Dad and Grandfather last week when you were in the hospital. Are these the same Bigfoot that you encountered in the mountains and at your girl's homes too?" He asked and nodded to Amanda and Trina who actually seemed a little shaken by this.

"Yes Uncle Jared or do I need to call you Sheriff while you are investigating?" I asked trying to lighten the mood.

"Uncle is just fine. How are you girls doing?" Uncle Jared asked Trina and Amanda who hadn't let go of Terry and Jerry's arms since we got inside, they even managed to eat while still holding on. I just had Harry hovering over me and checking doors and windows every so often, plus Mongo in my lap almost. He wasn't letting me out of sight either.

"We've had one hell of a scare that's for sure." Amanda was saying when she answered the Sheriff.

"I can't believe they are still following us!" Trina said as she perked up a little knowing that Jared was paying her attention right now. I guess she never got over her crush.

"We are here to protect you girls, no need to worry." Terry piped up to make sure that the Sheriff knew that the girls were being protected. I think he saw the spark of interest from Trina toward Uncle Jared.

"When can we take the girls back to the property?" Terry asked as he put his arm around Trina's shoulders to pull her in closer to himself, now I know he was showing that Trina was with him. I must have rolled my eyes because I know Uncle Jared smiled and pocked my side while no one was looking.

"As soon as you guys tell me or my deputies what you saw out there. And I was told that some of your crew took some video of what was out there?" Uncle Jared was saying as Harry came back to sit next to me again.

"Uncle Jared this is Harry, he is also with the Bigfoot Getters but he is also my boyfriend and has been taking care of me. He and Mongo got me in here just in time when the Bigfoot was coming to get me." Oh my gosh could that sound any more like a damsel in distress? I had a gun for god's sake!

"Nice to meet you Jared, I have heard great things from James and Janet about you. I'm glad we got to meet but it kind of sucks that it was during a situation like this." Harry said as he shook Uncle Jared's hand and then sat in his seat on my other side taking my hand in his. Mongo was in between us on the floor.

"Sheriff, we have all written done everything that we could remember, most people just saw the Bigfoot and ran back inside. Our crew has sent the recordings to our cloud server so you can come on by the trailer that we have all of the recordings. You're welcome to see everything we have as well." Terry was saying as he looked around at the crew who were all still sitting at the table. Everyone seemed to be in a bit of a shocked phase. They have followed Bigfoot through the woods and this time he followed them back. What the hell is up with that and why are they focused on me?

"That would be great Terry, please call me Jared. I would like to come out tomorrow if that fits with your schedule. Who is in charge of the video feeds?" Uncle Jared asked as he stood.

"That would be me Sheriff, names Jerry." Jerry said as he and Amanda stood up together. When the crew noticed Terry and Jerry standing, they all looked around and they stood too. I think everyone just wanted to get back to their trailers to try and get some sleep. It was defiantly a scary evening and not a relaxing one like we had all hoped.

"Oh, yah sorry! Jared, my boyfriend Jerry from the Bigfoot Getters." Amanda said as she let Jerry's arm go so that he could shake hands across the table with Jared.

"Jerry, nice to meet you." Jared said and then he got this huge smile on his face and turned to me.

"Are you guys joking with me right now?" He was smiling and started to laugh but no one else was.

"What are you talking about?" I asked kind of confused. No one understood what was so funny.

"What so are you telling me this is real, no joke?" Uncle Jared asked me, now he was looking confused.

"What is so funny? We aren't joking about anything, what's going on with you?" I asked and I was trying so hard not to get mad at him. Did he really think we were lying about the Bigfoot that it was all a hoax?

"So their names are really Terry, Jerry and Harry. So Harry is with Carry while Trina is with Terry and Amanda is with Jerry? Okay the Amanda Jerry thing doesn't rhyme but still this has got to be a joke with the names, right? And all three of you girls are dating Bigfoot Getters? Wow I did not see that coming!" Uncle Jared wasn't funny but now I get the name thing is kind of funny. At least Harry, Terry and Jerry were all laughing about it now. Amanda wasn't laughing and Trina was still just kind of dumb founded that Jared was laughing at us.

"Dude, not funny! None of us got the name weirdness until now, thanks a lot!" I said to Uncle Jared as others in the pub were starting to stare at us.

"Okay guy's we better stop laughing, the girls are not amused with it." Uncle Jared said as he pulled me out of my chair and gave me a hug.

"I am glad you are okay though. You did have your pistol, didn't you?" Uncle Jared asked me in my ear.

"Always!" Was my only response. He knew I didn't go anywhere without one.

"Good girl. Your Man is a good guy? Everyone on the crew are all trustworthy?" He continued to whisper in my ear as we hugged. I was sure Harry could hear him but I didn't think anyone else could.

"Of course, do you think I would be with them if they weren't?" I whispered back and then he held me at arm's length and smiled.

"Good enough for me." Uncle Jared said as he turned around to give Harry a hug too, which took a little longer than you would think it should. I am pretty sure he was telling Harry something, probably a warning of some kind knowing Uncle Jared and how protective he is of me. When they separated Uncle Jared talked to the whole table.

"Okay you guys can all go home but, make sure to lock your doors tonight. I will collect your written statements from the table when you leave. Jerry, Terry I will see you guys tomorrow. Be well and be safe going home. Good night." Uncle Jared turned back to me and gave me another quick hug and then he turned and petted Mongo who had been waiting to see him.

"Good boy Mongo." He whispered to Mongo and then he went back to talk some more to Miss Mary, Miss Karen and Big John who were all sitting at a table next to the door.

We collected what we brought with us; Terry went up and paid the bill for the whole crew and all of us. Then we all went out to the trucks and left together in a convoy yet again to go back home. We got back to the house and Harry did a walk through to make sure there were no Bigfoot around. Everything was clear so he came back for me and Mongo to go into the house, Mongo went potty really quick before we went inside. We were exhausted by the day's revelations and all the actual drama. Harry walked Mongo and I back to the bedroom and then he kissed me goodnight.

"I will make sure the house is secure from the inside as well as from the outside. No one will get in and you won't be sleep walking out. Good night Carrie, I will keep you safe." Then he closed the bedroom door and I heard him walk down the hall.

"We both protect you!" Mongo said in my head as I got my night clothes together so that I could change.

"I know Mongo, I know." I changed and was feeling so drained of energy. I went to the bathroom and then Mongo and I went to bed. He was my cuddle bug tonight.

## Chapter 15

I didn't sleep walk last night and there were no dreams that I could remember. It was a good night and the morning was very beautiful. Mongo and I got up and I took him through the living room to let him outside to the back yard to go potty. Harry was once again in the kitchen cooking me and Mongo breakfast.

"Morning!" Harry said when he saw me. It was a good thing I had a hairbrush on my night table because my hair gets wild at night and right now I know it wasn't.

"Good Morning!" I said as walking into the kitchen to give him a side hug and a kiss on the cheek. "You are too good to me." I said as I saw that he was making us omelets with ham and cheese, yummy.

"Just for you, Darling." Harry said and kissed my cheek, then looked at the sliding door and said, "Looks like Mongo wants in now." I turned to see Mongo with is snout on the glass door and he was licking the window.

"Mongo, are you a window licker?" I said as I walked to the door and opened it for him. He looked at me and headed straight to his food dish that Harry had obviously filled for him this morning.

"I guess he was just hungry." I said as I closed the sliding door. Mongo stopped eating for a second and then he walked to the front door. That's when I heard the vehicle in my driveway.

"Uncle Jared is here." I said to Harry as I walked to the front door. Harry had not only locked the main door knob but the deadbolt too. He also put the shoe bench in front of the door. He came out of the kitchen and was passing me in the living room before I could get to the door to start the opening process. He grabbed the shoe bench and moved it back to its spot and then he set to unlocking the deadbolt and then the door knob just as Uncle Jared knocked. Harry opened the door for me.

"Well, hello. I wasn't expecting you to be in here." Uncle Jared was a very nice guy and you could tell that Harry staying with me in the house kind of threw him off.

"I am an adult Uncle Jared, be nice. Harry and Mongo are my protectors. Aren't you Mongo? Harry?" I said as Mongo came up beside me to see Uncle Jared. I rubbed his ear and then he went to Uncle Jared. Uncle Jared is the one that gave Mongo to me. A friend of his had puppies so he took me to pick one. Mongo has been with me since he was a baby. I think that is why we are so in tune with each other also.

"I'm here at your command Lass." Harry said as he kissed my cheek heading back to the kitchen to finish breakfast. Then he asked from the kitchen, "Jared, have you eaten? Do you want a ham and cheese omelet too?"

"No thanks Harry, I already had breakfast. But thank you though." Uncle Jared said as he stood back up from Mongo. "But I will take some of that delicious smelling coffee though." He said walking past me and into the kitchen where Harry was right at home it seemed. Uncle Jared got coffee and joined me at the island as Harry served me and Mongo breakfast. Then got his plate and joined us.

"So Jerry and Amanda are early risers if you want me to take you out to the trailer where we have all the footage of everything that has been going on since we encountered the Sasquatch." I said after I swallowed a mouth full of my heavenly ham and cheese omelet.

"That would be great. You're Parents and your Grandparents told me all about what has been happening, I would just rather see if for myself. I did stop in at the hospital while you were in there, just your Mom was sitting with you at the time and I had already talked to Grandpa Hunter so I knew what to expect when I got there. You sure did heal fast though. Have there been any complications or strange issues come up since you've gotten out?" Uncle Jared asked as he drank his coffee. I took a sip of mine and thought for a minute on whether or not to talk about the sound, hearing and vision sensitivity plus the sleep walking. But in the end my Uncle Jared has only the best intentions.

"Well, if I confide in you then you cannot tell anyone. Do you understand?" I was very serious and he knew I meant it too.

"Okay now you are scaring me more than the thought of Sasquatch being after you. Spill I won't tell a sole." Uncle Jared said as Mongo came over for his part of my breakfast which I was sad to say I had finished every bite.

"Sorry Mongo I ate all my breakfast this time buddy." I petted his head and then he went to Harry. Harry got up and went to the stove and spooned the last of another omelet onto a plate and set it by his food dish.

"There you go buddy, I almost forgot your breakfast." Harry said and then sat back down with us again.

"Okay Mongo is fed, now spill!" Uncle Jared was very interested to know what was going wonky with me, very interested.

"Okay, Okay! It actually started in the hospital. When I woke up my hearing was a lot more acute along with my vision and my sense of smell. I have an actual appetite that I have never had before and then there is the sleep walking." I paused for effect.

"I sleep walked the night I came home and the video cameras that are positioned outside went off line during the time I was in the backyard. Now here is the kicker, I had a very lucid dream that I was in a fur coat and hat walking in the woods during this dream. Then I come upon four guys sitting around a campfire drinking beer and talking about Sasquatch. Then last night I saw and spoke to the same four guys from my dream. They are real and they were in the woods here on the property that butts up to the

Forest Service land.  They said that Grandpa Hunter gave them permissions to be there along with their Grandfather's years ago.  I actually talked to them and they remember hearing me sneezing which also happened in my dream."  I was looking into my hands not sure where else to look when Mongo came over and placed his head in my lap for love.

"The other mystery is when the cameras started working again I was in the backyard and Mongo followed me into the house again."  I could tell by the look on Uncle Jared's face that he actually believed every word I said.  He looked astounded but also a little in awe.  He didn't say anything right away and neither did Harry.  I hadn't told Harry about everything until now.  He also looked a little astounded but also a little relieved maybe.

"Okay well at least you are not a serial killer, right?  I mean there are worst things that could be going on.   So I know of some medications that could have these side effects.    What are you currently taking right now?"  Uncle Jared asked trying to look at this logically first.

"Nothing since I left the hospital, the bite was completely healed by then."  I said as Mongo looked up at me.

"Are you going to tell him about me and your hair incident too?"  Mongo asked in my head.  I hadn't thought I would, but maybe later I will.  It's not something that I wanted Harry to know yet.  It was all just so weird, I swear weird is the new normal for me!

"Okay.  I will make some phone calls and I may have something for you by the end of the week.  Do you want me to talk to you before, after or during the Grandparents Sasquatch BBQ?"  He asked as Mongo got back down and walked over to him.  Mongo needed more petting; he almost seemed upset that I wasn't telling Uncle Jared about his being able to communicate with me.

"Before or after but please not during.  There will be way too many people and I want to have fun.  Did you here Cousins Koda, Caleb, Christoff and their friend Jody are coming to play?  And Uncle Berry and Aunt Maggie will be there and maybe even Aunt Nova and Uncle Adam too."  I was rather excited that they were coming; I hadn't seen them in a while. I know Harrisburg isn't that far away but everyone has such busy lives. Especially the band, 'Right Around the Cornerstone' is great to listen too. Grandpa Hunter loves their Sasquatch song; I hope they play it for the 'Bigfoot Getters'.

"Sounds great to me! I can't wait to see the family again. Let me know right away if anything else happens, I don't care how small if you think it's out of the ordinary for you and your body then you tell me. Do you promise?" Uncle Jared was saying as he placed his coffee cup into the sink, Harry took care our dishes.

"I am going to go get dressed and then we can head out to the trailer." I said as I started toward the bedroom. Harry started to talk so I stopped to listen.

"It's okay Lass; I can take him out there then be right back for you." He was smiling and it seemed like he wanted to talk to Uncle Jared by himself or something so I shrugged my arms.

"Okay. Take your time. Mongo come on buddy!" I said as started walking again toward my bedroom. I wouldn't have to rush this way.

An hour later Mongo and I were sitting on the couch fully dressed and I was on the phone with my Grandma May. She called me to talk about how I was doing.

"Yes Grandma I will see you at the BBQ. Is there anything you want me to do or make for this thing?" I asked for the second time. Grandma May was so excited that the family was getting together that she was just going on and on about who was coming. Some of the family I hadn't seen for years and who knows how many will actually show up. But Grandma May and Grandpa George were known for their great family get-together's, where there will be lots of food and entertainment. Since they were having most of it catered by the local catering company called Mama Hogg's BBQ Catering that everyone around these parts absolutely loves their brisket and ribs. Grandma May and Grandpa George are going all out this time. Even having a stage built for the band to play on too. Grandma May is a fountain of information because she loves doing these kinds of things.

I was trying to cut this long story short so that I could get off the phone since Harry finally returned for me. All the guys said I shouldn't leave the house without at least one guy with me in case the Sasquatch tries taking me during the day. This is a good plan and the only reason I am still in the house.

"No Dear, I have everything covered. Will Harry be bringing you when its time? We all sure do like him Carrie." Grandma May was saying about Harry. Apparently when they came to the hospital Harry wouldn't leave my side except to go to the restroom. It took an act of Grandma May to get him to go and take a shower.

"Yes, Grandma May. Harry will be bringing me; he's always by my side taking care of me still. And everything sounds great! Harry just came in to get me so that I can go and visit with Uncle Jared some more before he has to leave." I said trying to get off the phone.

"Okay Dear. Tell your Uncle that if he wants to bring someone then he should. Tell Harry I said hi also. Love you!" She knew he was right there with me. So I told him, "Grandma May says hi!" Then he in turn said hi back of course.

"Okay Grandma he said hi. Love you too. Bye." I was finally off the phone. I am not a party planner. I do not need to know every detail of what is being done. But I do love talking to my Grandma May though. Now I needed to find out what took my boyfriend so long to get back to me. My boyfriend, huh! It sounds rather good to be able to say that again.

"So, what's going on now?" Was the only thing I could think to ask that didn't sound bitchy, which for me is an improvement.

"Not much, Jerry got him started on the video from the night you were sleep walking. Then I came in to get you but I heard you on the phone so I didn't want to interrupt, so I stood outside and waited." He said as he sat down on the couch next to me.

"Oh, so we don't need to be out there with him while he goes through the footage?" I asked and Harry scooted closer to me on the couch.

"Nope, he just needs Jerry. Amanda is also out there. All the footage from the cell phones has been uploaded and ready for anyone to view." He said as he leaned in toward me.

"So we are good in here all alone?" I asked as I slowly moved toward him.

"Yup, all alone." Harry and my lips met and it was one of those kisses that spark on contact. It was like our lips were meant to be together. The feelings the passion and the sparks were like nothing I had ever felt before. The two of us kind of slowly moved into the couch for a make out session that lasted so long you would think we were in high school all over again. We just kissed and held each other as our bodies fit so perfectly. Harry didn't push for anything more but my hormones were in overtime. I wanted to go further and my body defiantly wanted to go further, but my brain was there to make sure we didn't and so was Mongo. I guess he had had enough of us because he tried to get into the middle of the kissing with his own kissing. The licking on the side of my face and Harry's kind of put a stop to what we were doing. But like anything good, it must come to an end at some point, right? Right? Yah I know, right!


The day flew by while Harry and I spent time just talking while I was doing some of my household chores. I washed and dried the laundry and then Harry helped me to fold it all. He cleaned the kitchen so I cleaned and vacuumed the living room. Mongo spent most of the day out in the backyard either playing with butterflies or sleeping on the patio. The next thing we knew we had skipped lunch and it was almost time for dinner. We were trying to figure out what we wanted to do for dinner when Harry got a call from Terry.

"Hey buddy! What's up?" He asked over the phone. I could only hear one side of the conversation so I just stood and waited to find out what was going on.

"Sure, sounds good to me. I'll ask her." Harry put his hand over the phone.

"So Terry and Jerry feel that you girls probably shouldn't go out anywhere for a while and wanted to know if you would like them to pick up food from the food truck and they all will come in here and we all have dinner together?" He looked like he was interested and I hadn't gotten a chance to talk to the girls all day, which is totally not like us.

"Sure it sounds good. I'd like something meaty though, but not another burger. Should we let them choose?" I was sure if they had the cooks making dinner it was something good. I was really hungry all of a sudden too. Harry turned to the phone.

"Yah she's up for it. She said something meaty but not another burger. Yah, me too. And don't forget something for Mongo. He would not be happy. Okay see you guy's shorty then. Bye!" Harry got off the phone and walked to the sliding door to let Mongo back in the house. It appeared that Mongo also knew it was dinner time. I had filled his bowls earlier; I like to keep them full so he can eat whenever he gets hungry, which I have been told is not a good thing to do to a dog. But Mongo is not fat in the least and he loves to run and play, it's probably not something I have to worry about until he is old and gray.

"Well I guess it's a good thing we cleaned the house today then, huh?" Harry asked as he unloaded the dishwasher.

"My cleaning shores are always quick because it's only Mongo and me living here. Mongo is the messy one of the two of us." I said laughing as Mongo stopped eating and turned to look at me which made Harry also start laughing.

"It's almost as if he can understand you and you just ratted him out." Harry had a wonderful laugh. Something I have learned over the last few days. He had a great sense of humor and was a very caring and honest man. I just wish I knew what the future had is store for us.

I hadn't gotten too dirty while cleaning the house today but I decided to go and at least change my clothes before we had company. Mongo followed me back to the bedroom and jumped on the bed. He lay down and closed his eyes like he always has when I was dressing. I just realized why he always did that. I closed my bedroom door so I could change in private; Harry was changing in the hallway bathroom.

"I just realized you have always closed your eyes whenever I change my clothes or I am naked." I said to Mongo in a lowered voice than I would normally use. Mongo opened his eyes and lifted his head.

"I have always been respectful to you. You are my Mom, my partner and my responsibility. Plus, you have no fur, but I love you anyway." Mongo said and he did his pitbull smile.

"Ahhh, Mongo! I love you too buddy!" I walked over to the bed and sat on the edge and took his face into my hands.

"You are my baby boy and my partner and I will protect you always." I said then I kissed him right between the eyes in that little indent, my favorite place to kiss my Mongo.

"Okay, now get dressed. Trina and Amanda will be here soon." Mongo had just told me he loved me, told me! How many people can say that? Not many I would wager.

"Okay, okay! Now what do I wear?" I started looking through my drawers and then I pulled out a pair of jeans and a gray t-shirt that said 'Your opinion matters, Just NOT to me!'. It makes people look that's for sure. I love to order these funny t-shirts off of Amazon, they have everything.

When I was finished washing my face and then changed into the clean clothes I could hear voices coming from the kitchen area. I knew my island in the kitchen is too small for all of us so we will have to sit at the dining room table. Mongo and I headed in the direction of the kitchen when we saw everyone. Harry must have changed in a hurry; he was in a nice pair of wrangler jeans with cowboy boots and a white, form fitting t-shirt that definitely showed off his muscles and his 6-pack abs. DAMN!!!

Anyway, as I do a mental shake of my head. Harry must have changed fast because he already had the dining room table ready for us with cups, silverware and he even found the candles and lite them. The dining room is on the other side of the kitchen and isn't to big but is big enough for my oak table that fits 6. My Mom and Dad gave me theirs when they decided to downsize, I really love this table. At the end of the dining room was the closed in solarium with all my herbs that my Grandma May has decided that I need to grow because the herbs in the store have too many chemicals in them. It has a self-watering system that runs off of solar power and I love just sitting in there sometimes. I don't even have to really take care of them they take care of themselves, which works great with my job.

"Hey Lady, how are you doing today?" Trina asked me as I walked into the dining room with Mongo on my heals, figuratively speaking. I was wearing my leather moccasins that Grandma May made for me last winter. Have I told you my Grandma loves to stay busy?

"I'm good. How are you guys doing? You, Amanda and Jerry are getting all the video together to make a great couple of episodes?" I asked as Harry came around and kissed my cheek and then pulled out a chair for me to sit at the head of the table then he sat in the chair on my right.

"We definitely have a lot of footage and we still have so much to go through. But I think we are totally going to make a great couple of episodes because there is way too much just for one episode of the 'Bigfoot Getters' show with my expose on Sasquatch has been found! Sorry I get over excited about my work." Amanda was saying as she took the chair on my left and Jerry sat down right next to her. Terry took the chair right next to Harry which left Trina with the end of the table. Trina didn't look very happy right now.

"Trina, how are you doing?" I had to know if she was okay since we have been having so much excitement with the Sasquatch and other things going on.

"I'm good. Terry and I have been working on some schematics to make a better Sasquatch trap then what we used before along with a way to record my voice doing the primate mating call to see if that can be used instead of me sitting in the hot seat again. We think we have come up with a perfect plan." Trina was saying with a small smile on her face. She was usually more upbeat than this.

"You seem kind of sad, is there anything else?" I asked her now but I wasn't sure if she would talk in front of everyone or if maybe Amanda and I should take her aside and see what was really going on with her.

"I'm okay. I was just really scared when the Sasquatch came into town. What if they had gotten one of us?" Trina looked wide eyed and scared all over again.

"Trina has been having nightmares ever since she watched you get bitten, last night was really bad. She's not getting much sleep. But we do think we have the solution and when we are ready we would like to take it out to try and catch a Bigfoot again. Except this time, we will be leaving those who want to stay behind. That's any of you girls plus, any of the crew that doesn't wish to be there." Terry was taking this whole Sasquatch thing seriously and I was glad for that but he was also very concerned about Trina too.

"Why don't we table this discussion until a later date for right now Terry? Let's just have a nice dinner with great company and just relax. After dinner if you guys want to we can watch a movie and pop some popcorn!" Harry was trying to defuse the situation the best he could. Trina started to relax a little after that. Dinner was wonderful, the cooks had made up spaghetti and meatballs, and I swear the meatballs were the size of a baseball. The sauce was divine, the noodles were perfectly cooked, the garlic bread was perfectly garlic buttered for every bite and there was a side salad. Everyone was in good spirits while eating and talking.

Terry brought a bottle of red wine so we all have some, I didn't drink very much but it was nice. Later I switched to iced tea my usual drink of choice, freshly brewed this morning. When the wine was finished everyone switched to iced tea for the rest of the evening. We sat at the table so long after dinner was eaten that we hadn't even noticed the time. Everyone just started yawning almost at the same time.

"Well, I think we are going to pass on the movie this evening." Jerry said as he and Amanda stood and helped to clear off the table.

"Us too, I am afraid. But we will help clean up from dinner first." Then Terry stood and started helping. Harry stood and took our plates following the others to the kitchen. I stood and walked down to the end of the table to talk to Trina.

"Are you really okay?" I asked her in a lower voice. Mongo came over and put his head in her lap.

"I'm really okay. Terry has been great about everything. I do feel safer with him than without him. I can't go back to my place because the Sasquatch has been there, I know if we just catch one then maybe the rest will leave us alone." Trina was saying as she was petting Mongo on the head.

"She is scared. She is shaking." Mongo said in my head.

"Trina, do you want to stay in here in the spare room?" I asked her. She looked up at me with sadness in her eyes.

"No I just want to be with Terry. I don't know how it happened so fast but I have to be with him. Terry is so great and I haven't felt this much love for a man or from a man in, like, ever! I know he will keep me safe." Trina was really in love with Terry, I would not have seen that coming. Then Terry came into the room and walked down to the end of the table where Trina and I were. He got down on one knee next to her. Mongo moved aside so that he could be closer to her.

"And I have never felt this much love for a woman either. Oh, Trina you are the most amazing woman I have ever met. Even though you were scared you still stuck by my side through all of this Bigfoot stuff. You are great at what you do; you are smart, funny and so amazing that I never expected this relationship to bloom as fast as it has. I love you, Primate Lady!" Terry leaned in and Trina met him halfway. Their kiss was so sweet and I think Trina was crying. I turned to see that Jerry, Amanda and Harry were standing at the entrance to the dining room. They all started to clap for the new couple.

"Wonderful, Congratulations!" Harry yelled at the happy couple smiling.

"It's about time!" Jerry was saying as he too was clapping with a huge smile on his face.

"I'm glad to see that Jerry and I aren't the only couple that has proclaimed out love for each other." Amanda said sarcastically with a smile on her face.

"Hey now, the Lass said she loved me last night! Didn't you?" Harry was saying as he walked to me. He looked like he couldn't wait to tell everyone and he figured telling them jokingly wouldn't make me upset. I know I love this man. When he got to me he encircled my waist with his arm and I followed suit. Then he leaned in for a quick kiss.

"Yes, my love I did and so did you if I recall?" I said in good humor.

"Well I guess there is a whole lot of love that has come out of this adventure so far and we still have so much more adventure to come." Terry said as he stood and brought Trina up with him. He held her in his arms and they kissed again, which made Amanda and Jerry kiss so Harry and I started kissing too. There was a lot of love here. But the night had to end here for everyone. Tomorrow will bring another day of fun and love.

Everyone helped finish cleaning up after dinner and Trina was in a lot better mood now. Who wouldn't after having your boyfriend proclaim his love for you but to know that your two best friends were also in love at the same time?

With the entire cleanup done and the others said their goodnights heading out to the trailers again it left Mongo, Harry and I all alone again. Being after midnight Harry and I said our goodnights after he checked the house and locked all the doors. Mongo had gone out and went potty when the others left so he was ready for bed now.

"Thank you for a wonderful evening Harry." I said as he led me to my bedroom door. He was looking so good to me right now in the tight shirt and tight wranglers that I know if he walks me into my room, poor Mongo was going to be the one to sleep on the couch.

"Thank you for a great evening too, Lass." Harry said as he suddenly pushed me up against the wall just before the bedroom doorway. His hot lips were on mine so fast I didn't even have a chance to make a noise. My hands were around his chest as he put his hands into my hair and held my face as he kissed me with so much passion I swear my toes curled. This man knew how to kiss a woman senseless! And then he stopped. We were both breathing very heavily and he was looking into my eyes so intensely, then he just smiled and slowly let me go.

"I just wanted to give you something else to dream about tonight Lass! See you in the morning." Harry said as he pulled away from me and walked no he strutted back down the hall to the living room. I was still in shock and I was still leaning against the wall. I had watched him go all the way down the hall before I pulled myself away from the wall. I walked into my bedroom and closed the door. Oh I definitely will be thinking about him when I dream tonight, and all I can say is DAMN!!!!

## **Chapter 16**

I slept so well dreaming about Harry and all the naughty things I would love to do to that man. Poor Mongo was laying on the floor next to the bed when I woke up.

"I'm sorry buddy, was I too restless for you to sleep on the bed last night?" I asked when I got up and petted his head. He got up and sat then sat back down again and whimpered. I know that sound he had to go potty.

I brushed my hair really quick and put on my slippers and then not thinking I opened the bedroom door to let Mongo go out in front of me to the sliding door so he could go out to go potty. I was only in my night clothes, but it was early so I didn't think Harry would even be up yet. So I tip toed past the backside of the couch to slide the door open after unlocking it. Mongo bolted out and squatted almost right away.

"I guess he really had to go?" I must have jumped a mile high when I heard Harry say from right behind my ear.

"Harry! You scared the crap out of me!" I said as I took a little swipe at his arm. He of course was all smiles and leaned down to kiss me. It was a quick sweet kiss, nothing like the fire from last night.

"I think he's ready to come back in now." Harry said as he reached past me to slide the door open for Mongo who then pushed himself right through and into me like a freight train knocking me into Harry's arms as he caught me. He was hungry and I was obviously in his way.

"Really Mongo, manners?" I said as he stopped and turned his head and smiled at me the little brat. He was trying to put the two of us together after all. And here I thought he was trying to keep us apart. He must have learned something last night during dinner.

Harry kissed the end of my nose and smiled down at me.

"What do you want to do inside today?" Harry asked in a very sexy gravelly voice and wiggled his eyebrows at me. With his accent on top it just made me melt into his arms. He held me for a few minutes and then he said, "What else do you want to do today?" His laughing vibrated my ear that was currently resting on his chest.

"How about I go take a shower and get dressed first? I don't know what we can do right now and I am getting cabin fever something awful. Can we go get food from the food truck and visit with everyone?" I asked as I slowly pulled myself out of his arms.

"Sure, we can do that. I'm starting to get cabin fever myself; I'm not used to being inside so much." He smiled as I turned toward my bedroom and started walking down the hallway.

"I'm not used to it either. I'm usually working all week, mostly in the woods and then on the weekends I'm usually hiking in the woods for fun. Right now I can hardly go outside without worrying if a Sasquatch is coming to get me, day and night!" I wasn't mad at anyone as much as I was mad at the Sasquatch that seems to have the hots for me.

"Well, hopefully in a few days we can fix that problem. But for now we will go and see the crew and then we can decide what to do after that." He had to talk louder because I was almost in my room by the time he finished talking. I wasn't being rude on purpose I just wanted to hurry up and get dressed is all.

"We can talk more when I come back out." I said as I closed my door. I hadn't even seen Mongo go to my room until I closed the door and he was laying on the bed again.

"You are twitter pated!" Mongo said in my head, with a smile on his face.

"I do believe I am." Was all I said as I started the shower and jumped in quickly, it doesn't take me very long to shower. Once I got out and dried off I went through my drawers getting out my clothes for the day. I love my jeans in case you can't tell. It's pretty much all I like to wear, so as usual I put on a pair of jeans and a t-shirt; this one was one of my favorite. It was a black shirt with wolves on it, I love the colors. Then I put on my tennis shoes with my fuzzy socks. By the time I was done dressing Mongo was sitting by the door again. He must have drunk too much water.

"Come on Mongo let's take you potty again." I said as I opened the bedroom door and Mongo bolted for the front door instead of his usual slider door to the backyard. That's when I heard a vehicle pull up in front of the house, it sounded like a bigger truck. I walked down the hall to have Harry meet me as he came out of the living room with a questioning look on his face.

"Were you expecting company?" He asked as I got to the door and stood on my tip toes to look out the peek hole.

"Not that I know of. I don't recognize the truck either." I said as I sank back down on the flats of my feet. Then Mongo started growling and he wasn't happy.

"Men at door, strange smelling. I know their smell, not sure from where." Mongo was talking in my head with more broken speech when he is in protection mode so I have noticed. When we talk he has complete sentences but when angry or weary of a situation is more broken up.

"Okay guys, let's just calm down and see who is at the door." I was saying just as someone starting knocking at the door. It was a hard knock but not like a police knock. Mongo was at the edge of the door waiting to pounce on whoever was out there. This was weird because Mongo is usually very reserved for a dog. He usually waits for commands; I guess the link between us has made me a little lax in being the one in control.

"Mongo, sit!" Mongo turned to me and then sat at my feet. He didn't look happy about it but he did it. I reached for the door knob when Harry said, "Would you rather I open the door? That way you can hold

Mongo back. He doesn't seem to like who is on the other side of the door, Lass."

"No I got this. Mongo will listen to orders like he always does! Right Mongo?" I said and looked right at Mongo. He lowered his head for a second then nodded. Mongo would stay put at my feet until told otherwise.

It had been a few minutes since the first knock but the person didn't knock again. They knew we were standing here and were going to open the door. I turned the knob and pulled the door open very slowly and took notice of everyone that was standing there.

First I see a very handsome man with a light beard and I know him. He was the guy that stopped and said hi to me outside the market the other day, which means he was Tom of the Weird camping brothers and CEO of Emerald City Security. And he was at my house with four of his brothers behind him along with most of the Bigfoot Getters crew; I guess they were my protection detail as well? It appears that Tom has not shaven in a few days and neither have his brothers that he brought with him.

"Ma'am, I'm Tom Johnson. We were the brothers that were camping up at Waldo Lake the day you had an accident. I didn't think you recognized me when I saw you at the store the other day." Tom said with his cowboy hat in his hands. He made no move to walk forward or ask to come in the house. He was nervous but I figure that was because he hadn't expected so many people to be at my house.

"Hello Tom, no I didn't recognize you without your beard, which it seems you are growing one again." I wasn't sure what else to say. He was standing on my front porch with his hat in his hands and he just looked like the typical cowboy that you would see in town. He and his brothers were all dressed in wranglers with varying shades of blue button up dress shirts and yes they were all wearing cowboy boots.

"Yes, Ma'am I thought you would be more comfortable if we had our beards on and you would recognize us better this way." He said looking from me to his brothers and then back at me. Harry was standing off to my right so I don't think that Tom could see him.

"So what can I do for you gentlemen? I'm not working this week so if it's a forestry thing you can see my boss Johnny Case at the office. It's down on Thatcher Lane just off the Willamette hwy."  How did they know where I live if they didn't know I wasn't at the office?

"No Ma'am this isn't a forestry matter. I was hoping to talk to you privately if I could." He said and was getting more nervous by the minute. I think he could tell that I was putting things together in my head. The fact that they knew where I lived meant they had to have been the trucks following us back from the market the other day.  They had to know who my boss was since they knew I was a Forest Service Ranger and with that information they would also know where I worked. So they knew I was home and not at work. Am I being paranoid here? That's when Harry walked around the corner and put his arm around my shoulder.

"Sorry, Tom is it? Carrie and I have plans for today and we have to get some things together before we do. So if you don't have anything else, now is not a good time." Harry was saying as I looked from him to Tom to see not only Tom's face change a little but also his brothers too. They were getting angry, and I don't mean like a little upset but they were kind of pissed and I could swear I saw the irises of their eyes flash to yellow. What the hell! Mongo could feel the tension in the air because he stood next to me and then he was at a slow growl. The kind that starts really low but once you hear it you know trouble is coming.

Tom did a sort of body shake and the tension seemed to leave him along with his brothers who had done the same after he did.  Then Tom looked back at me.

"I'm sorry Carrie; I didn't know you had company."  Tom then reached into his shirt pocket to pull out a business card then he handed it to me.

"When you have some time and would like to know what is going on please give me a call. We are staying at the Oakridge Lodge & Guest House for a few more days then we have to get back to Eugene for work. Please call me." I took his card and he looked into my eyes with a pleading sort of way. Then he turned walking away with his brothers toward the large dark blue almost black Dodge truck that they came in. It was the truck that had followed us home I knew it had the license plate number, CTY112. After they started to drive away the crew seemed to relax again so they headed back to the trailer area again with a smile and a wave. I glanced at the card, wondering what this strange visit was all about. The card read;

Thomas Johnson, CEO Emerald City Security<br>tomjohnsonemeraldcity@yahoo.com<br>541-555-1961

"So he wanted to talk to you privately? I noticed his license plate; he's the one that followed us home the other night too! Lass, he is stocking you! Are you going to call your Uncle Jared about him?" Harry seemed upset but I was a little shaken by the day's events so far and I hadn't even had breakfast yet.

"Yup, I plan on doing that right after we have breakfast. Come on Mongo!" I said as I closed the front door and slid the card into my back pocket. Uncle Jared isn't going to like this. He was always protective of me; I was more like a little sister than a niece. But I am hungry now and I will deal with it after breakfast. Mongo was right beside me all the way through the house to the sliding door. I let him out to go potty and then he went out through the side gate to the food truck. The picnic tables were set up in a circle and we made our way to the window to get food. I was getting everything I could and Mongo was getting half. I petted his head as he sat beside me while we ordered. Harry hadn't said another word to me and he was a little stand offish to me right now too. This was going to be a great day. NOT!

Sometime later I went into the house with Mongo to call Uncle Jared. He answered on the first ring.

"About time you called me; Harry already called me and filled me in on what happened with the Johnson brothers. Why didn't you call me when it happened?" Uncle Jared went head long into telling me. Which Harry wasn't very far from me the whole time we were with the crew and eating breakfast, but I guess I did take my sweet time in calling.

"Sorry I was starving and I wanted to talk to you alone about this without too many ears listening. I can't believe he called you!" I was not happy and the more I thought about it the more I got pissed and I'm really not the type to get pissed off easily.

"Calm down he was only looking put for you. Do you really think these guys are stocking you?" He was defending Harry, he must like him.

"I don't know what to think. They did follow us home the other night and they were up camping at Waldo Lake but they left the morning we did according to Tori and Don. But I don't want to take this too lightly after what happened to my friend Jessica Langly from Paisley, you remember her don't you?" I know I was babbling but I was not really thinking but I was feeling and I didn't even know exactly what I was feeling either. I am a mess!

"Yes, I remember Jessica but you are not in that situation right now. You have the crew, Mongo plus Harry staying with you. From what Harry said this Tom guy didn't like seeing him with you either. Do you still have his card?" Uncle Jared was in Sheriff mode now.

"Yes, I have his card still. It was weird though the way he gave it to me. He said that he wanted to talk to me privately and if I wanted to know what was going on to call him. He and his brothers are staying at the Oakridge Lodge & Guest House for a few more days then they have to get back to Eugene for work." I said as I pulled the card out of my pocket.

"Why don't you give me the number just so I have it?" He said, so I rambled off the number off the card to him.

"Okay, so just put the card away and don't call the guy until you talk to me first. I am going to be doing some research on him and then you can call him if you need to. He may know why all your senses have heightened.

Or he could just be a whack-a-do, either way let me find out first." Uncle Jared said.

"So Amanda has already done some research on them so I would give her a call and see what she has, that way you aren't redoing work that you can get from her, right?" I was getting into a better mood now.

"Okay good. I'll call her now. Love ya kid. Bye!" Uncle Jared said and then hung up. I put the card back into my back pocket and was about to turn around when I sensed someone coming up behind me. Then I could smell him and I knew it was Harry. He put his arms around me and hugged me from behind placing his face into my hair and breathed deeply.

"So I guess you aren't mad at me anymore?" I said as I turned in his arms.

"I was never mad at you. I was just confused on why you would take his card knowing that he and his brothers, who were not only weird at the campsite but then they stocked you back home. I was jealous I guess. That Tom fellow was very into you seeing how he got pissed upon seeing me with you, well that says too." Harry said as he kissed my forehead.

"I'm not interested in him, I just really want to know what kind of information he thinks I need to know. I'm having a hard time with all of this. I had a friend in college that was hurt and stocked by a friend of ours. We never thought he would have done that to someone but he did it to her. He's behind bars now and she's happily married but she went through a lot to get to that point. I just don't want that to happen to me too. I am not taking this too lightly but I also don't want to go off halfcocked and cause problems for someone just because they were interested in me and I didn't return the feelings back." I said as I saw the realization in his eyes of what I had gone through with my friend.

"I heard you talk to your Uncle; did he mention that I had already called him?" He asked with his sad little puppy dog eyes, he was hoping I wasn't pissed at him, which I wasn't anymore. He seemed to have that effect on me.

"Yes he told me, which really pissed me off. I'm an adult woman and I don't need you doing everything for me like I'm not. That being said I also realized that you are just trying to protect me. And I just can't seem to stay mad at you, not for very long anyway.

"That's good to know." Harry said as he leaned in and kissed me on the lips, just a quick peck but there was still a spark.

I smiled at him and put my arms around him and we just held each other. The day was starting to get better.

## **Chapter 17**

When the day was coming to an end Harry and I had just stayed in watching movies yet again I was starting to get a little down. We had a quick lunch and watched The Hobbit: An Unexpected Journey. We had dinner from the food truck delivered by Alvin when we were halfway through The Hobbit: The Desolation of Smaug which Alvin stayed and finished watching with us. After Alvin left and we popped some popcorn and watched The Hobbit: The Battle of the Five Armies and then we decided it was time for bed when my Mom calls me. I answered and told her to hang on.

"I'll just take this to my room and go to bed. I will see you in the morning, Night!" I gave Harry a quick kiss.

"Okay Lass I will see you in the morning. We will do something else tomorrow I swear, Night!" He said as Mongo followed me into the bedroom where I closed the door on another home date.

"Okay Mom, what's up?" I asked as I pulled my night clothes out from under my pillow so that I could put them on while I had Mom on speaker phone.

"So your Dad just talked to your Uncle Jared. Why haven't you called to update us on what has been happening? I know you're super busy with everything going on with the Sasquatch's. We are your Parents; we would like to be kept in the loop with all that is going on with you!" I hadn't heard my Mom yell at me for years. I was always a good girl, always did what I was supposed to do. Since I have been out on my own I have only had to make sure I have done everything for myself. I mean yah I call or went to see my Parents and Grandparents a lot and they were filled in on my boring life as it was but now....

"Sorry Mom, I just haven't been thinking straight being on my own I haven't had anything exciting happen to me in a long time so I guess I forgot to share." I was sorry and Mom doesn't usually yell at me or anyone really.

"Well, I just wanted to make sure that you are being careful and we feel safer know that Harry is there with you along with all the crew taking care of you but Babygirl, you've got to keep us informed on what is going on. Okay?" Mom was done with her rant and she knew I got the point, I'm not that hard headed.

"Yes Mom, I know." I was really feeling like a child again here.

"Okay that being said, I have to go into Eugene tomorrow to get some supplies for the party that your Grandma wanted me to pick up from Heavenly Chocolate Company on Stewart Road, I have to stop at the Whole sale Grocers, so I thought two birds one stone. Anyway I know how much you love that place so if you want me too I can get you your favourites?" Once my mom said Heavenly Chocolate Company my tummy did a summersault that is my Disneyland and 6 Flags for my tummy. I love everything they make from the truffles to the chortles to the Black Forest Caramels not to mention the chocolate covered cereals. My Mom always gets me an assortment of everything when she goes there for me she has them put it into a special gift box for me, I go over board when I go alone.

"I would LOVE some Heavenly Chocolate Company's special box you get me Mom that would be amazing!" I know it doesn't look like I eat a lot of chocolate but these chocolates are worth their weight in gold. They always make me feel better no matter what's going on in my life.

"Okay well I will be leaving early in the morning; you know how much of an early riser your father and I are. When we get back I will let you know. Maybe you, Harry and possibly the crew can come to the Pizzeria for lunch or dinner and then you can pick up your chocolates. Sound good?" This was her way of getting the crew to come into the restaurant and that way she can get information out of them at the same time.

"I will ask tomorrow Mom, I was just headed to bed and I am sure everyone else is too. Isn't this late for you too?" I asked as I finished putting on my nightshirt and then folded back the covers.

"Well it was a late night at the restaurant and your Dad and I were relaxing watching a movie when I remembered that I hadn't talked to you yet. Anyway, we are heading to bed too. Just send me a text letting me know if you and the crew are coming so I can have a table reserved for you guys. Okay honey I will let you get back to Harry then." Mom said and I know she was fishing for Harry information.

"I'm going to bed alone with Mongo, Mom. What kind of girl do you think I am?" I asked a little insulted.

"Sorry Honey, I just figured you inherited my hormones and libido I wasn't meaning anything by it. And I would never judge you if you had done something either." Mom was still fishing.

"Mom we are taking this slow and I don't need any help here. I love you and I will see you tomorrow one way or the other. Good night." I said as I was about to hang up on my Mom.

"Okay, okay fine. I will see you tomorrow. I love you too. Goodnight." My Mom hung up the phone. I started to lay down and I swear I heard laughing coming from the living room. I think he heard my conversation, was I really talking that loud? Oh, well.

You know when you are having a great dream and then something starts ringing in your dream and you can't find it? It's usually your alarm clock but this time it was my cell phone that was recharging next to the bed. I woke up enough to look at the phone to see that it was my boss Johnny. So I answered it.

"Hey, Johnny what's up?" I said answering my cell and putting it on speaker.

"I hate to do this to you Carrie but I'm going to need you in the office this morning. We have an issue that I am going to need your help with." Johnny didn't sound like himself so I sat up straight in the bed and threw the covers back.

"What's going on Johnny?" I had to ask.

"Well, Terry warned when they came into town that once the Bigfoot hunting community found out about what they were doing here that a lot of the hunter types may show up here in town." Johnny said and then paused.

"Let me guess they have started showing up? How did they know that the Bigfoot Getters had even found anything yet? They are still going through footage!" I was out of bed opening the bedroom door to find Harry standing there in his boxers with a grim look on his face. He must have heard my phone ring and then heard the conversation because I had it on speaker.

"Someone from the pub the other night posted it on Facebook and then it flew all over the internet. They are coming in to Oakridge in droves; Miss Mary said they had people as early as last night come into the pub to ask questions!" Johnny was sounding very flustered.

"Okay so they know about the pub but what about Waldo Lake is that still safely closed?" I hadn't even thought to check in with Johnny for an update.

"I had to reopen it on Monday, Don and Tori are back up there. We have a couple volunteer rangers staying up there in case of any issues. But Waldo is not what I am worried about. There are trucks and SUV's all over town asking questions about what happened at the pub and if there were any other places that the Bigfoot had been seen. Your name has been tossed out there as being with the Bigfoot Getters from the beginning of this mess. People are talking about the Bigfoot Getters being here and filming their show. I thought I had a plan but it fell through. Can you come in to help me figure this out Carrie, I know it's a Friday but please?" Johnny was in a pickle and he thought I was the one to help him out, me? Before I could say anything Harry had to talk to Johnny as well.

"Hey Johnny, Harry here, I will get Terry and the crew to come on down to assist you. Maybe there is something we can help you with and I don't leave Carrie's side." Harry was grinning at me as he pulled out his phone and started dialing Terry.

177

"Johnny, we will be in at the office a.s.a.p. Do I need to bring anything?" I asked before I turned to gather clothes for a workday.

"Great! Yah bring that food truck with you guys, those guys can cook. Thanks again Carrie, I know I kind of got you into this but I am glad that something is working out for you in all of this." Johnny said and I knew he was talking about Harry.

"Yah, some things are coming up roses. See you in a few Boss! Bye!" I hung up before he could say anything else because Harry was walking back with his phone and he had his jeans on this time.

"Okay so Terry is waking up the crew so everyone will be going with us to your office. Did Johnny need us to bring anything?" Harry asked as he saw me put my clothes on the bed where Mongo was now wide awake but didn't want to move off the bed yet.

"Yah, he asked if we could bring the food truck, he really likes their food." I said laughing.

"I can make that happen." He smiled and then sent a text to someone; I am assuming one of the wonderful cooks. A second later he got a response.

"Ha, they said they would be happy to. Well I guess the whole gang in coming in. I'm going to go and get dressed while you do the same. Mongo, need to go potty?" Harry said as he headed for the door. Mongo looked at me and then at Harry, jumped off the bed following him out the door which Harry closed behind him.

"Huh, well that's new." Was all I said and then I took my clothes into the bathroom for a quick shower and to get dressed. I didn't take too long in the shower and applying my makeup is a breeze so I brushed my hair up in a ponytail my favorite style to wear it. That is until I met Harry who likes to run his fingers through my hair every time he kisses me with those toe curling kisses of his. Okay mental shake, got to work today. At least the cabin fever will be over, right?

An hour later we were all at the Forestry office sitting around a table waiting for the food truck to be done making the breakfasts that make every day.  Now we are just getting the low down on who is actually in town.

"So I have been doing some Facebook research on the Bigfoot/Sasquatch hunter's sites and have found at least five different groups are here.  All of the groups except for one are the research types.  They what to conduct interviews, possibly go out for a night investigation.  The last group is the worst of the worst.   Terry here told me some about them when you guys came to town.  Not The Sweethome Mountain Men Bigfoot Hunters!" Johnny was saying as he pulled up a photo of the group from their Facebook page.

"We have Jedidiah, Jed for short and Cletus Monroe they are the leaders of the group, according to Terry.  Jed may be a redneck but he is a smooth talker and can convince people to let them hunt on their private lands.  Cletus is the trap maker; he makes contraptions to grab the Bigfoot, bear traps on steroids.  Their three friends Billy Bob Brockman ex- army ranger, is their Weapons specialist.  The Munster twins Tray "the tracker" and Ray "the mechanic" Jones.  The Jones twins are called the Munster twins because they look like an older version of Eddie Munster who likes wearing black from head to toe including combat boots and black dyed hair.  They do their hunting at night only with real guns!  They just want to kill Bigfoot for the bragging rights, not for research.  They all grew up in the Sweet Home area.  They are bad news, the worst of the worst in the Bigfoot hunting community.  Terry, do you have anything to add about these guys?" Johnny finished his short presentation.

"Yes, these guys are your typical rednecks.  They will shoot first and think later, Harry almost got shot by them when they came in on our investigation site a while back.  Please do not underestimate these guys.  They are dangerous!" Terry said as he stood behind Trina with his hands on her shoulders.  She hadn't been very far from him since the pub incident.  I am sure she will get her mojo back; she has worked with primates for a long time now.

A few minutes later Monica Casey, a transfer park ranger from Three Sisters Station came in to talk to Johnny.

"Sir, the owner of the Oakridge Lodge & Guest House called to let you know that the people they were expecting have arrived.  He wants to know what your orders are, Sir." Monica was super serious about her job. She took pride in her work as well as her uniform that was always spotless and she was perfectly groomed. I don't know how she does it. But otherwise she was a nice person outside the office.

Thank you Monica, please let them know that I will be calling them in a little bit to let them know." Johnny said and Monica whirled around and was gone again presumably to relay the message. Terry got a text and smiled.

"Okay everyone our brain food is ready let's go get in line and get some food. Johnny, are we meeting right back in here with our food?" Terry asked as everyone started to get up to walk out to get food. My tummy was rumbling, and I know Mongo was hungry even though he scarfed down some of his dog food before coming back to me in the bedroom this morning.

"Yes, please as many as can fit in here. If needed, we have to we can move the other conference table into here as well." Johnny said as people filed on by him next to the doorway.

Harry and I were the last to get out to the food truck so we were at the end of the line. Then my Uncle Jared and his two deputies pulled in to the parking lot. They got out and headed straight to us.

"Is this were we can get some free breakfast?" My Uncle Jared joked as he gave me a hug.

"Why yes it is!" Harry said as he shook Uncle Jared's hand that he offered.

"Great, because we have been on disturbance calls all night with these Bigfoot hunters in town causing problems. Miss Mary and Miss Karen had to actually shoot at some guys who were trespassing on their property at three am this morning. They thought the Bigfoot came back because the dumb asses were howling in the backyard!" Uncle Jared was laughing and so were his deputies. Gabe and Luke Bronson had been deputies here in Oakridge since they got out of the Marines four years ago. They are the brothers that did everything together. They were on the shorter side only about 5' 10" or so, both had blonde hair and blue eyes they obviously have some Scandinavian in their blood. They grew up in Junction City, Oregon and were in Uncle Jared's platoon and they were together for a while. None of them talk about it much, but he helped them get their jobs here so that they could all still work together. Great guys and always in a good mood too they go almost everywhere Uncle Jared goes.

When everyone had their food we all went into the conference room to eat while we talked about the Sweethome Mountain Men Bigfoot Hunters or SMM Bigfoot Hunters. Uncle Jared had done his research as well.

"Those guys may act stupid but they aren't. They have a few charges against them for trespassing along with breaking and entering but no felonies which is why they can still have their guns. Now I made a call to the Sweet Home PD and they say these guys are very aggressive when it comes to going where others have had luck with anything Bigfoot, be it recordings of sounds or what have you. They push themselves into other people's areas which wouldn't be too bad except these guys are packing guns and real ammo where most of the Bigfoot researchers are only carrying tranquilizer guns. The Sheriff in Sweet Home actual said good luck with them when I spoke to him. They are glad for the break when they leave the area." Uncle Jared said with a little laugh.

By the time Uncle Jared was finished talking most of us were finished eating. Mongo got almost half of my breakfast, he was so happy. He was lying underneath my chair while we were all in the conference room.

"Okay, so we know these guys are a little rowdy and have no boundaries when it comes to Bigfoot hunting. What else can you tell us Terry?" Uncle Jared said before he sat down to eat his cold breakfast burrito. Terry stood up and looked around at the table.

"My only input is that we need to keep these guys away from our Bigfoot investigation at all costs. We know for a fact that the Bigfoot is not only here in the area but are also willing to come into town. It seems like they are in some kind of a mating frenzy because they keep going after Carrie, Amanda and Trina because of the mating call we did in the mountains during our first hunt. I blame myself for that one. But we did get a lot of real evidence even without capturing a Bigfoot, which I think we should try again. We will have to be somewhere that the Jeb and his SMM

Bigfoot Hunters can't go at all." Terry was saying as he was rubbing Trina's shoulders, she did look a little tense.

"What if we gave them false information or if we talk to Miss Mary and Miss Karen and see if they will let them investigate the pub area?" Trina asked as she started to be more like her old self.

"That just might work." Uncle Jared said as he finished his breakfast and gave Mongo the last bite. I hadn't seen him crawl under the table toward him until he popped out to eat the bite Uncle Jared offered him. Then he walked around and back under my chair.

"Yes, I think we can get them to help us out and make them feel safer knowing that the Bigfoot is no longer in the woods behind the pub anymore." I said as I pulled out my phone.

"Do you and your deputies want to talk to them or do you want me to call them?" I asked Uncle Jared as I set my phone down on the table.

"I think we will handle it. We will head over there as soon as we are done here. Now as for them staying at the Lodge, I think my deputies will pop down there and give them a little warning about how to behave in our town. Right, Boys?" Uncle Jared asked Luke and Gabe.

"You got that right Boss." Deputy Gabe said as he stood as well as Deputy Luke.

"Yep, we are on it right now." Luke said as they grabbed their jackets and headed out.

"Good. Let me know if you have any problems." Uncle Jared said as they walked past him.

"Okay I'll be on my way over to talk to Miss Mary and Miss Karen and then they can contact the SMM Bigfoot Hunters to do an investigation at the pub tonight." Uncle Jared said as he stood and grabbed his jacket. It may have been a spring day but the warmer weather still wasn't here yet, we still get cold gusts off the mountain tops.

"Well, okay we have a plan then. Is there anything we should do about the other Bigfoot hunters Sheriff?" Johnny asked before Uncle Jared could leave.

"No they are all pretty harmless, let them talk to people and do their research. Just stay out of their way as much as possible unless you want others to take your research I would suggest getting your stuff done a.s.a.p.?" Uncle Jared said as he came over to hug me goodbye. I stood up for that and Mongo was already out from under my chair and under the table again. He's not used to so many people in one small room where he is underfoot so to speak.

Uncle Jared hugged me, petted Mongo and shook hands with Harry, Terry and Johnny then he left for Miss Mary's pub. We all sat back down to talk more about Terry's idea about a capture mission again. I wasn't in a big hurry to volunteer to be the bait again and neither was Trina.

"What about using Grandpa's property where it butts up against the wilderness that basically leads to Waldo Lake? I mean it's private and Grandpa is NOT going to let anyone else in, plus we would be in an area that we know they have been because they have come to my house. What do you guys think?" I was pretty sure that Grandpa Hunter would let them do it; he may even want to be there too.

"Do you think he would let us do that? I know he likes us and all but to be on his land and capturing a Bigfoot that would be amazing!" Terry said getting very excited.

"All I can do it ask him." I said. My phone was still out on the table.

"I would need to know when you would like to do it because they are having that party this weekend so it would have to be before or after that." I said looking around at everyone. Harry leaned toward me and took my hand in his. I noticed he was careful with the public displays of affection, PDA when he is around my family, especially Uncle Jared.

"Tomorrow is Saturday and the BBQ Party starts tomorrow after noon, so we either have tonight or we wait until Monday night? What do you all think?" Terry asked everyone at the table.

"You do realize that tonight is the New Moon, Terry? Another of the nights that the Bigfoot are known for being active, which I am not even sure that it really counts with these Bigfoot since they have been active in town. Carrie, Lass, do you think you can make the phone call to your

Grandpa Hunter and find out what he thinks?" Harry said as he rubbed his thumb across the knuckles of my left hand.

"I haven't even been paying attention to the moon the last couple of weeks. What do you think Carrie?" Terry asked, he looked a little flustered. Had he been sidetracked with Bigfoot research or Trina?

"I can call him right now." I picked up the phone and dialed Grandpa's number. He always answers right away.

"Hello Babygirl! What going on today?" He always answers the phone that way whenever I called.

"Well Grandpa I am here with the Bigfoot Getter Crew and we wanted to know if we could do a Sasquatch hunt to capture on your land where it butts up against the forest land tonight? We have either tonight or Monday night with the group of Sasquatch hunters in town that are out to shoot them not capture we kind of have a small window of time. Plus, everyone wants to be at your party tomorrow too." I know I was rushing though what I wanted to say but I wanted to get it all out there before he said yes or no.

"Tonight would be fine or Monday. I've grown very fond of those guys and they are welcome to do whatever they need to on our land. I would love to go along but I think your Grandma would kill me." Grandpa said laughing. He always has the best outlook on everything and when he makes friends you are friends for life. Everyone at the table was all smiles.

"Well Grandpa I think they really like you too. Can you let Mom and Dad know what's going on please? We have things to get together and I am not sure if I will have time to call them before we head out on the hunt to capture a Sasquatch." I said seeing everyone around the table getting excited; even Trina and Amanda seemed to be getting into this hunt.

"Just make sure that you call me when you capture one because I really want to see one up as close as possible. I have heard and told all the stories; it's about time I get to tell one of my own too." Grandpa was great and Terry was nodding his head.

"Terry says no problem Grandpa. It may be late tonight or early morning when you get the call though. Okay we got to go get ready for the hunt. Love you! Bye!"

"Okay Babygirl, Love you too. Bye!" Grandpa said then we hung up. The room was filled with excitement and Terry stood and looked around at us all.

"Well, what are you all waiting for an invitation? Let's go capture us a Bigfoot!" Terry yelled as everyone even Johnny got up. We all funneled out of the room and out to the trucks to head back to the property. Tonight was going to be a wild ride, I guarantee!

## Chapter 18

We headed back to the house and trailers right after the meeting. Johnny was excited to be included; he left Monica in charge of what was happening with the Bigfoot hunters that weren't in the SMM Bigfoot Hunters group. Besides the Oakridge Police Department, we will be taking care of most of the issues, it's when they are in the woods causing problems that it's the Oakridge Forest Service issue.

Once we got back to the house it was a little before 11am. Everyone had their specific jobs to do and things to gather together. We all stopped to eat a very quick lunch and were ready to go a little after 1 pm. We had everything we needed for the hunt tonight. All we needed were the SUV's. The food truck went with us just in case we were up there really late and need any food. I think the cooks just wanted to be in close to where the action was going to be. Grandpa said we had free rein to go where we thought the best spot was to have our capturing site set up. We all felt like we were on a time crunch and I guess in a way we were.

We used the driveway that ran along the river toward the wilderness part of the property. Grandpa and my Dad had made a rough road through there a couple years ago just in case a fire ever broke out so they could get a water truck back in there to help put it out. We drove a good 5 miles back where I knew there was a small meadow that all the trees had fallen a few years ago during a very bad winter. Most of the trees had been utilized for firewood but there were a few that still laid on the ground. Once we stopped is when the work began.

We moved all the supplies to the edge of the meadow so that they were a little inside the tree line. Jerry and Amanda were out with Alvin putting cameras everywhere. They had them in the trees on the ground and on everyone. Once everything was set up to Terry's satisfaction we broke for a quick dinner before it turned dark. Terry didn't want any food smells from the grill or ovens so the cooks made everyone sub sandwiches with chips, fruit and veggie trays and soda pop or water bottles. Mongo was helping people eat this time. I think he liked the crew too; he hadn't talked to me much since we got the go ahead from Grandpa but that could just be because he was trying to stay out of everyone's way and yet still be here for me.

When everyone was pretty much done eating, Terry stood in front of everyone.

"It is almost dark and the New moon is getting fuller. I don't know what is going to happen tonight so I just wanted to say that I have had a great crew and a great time Bigfoot hunting with all of you. I want to thank Johnny here for letting us steal Carrie and her friends, including Mongo, to help with this amazing adventure." Terry nodded to Johnny and Johnny smiled.

"That being said, please everyone be safe. The Bigfoot are known for their strength and agility. I don't want to lose anyone tonight, if we catch one then we catch one, if not then we try again another time. We got lucky the last couple of times this time we will be smarter and outsmart them." Then Terry turned and looked at Amanda and I, then at Trina.

"Ladies I know you're scared about this but the recording that we have should be enough to bring the Bigfoot in without using you ladies as bait. I am sure Trina and Carrie both are very happy about. We are calling them right into the cage and hopefully we can close the door this time before any get back out. The tranquilizer guns have been increased from the last time because that just wasn't enough to knock them out, this time it should be good." Everyone was hanging off of every word that Terry was saying. Trina was by his side looking the best she had in days. She looked confident and in control again.

"Okay if everyone is ready, you know where you are supposed to be so please take your positions. Ladies you will be over next to the food truck out of danger. The cooks will be armed with tranq. guns to protect you while we are all doing what we need to do to get a Bigfoot in the cage. If anything goes wrong get into a truck and leave, please. We are trained professionals and we will be fine. They are after you ladies so just get out of here. Okay. Is everyone ready for this? The sun is going down fast. Everyone get into place let's get this show started!" Terry was super excited and you could feel the excitement in the all around us.

Our guys walked Trina, Amanda and I over to the food truck so we had could say our goodbyes. We walked two by two until we got to the back of the food truck for safety. It seemed like everyone had a job but us so we had to stay out of the way. We girls and Mongo didn't mind that at all.

"Just be safe and don't take any chances. No matter what you hear out there, Lass stay put!" Harry really wanted to make sure that I would be safe, I get that but come on, I am a big girl and I could do something? He kissed me with one of those super passion filled kisses that curled my toes and melted my brain I swear. My arms went around him and his hands were all over me. Then he let me go and leaned his forehead against mine. "No matter what, you are mine."

"Okay my Love." Was all I could think to say after he let me go? My brain was mush!

Amanda and Trina were getting the same from their men, I was trying so hard not to hear them, but with my senses so heightened it was hard, but I really think I was getting the hang of it though. They let us go at about the same time and looked back only once on their way to capture a Bigfoot.

We Ladies were in the food truck.  Which was fine, no problem.  I always had my handgun if I needed it and I had Mongo.  I was sure we would have no problems being out of the way and all.  Once the sun had gone down and darkness had taken over the land that is when the fun would really begin.  Terry had Trina's primate mating call on an audio loop was what we started hearing.  The howling started low and then got louder and louder then it stopped for a few minutes so everyone could listen.

The first hour we didn't hear anything.  According to Stephen Jefferson, one of the cooks this is not unusual.   Stephen had worked for the Bigfoot Getters from the beginning, even before the food truck.  So he would know, so now we waited.

After a while I thought I heard something far off in the distance, but wasn't sure if it was a howl or a coyote in the distance.  Mongo just sat at my feet and we waited.  The guys made sure we had camping chairs to sit in while we waited.  My hearing was defiantly intensifying even more.  Now I heard something heavy running through the woods.  But it wasn't coming from the direction of the forest; it was coming from behind us.  Mongo turned his head in that direction then looked at me.

"I can hear it too Mongo.  Stephen, tell Terry they are coming from behind us, quick!"  I turned in my chair to look into the woods on the backside of the Meadow that was closer to our property.  Why would they be coming from the direction of our property and not the forest?  Did they stay in town somewhere or were they staying on our property watching us?

"Harry, Carrie said they are coming from behind us, not the forest direction!"  Stephen said into the walkie talkie.

"Shit!  Get the girls inside the truck and lock the doors!  We may still be able to salvage this!"  Harry yelled into the walkie so we girls and Mongo go up really quick and followed Stephen and the other cooks into the back of the food truck.  They pulled the metal side panels down over the serving window and then they closed the metal partition door to the front of the truck as well as locking the door in the back that we came through.  Mike Stone, James Peterson, Brad Summerly and Stephen all seemed a bit rattled at what was happening right now.

"Okay, we all just need to stay calm and quiet. They will probably just pass us by and head straight for the recording in the trap. We will be fine in this metal truck with tranq guns and I have a pistol if anything gets out of hand. Just listen since we can't see anything anymore." I was saying as we all tried to get more comfortable sitting on tiny stools they pulled out of a cubby.

"Yes Ma'am." Is what all the guys said almost as one. Trina and Amanda knew not to talk when I said no talking. Mongo sat by the back door listening. It got very quiet outside then Terry must have started the howling audio again to make sure they went passed the truck we were in. This went on for about 15 minutes and then they stopped again, so we waited.

"Something is outside the door." Mongo said in my head and then we felt the truck move a little bit, like someone was pushing on the side of it to see if anything was in it. The howling audio started again then the moving stopped.

"Not sure if they left. There are lots of them out there." Mongo said in my head. I reached over and started to pet his head, more to calm down me than him. That was when I saw that my hand was rather furry. It had to be a trick of the light, wait there were no lights on. I took my left hand and rubbed the back of my right, there wasn't any fur there now. Wow that was weird!

This time when the howling started you heard guys yelling and it almost sounded like celebrating for a second then it sounded like all hell broke loose! Men were yelling, guns were going off and the food truck we were in started really being shook. Mongo almost fell to the floor; they were pushing us or something! More gun shots along with more yelling and high power search lights so bright the light was coming through the cracks in the door and cover panel. Then there were a couple howls and a scream. I was actually getting scared.

"It's that damn Jeb and Caleb and his SMM Bigfoot Hunters group! They came in shooting at the Bigfoot that we almost had in the trap! Call the Sheriff someone! Carrie!" Terry was yelling into the walkie talkie.

That's when the truck was pushed really hard.  Then the back door was pulled open. Mongo was on the floor and I was yanked out in seconds! I never saw by who or what but I had a bad feeling that I was being kidnapped by Sasquatch!

I must have hit my head because I don't remember hearing or seeing much of anything until I was being pulled through the woods and the tree branches were hitting me. I was being carried by something very big and furry; I knew it was a Sasquatch. I pretended to still be out, but I was trying to take notice of what was happening around me.  I hadn't been out long because I could still hear the Chaos of the guns shooting, men yelling and a lot of trucks driving around.  I could still see the search lights in the meadow, that's when realized that I was not alone, there were other Sasquatch with us. Damn it, there were maybe 5 or 6 others. My eyesight right now was heightened so they were not just shadows to me.

I was starting to breath heavier and if I didn't get myself under control before the Sasquatch knows I'm awake. Calm down Carrie, Clam down.  I closed my eyes to try to get myself under control.  Then I heard something big running right behind the Sasquatch carrying me away. I opened my eyes to see a very large Sasquatch with more of a dark red in color than the one carrying me that was a darker brown. The Big Red one howled.  The one carrying me stopped, turned to look at the Big Red one.  I could see was the other Sasquatch stop and walk back toward us. Then I heard the damnedest thing!

"MINE!"  The Big Red Sasquatch yelled.  The one carrying me shook his head.

"Mine!"  He yelled, turned around and started walking again.  Big Red howled again and this time Mongo came out of nowhere to stand beside Big Red and he howled too.  I felt this urge to howl back without even thinking.

The Sasquatch carrying me stopped and pulled me off his shoulder to look at me. Mongo let out another howl and then I did too matching his. The Big Brown Sasquatch set me on my feet in front of him and turned to face Big Red.

"Why yours?" Big Brown asked.

"Mine by choice!" Big Red said pointing at me then hit his chest where his heart was. Mongo was right beside this Sasquatch like he was his buddy. What the hell, what about me, I wasn't scared I was, flattered? Big Brown turned and looked at me again.

"You choose him?" He pointed at Big Red and Mongo. All the Sasquatches were coming to where we were standing, circling around us. If I say no, then they would take me away. If I said yes then the Big Red one would take me away. Were they all part of the same group? No, there was something different about the Big Red one and Mongo was at his side. My hands started itching and I could feel a warm sensation all over my body. Was it because I was nervous? I looked at my hands, the fur was back on the backside of my hands and my finger seemed to be longer. Was it another trick of the light? My feet felt very tight in my shoes too. Big Red took a step forward.

"Lass, mine?" Holy Shit Harry was a Sasquatch! I felt like fainting. I put my hand over my heart then I pointed to Big Red, Harry.

"My Choice!" I yelled with my voice a little gravelly. What the hell was going on? Big Brown looked at me and then looked at Big Red Harry. He leaned in and sniffed me. I don't mean a little sniff either. He grabbed my hair sniffing it and then my neck.

"Not fully yet! May choose another!" Big Brown said as he stepped back from me. Then he motioned for all the Sasquatch around us to go ahead and leave. He leaned down and looked me in the eyes and whispered to me.

"Call me Tom." And then Big Brown took off after the others. I was about to faint at all the things I had just discovered. Big Brown was Tom

Johnson, Big Red was Harry and Mongo obviously already knew that!!!! I watched Big Brown leave and then turned to find Big Red, my Harry standing next to me and Mongo was sitting panting at my feet.

"Harry? Is that really you?" Harry nodded his head.

"Mongo you knew about this didn't you?" Mongo turned his head away giving me that I'm in trouble look.

"Yes, he has talked to me for a while now. I liked his smell but wanted you to find out on your own what he was and what you are now." Mongo said in my head.

"Talking hard in this form." Big Red Harry said in that gravelly voice that was so not his. Then he started to change from Big Red Sasquatch into a very naked Harry in human form. That was all my brain could take, I passed out. The world around me went dark and I welcomed it.

## Chapter 19

    When I awoke I knew I was at home again. I was in my bed with Mongo by my side. I had no clue of the time I think it was till dark outside. I really had to go pee so I rolled out of bed and walked to the bathroom half asleep. I turned on the light, closed the bathroom door and walked over to the toilet, grabbing at my night clothes pants and dropped them to the floor to sit and pee. Am I still dreaming right now? Was I wetting my pants somewhere in the woods because I was dreaming? Am I really peeing while on the toilet? I shook my head just to make sure to knock some of the cobwebs out. Looking around is this my bathroom? Nothing was out of the ordinary. Except for the fact that I had passed out with my pants on and now I am in my night clothes.

    I finished, wash my hands and then head back into the bedroom. Mongo is asleep on the bed or he was pretending to be anyway.

    "Mongo!" I said in a yelling whisper. He lifted his head and looked at me.

    "Come back to bed, it's not time to get up yet." Mongo said in my head.

    "Mongo, how did I get home and how did I get changed into my night clothes?" I was a little louder in my whisper.

"Harry and Johnny brought you and me home after you passed out. Amanda and Trina helped change you. Boy you were out!" Mongo said in my head and smiled at me, he actually smiled at me! I walked over to the side of the bed to look at my alarm clock, the time was 4am.

"What happened when I passed out?" I asked as I sat on the edge of the bed feeling foolish and suddenly getting tired again.

"Do you remember everything you found out last night?" Mongo asked in my head in a very hesitant way, he thinks I don't remember what happened.

"I mean after I was out what happened with the crew and who was shooting at us?" I asked Mongo and then Mongo turned his head looking at the door just before I heard him.

"Lass, I think I can fill you in on all the details about last night more than poor Mongo can. He was beside himself when you found out he had kept a secret from you when you passed out. He thought you were dying!" Harry said as he crossed the bedroom and crouched in front of me. He was in nothing but a pair of green sweatpants with a white draw strings in the front that dangled and I so wanted to grab it. My mind has moved on but my eyes are getting droopy.

"I think I am going to pass out again but I think it's just because I'm so tired. Can we talk in the morning please?" I slowly lay down and placed my head on the pillow and was out. This time I was sleeping and dreaming. This was a recap for my brain, not a dream about anything funny or silly. I dreamed of Sasquatch that talked to me, of Harry revealing himself and Mongo knew. Why wouldn't Mongo tell me? I felt like Alice in Wonderland, I had slipped down the rabbit hole and Mongo was my white rabbit.

When I awoke this time I was in my bed alone. No Mongo which has NEVER happened before. I could hear Harry talking in the kitchen, I just wasn't sure if he was talking to a person or to Mongo. I guess the only way to find out is to get dressed and go see. I went into the bathroom with my jeans and t-shirt, went potty, got dressed then brushed my hair, put on a light makeup.  Then I headed to the kitchen in search of food, Mongo and answers!  Just before I reached the kitchen I heard Uncle Jared talking to Harry.

"Should we check on her again?  I know she's had a trauma but she should be up by now.

"She is up and about to walk around the corner right now.  Good Mornin' Sunshine!  Do you feel better after a good night's sleep?"  Harry was awfully chipper this morning.

"Not really.  I woke up and Mongo wasn't in bed with me. He never leaves me." I said kind of pouty turning to see Mongo outside playing by himself in the backyard with his braided rope toy.  I couldn't help but smile he was being so cute out there.  Uncle Jared got out of his seat and came over to me.  He seemed to be checking me out from head to toe then he placed his hands on my shoulders and looked in my eyes.

"Are you sure she shouldn't go to the doctor's?"  He was still talking to Harry.  I am standing right in front of him and he asks Harry if I should go to the doctor's?

"Uncle Jared!   I am fine it was just a little too much for my brain to handle last night.  I still have questions but I am sure everything will get better."  I looked at Harry when I said the last part.  I wasn't sure how much Uncle Jared knew about the whole Were-Squatch thing.  That is what I am after all, and Harry and the Johnson brothers obviously were too.  Harry and I need to talk, in private!

"Well, all right!  Your Mom and Dad will be by in a little while with your Grandpa Hunter.  They want to see you for themselves before the party tonight and to make sure that you are able to even go after last night."  Uncle Jared said as he walked over to let Mongo in.  Mongo ran over to me very happy and excited.   He was smiling and wiggling his whole butt.  I crouched down to dive him a hug and he licked my cheek.  Then he ran over to his food dish which had his dog food in it and a plate next to it with scrambled eggs and fruit.  There were even sausage pieces in his scrambled eggs; I could smell them from here. I heard Harry give a small chuckle turning to the stove. When he turned back around, he had a plate of the same food as Mongo's but it was piled high with everything.

"I'm starving!" I sat down where Harry had set the plate for me on the island.

"Thank you Harry, it looks wonderful!" Not another word was uttered as I shoved food into my mouth. You would think that I hadn't eaten in a week.

"Slow down their kiddo! You might get a tummy ache if you eat too fast." Uncle Jared said as he refilled his coffee cup and then sat back down in his chair. Harry poured me an orange juice and a glass of iced tea.

"Thank you Harry, everything is great!" I said around a mouth full of scrambled eggs that almost melted in your mouth.

"Okay, you guys need to fill me in on everything that I missed last night. Uncle Jared, you weren't there but I have a feeling you came in later on because of the shooting, right?" I said as I took a bite of toast.

"Yes, your Grandpa Hunter called to let me know he heard gun shots and he knew it wasn't the Bigfoot Getters doing the shooting. Jed and Cletus's group the SMM Bigfoot Hunters were in the area so we had to follow up on it." Uncle Jared was saying as Harry walked around the island to sit down next to me.

"They were supposed to be at Miss Mary's Pub doing an investigation but they never showed up." Harry said and then took a sip of his coffee.

"It seems that someone clued them in on your hunt on private land last night so they took it upon themselves to crash it. When they saw the Sasquatch they just started shooting. They even saw the Big Brown Sasquatch rip off the food truck door and yank you out and run into the woods. People are freaked about that one. I'm still not sure how you got away from him and the others with him too. Do you remember anything?"

Uncle Jared was just concerned about me; I wasn't sure how much we could really talk about with him right now.

"I don't remember much at all. I think he knocked me out when he pulled me out of the truck. Anything after that I'm not too sure of either." I said as I finished my breakfast. Keeping my mouth busy.

"Well, Jed and all of his crew have been arrested. Your Grandfather is trying to decide on whether or not to press charges against them. They did shoot their firearms but luckily they didn't hit anyone that we know of." Uncle Jared said as he looked down at Mongo who had decided to sit at my feet and put a paw on my leg for some love.

"Hello Mongo, everything okay buddy?" I asked as I petted his head and rubbed his ears.

"Uncle Jared needs to go so Harry can talk to us about last night." Mongo said in my head as he got back down. Then he went into the living room and climbed on the couch and laid down.

"Anything else that I missed?" I asked Uncle Jared and Harry looking first at one and then the other.

"Let's see, you were kidnapped by a Sasquatch and passed out, Harry and Mongo went after the Sasquatch to get you back which they did. Crazy Bigfoot hunters were shooting at everything in the woods but managed to miss everything that was important. We arrested them all and your Grandpa hasn't decided if they are going to be charged or not. And last but not least your Parents are freaking out about all of it! I'm surprised they aren't here already. That about covers it!" Uncle Jared seemed a little on edge.

"Good so I didn't miss much?" I tried to keep a straight face but couldn't help but laugh at the look on Uncle Jared's face. Harry started laughing too and then of course Uncle Jared got it and started laughing too. He got up, put his cup in the sink and came back to stand beside me. Looked me in the eyes once more and then he hugged me.

"I hope your Mom and Dad spank you if you get cheeky with them like you just did with me young lady!" He pretended to be upset but I knew he wasn't. He loved me and I knew that he was joking with me.

"I love you Uncle! Let me know what you find out, would you?" I was saying as he released me. Mongo came over to say good-bye, he knew when people were leaving by the body language or so I thought. He actually understood everything being said.

"Oh so cheeky! Later Harry, see you at the party." He said as he shook Harry's hand and then he leaned down to Mongo.

"You are such a good boy Mongo! Keep her safe Buddy!" He rubbed his ears and patted his butt then stood up to go.

"Bye!" Was all he said as he walked himself to the front door and was gone.

I waited a few minutes until the sound of his SUV was gone. It sounded like he was going to Grandma and Grandpa Hunter's house, probably to find out what their decision is on the trespassers. Which leads me to the talk that Harry and Mongo had for me? I turned to Harry, not realizing that I was turned to listen to the vehicle leave, Harry was staring at me with a strange look upon his face.

"Shall we go sit on the couch to have this talk? I don't need you fainting again or falling off your chair." Harry said as he walked around the island and took my elbow as I stepped down from my chair. He walked me into the living room and we sat on the couch together, Mongo followed us and sat at my feet facing me so that he would be included.

"Okay guys spill it, from the beginning." I said as I leaned back into the couch.

"Where do I start? Do you want my beginning or yours?" Harry asked a little nervous it seemed.

"Tell me about your beginning, let's start there and then Mongo can fill me in on my situation. Okay?" They both nodded then Harry sat a little straighter as he too set back further on the couch.

"So I am what you call a Were-Squatch. I was bitten by another were-Squatch on the first Bigfoot hunt I went on with Terry and Jerry. It was only the three of us guys out trying to find evidence but we kind of found more than we were bargaining for. Yes, they both know what I am and no they are not Were-Squatch's, I was the only one bitten." Harry stretched out his legs a little but I could feel the tension coming from him.

"We were in the Bluff Creek area of California trying to find the Patterson area that they took the famous video footage. It got dark so we camped out there. That night we had a visitor that was throwing rocks at us while we were in our tent. After so long of that, we decided to rush out to possibly scare this thing away. Well, it was a Were-Squatch so it understood what we were saying. When we ran out it was ready for us. Terry got a broken arm; Jerry a concussion and I got bit causing an almost comatose state for a week. That is how I knew your bite was going to lead to you changing." He took my hand in his, like he needed a connection between us.

"Anyway, the day after we were attacked the were-Squatch in his human form came back to help us get out of the woods. Some of us don't have very good control when we change, but there are a few of us that are what we call pureblood or as close to as possible when it comes to these things." He said when he pulled my hand to his lips and kissed it.

"I was bitten by a pureblood, which means either one or both of his Parents were also Were-Squatch's. Most Were-Squatch's have Native American blood, at least the ones that I have met do, so far." He was saying and my mind was ready with a question.

"How many have you met?" I asked leaning forward, this was fascinating.

"In the years since I have become one, I have come into contact with eight other Were-Squatch. Until I met the Johnson brother's last night anyway. The Were-Squatch that turned me didn't teach me very much. He had become a nomad because of all the people that became interested in Bigfoot hunting the in recent years. He stuck around for a couple of months and then he left me on my own to figure out everything there was to being a Were-Squatch." Harry stood up walking around the living room like a caged animal, which I suppose on some level he is. I waited patiently to see if there was more to his story.

"That's when we started using me to find the difference between a real Sasquatch and a Were-Squatch. That was in the show we were doing. You see we were recording on our own when the Animal Channel offered us the opportunity to research and find a real Bigfoot. I would change while I was supposed to be tracking them when we did our howls and such to bring Bigfoot out in the open." Harry sat on the coffee table in front of Mongo and I.

"You see, I would stop them before they got to close to the cameras to find out if they were real Bigfoot or a Were-Squatch. A Were-Squatch would usually leave and the real Bigfoot usually didn't understand me and would keep going. We may be very close in species but I think our human brain is still more in the forefront even while changed but there is not. Don't get me wrong I have met a few real Bigfoot but they didn't really want much to do with people or Were-Squatch." Harry moved back to the couch next to me.

"That is how I became a Were-Squatch. You know it was Tom Johnson that bit you, right?" Harry asked as he took my hand.

"I kind of figured as much I just don't know why he bit me." I said as I shrugged my shoulders.

"When the Were-Squatch Brother's came in that night I knew they were Were-Squatch but they wouldn't listen to me because they were in a mating frenzy. I haven't had one yet but I am not a pure blood either. You see every year purebloods and real Bigfoot have a primal pull to the woods to mate. I have never met a real Bigfoot female or a Were-Squatch female. I was taught that Were-Squatch females that are bitten but do not have a Sasquatch gene in them usually die. So there must not be very many females out there. I don't know why I haven't met any female Bigfoot either, they are scares too. He told me that the females have to have the Sasquatch recessive gene in them. He also taught me about the telepathic connection we share with all animals. That is part of the reason Mongo knew what you were saying, thinking and feeling. This may not be the case with others of the Were-community. A female can be bit and made into a Were-whatever. For us Were-Squatch though, there has to be the recessive gene of any Were-creature. I don't know why I haven't met any female Bigfoot though, they are scares too. When you and Trina were howling they thought you were the real deal and they wanted you girls for mating but mostly, they were after you Lass." He said as he scooted closer to me and Mongo put his head on my lap. I looked at Mongo.

"Why didn't you tell me Harry was a Were-Squatch or that I was going to be a Were-Squatch, Mongo?" I asked my Buddy, My son, my partner.

"Harry asked me not to say anything since you had no clue what you were yet. He wanted to tell you. We talked that first night about him and you. I was protecting you because I love you." Mongo said as he lowered his eyes, licked his lips like he was in trouble. I put my hand on either side of his big ol' head and kissed his forehead.

"You're not in trouble Mongo. I love you too." I was petting his head when Harry started talking again.

"I hope this doesn't hurt what we have starting between us Lass. There is more to your story than you know yet." Harry said as he took my hand yet again and then sat up straight and looked at me.

"I'm okay so far with everything. Bring on the rest." I said as I scooted to the edge of the couch as well.

"I think we are even more compatible now?" And I winked at him which made him smile; I swear I could physically see a wave of relief wash over him.

"Now is the difficult part to explain. You know how you and Mongo have been kind of linked since you got him?" Harry asked and reached over petting Mongo on the head.

"Yes, since he saw me he has been the perfect dog. He listened to all commands, most of the time he knows what I'm thinking and feeling before I do, all without any training." I said as I pet Mongo too.

"That's because you have a Were-Squatch recessive gene. Someone in your family is a Were-Squatch. Now with Were-Squatch we are a little difficult for one another to feel. I had no idea the Johnson brothers were Were-Squatch. Since Mongo could understand you and you could only understand him after you were bit means that one of your parents or grandparents is a Were-Squatch. Your parents were at the hospital and were genuinely surprised that you healed so quickly, but your grandparents didn't seem to be I would say that by process of elimination that you're Grandpa Hunter who is more Native American that your Grandmother is a Were-Squatch!" Harry was saying almost like he was Sherlock Holmes.

"My Grandpa George could not be a Were-Squatch. Grandma May could not be a Were-Squatch. And my parents? Never!" It was ridiculous! There was no way with as much as this family is in everyone's lives that one of them could keep this a secret from the others! Harry looked at me like I was going to blow up or something. He stood very quickly and even Mongo took his head off my lap and looked at me.

"What is wrong with you two?" I asked as I felt the warming sensation run over my head and down my back. Then I looked at my hands that started to get warm. Oh, SHIT! I was growing fur!!!

"Lass, I need you to calm down now. I know you haven't fully changed yet and you shouldn't do it with so many things going on. Your parents will be here any minute and you don't want them seeing you this way if they know nothing about a Were-Squatch. Please sweetie, calm down." Harry was using such a soothing voice to talk to me. It made me want to sleep, I was getting tired again.

It's okay Lass, the first few times you turn you will get really tired afterward and you will just want to sleep. It's okay, you can take a nap right here on the couch until your parents get here. Mongo will even climb up there to sleep too, won't you Mongo?" Harry was saying as my eyes drooped, I felt Mongo climb up on the end of the couch. Then the warming sensation kind of just went backwards from my hands then up my back and all the way to my head again. I laid my head on the arm of the couch and I was out in no time at all. I sure was fainting and sleeping a lot lately. Maybe Harry is wrong, maybe I'm not a Were-Squatch, I'm just narcoleptic. And the world went silent yet again.

## **Chapter 20**

When I awoke from my nap, Mongo was curled at my feet and we were sharing the soft quilt from the back of the couch. I was nice and warm but boy I had to pee. I popped my legs over the side of the couch to sit up. Not hearing anything out of the ordinary I got up and made a bee-line for the bathroom. Barely making it!

As I came out of the bathroom I heard the whispering voices. They were coming from the solarium. It sounded like Mom and Dad talking with Harry. I walked around the corner and they saw me, so they all filed out to me in the dining room. It looked like Mom was watering my herbs.

"Hey Babygirl, how are you feeling?" Dad asked as he took me in his arms for a great big hug. Then Dad stepped back as Mom took his place.

"Oh, Sweetie I heard you have had a couple of bad days? How are you feeling right now?" Mom asked while hugging me like I was a little girl again.

"I'm okay Mom. I've just been super tired lately." I said as she let me go.

"Are you still feeling up to going to the family gathering today?" Mom asked as she turned me so we could all go into the kitchen and sit down at the island. Harry went to the refrigerator and poured everyone glasses if iced tea, then he joined us.

"So, Harry and your Uncle Jared have been filing us in on a few things that have been happening around here." Dad said then he took a sip of his tea. I looked at Harry and he shook his head no.

"I just reaffirmed what your Uncle Jared said about last night and that you were safe. Mongo has to go potty, I'll let him out." Harry said as he walked around the island and opened the sliding door for Mongo to go out into the back yard.

"Thanks." I said as I watched him. He was still a good Man; he was leaving the Were-Squatch issue up to me. But I think I will talk to my Grandpa George first. What better time than tonight, right?

"So what time are we supposed to be at this thing anyway?" I asked taking a drink of my tea.

"Well, some of the family is already here. Your Grandpa is dealing with those Bigfoot hunters from last night. I guess he has decided to have a talk with them instead of pressing charges, yet! Your Uncle Jared said he can still press charges if he chooses to at any time." Mom was saying as Mongo made a noise at the slider door, the goofball was licking the window. I got off my chair this time to let him in. He went straight to his food and water dishes.

"Your cousin and his band are already here and setting up. Their folks will be here shortly too. Maybe we should take the crew up there now so that they can meet everyone as they get here. This is going to be fun tonight!" Dad was saying as he finished his iced tea, he looked like a little kid getting ready to play with the neighborhood kids.

"Tell you what, why don't you go out and talk to the crew about that Honey, I will meet you there in a few minutes." Mom was saying to

Dad then she kissed him and he was off. He stopped in the doorway just in front of the front door and turned.

"Harry, do you want to go with me?" Dad asked Harry, who then looked at me with a smile.

"Go ahead and go. Mom will be with me and Mongo." I said as Mongo gave a woof. Harry came around the island gave me a quick kiss then headed out the door with my Dad. Guy bonding thing I guess.

"Okay there are a few things we need to talk about before we go to the Family get together." My Mom was saying now in her no nonsense voice.

"Okay Mom, what's up?" I said not quite sure what this was going to be about. Harry is still with me? The whole Bigfoot kidnapping thing! The guys following me! This reminds me I think I need to give Tom Johnson a call after last night.

"So how much do you know about what you are now?" My mouth dropped and I was in shock.

"What are you talking about Mom?" She couldn't know about Were-Squatch, right?

"Honey, I know you were bit, I know about the fainting, tiredness as well as the sleep walking. So you have either been turned into a Were-Squatch by the Sasquatch that bit you or you are pregnant? Which is it??" I was so in shock now there weren't any words for this.

"What the hell Mom! How do you know about Were-Squatch's? Why didn't you tell me there was a possibility that I could be one?" I just couldn't sit still right now. I hopped off the chair and walked around to the refrigerator to pour myself and Mom some more tea. I was trying to stay calm so I wouldn't change.

"I didn't know until after I had you that there was a possibility that you could have the recessive gene, which for me being from a pureblood. I was happy you hadn't changed when you hit puberty. Your Grandpa

George is a pureblood too. He wanted to change your Grandma May but couldn't because she had no recessive gene and it would probably kill her. I am a Were-Squatch; your Aunt Nova and Aunt Maggie were born human but carried the recessive gene like you. They are now Were-Eagle's though. You and I have a whole lot of talking to do about this Were-issue. There are more Were's out there that just us. They are not all family and they are not all nice either. There are different Native American Tribe's that each has their own thing, but when you mix two Were's you get one or the other. There are no half Squatch- half Eagle or half Cougar or Bear, you are only one type. By the severely shocked look on your face I would say that you had no idea there are other Were's out there, huh? I thought you paid more attention to your Grandfather's stories then that?" My Mom has just told me more shocking things than when Harry told me I was a Were-Squatch and that my Grandfather was one too. Now I find out my own Mother!

"Holy Shit Mom! I can't believe you wait until now to tell me. I was bit over a week ago and you had plenty of time to tell me. And where is my Heavenly Chocolates?" I was freaking out and some Heavenly Chocolates would help me calm down right about now.

"Oh, I put them in the cupboard over there next to the fridge were you keep your teas." Mom said as she got up and went to the cupboard and pulled out the box of goodies. Each tiny box has an assortment of chocolate treats whatever Mom had them fill it with. Milk chocolate, dark chocolate, and white chocolate I love them all. This will help me…..

"Thanks Mom." I opened the first box and inside is a milk chocolate truffle so I take a bite right away and inside is strawberry truffle filling, my mouth waters with every chew. Heavenly chocolates and tea are my weaknesses. Feeling calmer now I was able to sit down with Mom to talk with a clearer head.

"So we are Were-Squatch, and there are other Were's out there. You were one from birth because Grandpa George is one from birth. Grandma May is not because she could die from the bite having the recessive gene which you need to change if a Were-Squatch bites you like when Tom Johnson bit me in a mating frenzy that night." I was recapping for my own brain to retain everything.

"Wait what? You know the man was Tom Johnson that bit you? His Grandparents used to live here in Oakridge. They were friends of your Grandpa and Grandma's, I bet that is why they go up to Waldo Lake so they can change and run in the forest. They are pure-pure bloods. Their family was part of the same tribe as your Grandpa's when he was a kid. They wanted to make sure their son married a pure blood Were-Squatch but, since I wasn't a pure blood because of Grandma May being human, they left town to find a mate for him. We are the only other family here in Oakridge that are Were-Squatch. Wow, small world." My mom was both excited and a little weirded out by this news.

"Okay, but I still need to call him to let him know what I am. That I know all about being a Were-Squatch." I was saying as I pulled Tom's card out of my back pocket, I was carrying the thing around with me.

"There is more that you need to know before you do that." Mom said as she put her hand over mine.

"What more could there be?" I waited with an ache starting in my head.

"Your Dad knows everything, I hide nothing from him. Your Grandpa and I change and run on our own property and now you can run with us. But there is more." Mom was saying as she straightened herself in her chair.

"When Tom bit you during a mating frenzy, he marked you as his own. Which means when the full moon comes in two weeks he will come for you to mate. Were-Squatch, like were-wolves mate for life. If one dies that has been mated then the other may find another mate. We are usually so heartbroken that we don't last much longer after our mate passes. I don't know about when our human mate dies how it will affect us?" Mom was trying to say in the nicest way, she didn't know about Harry.

"Mom, Harry is a Were-Squatch too." I said and I swear my Mom had the same shocked look on her face that I had earlier.

"Holy Shit! Are you serious? That changes everything!" Mom was so super happy right now she jumped out of her chair and hugged me doing a little wiggle jumpy thing while she squealed.

"What do you mean?" I asked her after she calmed down a little bit.

"Do you Love Harry? And does Harry Love you Babygirl?" She asked trying to hold in more excitement.

"Yes, we love each other; we were attracted to each other before I turned into a Were-Squatch. Why?" I asked but the wheels in my head were stating to click back to the Bigfoot kidnapping incident last night.

"It means that if you mate with Harry before the full moon, then you two will be mates for life and Tom has no claim on you anymore!" Mom jumped up doing that wiggly jumpy squealing thing again. Poor Mongo was lying on the floor with his paw over his ears.

"Okay Mom, okay! That makes more since then with what happened last night. When Tom took me, he was making his get away with me and his brothers. It was Harry and Mongo stopped him. When Tom was carrying me over his shoulder I heard the Big Red Sasquatch which was Harry yell "MINE" and then Tom who was the Big Brown Sasquatch carrying me, yelled "Mine" and then Harry howled and Mongo joined him and it was automatic for me to join in with the howl. Then Tom put me down on my feet and asked Harry why I was his and Harry said by choice with his hand over his heart. Then Tom turned to me and asked if I choose him. I didn't even know it was Harry until he called me "Lass" and Mongo was with him. So I said "Yes by choice" and I put my hand over my heart like I saw Harry do. Then Tom sniffed me and said that I hadn't chosen yet and that I could still choose another. Then he told me to call him Tom. Then he left with his brothers, leaving me there with Harry and Mongo." I paused to take a breath and then started again.

"That's when my brain started to connect the dots and I sort of passed out. Harry filled me in on him being a Were-Squatch and how he became one as well as the fact that I was a Were-Squatch now too. I didn't take it well when he was telling me that Grandpa was a Were-Squatch and hadn't told me and I think I started to change because of it. He talked me down again and then I fell asleep. Now you are up to date on most everything so far." My Mom was literally sitting on the edge of her chair with her facial expressions going between surprise, excitement and a little bit of shock and awe included. I do believe my Mom is speechless and that is hard to do.

"Wait until the family hears this! This is going to be one of the best family get-togethers we have had in years Babygirl!" Mom had snapped out of her condition quickly enough.

That's when Dad and Harry made their entrance back into the house. Mom went straight up to Harry and agave him a huge hug. He looked at me over my mom's head and I wasn't sure what he was asking so I shrugged my shoulders. He then looked down into my Mom's eyes, her eyes turned yellow and back again, Harry looked up at me and his eyes went yellow and back again very quickly. Then Harry looked at my Dad and he just smiled and raised his hands in the air.

"Unfortunately, I am not a part of this club that it seems to have new members." He said as he walked over and gave me a side hug as we watched Harry.

"Janet, how long?" Harry asked as Mom pulled further out of Harry's arms.

"All my life, I was lucky. Both of my sisters are Were-Eagles, they were born human but chose to be what their husbands are. My Dad which you figured out that Carrie's Grandpa George is a Were-Squatch; you are pretty smart cookie Harry. I think we like you for our daughter." Mom said with a giggle and she walked over to join me and Dad.

"Slow down guys, Harry and I are taking it slow. We love each other but have to wait until we are both on the right page for a relationship." I was saying as I pulled out of the hug and went to Harry to be held by him. Mom looked at Dad and then they looked at both of us. Then Harry looked down at me as well.

"Lass, they are giving their blessing because of the time issue." Harry said and then kissed my forehead.

"What time issue, I just became a Were-Squatch. Now we are telling the family at this big family gathering thing today." I said as I looked at him then at my parents. What did they know that I didn't?

"Because you were bitten on the full moon, you have until the next full moon to take a mate other than the Were-Squatch that bit you. In other words, it's either Harry or Tom dear. Tom will come and try to claim you on the full moon. He changed you and even though you are a pure blood it was still the bite that changed you in the end." Mom was saying as she looked at the two of us.

"The guy that changed me didn't tell me any of that at all. He just told me never to bite a female human because most of them don't have the recessive gene to be able to change and then they would die. I had no idea that Tom would have a right to Carrie if I didn't take her; I thought we would have time to get to know each other better. So she knew what she was getting into with me." Harry said rather sad as he was looking deep into my eyes. I looked at Mom and Dad and they were always so happy together even though Mom was different.

"Mom, what should I do? I love Harry but we still don't know that much about each other. And I know nothing about Tom except what Amanda found on the internet about him." I was asking my Mom for her honest advice.

"Tell you both what you should do. Don't make any decisions until after your Grandpa's party. There are a few things that both of you need to know before you decide. But I also think that Tom should at least get a phone call from you Carrie. He had you and if he was a bad guy he would have made you go with him whether you chose to or not. But I also must remind you both that we have some bad people in town that are hunting our kind right now. Do not leave the property to change. This is the only safe place for our kind right now.  And yes, I know they got in here last night but it will not happen again, trust me! Your Grandpa has made arrangements to make sure of it." Mom said and then she and Dad hugged both Harry and I before they headed out the door. Grandpa expected them up at the main house before the rest of the people started to show up.

"Well, I guess I have a phone call to make." I said as I pulled the business card back out of my pocket. Harry looked a little green when he saw it.

"Do you have to? Couldn't we wait until we know what we are doing or at least until after the party today?" Harry was begging me as he took me into his arms again. I do so love being held by him.

"I tell you what, I will wait until after the party today just because of the way my Mom said that we had more to learn from it. Who knows you might even run away from me when you meet my whole family. Grandma May said we have family and friends coming in from all over the state." I said as he started to smile thinking he had won.

"I hate to tell you Lass, I don't scare easily and I don't think I will be going anywhere. Unless you are going with me that is." He said as he wiggled his eyebrows at me. He was so cute when he did that and I know he knew it too.

"Well, I hate to tell you Big Red but I don't plan on leaving Oakridge any time soon, so there is that we would have to deal with as a future issue." He pulled me closer and whispered in my ear.

"Minds can be changed Lass, yours or mine. Either way it would take a miracle to get you away from me." And then he pulled away from me a little and looked at my face.

"Why did you call me Big Red?" He asked rather bewildered.

"Because when you are in your Sasquatch coat, you are Big and Red. And that is what I called you in my head the first time I saw you when you and Mongo rescued me." I said trying not to smile and giggle at his facial expression.

"Oh, right. I guess I never really looked at myself when I was a Sasquatch. It must have to do with my Scottish ancestry which gave me my red hair." He said as if he just figured out something amazing.

"That means that when you change you will also be a red color, probably close to mine! This also means that we should be together!" He sounded so surprised and excited about it too.

"Well, we don't have very long before we are supposed to head up to the party so we better go and get ready." I said as I started to move myself into the direction of my bedroom, but Harry wasn't letting go of me yet.

"Not until I get another of your wonderfully exciting kisses Lass." Harry said just as he pulled me to him again. His hands went to my hair and my face as mine went around his chest and rubbed his back and then my wondering hands decided to move a little lower and cup his perfectly shaped butt. His butt cheeks were the epitome of buns of steel. He broke from the kiss when I squeezed his butt cheeks and then he looked at me.

"You know that could be considered teasing don't you?" Then he picked me up and took me to my bedroom. He set me back down on my feet and kissed my forehead instead this time.

"Next time I will not be stopping and then you and I will be true mates. But right now we have a party to get ready for." Then he stroked my right cheek with is hand and turned around and left me standing by myself in my bedroom. Now he was the tease in my book.

## Chapter 21

When I was finished getting cleaned up and dressed for the party with the family I headed into the living room to find Harry and to see where my Mongo was. Mongo didn't come into the bedroom while I was getting ready which is not like him in the least. I found the two of them in the kitchen snacking before we went to a party with lots of food, how like them.

"So are you guys ready to go? Are we going with the crew or are they coming later?" I asked as I looked around outside the sliding glass door.

"They were asked to come up now and I guess the crew will be turning in early so that your family can show us what they need to show us so that we can make a decision on what to do next." Harry said as he moved around the kitchen island and took me into his arms. Then he looked deep into my eyes.

"You know that I have made my decision, we just need yours. Which, I am not rushing you to decide right now. But I am telling you that whatever your family has in store for us, I am not going anywhere. I have chosen you, you are my heart, we were meant to be together." He said as he put his forehead against mine. He had the most beautiful voice and accent. I am really surprised that I have held out for as long as I have with him and this whole seduction thing.

"I am pretty sure I know what I want, but yes I need to know what my family has to say too. I love you Harry." Was all I said, then he kissed me and we separated to that I could let a very anguish Mongo outside to go potty before we headed up to the party. My tummy was rumbling and Harry must have heard it because when I turned around from closing the sliding door he put a piece of my blueberry chocolate from Heavenly Chocolates into my mouth which watered right away. I closed my eyes to fully enjoy it too.

"You keep doing things like that and we may not make it to the party after all." Harry said as he gave me a peck on the lips.

"You found my chocolates." I said as I took a seat to wait for Mongo to come back in.

"Yes, and I know how important they are to you, so before you ask, no I did not eat any of them." Harry said with a smile on his lips.

"You can have some, I don't mind sharing." I said as he put another one in my mouth.

"Lass, I get more out of feeding them to you than I ever would eating them myself." He smiled and wiggled his eyebrows again.

"Now who's teasing?" I asked as I got up to let Mongo inside. It was time to stop teasing each other before something happens so we can get up to the party were we are expected. I had family to see and food to eat and I think in just that order too. Fun, music and eating, it's the perfect party and if we learn something too, then so be it. Okay family here we come!


Harry parked my truck up where the family had parked by the main house. The whole backyard was lite up with all kinds of lights from Christmas to straight up decorating lights that had pink flamingos on them. It wasn't dark yet but when this place does get dark you won't be about to tell. When you walk into the backyard where everyone is gathered it's like walking into another world.

Going through a 7' tall wooden gate that has the old iron hinges and latch to a cobble stone pathway that led past the house. The house is a very old three story log cabin that Grandpa George has renovated a couple of times to add more rooms and floors for kids and grandkids plus guests if they chose not to stay in the guest house which was a more modern single story manufactured home.

They had originally gotten it for Grandma May's Mom 'Nana' before she passed away 10 years ago. Now it was for the occasional guest. This is where the caterers had set up the outdoor buffet and the Grill was being manned not too far from there on the cobblestone floored BBQ pit area.

The pathway leads to the beautiful backyard garden that was filled with herbs of all kinds. There were rosemary trees, sage and lavender bushes and lots of beautiful cedar beds of oregano, basil, mints and spearmint, thyme, marjoram and lots of other ones that I couldn't remember the name of.

People were everywhere talking, eating, drinking and laughing. My Aunts and Uncles had made it from Harrisburg, and some family from Philomath, Brownsville, Monroe and there were people I knew that were family friends as well from Lincoln City and Alpine. I saw Miss Mary and Miss Karen where here with Big John too.

What an amazing assortment of people and the crew looked like they fit right in with everyone. The food smelled amazing and my cousin's band was up on the stage that Grandpa had built for them. Everyone was having a good time and I couldn't wait to join in and catch up with everyone. I hadn't realized it until now how much I had missed them all.

"There you guys are!" My Mom came up behind as we stood there. I jumped a little because I was busy looking at all the people.

"Hi Mom, wow it seems like everyone made it. There are family here I haven't seen in years along with some people here I am not sure if I remember their names." I said as I leaned down to pat Mongo on the head. He looked up at me and then sat at my feet.

"Yah it's a historic event so everyone that could be here is here. Some drove for a long way to get here. You see the Man standing beside your Grandpa?" Mom asked as she came up beside me to point to a very attractive Native American man standing next to Grandpa George. He seemed familiar but I couldn't place him.

"That is my Cousin Jacob Thompson's youngest son Dan; they are members of the Siletz tribe in Lincoln City. Dan is about your age too. He went to UCLA to become a Marine Biologist which kind of suits him. They are Were-Orca's, the largest predators in the whole family really. I haven't seen him since you two were little. Do you remember how much you two loved going swimming at Waldo Lake and Odell Lake together? We had a terrible time trying to keep the two of you out of the water. My, he has gotten handsome hasn't he?" Mom was saying as we starting walking a little closer to everyone.

"Wow a Were-Orca, like as in Killer Whale? Huh, it makes since why he was such a good swimmer now." I said as we kept walking.

"Yes it does, doesn't it? Let's see where all the family is that is close to your age. Over there are your Cousin's Koda, Caleb and Christoff, but you already know them. You know they are part of the Siletz Tribe because of their Fathers. They are Were-Eagles and they sure have they have grown into fine young men." Mom said as she swiveled just a little to move on to the next family members like telling me about Were-Eagles is no big deal, she didn't even wait for me to react.

"Over there by the buffet is your Cousin Yancy and her twin brother Shawn, they are from the Davidson side of the family, your Grandpa George's Uncle Jr's side. They live in Monroe, which is between Corvallis and Eugene, I am sure you have driven right through there once or twice. They are part of the Muddy Creek Kalapuya-Chemapho Tribe. Her name literally means Sassy Woman. They are the Were-wolves in the family and are next in line to be the pack leaders after their Parents. Because they are twins one of them has to mate before the other to be the actual leader. The second one gets to be second in command unless their sibling's mate is also an alpha." Mom drops another Were bomb, Were-Wolves are in the family as well. Okay what's next?

"Then the Jamison triplets are in from Philomath which is next to Corvallis. Let me see if I remember their names? Oh yes, Darrin, Donavan and Deidra. They are from your Grandpa George's Uncle Derrick's side of the family, they are Hunter's too. They are from the Alsea Tribe and as you can tell they are Were-Cougars. Very quiet family, they don't come to these things much but I guess the younger generation is more open to mingling with other Were's besides their own. It may also be because we Were's are in shorter numbers too. It makes it easier for the Were-Council to get new members too." Mom was saying and I know she just told me about not only Were-Cougars but that there is also a Were-Council? And the only thing I can think to ask is this.

"Wow Mom our family is really into multiple babies, why didn't you and Dad have more?" I asked as we meandered through everyone. Harry and Dad had wondered off to talk with the crew that parked themselves at one of the many picnic tables that were in a large circle around the fire pit that hadn't been lit yet I am sure that it will be coming soon. We are big on Indian traditions around here; it isn't a gathering until someone has lit the fire.

"We weren't sure how life was going to be for you so we didn't try for more. We made the perfect child with the first try, it just so happens that you finally follow more of my side than your Dad's is all. Too bad it took a bite to do it though." Mom was saying as she looked me in the eyes and then she pulled me in for a hug. She almost spilled her drink as she did it. Poor Mongo looked like he would rather be with the guys than listening to us talk. I leaned down rubbed him behind the ear when Mom let me go.

"Would you like to go hang out with Harry and Dad?" I asked Mongo.

"Yes please! You are safe here." Mongo said in my head.

"Go ahead Mongo." I said and it didn't take him long to high tail it to Harry's side and lay under his feet after getting a head rub from him.

"I was so happy when your Uncle Jared brought Mongo home for you. I was hoping that him talking to you in your head would have made the Were in you pop out sooner. But at least he was in tune to you even though you didn't know it. That's what made him such a good dog and a fur baby grandson for me. All of us being able to communicate is key." Mom said with a smile.

"Does Uncle Jared know about us?" I hadn't thought to ask before now.

"Yes, he has known for a long time now. I think it helped him when it came to his deputies too." Mom was saying as she pointed in the direction of the BBQ area where Uncle Jared and his two deputies were helping out.

"Why are the deputies Were also?" I asked because at this point I would not be surprised who was or wasn't a Were around here. We started walking and talking again.

"Yes, but they weren't born that way like we were. When they were stationed somewhere that they can't talk about, I guess they were ambushed by another American platoon that had no idea they were American too. There platoon was mostly made up of Were-Coyote's, so when one of them was injured, the Bronson brothers tried to help, they both got bitten by the guy who turned out to be the other platoon's commander and he is from Brownsville, Oregon of all places." Mom kind of giggled but it wasn't really funny was it? She took my arm in hers and we continued to walk around and talk.

"The Bronson brothers still check in with him from time to time, I guess they are still technically part of his pack since he turned them and all. What was his name? Oh, yah Larry Erickson! He and his brother Dwayne run that pack together; they were both in that platoon. You know I still don't know if the Military knew that they were Were's or if they just so happened to put the Were's together because of their fighting abilities? I guess that is something to ask the Bronson brothers someday." I know my Mom wasn't talking very loud but when the Deputies looked our way I have a feeling it was because they heard her. Were-animal hearing is pretty intense. We walked a little further and then Mom waved at Miss Mary, Miss Karen and Big John. They waved back and Big john smiled, he didn't smile much unless he was looking at his wife.

"Mom, are they Were's too?" I asked as we turned a little and heading to the other side of the party making our way back where Dad, Harry and Mongo were sitting.

"Not all of them but Big John there is a Full blood Sun'aq Tribe of Kodiak Island, Alaska. He is a Were-Bear Honey. He has some friends sitting over there by the crooked willow tree that we thought you might like to meet tonight. They are from Veneta and they are also Were-Bears, they're from the Long Tom Kalapuya – Chelamela Tribe. They are about your age and well when we have a family gathering event of a Were-kind it means that we have the opportunity to introduce the younger generation to each other so that way you won't feel as alone, which does happen." She was saying as we passed pretty close by the small group. There were four guys about my age and two girls too. Mom stopped in front of them and nodded her head. They all stood. The eldest of the group that looked to have the most Indian heritage of the group came forward and lowered his head to me and Mom.

"Ma'am, we're thankful for being included in this occasion." He was very formal acting which I thought was a little strange but I guess I don't really know that much about Were-customs.

"My name is Dominic Black," he placed his hand over his heart and then he turned and with a show of his hand pointed out each of his siblings to us. Dominic was pretty close if not a little older than me. He was roughly about 6'4" tall with a very typical Native American build, all muscle and very tan. He wore jeans and a nice Indian print short sleeve button up shirt in light blues and gold's with a very well used set of cowboy boots. He was defiantly darker than his siblings but now knowing that they were siblings then I can only guess he has an outside job like me to enhance his tan, his long black hair hanging loose to his shoulders and dark brown eyes that reminded me of melted chocolate.  He also has laugh lines so I knew he wasn't always this serious and his smile was infectious.

"My younger brothers Steven, Wayne and Galvin and my sisters Lana and Ava." As he introduced them they each lowered their heads and did not look us in the eye.  His brother Steven must be the next oldest he was almost a perfect copy of Dominic except he had an extra 20 pounds on him instead of all the muscle.  He had his Black hair in double braids hanging on either side of his face. He too was wearing jeans and a nice Indian print short sleeved button up shirt but his was in reds and gold's.

His brother Wayne was a little lighter in the skin and a bit shorter than both his older brothers; he too was heavier but not as much as Steven. Maybe Steven doesn't get out as much as his brothers do?  Wayne's hair tied back with a leather thong and not braided at all, they all shared the same chocolate eyes even the girls.  Something about Wayne made me think that he and Galvin were twins because they were even wearing the same shirts, an Indian print short sleeve button up shirt with a black bear on the back on a high mountain top with lighting in the background and the bear swiping at it.

The only difference between them was the hair style and Wayne seemed to have a smile that he couldn't stop.  Galvin was too busy watching my Mom to really pay much attention to me.  He struck me as the baby even though I think he is Wayne's twin.  He still didn't make eye contact but you could tell the kid was checking out my Mom.

Then the girls Lana and Ava were definitely twins.  Their hair was raven black where the color changes a little in the light of the campfire Lana had a blue streak in her hair and Ava had a Red steak.  They have the same melted chocolate eyes as their brothers.  They were both dressed in pink camo skirts that were barely made it to their knees.  Their shirts were pink tank tops that barely contained their ample breasts and don't get me started on the makeup, they kind of had this punk rocker thing going on.

From the way they were dressed I have a feeling these two are the wild ones of the bunch.

"So I guess your family has multiple births too huh?" I said jokingly, it made Dominic smile. He had a very nice smile too.

"Yes, a lot of the Were-community have multiple births. I have always wondered about the Were-Squatch, is it typical to have a single birth?" Dominic asked my Mom.

"We also have multiple births as well. My sisters are twins but I was a single birth and so was Carrie. My twin sisters are not Were-Squatch's though. My Mom was human and that gave us kids a 50/50 shot. I am the only Were-Squatch from my Father and Carrie is the only Were-Squatch from me. It's that whole recessive gene thing. My twin sisters were bitten after they married their husbands who are from the Harrisburg side of the Siletz tribe; they are Were-Eagles." My Mom was very at ease with talking about our family heritage but I guess you would be able to when you are surrounded by Were's.

"That is interesting, I thought this as a Becoming Ceremony this evening for Carrie but she looks to be my age. Did she only now go through puberty or does it not work that way with the Were-Squatch?" Dominic was defiantly interested in us that was for sure or maybe he is just interested in talking with my mom? His whole family was listening to my Mother like she was teaching a class or something. Maybe all Were's weren't as open as my Mom?

"With Were-Squatch it usually does come out at puberty but with Carrie she is a special case. Since she had the recessive gene she turned when she was bitten by a Were-Squatch in a mating frenzy. She is now a pureblood Were-Squatch and may pass it down to her children because now she has the Were-Squatch gene as a dominate gene now. She will have to choose between her boyfriend Harry who is also a Were-Squatch or the Were-Squatch that bit her before the Full moon in two weeks." My Mom was really talking too much now. She was telling them about my live issues and I really don't know these people. I know they are Were-Bears and they seem nice but other than that I know nothing about them. I was getting very uncomfortable and I could tell that the Black clan could tell. They had managed to skootch in on me and my Mom and now they were slowly backing away, giving me some space at least. Did I have a look on my face that said 'That's enough Mother? 'cause I sure felt like I did and they acted as if I said something too.

"Well anyway, enough about our family drama, have you kids eaten yet?" My mom was pretty good at catching my moods and I am glad I didn't have to say anything this time.

"We were going to get some now Ma'am." Steven spoke as he looked at the ground again. It was kind of irritating that they would not look us in the eyes. I will have to ask Mom or Harry about that later.

"Our Father and Mother are talking with Chief George and then we will eat as a family." Dominic said as he stepped back from me and my Mom even further. Was I putting off some kind of pissed off vibe or something? Wait, what did he call Grandpa?

"I'm sorry did you say Chief George as in George Hunter my Grandfather?" I asked Dominic and then turned to my Mom as he answered.

"Yes, Ma'am. Chief George has been the Council Chief of the many Were-kind Indian Nations. His Grandfather started it and the position has been passed down." Dominic said as I looked back at him and then his brother Wayne said.

"Your Mother is next in line to take over the council and then you since you are her only Were-Squatch heir, Ma'am. It is a position of high regard and respect; you are our Were-Royalty." I couldn't help but look at him with shock, this was the first I was hearing of this.

"The Council of the many Were-kind Indian Nations keeps all Were's safe from each other as well as from the humans that want to harm us." The twin girls said in unison like some freaky movie or something. They knew this stuff and I had no clue. I looked at my Mother and she had a look on her face that told me she knew she messed up by not telling me these things sooner.

"Well, Black Clan I will be taking my daughter to sit and process this information for a minute before her head explodes. Have a nice evening and it was nice meeting you." Mom said as she started to lead me away from them all.

"Nice meeting you as well, Ma'am. It was nice meeting you too Carrie!" Dominic said as he went around them and headed toward the table that Dad and Harry were sitting with Mongo. That's when I felt something that didn't seem right. There was something happening in my brain and in my body. I was getting a fuzzy head and I was getting warm all over. My Mom seemed to pick up the pace to get me to Harry when I stared to grip her arm a little tighter and my breathing started getting heavier, it was like I was breathing from inside a wet cloth or something. Was I changing right now? Oh, God and the crew was all here!

Harry must have seen the look on our faces, he popped up from the table and touched my Dad on the shoulder to turn around and then snapped his fingers, Mongo was up and running toward me almost as fast as Harry was. Harry was up in my face and he nuzzled my nose with his.

"Breathe slowly Lass. I'm here and so is Mongo, no changing in front of the company and crew Baby. Just breathe." Harry was saying into my face and slowing my breathing with his. I automatically wanted to breathe like he was, it was weird. Mongo nudged my right leg and I could hear him.

"Carrie you will be fine. Calm down and listen to Harry breath. You got this!" Mongo nudged me again and then I felt him lick my hand. Harry's and my bodies were very close at this point and I am sure people probably just thought we were dancing. My Cousin Koda's band had been playing for a while now and there were people dancing all over the yard. Mongo stood up and put his front paws one on each of us so that it looked like he was trying to get in between us dancing.

"Carrie, rub Mongo. Rubbing Mongo calms you down all the time, remember?" Mongo was saying in my head. I took my right hand and started rubbing mongo's head and then his ear and then his back and Harry continued to talk to me.

"Just keep breathing Lass, Mongo is a big help. How are you feeling?" Harry asked as he kissed my nose and took his head a little bit away from mine.

"I'm cooler now and it's not as hard to breath. Thanks guys that would not have been cool." I said and Harry leaned in for a quick kiss.

"What happened to make you so upset you almost changed Lass?" Harry looked worried. He had been watching us talk to the Were-Bears for a while.

"My Mom and Grandpa kind of forgot to let me know that we are Were-Royalty is all. My Grandpa is the Chief of the Council of the many Were-kind Indian Nations. Apparently my Mother is next in line and then me for that position, since I am now a Were-Squatch as well." I was starting to get upset again. Harry leaned forward and kissed me a long heart pounding kiss. I felt Mongo get down and sit at my side on my right foot. He was making sure no one came close to us; I knew this in my mind.

I was calm again now. Harry, Mongo and I started to walk toward the food. I was starving and I knew Harry and Mongo were as well. It had been a while since we ate and the night was starting to get dark. I just needed food, my dog and my Man then I will calm down.

## Chapter 22

After getting something to eat and relaxing at the picnic table with Harry and the crew and my friends Amanda and Trina, I was feeling a bit better and was able to talk to my Mother without freaking out.

"Okay Mom, let me get this straight." I said as Harry and I walked away from the picnic table with my mom and Dad. We were walking around the partying people to stay as much out of ear shot of the crew as and other Were's here.

"Our family is Were-Royalty in the fact that Grandpa George's Grandfather started this Council of the many Were-kind Indian Nations to protect not just us Were-Squatch but all other Were-types? There are really Were-Wolves, Were-Bears, Were-Eagles, Were-Cougars, Were-Coyote's and Were-Orca along with us Were-Squatch, am I leaving anyone out?" I was a little touchy but I was staying calm hang on Harry's arm and Mongo by my side. Guessing from Harry's body language I would guess he didn't know about all the other Were's either.

"Thant's about all that I know about anyway. Harry, son I can see by your face this is a surprise to you as well?" My Dad was asking Harry as we got closer to Grandpa George and Grandma May who were sitting in a circle with some Elders I had not seen before.

"Yes, Sir a bit of a surprise. I thought maybe Were-wolves existed because, well Were-Squatch's did but I had no clue about the others or the Council of the many Were-kind Indian Nations. But I don't think I would have since I am not Native American but a pure Scot from the Scottish Highlands were we had stories about Were-Wolves as well but nothing concrete." Harry was saying as his accent always gets a little thicker when he talks about home. Mom saw me looking at Grandpa and Grandma and the Elders.

"Yes, Honey those are the other Council members, there are always 1 or 2 don't come in case anything happens to the Council when they are all in the same place. It's a security thing, that's also why we have sentries out around the property as well. You won't see them or hear them unless something is wrong." Mom was saying as she looked around the party.

"Mom are you also the security for the Council meetings when they are here as well?" I was finding all these things out about my Mom that I am not sure she ever would have told me if I hadn't been bitten and became a Were-Squatch like her.

"Yes I have many rolls in the Council until I become Chief someday. It is so that you better understand your roll as Chief when you are the Chief. That way you don't do things that are not safe or against the laws in which you helped to make. Since you and Harry both did not know of the Council of the many Were-kind Indian Nations, you will have to learn the laws and make sure to uphold them. The penalty for most of the laws is pretty stiff and you have to go before the Council to plead your case if you ever break one of these laws. We govern ourselves and have our own law-enforcement which is also made up of a few different Were's that way there are no favoritisms when someone does something wrong." Mom was telling this to us as we walked closer to the dance floor.

The music seemed to get lower and slower and many of the people who were just standing around started to move to the dance floor. We could see from where we were standing that many of the crew had tried to ask Lana and Ava to dance but their brothers got in the way. Alvin got the go ahead to dance with Deidra and they looked to be having fun. My Aunts and Uncles were all on the dance floor as well as Mike Stone, one of the crew's cooks was dancing with Yancy and they looked very cozy together too which was making her brother a little upset. There were more people here now, not sure when they came in but there were quite a few that I didn't know. Mom must have felt my anxiety because she bumped me like Mongo does.

"Hey, the random people you are seeing are the families of the other Council members. A mix of all the Were's but not any Were-Squatch's in the council. We actually thought your Grandpa, you and I were the last until you found Harry and then Tom and his brothers found you." Mom said with a little of a giggle. Then she turned serious again and stopped walking and then she and Dad turned to Harry and I.

"Which leads me to tell you something that you may not want to hear." Mom looked at Harry and I as we stood stock still in front of them. Mongo bumped my leg and licked my hand. Oh, crap that means this is going to be a doozy.

"I just want you to know it was not my idea! Your Grandfather spoke with the Council about what happened to you and about the choice you have to make and well the Council has decided that you should also spend some time with Tom Johnson as well." Mom made a cringing motion and Harry's whole body stiffened, as she not only looked at my face but also Harry's.

"Now I don't want you to take this personally, either one of you." My mom was not making any brownie points right now with either one of us.

"Are you kidding me? He bit me and then took off without even explaining to me he was a Were-Squatch. He and his brothers stocked me and then he finally introduces himself to me only after Amanda found out who he was and that they were all following me whenever I left the house. The council seriously thinks this is a good idea? What if I say No?" I know I was starting to yell and I am sure more than one set of eyes were watching us as well as Were-ears hearing everything that was going on. My Mom actually cringed a little, then she looked behind me and I knew, I just knew my Grandpa was coming to talk to me. Mom and Dad moved past Harry and I and left us there to talk with Grandpa. I started to turn around and instead Grandpa took my right elbow and whispered into my ear.

"Why don't we take a little walk before someone over hears something they shouldn't shall we Babygirl? Harry you and Mongo are welcome to come with us of course." Grandpa George smiled at me and then at Harry as we started walking to the side of the house that lead into the small garden that Grandma took such good care of. It was packed full of her herbs and veggies that she had recently planted in the ground after germinating in her greenhouse at the back of the yard inside the small wooden fence that surrounded their private area.

"I know you are upset right now but you must understand that it is not something that we take lightly. Yes, we understand the situation in which you were bitten but we also need to take into consideration that there are very few Were-Squatch left Babygirl." Grandpa was saying as he unhooked the small wooden gate for us to go inside the garden. Grandma had 4 chairs circling a small table on the small wooden patio next to the garden. He walked us over to it and motioned for us to sit with him.

"Grandpa, you and the council cannot be serious about me spending time with someone who bit me and then he and his brothers stocked me. That's just insane!" I was not taking this very well. At this point I was mad but at least I didn't feel like I was going to change right now, maybe I was starting to get a handle on this?

"Once you told me about what happened I reached out to the council. After talking it over with them I then contacted Tom Johnson and wanted to hear from him what his thoughts were on what happened. You have never experienced a mating frenzy Babygirl, but all males do at some point until they are mated. He did not have total control over what he was doing; all he knew was that he was being attracted to a female that sent out the mating call not once, not twice but 3 times counting last night. That is why he came for you each time. Because he bit you he has claim over you at the next full moon, unless you have chosen another and mated before the full moon that is our way." Grandpa was saying as he held my hand, he didn't look too happy about it either really.

"I am not saying that you have to give up Harry by any means. The council just feels that you need to give Tom equal time to get to know you as well since both men are Were-Squatch. Now I need to ask a delicate question to make sure but I can pretty much already tell by your smell that the two of you have not mated yet, have you?" Grandpa looked into my eyes and then into Harry's. We looked at each other and I looked down at my hand in Grandpa George's.

"No." I said rather sadly.

"No, Sir." Harry sounded even sadder than I did.

"But it was only because I never go very fast in relationships, I didn't know there was a time crunch for us either or else I would have already by now. I love Harry, Grandpa. And Harry loves me too." I looked him in the eyes and then I looked at Harry he was also nodding his head and looking at me.

"I was giving her time, Sir. I would never rush a woman into bed and we didn't know about the rules of being changed. The man that changed me never said anything about that at all, just that I should never bite a woman unless I knew she had the Were recessive gene and how would I know that, ask her about her DNA?" Harry gave a little smile with his sarcastic response. Mongo came out from under my chair where he was laying and sat in between Harry and I and put his left paw on Harry's lap and looked and Grandpa George. I waited a few minutes and then looked at Grandpa.

"Is he talking to you right now?" I asked, I knew he could talk to others of our kind, why not Grandpa too?

"Yes, and he said he chooses Harry for you too. But the council has spoken and we all must follow the rules to keep everyone safe. Tom and his brothers will be coming to your ceremony this evening." Grandpa started with and I gasped. But he kept on talking.

"Once the ceremony is over Harry is to move back into his trailer and leave you alone in the house. Tom will com courting you and you will give him a chance to show you his life. You must give it a chance Babygirl, a real chance. Harry you will not contact Carrie unless you have to about business only." Grandpa continued and even after I heard Harry grunt his disapproval.

"Tom will be given 1 week to see if you two are compatible and if you wish to choose him. After that 1 week you will then have 1 week without either one until the night of the full moon in which the council will return as well as both men and you will then make your decision. Both men will accept your decision without any issues. And you will be free to go with either man that you have chosen." Grandpa was saying as he was not only talking to me but to Harry as well. Mongo didn't sound happy about it much either by the noises he was making.

"I know that neither one of you wants to go through this but with the shortage of Were-Squatch's out there we have to make sure that the bloodline keeps going." Grandpa was still talking but I was starting to not want to hear him talk anymore.

"But Sir, there are more Were-Squatch's out there they just have no idea about the council and how to even contact them. Like I said, the man that changed me had no clue there was a council for our kind or he might have told me, plus you would have known who he was also. And how do you find them if they are all over the world? There are Sasquatch and Bigfoot sightings in every continent and they can't all be real because I haven't found too many myself and I go looking for them for a living." Harry was trying so hard to reason with Grandpa abut I could tell by the look in his eyes that he was not changing his mind and neither was the council.

"I and the council will not falter from this decree, but I will discuss with them what you have said. There may be more of us out there but they have no way of getting ahold of us so that we can count them and council them as well." Grandpa's eyes did change a little and I know that what Harry said had made sense to him as well and he would make sure that the council knew as well. I think he really like Harry, this was going to be tough but I have a feeling that everything will be okay once the full moon gets here. Grandpa reached out and shook Harry's hand and they looked each other in the eyes with respect, something that most men don't have much of anymore now-a-days.

Once Grandpa had made up his mind there was no changing it without further investigation into whatever I wanted changed. I felt so defeated and Harry looked it too.

After the conversation we had with Grandpa George we decided to stay at the table while Grandpa had to get back to the council and get things going for the ceremony. Which meant that the crew would have to leave as well as anyone that was not Were or Were family. Now I wasn't looking forward to what happens next.

"Listen, I hate the idea of you spending any time with that guy Tom, but you have to follow the rules and so do I know that the council knows I am a Were-Squatch. So, I will move my stuff out of your house and go back to my trailer with Terry and hopefully Trina doesn't get too upset that I have to move back in." He bumped my shoulder as he was talking trying to get me out of this funk that I was in now.

"I was really hoping that you and I were getting better acquainted with the next couple of weeks we had until the full moon. I don't want to see anyone else, you are my boyfriend! Aren't you?" I could feel my heart breaking.

"Because I was raised you didn't cheat on your boyfriend, girlfriend or spouse whichever the case may be. That is exactly what the council is asking me to do, go out dating another guy." I couldn't hold back my tears now, I just couldn't. Harry took me into his arms; I was leaning over the arm of the chair to get to him.

"Awe Lass, I know how you feel. I still consider myself your boyfriend but if you are to give this a real try, which is what the council wants you to do then I guess we aren't actually together anymore, at least not for the next week!" He held me in his arms while I cried. His voice wasn't very far from my ear and I could tell he was very upset as well without the crying. Some men just don't cry I guess.

"Now listen, you have to give, Tom a real couple of dates but after that week I am here if you still want me. I just need you to know that whatever decision you make I will stand by it. But I really hope you pick me in the end." Harry said as I picked up my head to hear him fully and he winked at me. Then he kissed me one of those fire starting, toe curling kisses that I was too stupid to take him up on earlier then this would not be an issue I would be already mated to Harry.

After being in his arms for a few more minutes we came up for air. That's when we noticed that the music had stopped. And the voices were getting louder as if they were coming this way. Then it dawned on me that Grandpa was sending the crew back to their trailers, it was time for the ceremony and that meant that Tom and his brothers were here as well now. Another wave of pure despair went through me.

"It sounds like the crew is heading back to their trailers now, it must be time?" I said as Harry started to stand and brought me up with him.

"I'm still going to the ceremony with you and your family Lass. I will not leave you." Harry said and then hugged me to him again. I hadn't heard anything out of Mongo this whole time until now. He was clawing at the gate we had to go through to get back to the group so we could all go the ceremonial area at the back of the fenced in yard. That's when I heard my Mom.

"Carrie, Honey! It's time for the ceremony. Is Harry still coming with you?" She said as she slowly opened the gate. I looked from her to him and saw the expression on her face. She knew what this was doing to my heart, she had to know.

"I will be by her side until she tells me to not be, Ma'am. We will abide by the council's rules and do as we are asked but I will continue to support her anyway I can." He gave me a sideways squeeze.

"I just wanted to make sure you too knew this was not coming from me or you're Father, Carrie. We too have to follow the rules of the council. That being said, Harry you are a fine man and I really hope my daughter chooses you after she has given Tom a week of her attention." Mom

232

nodded her head as if saying that was all we needed to say about that. Then she turned.

"Now if you three will follow me we will be joining the ceremony along with everyone else. Just so the two of you know, Tom and his brothers are already here and with the council answering some questions of their heritage right now. Since the council had no idea they even existed." Mom said that like they were in trouble or something. But I guess them all being pure bloods would mean that their parents were as well and that means that the council should have known they were in the area beings that there are so few Were-Squatch's left and all. Not my problem, not right now. Now we go to the ceremonial area and wait to start.

## **Chapter 23**

Terry and the girls knew that Harry was staying with me so they didn't wait for Harry to join them when they left to go back to the trailers. Just wait until they find out what is going to happen this coming week. Even they know how I feel about Harry and about dating other people while in a relationship.

We followed my Mom along the path meeting up with my Dad along the way. It seemed like everyone else had already made their way to the area and were sitting on various blankets set out in a very large circle. Inside that circle was a large circle of stones that were about the size of bowling balls. And inside that circle was a small fire pit in the very center that had already been lit. The smoke was white and almost spiraled out from the flames in a very hypnotic way.

Mom stopped at an empty blanket and kissed my Dad then turned to me and Harry.

"This is where you say good bye to each other. Once you enter the circle you will not see him again until the week is over. Your Grandfather usually would be doing this but I volunteered to be the one to lead you." Mom said as she turned her back on me and waited. I was in shock I thought we would have at least this night to say goodbye.

"They don't want you to mate with Harry out of spite. The council is upset that you were allowed to be alone with Harry after your Grandpa George left you in the garden." Mongo said in my head. Mongo was very observant of people around me. I didn't want to reply out loud so I nodded my head and then rubbed Mongo behind the ears. Then I turned to Harry and gave him a huge bear hug. When I started to pull away he pulled me back to him and buried his face in my hair and took a deep breath.

"Just remember that I love you know matter who you choose, I am here for you." Harry said in my ear then he started to pull away from me and gave me a quick kiss on the lips as we separated. My Mom tapped my shoulder and I turned toward her. Dad gave me a quick hug too.

"I am in you corner too, Babygirl." Then he let me go and I nodded my head that I understood. Mom led me away from them toward the entrance of the large circle. When we were almost to the opening I turned my head and looked back at Harry, Dad and Mongo. All three of them were sitting together on the same blanket. And they were talking while they watched Mom and I. Well, at least Dad knows some of the things that Harry should expect from this ceremony.

Mom and I stood at the entrance to the main circle of stones for a few minutes until the council came and sat at their special blanket set up to view the ceremony. Grandpa and my Mom would be the two that were doing the actual ceremony with me and leading me through it. I didn't have a clue on what to expect.

Grandpa George came up on my left side and Mom on my right, they each took my hand and we walked into the center of to circle the fire pit. No one was talking; there wasn't a sound to be heard. Then the drums started, the rhythm was slow and steady. My Mom stared moving to the beat and then Grandpa did too, which made my body also feel the need to move in time with the beating of the drums. Then the council started chanting, I didn't understand what they were saying at all, but I felt it in my body. The drums went faster and we danced faster too and started moving around the fire pit in a clockwise circle. They let go of my hands and we all started to dance around and then do a spin every few seconds, like it was programmed into us.

I felt like I was going into a trance of some kind. My body was getting warmer, it started in my feet and was radiating up my legs and into my lower body. Then my tummy started to tingle and my breasts felt like they were being dipped into a hot tub the way it moved was like a liquid was running up my body and covering every part.

I closed my eyes to feel the heat and the music go through my whole body. My shoulders were feeling it now and my arms were too. Then it was going up my neck and over my head like I was putting on a nice warm hoodie. I was warm all over and it wasn't a warmth from a fire even though I was always mindful that we were still dancing around the fire pit, never getting too close. Last was my face, it got really warm like a blush and then it wasn't anymore. In the back of my mind I knew I was changing into the Sasquatch I was meant to be, even if it did take a bite to get me there.

The drums started to slow as we slowed our dancing with them. I started to open my eyes but they felt so heavy and just different. But I opened them anyway. As I stopped dancing my Grandpa took my left hand and my mom took my right hand again. I turned my head to look at Grandpa first to find that he had changed into a very large dark brown Sasquatch. He smiled at me and then he looked at my Mom, so I turned my head to look at her too. Mom was a little taller than me and she was sporting a lighter shade of brown with what looked like streaks of auburn running through it.

Then I looked down at myself and I saw myself covered in a beautiful auburn fur, all of my clothes were gone and I was covered in fur. I took both of my hands away from Mom and Grandpa so that I could touch my fur, yah, my fur. It was soft like a rabbit pelt but long like a sheep dog. And my fur was all over me, except for the palms of my hands and my toes and of course the bottoms of my feet which were huge by the way. I had never had big feet but let me tell you I was a size 15 or 16 in men's shoes for sure. I was taller that I normally am I could just feel the difference.

I touched my face and found it was definitely different but I had some of the same features as before. I didn't have a huge nose or lips but they were perfectly proportioned to my face, which was bigger to fit into my big head. Then it dawned on me that I wasn't wearing any clothes anymore! My hands went to my chest and yes my breasts were there but they were so covered in fur you couldn't really see them, except for my nipples which I made sure were covered with fur. How embarrassing, but wait that means that my girly area and my butt are covered in fur as well, so I reached around and grabbed my butt to feel a whole lot of fur there as well. I really hope no one saw me do that. Mom isn't worried and she has done this before, just act natural.

I had changed on my own for the first time, without sleep walking. I looked around at everyone that was sitting on the blankets. I was looking for Dad and Harry. I saw Dad sitting on a blanket and then I looked where Harry was sitting, he had also changed into his Sasquatch self. Grandpa saw who I was looking at then he took my hand and turned me to the council.

"I present my Grand Daughter Carrie as the newest member of the Were-Squatch pure blood line of the Hunter family, Molalla Tribe of Oakridge!" There were a lot of hoops and howls as everyone present on the blankets were cheering. My Mom came to my side and raised my other hand in the air.

"I present my Daughter Carrie, the newest female Were-Squatch pure blood Line of the Hunter family, Molalla Tribe of Oakridge!" Then both my mom and Grandpa dropped my hands and bowed to the council. Then I also bowed to the council.

"As speaker for the Council of the many Were-kind Indian Nations I welcome you Carrie, newest Were-Squatch of the Hunter family, Molalla Tribe of Oakridge!" A very friendly looking woman said that was part of the council with Grandpa. She was someone I had never met before so I was looking forward to meeting each of the council members now that I was an official Were-Squatch pure blood and all. I merely nodded my head to her; I wasn't sure what else I was to do. The speaker sat back down on the blanket with the others and she nodded her head.

The drums started again, this time they had a different beat to them. Mom and Grandpa took my hands yet again and we started to walk the inside of the circle of stones. We walked with the beat of the drums and I was looking around at all the people that used to be on the blankets. Now there were huge grey Were-Wolves, happy Were-Coyote's, beautiful

Were-Cougar's, huge Were-Eagles and even bigger Were-Bears. Most of them were in a kind of middle phase standing on their blankets. They were not fully human and not fully animal, it's like the horror movies when the Were-Wolf is standing on his back legs with huge arms and yet has the head of the wolf with the mouth full of teeth and you can see the tail hanging from behind them. That is how most of them were; I was watching them and not paying attention to the drums.

That's when I saw the blanket full of Were- Squatch's like me. It had to be Tom and his brothers, the one standing at the front of them just stood there watching me like he was in awe or something. Then he raised his arm and simply waved at me and smiled. He was the Were-Squatch that tried to take me away the other night. It was Tom! I turned to look at Harry who was still on the blanket with Dad but he was changing back to his human self before my eyes as I was dancing in the circle headed to the side they were on. I saw how the change went in reverse on him and I saw his clothes come back over his body and then he sat down next to Dad.

Well, at least I found out by watching him that my clothes would return as I changed back. I looked down to see how much fur was on me to see that I had already changed back and hadn't felt a thing when it happened. I guess being a Were-Squatch wasn't going to so bad after all.

I turned to look at Mom and she had already changed back too. So I looked at Grandpa and he had changed back. By the time we had made it back around to stand in front of the council again everyone was changed back to who they were before. This means that my just seeing Harry was that last time for a week that I would be seeing him. This made me turn around to look at him again to see that he was gone. Dad sat on the blanket by himself with Mongo who also didn't look too happy. So now my week of hell starts, great!

I was so depressed once Grandpa and Mom walked me out of the ceremonial circle that I wasn't really paying much attention to what was going on around me. My Cousin's Koda, Caleb and Christoff came over to me right away for hugs. I hadn't seen them since last year. They took me to a place in Junction City called Bugsy's, great burgers and they had a band playing. They were friends of my cousin's but they were no 'Left behind the Corner Stone'! But we all had fun and no one got hurt, too much. I had a really bad hangover after that but I survived it. I think that's why I don't really drink much now though.

"Wow you did great Cuz!" Koda said as hugged me again.

"You guys looked awesome, Were- Eagles! That has to be cool!" I was amazed at what they became.

"It's okay when you want to fly somewhere but you get to be huge and strong. And I bet your hearing and eyesight are great too." Caleb said with his big hug.

"Yup, everything is a lot better." I smiled as Christoff came in for his hug; he was always the shy one.

"Hey Cuz, does this mean we don't have to hide our strength and all around coolness from you anymore?" He was always the joker in the family.

"No more hiding anything from me. How are you guys doing? I haven't gotten a chance to talk to you guys in a while." I said as I saw Tom and his brothers coming my way to talk as well.

"We are doing great, we have our own u-tube channel and we also did a gig at Cosmic Pizza in Eugene the other night." Koda was saying as Tom and his brothers made their way to us.

"We, we know that place! It's not too far from our apartments." Tom was saying as they joined us. Koda, being the well-mannered person that he is held out his hand.

"I'm Koda, Carrie's cousin." He said and Tom took his hand in a shake.

"Tom Johnson, I'm a kind of friend of Carrie's." Tom said looking at me for confirmation. It just kind of rubbed me the wrong way for a second. So I turned to Koda, Caleb and Christoff.

"He's the Were- Squatch that bit me." I said without thinking it through. Koda dropped Tom's hand and then looked at his brothers.

"And now we are friends?" Koda asked me with a little of the fire he got in his eyes whenever he was about to let his temper fly, which now makes sense him being a Were-Eagle, very territorial about family. I saw my mistake and had to change it.

"Yes Koda, we are friends. There is more here than meets the eye." This was a phase that we used to say when we were kids and talking about something that couldn't be talked about in mixed company. Koda and the boys understood what I was saying.

"Well, I guess if he is your friend then he is our friend as well." Koda nodded his head at Tom who seemed to take a breath; I hadn't realized he was holding it. I guess he was taking this seriously; maybe I should too, for a week anyway.

## Chapter 24

My cousin's didn't stick around very long because there was a line forming to meet the newest Were-Squatch officially, it was something like a receiving line after you get married from what my mom was saying in my ear.  Mongo was back at my side and it seemed that Tom Johnson was now staying close to my side as well.

We were all standing outside the stone circle, the fire torches that Grandpa had stationed all around the area for these kinds of occasions was a very good light source.  It was lit up perfectly so that you could see everyone but it wasn't overly bright so that you could still see the stars overhead.

I had hugged my cousins and then my Dad and Mongo came over to Mom and me.  Mongo was at my side and was at attention, something he always did when we went into the woods alone or we were in a tricky situation.  I felt better having him by my side.

"So, I let Harry take our car so Carrie can give us a lift down to her house where Harry will leave our car.  The council asked him to leave now instead of prolonging him being around Carrie while she meets all the tribe members around her age."  Dad said as he gave me a hug and then held onto Mom.

"That's fine, Dear.  Is he okay you think?"  Mom was actually worried about Harry; maybe she did like him more than she was letting on?

"Not really but he knows what is at stake for the family and he will do what he needs to do to make sure Carrie is happy."  Dad said as he noticed the line starting and drew my attention to it with a nod.

Mom pulled away from Dad and took me by the hand and led me over to the area we are in now for the receiving line thing. And of course Tom followed me over there as well, while his brothers went to the end of the line that was forming. Mongo was once again by my side now that I was outside the circle of stones. And Tom must have known to keep his distance from Mongo because Mongo was throwing him some wicked glares and a few growls mixed in. He was showing him who was boss here and who I belonged to as well.

When the line started up after my cousins then I got to meet everyone Mom had been pointing out to me earlier. The Were-Wolves from Monroe, Shawn and Yancy. Shawn was a very tall and very good looking man. He was over 6 feet tall and was not showing as much of the Native American heritage as a lot of the others. His hair was dishwater blonde with darker blonde highlights; his eyes were a midnight blue and very mesmerizing. He was very muscular and tan but you could tell it was from being outside and not from his Indian heritage.

Yancy was a little bitty thing not more than 5 feet tall but she too was very muscular. These two were twins you could see that but it seemed like Shawn got all the height and Yancy the beauty. Yancy had the same eyes but the hair was a little blonder and she had blue highlights in her hair. But you could tell by the look in her eyes that she was a take charge kind of girl no matter what size she is.

"It's nice to meet someone our age again, I'm Shawn Davidson, Were-Wolf." Shawn said as she took my hand for a nice hand shake.

"And this is my Sister Yancy; she couldn't wait to meet you." He said as he smiled at me.

"Nice to meet you both, I think I have driven through Monroe a few times. I went to college at the U of O in Eugene." I said as I shook Yancy's hand too.

"Well, we won't hold that against you." Yancy giggled a little.

"You see Monroe is pretty much Beaver country and you have just admitted to being a duck." Yancy did laugh at that one and so did I.

"That just put a picture in my mind of a half duck and half Sasquatch!" I was laughing at that as well as Shawn and Yancy. Then I heard Tom laughing a bit too. I guess he found that funny.

"I like you! We will be friends!" Yancy was saying as her brother had to take her by the shoulders.

"Yes we shall! We have to move on so that Carrie can meet other Were's Sister dear. See you again Carrie." Shawn said but in like a weird way. Was he in heat too? Was all I could think in my head.

"No but his sister is." Mongo said in my head. I smiled and had to chuckle to myself and so did Mongo.

Next to be received in line were the Were-Bear's that Mom had introduced me to. Dominic was the first to take my hand and he actually pulled it to his lips and kissed my hand with a small bow. Wow he was treating me as if I was royalty or something, but I guess I am. Before when we were talking I could have sworn he was watching my Mom but now he was definitely giving me his full attention.

"Miss Carrie, we meet again. I was very happy to have talked with you before the ceremony so that you could meet me as well as my brothers and little sisters." He said as he waved his arm down the line to his Brothers and Sisters who were waiting to shake my hand as well.

"I do have to say that the apple does not fall far from the tree. If you don't mind me saying so, you are a very lovely young woman." He grinned and leaned forward to whisper in my left ear.

"And I kind of wish I had bitten you, then you would be a Were-Bear and fall madly in love with me." He pulled away but I was sure that even though he whispered his brothers heard for sure because they were all grinning as well.

I decided to lean forward to whisper in his ear as he had in mine.

"Well it's probably for the better since I was born to be a Were-Squatch. Besides I already have one to many men in my life." As I leaned back out I could hear his brothers barely able to keep their laughter intact.

"Well, you can' blame a Bear for trying." He shrugged his shoulders, smiled a very nice smile and then winked at me before moving on so his brothers and his sisters could talk to me as well. Dominic's brothers Steven, Wayne and Galvin went by me very quickly. Each took my hand gave it a good shake and each and said something like welcome or good to meet you. Dominic's sisters Lana and Ava both came up to me at the same time. They were more open than they had been before when I met them.

"Nice to meet you again, Carrie." Lana said as she took my right hand and Ava took my left and they both shook me at the same time.

"We are very happy there is another female in the Were-Community now. We know we are a little younger than you but we would really like to be friends and maybe go out and do things, just us girls?" Ava was saying so fast I was trying to keep up with her,

"Sure I would love that. I do have to warn you that I am a tomboy at heart so I don't really wear all the girly clothes and things." I was saying as the girls were taking my hair and playing with it. I was beginning to see that these two had no personal boundaries, but that is the Were way and all.

"Oh, we can help with that! We could give you a total make over and we can dress you up and everything. We love doing that!" Lana was squealing with her sister over making me into a girly girl, and they do it for fun.

"That would be fun." I was saying as Dominic came back for his sisters that were in no hurry to leave me.

"Girls, she has a lot of others to receive. Let's get a move on! Carrie, until we meet again." I think Dominic thinks he's a Rico Sauvé or something. He actually winked at me again as he pulled his sisters off of me. But before Ava was pulled to far she put a note in my hand. Then she smiled. I put it into my pocket before her brother could see it; I would look at it later.

Next in line to see me were the Were-Cougars from Philomath that Mom had pointed out to me on our walk. Darrin, Donavan and Deidra Hunter not sure how many cousins separated but if their Grandpa is my Grandpa's cousin, then their Dad is my Mom's second cousin and that would make us third cousin's.   I think that is how it goes?  Oh, well they are family and they have the Hunter name, that's all that matters for me.

"It's nice to finally meet you, cousin." Deidra said as he took my hand and pulled me in for a hug, she was very strong for a girl.

"It's nice to meet you too, Deidra. My Mom was showing me the family on our walk around the party earlier." I said as she pulled away from me a little in surprise.

"Oh, yah I saw you two talking.  I wanted to say hi but I thought she was getting you ready for the ceremony." Deidra said as she stepped aside and both Darrin and Donavon hugged me and picked me up off the ground at the same time, making us all laugh.

"We are so happy you have finally come into your real you Cousin." Darrin was saying as they set me back on the ground.

"Yes we are.  You will have so much more fun now that you can be with the hairier side of the family." Donavon joked as he and Darrin stepped back a little to give me space to breath.

"Well, thank you guys.  I am honored that you guys could be here.  I have wanted to see the family together for so long but there has always been something that came up at the last minute that we never made it to any of the family parties." I was saying as they started chuckling.  Then Deidra spoke up, it seems she was the spokeswoman for them.

"No, Honey they just didn't want you to get hurt if you played with us.  We Were's kind of play rough if you know what I mean." She laughed as she touched my shoulder. They made me want to laugh too. But now I knew the family secret, hell I was now part of the family secret.

"Well, we can do things together now!" Darrin said as he too had to touch my other shoulder. This made me a little uncomfortable, so of course I had to ask out loud.

"I have to ask about the touching thing and personal space, is it different with Were's because everyone really like to touch and I'm not used to that?" I said which made them take their hands off of me really quick.

"Yah, sorry it is a Were-thing. We are very touchy feely and we are always in a pack situation, we are hardly ever alone and to tell how someone is feeling or to sense danger or what not in a group we touch each other so when they get tense or strain then we feel it as well. Do you understand? I know that the Were-Sasquatch isn't really a pack animal but they are in family units like a pack." Deidra said as she looked back at the line.

"Okay, I get it now. Thanks Deidra." I said as she moved in closer to me again.

"We don't want to take up anymore of your time since you still have a few people to see and it's getting late for us. We have to head home back to Philomath. Your Mom has our numbers and I asked her to give them to you because we need some cousin time now that we can be around you." Then she leaned in and started hugging me when her brothers also got in on the hug as well. They were a lovey bunch, I like them too.

"Okay guys, we will have to have a visit that takes a little longer next time. You guys be safe going back home." I said as they started to turn away from me. Then Donavon turned around and looked at me kind of funny.

"Don't you know about the Were invincibility? The only things that can hurt us are fire, silver poisoning and decapitation and aging slowly, otherwise we are pretty much indestructible." Donavon was saying as my mouth dropped open.  Then he whispered, "And we live longer too."  Then he kissed my cheek really quick and ran to catch up with his brother and sister who had already walked away.

"You seem surprised at that?  Are you okay, Cousin?"  Dan Thompson said as he took his place in front of me.  Mom had pointed him out as well, he is Mom's Cousin Jacob's youngest son Dan from Lincoln City, a Marine Biologist and my second cousin and he is a Were-Orca.

"Well yes I am very surprised.  My Mom hasn't told me any of that."  I was saying as I took his out stretched hand and he pulled me in for a hug.

"I'm sorry she hasn't had time to I am sure she will as soon as this is all over this evening.  So you do remember me then Cousin?"  He asked as he took a step back but still held me by my upper arms.

"I didn't until Mom pointed you out earlier.  We used to go swimming together in the summers.  Why did we stop?"  I was trying to remember why but I just couldn't.

"Well you see it's because I came into puberty before you did.  The last summer we swam together I was starting to change and I'm sure your Mom has told you by now that I am a Were-Orca, right?"  He was hoping my mom had filled me in on something at least about him.

"Yes, she told me earlier that you were a marine biologist as well as being a Were-Orca, which I thought was the perfect job."  I laughed a little and so did he.

"Right?  The perfect job for me and you being a Were-Squatch and a forest ranger, that is priceless too."  We both had a laugh at that one.  I did remember bits and pieces of the fun we used to have playing as children.

"So, we are going to have to get together again soon.  The family has been separated for too long now and we need family.  And before I forget you need to talk to your Mom because she should have told you all the amazing things there are to being a Were too."  Dan said as he leaned in and kissed my forehead and gave me another hug.

"I have a feeling there are a lot of things my mom and I need to discuss about my life now." I said as Dan pulled away.

"I will leave you now to visit with the rest of the line; I will not be leaving for home tonight. Your Grandparents have let me use the guest house for the evening. I will be heading back to Lincoln City in the morning; may I stop and see you before I leave?" He was asking as my Uncle's Deputies were kind of moving in the line to get closer to us.

"That would be great, we will talk more then." I said as he started walking away.

"I'm going to talk to your parents right now since my Dad is over there talking with them." And Dan was on his way, I hope he has a really good conversation with my Mom about keeping secrets. I was lost in thought for a few minutes before the clearing of the throat noises got my attention. I hadn't realized that I was staring at my Mom as Dan walked up to them to talk. When I looked back in front of me Uncle Jared's two Deputies Gabe and Luke Bronson were standing right in front of me.

"Hello!" I said as they stood there. Then they looked at each other then back at me and both of them came in at the same time to hug me. Then picked me up and turned me around then put me back in the spot I started from.

"We are so happy we can talk to you about everything now!" Luke said a she smiled at me like a puppy dog, which I guess he kind of was.

"Yah, it's just sad they we couldn't have dated you before you got bit by that Tom guy. You could have been a Were-Coyote and married to one if us. But you Uncle said you were off limits." Gabe said as he smiled at me.

"You guys seem so different when you are not on duty. And when did my Uncle say I was off limits?" I was trying to get information out of them as slowly as possible since Tom's brothers were next to talk to me.

"Yah when we are on duty we are, you know, working. Like Mongo is right now. We stay alert and watch for trouble. But when we are at Were functions we can be ourselves." Gabe was saying as he leaned down and petted Mongo on the head.

"And your Uncle said you were off limits because your parents were trying to find you a Were-Squatch suitor and we were to leave you alone so that no feelings got started. Your Mom may have let it slip that you had a small crush on me when we first got to Oakridge." Luke was saying as he leaned in for another hug. Was this another Were thing or was he saying something to me?

"Okay, that is rather embarrassing…" I said as Luke pulled away and then Gabe leaned in for another hug too. Then he whispered into my ear so low that I was sure only I could hear him.

"If you want to choose one of us then we can talk to the council. We can petition for the right to fight for your hand." Gabe was totally serious about this, I could tell. I whispered as low as I could back to him.

"Gabe as flattered as I am and as embarrassed as I am I already have two men to choose from and I really don't want anyone fighting over me. But thank you, both of you." I said and I kissed his cheek and then I winked at Luke. This made Luke come back in for another hug.

"I would like a kiss too please." Luke said in my ear, so I kissed his cheek and then they let me go. Both had a very big smile on their faces. Who knew they were just two big happy puppy dogs looking for love? The two of them looked back at Tom's brothers then they turned and looked at Tom with a look that said they better not hurt me or else. Even I could read that look. Then the two Deputies went off in the search of someone else to talk to. They really were social creatures after all.

Tom walked around me coming from my right side. I had known he was back there a few yards from me the whole time but I was not going to be someone I am not just to make him feel more comfortable around my family and friends. Tom's brothers came up to me still in an orderly line but now Tom was right in front of me.

"I had wanted to talk to you in private but the council said I couldn't, that we had to wait our turn in line. I wanted to tell you that what the council is doing about you and I was not my idea. I am not opposed to the idea of some one on one time with you but I don't want you to hate me for it either. That being said, I am here to officially ask you on a date for tomorrow afternoon, since you have family to talk to in the morning." Tom wasn't being mean or rude and he was actually rather humble almost. He was asking not telling me that we should go on a date, not like the council was doing to me.

"I would like that. I'm sorry if I have not been very nice about this whole thing. I was never very good at being told what to do. My only request is that we don't leave Oakridge and I have to take Mongo with me." I was saying as Tom's brothers were getting antsier in line next to him.

"Well, I would really like to take you to see where I work and maybe see a movie or something but we can wait until you feel safer being with me. And I don't mind Mongo coming along, but I don't think he likes me very much right now." He finished talking on a rough whisper like it was a secret or something which made me smile.

"I will concede to the later date of seeing your work place and movie in Eugene. I went to the U of O and still have some friends in town as well. Maybe we can date and visit also? And I don't think you have to whisper about Mongo, he kind of can hear everything anyway." I finished saying as I squatted down and gave Mongo a hug and he got very happy and wagged his tale and licked my cheek.

"Okay good to know. And friends are good too. I just wanted a chance for you to get to know me and my brothers too. I know I bit you, but I was in a mating frenzy which I know is no excuse but if we could just start with a clean slate from here on I would really like the chance to make it up to you." Tom was saying and even though I know he is the Alpha and leader of his family he was still begging me for attention. I guess I can deal with that.

"So, we are going out tomorrow afternoon. Would you like to start with a lunch at my parents Bigfoot Pizzeria?" I was trying to pick a place that I felt safe and I think he understood that too.

"Yes, I will pick you up at noon if that is an okay time." Tom said as he kind of shuffled from one foot to the other.

"Noon is good. Now would you like to reintroduce me to your brothers?" I asked as his brothers started to push each other again in line. They were the only ones left and yet they acted like they were in line to see Santa Clause or something. Tom turned and gave them a look and a little grunt left his lips. All 6 brothers stopped and stood up straight in line, standing very calmly. Mongo gave them a woof too.

"Carrie, these are my brothers. Frank the next oldest brother and my second in command." Frank came forward and took my hand and bowed then kissed my knuckles.

"Ma'am." Was all he said then he let go of my hand and went to stand at the back of the line again.

"Gary, the next oldest, he's the guy who gets us the most clients." Gary came forward and took my hand and bowed then kissed my knuckles.

"Ma'am." Was all he said then he let go of my hand and went to stand at the back of the line again.

"Abel the next oldest who is a wizard with finances." Abel came forward and took my hand and bowed then kissed my knuckles.

"Ma'am." Was all he said then he let go of my hand and went to stand at the back of the line again. It was like they were programmed to do this or something. Then I was introduced to the next brother.

"Zeek the next oldest is the charmer of the family." Zeek came forward and took my hand and bowed then kissed my knuckles and then he lifted his head and winked at me when he said.

"Ma'am." Then he let go of my hand and went to stand at the back of the line again.

"Kelly the next oldest is also the one that makes sure everyone else is taken care of before himself. He is the organizer and go getter of us all." Kelly came forward and took my hand and bowed then kissed my knuckles and then he said.

"Ma'am. We are all so happy you agreed to see our brother." Then he let go of my hand and went to stand at the back of the line again. Then we came to the last brother who was obviously the youngest of the brothers

"Then the baby of the family, Jeffery. He is the one that everyone has to watch out for. He is the most serious, most professional security guy I have ever known and that isn't just us but everyone we have working for us as well." Jeffery came forward and took my hand and bowed then kissed my knuckles; he lifted his head and said.

"Ma'am, don't believe everything you hear about me. I can have fun just as much as the rest of them and if you don't find my brother to your liking then I am sure you would like me." Then he smiled the biggest, whitest smile I have ever seen, then let go of my hand and went to stand at the back of the line again still having a smile on his face. All of his brothers were stunned in to speechlessness which I bet doesn't happen often with these boys.

"Thank you Jeff for the offer. And thank you all for being here tonight. I am looking forward to spending time with your brother as well as with all of you this week and I hope that I don't get in the way of you working though." I said and that's when it dawned on me that I had a job too. I had just started back to work, how was I going to tell Johnny that I needed another week off because the Council of the many Were-kind

Indian Nations has made me take the week to let a Were-Squatch court me. Somehow I didn't think that was going to pass for an excuse.

"Is everything okay Carrie?" Tom asked me, I must have zoned off there for a minute thinking in my head too long.

"Sorry, no I was just trying to figure out how I was going to get this week off of work. I don't think that my boss would like me to give him the real reason on why I need the week off." I was saying with a little sarcasm.

"No, probably not. Maybe if you told him that you had family from out of town or maybe that your bite had given you some side effects that were unforeseen?" He was rather good at the ideas I will give him that. But I prided myself in always being as honest as possible with people.

"I will see if my mom has any ideas. She and my boss Johnny have been friends forever." I said as I looked toward my Mom and Dad still talking with the council members that hadn't left yet.

"I am sure you will think of something. I best be getting my brothers back to the motel and I will see you tomorrow." Tom said as he held out his hand for me to shake. I took it and then he also bowed and kissed my knuckles like his brothers did. Then he released my hand and turned to his brothers.

"Alright guys let's get to the motel and get some sleep." Then he turned back to me again.

"Goodnight Carrie. I look forward to seeing you tomorrow." Then he looked down at Mongo and said.

"Goodnight Mongo, I hope we become friends soon." And he waved at me and then at Mongo, I am pretty sure he didn't even want to try to touch Mongo knowing how he felt about him.

"He's not that bad so far. I will hold my judgment." Mongo said in my head, which I replied to him.

"Me too, Mongo. Me too." Then Mongo and I headed to Mom and Dad since we had to give them a ride down to my house to retrieve their car. And Mongo and I will be returning to an empty house with no Harry to do things for me anymore. I was starting to get sad again; at least I was happy for a little while meeting all the family I had now.

# Chapter 25

Mom and Dad didn't say much on the ride back to my house. I guess Cousin Dan had mentioned the fact that I hadn't been told all the info that I needed to know about being a Were. Grandpa wasn't very happy about. He thought Mom had filled me in when we took our little walk around the party which is what she was supposed to be telling me not just who was who and how we were related. There were plenty of other people at the party that I had no clue that they were but I guess they were council member's families and I would get to know then sooner or later anyway.

"Well at least you know everything now, Babygirl." Mom said as she climbed out of the backseat of my 4 runner and into my Dad's waiting arms. They kissed quickly and then then moved and closed their doors.

"Mom, maybe that's your problem. You always think of me as your Baby girl not as a full grown woman? I should have heard all these things a long time ago, even if I wasn't a Were at least I would have been aware of the possibility that I could be changed. What if I had fallen in love with a Were-Wolf? Or a Were-Coyote, I was crushing on Luke pretty bad, and thanks for telling him by the way. Both he and Gabe were ready to fight for the right to marry me if I wanted them." I said as I was following Mom and Dad toward their car with Mongo right at my heels.

Both Mom and Dad stopped suddenly and turned to look at me in unison.

"What?" Mom practically yelled.

"What do you mean they wanted to fight for you?" Dad asked in a calmer voice.

"I mean just that. They said even though I was Were-Squatch that if I didn't like my choices they would be willing to petition the council for the right to court me and if they had to they would fight for my hand in marriage if I wanted to choose one of them." I repeated as I shrugged my shoulders.

"What was the big deal?" I asked them, they both looked dumbfounded.

"The big deal Honey is that you are a pure blood and we have been trying to find you a Were-Squatch to court since you turned 18. We figured that if you fell in love with one then you would be bitten on purpose and become who you were meant to be. I don't need to remind you that Luke and Gabe are Were-Coyote's and they are very brute force driven. If they made the offer, then they are actually thinking that you would be interested in marrying one of them. Which means you need to set them straight that you are not interested in them in that way!" Mom was totally losing her cool, something she never did.

"Chill out Mom, I handled it. They know that I have enough to deal with between Harry and Tom and Tom's brothers apparently. They think they have a shot with me if Tom and I don't work out." I said that last bit a little sarcastically but I was sure that Mom and Dad weren't happy with how I put it.

"But you actually told them you were not interested in them, right? They will only take the words that are specifically said Carrie. You have to be clear with Were-Coyote's!" Mom was looking like she might actually start changing any minute here. Dad walked behind her and started to massage her shoulders and that is when she realized what was happening.

"Calm down my Love. No need to change again so soon." Dad was calming her down like Harry was ding for me all this time. This made me look toward the trailers at the side of the house. I knew he was in one of them but I couldn't see anyone they were all dark so I guess everyone was sleeping now.

"You can't see him Babygirl." Dad said very sadly. I think he knew what I was going through.

"I know Dad, but it still hurts." I said as I leaned down to touch Mongo's head. At least he was always there for me.

"So just to be clear you told Luke and Gabe no, right?" Mom asked in a calmer voice.

"Yes Mom, I told them no. Besides Uncle Jared already told them I was off limits, period. That you guys had been looking for Were-Squatch for me anyway." I said with a little attitude.

"Okay then. Is there anything else that you need to tell us about the receiving line that we should know? Anyone else try to get you to have them court you?" Mom was asking like this was a seriously bad thing. Which it would be because I already had 2 but she made it sound like no one should be interested in my or something.

"There were a few flirts but other than that most of them are family so there wasn't anything there anyway. I got a note from Ava Black though. But the two girls want to get together and do a girls thing so it was probably just her number to get ahold of them. I will need all of my Cousin's numbers from you as well as soon as you can. We all plan on getting together and visiting soon. Oh and Dan is stopping by in the morning for coffee and a chat before he leaves to go back to Lincoln City with his Dad. His Dad has some council business with Grandpa early in the morning." I said as Mom and Dad were getting less interested in what I was talking about.

"Yah, your Grandpa is taking him fishing in the early morning hours, council business my butt. Okay well have a good visit with Dan. When are you going on your first date with Tom? Oh, and I've already talked to Johnny about this coming week for you not working. He understands that you need more time and he will see you when you have made some life decisions that you need to focus on. All righty?" Mom was getting ready to get into her car.

"Wow Mom what exactly did you tell him? Does Johnny know about us Mom? And Tom and I are coming down to Bigfoots for pizza at around noon. So Dad be ready with mongo's pizza, he has been a really good boy with everything that has been going on lately." I said as my Dad leaned over and hugged me goodbye. My Mom was already on the other side of the car and waved at me.

"Yes he does Dear, he is one of my oldest friends what do you think? Okay Honey, we will see you tomorrow then. Love you!" Then she sat down and closed her car door. So I leaned down and looked though Dad's open door.

"Love you too Mom. Love you Dad. See you both tomorrow." Then Dad said.

"Don't be too upset with you Mom, Babygirl. She's doing what she and the council think are right for you right now. Love you too Honey. Bye." With that he closed his car door and then started the car and backed out of my driveway. They were going home and now Mongo and I were going inside to our very quiet, very lonely home.

Once Mongo and I got into the house I just wanted to go to bed. That's when I heard a knock coming from the glass sliding door in the kitchen. Mongo headed back there first and I was right on his heels hoping that it was Harry breaking the rules and wanting to see me before I went to bed. When I got past the end of the hall and was able to see the glass sliding door that's when I realized that it wasn't Harry and I know my face must have fell from the exciting expectations of seeing Harry to seeing my friends Trina and Amanda at the door instead. I could tell by the looks on their faces that they had seen mine fall as well. Mongo sat next to the door so that I could open it. I still put a smile on my face because I was happy to see my friends it just wasn't who I was hoping for.

"Well, we are glad to see you even though we aren't the one you were expecting, but we are here to spend the night with you like old times." Amanda said as she slid through the door and took me into a hug, followed closely by Trina joining in on the hug as well.

"We know how you feel and we wanted to be have a sleep over with you tonight so that you weren't alone. No offence Mongo." Trina said as we all pulled apart and Mongo jumped up on Trina to say hello.

"Thanks guys. I'm happy you guys are here too." I said as Mongo jumped down and ran out into the yard since the door was still open.

"I guess he had to go potty before bed?" I said as I turned to the kitchen.

"Do you guys want anything to drink before we go to bed?" I asked as I took out the pitcher of iced tea and 3 glasses after each of the girls nodded when they saw the pitcher in my hand.

"It must have been something, the ceremony thing you had to do, cause you look wiped." Amanda said as she came around to help me add ice to the glasses.

"Did Harry tell you guys anything?" I asked not sure how much I should tell them, I have always told them everything but this was something I wasn't sure I could share,

"Yes, Harry, Terry and Jerry filled us in on everything including some things that we were sworn into secrecy. He told us what the council and your Grandpa are making you do this week as well." Amanda was saying when she handed Trina her glass of iced tea.

"Yah we think it's kind of crappy the way they are making to spend time with Tom, the guy who bit you when you and Harry are obviously in love." Trina was saying when I put the pitcher back in the fridge.

258

"Tell me about it. But I also understand that Tom does deserve a fair shot at courting me too. I just wish that Harry and I had gotten to do more with our time we had together, you know?" I said as I sat down in the chair at the island were the girls were sitting now. We were waiting on Mongo and then we should head to bed I am thinking since it is so late.

"Well, we are team Harry if you are wondering." Amanda said as she handed me a folded piece of paper.

"Harry asked me to give it to you." She said as she watched my face. I opened the paper to read his note.

*'Lass,*

*I just wanted to let you know I am here for you any time.*

*You can call me, text me or just yell for me and I am there.*

*Love Harry'*

"Oh, Harry." Was all I said before I started crying.

"I know this isn't forever and I know that at the end of the week I can see him again. But what if my feelings change? What do I do then?" I was so unhappy right now. Both Trina and Amanda were by my side hugging me again.

"What is meant to be it will be. You will follow your heart wherever it leads you. We really like Harry but if you can give Tom a chance then if you choose him we will too. Otherwise though we are still team Harry." Amanda was saying and then she and Trina started giggling, something we hadn't done for a while now. That's when Mongo came in through the sliding glass door to see what was going on.

"Alright Ladies! It is late and we need our beauty sleep." Trina said as she stood up and grabbed her glass and then leaned out the door and grabbed her backpack and Amanda's then handed it to her as well.

"Oh, guys I almost forgot to tell you. My Cousin Dan will be stopping by early to talk while his Dad is out fishing with Grandpa George." I said as I grabbed my glass and slid the sliding glass door closed.

"Wait, which one is your Cousin Dan? Is he the one we used to go swimming with?" Amanda asked as she double checked the lock on the front door, a habit she has always had.

"Yes, he's living in Lincoln City and is a marine biologist now. I will get all the info when we have a talk in the morning though." I said as I was the first in the bedroom I was also the first to grab my night clothes and I headed to the bathroom leaving the door open a crack so that we could still talk while I did my nighttime routine before bed.

"Cool, he was always cute wasn't he Trina?" Amanda said jokingly. I was brushing my teeth when Amanda came into the bathroom with her toothbrush also.

"That should be fun for you to catch up. Do you want us out of here when he shows since we aren't supposed to know too much about the Were situation?" Amanda asked before she started brushing. I finished and put my brush away.

"You don't have to leave right away. I am sure he's not going to jump right into talking about Were stuff anyway." I said as I left the bathroom and went back into the bedroom.

"So are we having breakfast with you or are we heading out to the food truck in the morning?" Trina asked as she started to straighten the covers on the bed. I sure am glad that I had the good sense to buy a California King sized bed. Mongo is usually a bed hog but with all 3 of us girls plus Mongo we should be okay for one night.

"You guys can eat wherever you like. I was hoping to eat before Dan got here but I'm not sure what time he is showing up. Plus, I'm not supposed to see Harry at all until the end of the week. Oh, and Tom is picking Mongo and I up at noon to go on our first date to Bigfoot pizza for lunch. I've already warned Dad that we were coming, I'm still a little pissed at Mom right now." I was saying as Amanda came out of the bathroom and slid in the bed just before Trina so that Trina was on the outside on the right side of the bed. They knew I Slept on the left side with Mongo lying on the outside by me.

"Well, at least that is a safe place for a date. And we can bring you and Mongo breakfast if you don't want to cook in the morning." Trina was saying as she yawned and climbed into bed next to Amanda.

"Okay, I kind of got used to Harry making us breakfast in the mornings." I said with a little sad huff as I sat down on the side of the bed.

"Everything will turn out alright, don't worry." Amanda said as she rubbed my back a little and then she laid back down. I laid down too and patted the side of the bed when I was comfortable for Mongo to jump us.

"At least I still have my Mongo." I said as he let out a huff trying to relax himself for sleep.

"Hey! What are we chopped liver?" Amanda and Trina said at the same time. We all giggled and then I shut off the bedroom light.

"Night everyone!" I said and closed my eyes.

"Good night!" Trina said. And then of course Amanda has to be the smart ass.

"Night John Boy!" Which Mongo had to reply with a woof and then a little growl, basically saying shut up and go to sleep which made me and the girls start giggling again.

## **Chapter 26**

    Sleep came fast, I knew I was exhausted.  The next thing I knew it was morning and someone was knocking on my door.  Mongo was gone out of the bed like a shot.  He always saved his barking until he knows who is at the door so that he can do a sneak attack.  If you don't hear a dog, then you don't assume one will come charging out at you when the door gets opened, right?  Well that's how Mongo thinks of it anyway, he always has.  Plus, we already knew who it was; I just wasn't prepared for him yet.

    I put on my robe and that's when I noticed that the girls were already gone.  They must have just let me sleep, I looked at the clock on the nightstand and it was after 9 am already.  I really did sleep in this morning; Mongo and I are usually up no later than 7am most mornings.

    "Dan is here!  Amanda took me potty already then they went to get us breakfast.  Yours is in the kitchen they left you a note on the counter too."  Mongo said in my head as I made it to the front door and opened it to find Dan standing there waiting patiently.

"Morning Sunshine! Did I get here too early?" Dan asked as he came in.

"No I was up a little later than normal plus my friends came to spend the night with me last night." I said as I closed the door behind him.

"So, the living room is through there and I am going to go and throw on some clothes. Be right back." I said as I pointed him in the right direction and then I went back to the bedroom to change and get my day started.

It didn't take me very long to throw on a pair of jeans and my green lucky shirt and then I went potty, brushed my hair and put on a little pit of makeup because I wasn't sure how much time I would have between when Dan left and Tom showed up to go out to lunch. I wasn't gone more than 20 minutes. Mongo had followed Dan into the living room and was sitting in front of him where he was sitting on the couch when I came in.

"So Mongo says you have a date this afternoon huh? My Dad told me what the council was doing to you and your boyfriend. I'm sorry about that; Dad said he voted against it. He said he voted for you to decide for yourself at least. I guess the elders of the council wanted your Grandpa and Mom to choose who you were to be mated to." Dan was saying as he looked between Mongo and I. I felt a little light headed when he told me that. So I sat on the end of the couch.

"Tell your Dad thanks for me. So what's new with you?" I was trying to act as if nothing was wrong but Dan could see right through me.

"Mongo said you need to eat your breakfast. Why don't you and I go into the kitchen?" Dan said as he stood and held out his hands to me.

"Mongo is a worry wart." I said as I stood with Dan's help.

"Well, I have taken great care of you so far." Mongo said in my head and I swear he laughed at me too.

"I am a little hungry. Have you eaten yet?" I asked Dan as we walked into the kitchen. Dan took a seat at the island and I found the note that let me know my breakfast burrito was in the microwave and that

Mongo had been taken potty as well as fed all before I even woke up this morning. They were out in the trailers working if I needed them. And the P.S. was that if I needed to get out of a date to text them and they would come up with a good reason for me to come back home. I have such good friends.

"I'm guessing that it was a good note?" Dan asked me as he watched my face.

"Yes, I have really good friends. You remember Trina and Amanda from when we used to spend time together during the summer when we were kids?" I asked as I went to the cupboard to get two glasses out.

"I think I do. As I remember it your friend Trina used to follow me everywhere. She was at that the party last night wasn't she? She didn't come to the ceremony so I would think she isn't a Were though, am I right?" Dan had a good memory, and he was smiling too.

"Yes they were there. Amanda and Trina both have found love this past month. Amanda is a journalist working for a News channel in Eugene and she also has her own Blog. Trina is a large animal veterinarian and she has worked at a couple of zoos with the larger primates which made both of them perfect to be included in the Sasquatch hunting that the 'Bigfoot Getters' were filming for their Animal Channel's show. That's how I met Harry, he is not only a member of the 'Bigfoot Getters' but a Were-Squatch as well. He has the most amazing accent that just turns me to mush whenever he talks to me. He's originally from Scotland." I said on an exhale that made my head float right along with my heart.

"But I am guessing he is the one that the council doesn't want you to spend any more time with, so you can have the Were-Squatch that bit you can also court you now. I'm guessing because he is a pure blood, right?" Dan asked with a sad voice. He understood what I was feeling.

"Yes. I have my first date with Tom at noon today." I said looking at the clock on the wall above the sink.

"Well, I for one think that you are an intelligent woman who can see right through any bullshit and you will choose the right man for you!" Dan said as he walked around the kitchen island and took one of the glasses out of my hand and set it on the counter. Then he took my hand and walked me around the island to sit on the seat he had just left.

"I will get your tea and warm up your breakfast. Mongo said it's in the microwave and that you need some tea, stat!" He said as he opened the microwave door and looked inside then he closed it and set the time for 45 seconds. Then he took both glasses and added ice to them and then my iced tea from the fridge. Everyone knew how I was crazy over my iced tea.

"Thanks Dan. Enough about my crazy life right now. Tell me what is going on with you?" I asked as the microwave dinged and he took my breakfast out and set it in front of me. Then he went to the fridge and opened the door and pulled out some mild hot sauce and set it in front of me as he walked around me and sat in the chair next to me.

"I'm good your Grandma May made me breakfast at like 6am this morning." Dan said rubbing his very flat, muscular tummy.

"I know Grandma May's breakfasts; I bet you had waffles with blueberries in them?" I asked him knowing what he would say already.

"Yes, I did." He said with a smile and then he looked at me.

"Let's see where do I start? You have heard I am a marine biologist?" I nodded my head as I took my first bite.

"Well, next summer I start working at the Aquarium in Lincoln City, which is a great job in its self. But there is a lady coming up from San Diego to also work there and she is bringing the new whales for the Aquarium with her. So naturally I am pretty excited but also a little freaked out." Dan was saying as he looked at his hands.

"Why are you freaked out if this is your dream job working with the whales? What kind of whales are they?" I asked between bites.

"So they are Orca's from their Orca rescue at OceanWorld. The lady that was working with them down there is traveling with them up here. They already have a connection to her, I guess I was just hoping to have one with them myself since I am also part Orca. Weird I know." Dan said and then took a drink of his tea.

"You will probably have a better connection to them than she can because of you being part Orca, Dan. I don't think you have to worry at all about that." I said as I put my hand on his arm. He looked so nervous about what was to come for his career, while I was trying to figure out my future life. Being a grownup sucks!

"You really think so? I have checked her out too. I mean she is really pretty and everything but she is also very dedicated to her whales, which I find really cool." Dan was getting a little nervous now.

"Dan! Have you been Facebook stocking her?" I said with a giggle.

"Maybe a little, she is really cute. Ad get this her name is Amanda Waters and she is a marine biologist! Is that fate or what?" He was smiling and if he wasn't so tan I bet you would see him blushing too.

"Okay, so you have a crush on her and she loves whales, Orca's to be exact. So what's wrong with that?" I asked him as I took one more bite of breakfast and gave Mongo the last bite. He was waiting so patiently next to me on the floor. He never begged but waited patiently.

"Maybe because she isn't a Were-Orca like me?" Dan said as he shrugged his shoulders.

"What does that have to do with anything? As far as I know the Were-Squatch is the only Were that has to worry about changing females. If you guys fall in love maybe she will want to be a Were-Orca too?" I said feeling a little better knowing that there are other Were's with love issues and not just me, is that selfish?

"I know but my parents have been trying to get me to visit with a Were-Orca family in Astoria because they have 2 daughters my age. But the funny thing is that neither one of them wants anything to do with marine biology which is not only a big part of my life but, hello being a Were-Orca you would think it would be a part of their lives!" Dan was so cute when he was trying to be funny as well as get his point across about compatibility.

"Then you remind your parents that with a love you have to have compatibility somewhere and not just in being a Were-Orca. Do they know about this lady you are Facebook stocking?" I asked giggling again.

"No they don't but it is a good point. I know my Mom is more of a push over than Dad is." Dan said as he glanced at the front door.

"Well, maybe after being here this weekend your Dad will be looking at this with different eyes also?" I said and then I heard the phone ring. I went and got my cellphone off the bedside table where I had left it to charge. It was Uncle Jared calling me. So I answered it.

"Hey, I just wanted to give you a heads up that your Grandpa has decided not to press charges against the SMM Bigfoot Hunters so they are being released today. So give every Were a heads up and I am also calling the Bigfoot Getters Crew as well to let them know." Uncle Jared was saying barely seconds after I even said hello.

"Okay good to know. Also, did your Mom or Dad fill you in on last night? The council's decision on what I need to do?" I asked not sure if Uncle Jared was on my side or not.

"Yes, and it sucks! I really like Harry but you need to know that I stand behind whatever decision you make, okay?" I always loved my Uncle Jared.

"Thanks Uncle. I have a date with Tom at noon and we are going to Bigfoot Pizza, I figured it was a safe place. And Cousin Dan is visiting me right now too." I said almost forgetting Dan was here.

"That's cool. Make sure to let him know as well would you. We don't need anyone getting caught up with these SMM Bigfoot Hunters before they leave town. It makes me nervous with so many Were's in town as well as Hunters. Okay Babygirl! Be safe! Love you!" Uncle Jared had to let others know what was going on as well.

"Okay Uncle, Love you too! Bye!" I said and then I hung up the phone to head back into the kitchen to let Dan know what was happening when Mongo heard someone at the door. Mongo was off like a shot heading to the front door. I looked at the clock and it was 11:45am. Where did the time go?

"Well at least the guy is early. That shows that he has respect for your time at least. Do you want me to answer the door?" Dan was saying as he slid off the chair and was heading to the door.

"Sure why not. I need to wash my hands anyway." I said heading to the kitchen sink. I heard the front door open and then the hesitation in Tom's voice.

"Is Carrie here?" Was all he asked but his tone in his voice was that of someone who thought he was going to be sent away.

"Yah, we haven't met. I'm her Cousin Dan from Lincoln City. Come on in she is in the kitchen washing her hands." Dan was saying and I could hear their voices coming closer to the kitchen, followed closely by Mongo sniffing him all the way into the kitchen.

"So, I'm new to all the different kinds of Were's. Can I ask you what you are?" Tom asked Dan as they same into the kitchen.

"Sure, I'm a Were-Orca. I would have changed with the group last night but I kind of need water to do that." Dan said joking with Tom to put him at ease. Even I could tell he was nervous.

"Hi Carrie! Sorry I'm a little early but I figured early is better than late especially in my line of work." He smiled at me and then just stood there on the other side of the island not knowing what he should do it seemed. He was dressed in a very nice pair of tight black jeans a button up dress shirt robin's egg blue and some very expensive looking cowboy boots that could have been alligator or some other kind of reptile. He did look good for a city boy and that is what he was compared to Harry.

"What line of work are you in Tom?" Dan asked him then offered him the chair that he was sitting in before that was right next to mine. Then I decided to walk back to and sit down and take a drink of tea.

"My brother's and I run a high security business called the Emerald City Security, we do mostly bodyguard and private security for famous people that come to Eugene to put on concerts and what not." He said with an almost but not quite bragging tone. He was obviously proud of what he does.

"That's pretty cool. How many brothers do you have?" Dan asked trying to keep the conversation going.

"I have 6 younger brothers." He said and then he looked at me, which made me realize that I hadn't offered him anything to drink, how rude of me.

"I'm sorry Tom, would you like something to drink? I have iced tea, some soda pop and milk." I said as I got up and grabbed another glass out of the cupboard.

"Iced tea would be great." Tom said as he appeared to have relaxed a little bit.

"Well Cuz, I think that I should head back up to your Grandparents house and wait on my Dad. They should be back anytime and that way you two can go on your date." Dan was saying as he once again left his chair. He walked around and gave me a huge hug.

"Walk me to the door?" Dan asked as he then shook Tom's hand.

"It was nice meeting you Tom. Please take good care of my little cousin." Dan said and then he and I walked around Tom and through the living room to the front door where of course Dan had to give me his advice before he left.

"He's a nice fellow and I don't get any bad vibes from him. I know you will make the best decision for you Cousin and not for anyone else. Be strong but also remember to have fun too." Dan leaned down and kissed my cheek then he was out the door stopping to pat Mongo on the head just before he left. I watched him get into his SUV and then I closed the door and headed back to the kitchen.

"So are you ready for lunch?" Tom asked as he stood up and took his cup to the sink and rinsed it. Then he put it into the dishwasher like he had been here before, or maybe he was just a guy who liked to keep things clean?

Even though I swear I just ate my breakfast I was actually hungry again. So I guess now we go on our first date to get some Pizza and see where it takes us from there.

## Chapter 27

So we left my house on our first date in Tom's black 2019 Cadillac Escalade SUV. It was very nice inside and I am sure it has more to do with his business than anything on why it was so fancy. It had all the bells and whistles. I didn't take Mongo's special car seat because Tom said he wouldn't need it with how comfortable the seats are in the back along with all the safety features built in.

"So this is rather nice." I said as I took in all the digital devices that seemed to be in every square inch of the SUV.

"Yah, we use these for clients. I figured that it would also work for keeping you and Mongo safe. Do you like it?" Tom asked with real interest.

"It's nice, I'm just not really into all the electronic gadgets is all." I said as I sat back and looked out the window as he pulled out of my driveway.

"They do come in handy sometimes with the stars that we are responsible for. And all the windows are bullet proof too." He said with a smile, like I need to be behind bullet proof glass?

"That's cool. I just prefer power over gadgets. Like this new truck they got for me to use at work, Big Ben! I just love that truck!" I know I get excited over that truck a little too much.

"So what is so special about Big Ben?" Tom asked as if he was really interested in what I had to say about my favorite truck.

"Well to start with Big Ben is the brand new 2019 DODGE RAM Big Horn Lone Star 4x4, with a 5.7L HEMI V8 and it's a CREWCAB in mint green. Which mint green is okay but if it was mine I think I would do a camo job to it!" I was getting excited about Big Ben again. I was so amazed Tom was smiling at me and I hadn't even realized that we had already pulled into the parking lot of Bigfoot Pizza already.

"And you drive a Toyota 4 runner in your off time huh?" Tom asked as he turned off the motor.

"Yah, she gets me places that some of the bigger trucks can't go. That is the only drawback of Big Ben and even this SUV. My 4 runner can go down some of the motor bike trails as well as a deer trail a time or two when I was chasing some poachers." I was happy to talk about things that I loved my trucks and my job were defiantly two of those things that brought a smile to my face.

"That sounds like a story I would like to hear some time. Are you ready to go inside?" Tom asked as Mongo got up from laying on the backseat and stepped down to the floorboard which had a lot of room for him to just stand there waiting for the side door to be opened for him.

"Sure, I think Mongo would like his pizza today too. Wouldn't you Mongo?" I said as I rubbed his head before climbing out of the SUV before Tom could run around to my side to let me out. He was trying to be chivalrous but I wasn't used to that from anyone but Harry. But I am not going to think about Harry right now. So I put a smile back on my face and then closed my door.

"So Mongo eats pizza too, huh?" Tom asked and since he couldn't help me out of my side he opened the door for Mongo to jump out instead.

Mongo was by my side in a second and then the three of us walked into Bigfoot pizza for a nice lunch.

"Yah my Dad makes a pizza that is just for dogs also. Mongo loves it; it has organic peanut butter and sweet potatoes and chicken on it. He doesn't share the recipe with anyone, he seems to think he can market it someday and maybe do a frozen dog pizza line and put it in the markets that cater to the fresh and frozen dog food market." I was saying as we walked in to the pizzeria. Mom was behind the counter when we came in. She remembered we were coming in for lunch and this was her chance to meddle a little bit. At least that is what I was thinking anyway.

"Hi, Mom. Did you get a chance to meet Tom last night?" I asked as a way of introduction.

"Not formally, no." She said as she held out her hand to shake.

"Please to meet you. I'm Janet; please call me Janet and her Dad is the pizza maker in the back. James will probably be bringing out your pizza so that the can meet you." Mom said and then looked down at Mongo.

"Mongo are you being a good boy?" Mom asked him and Mongo huffed at her and looked away. I know what he was saying, probably something like, 'Please I am always good.' Then my Mom laughed so I am sure it was something along those lines. Mongo looked up at me and winked. He was being a very good boy.

"So Mom, Mongo needs his usual. Tom, what kind of pizza do you like?" I asked him as I looked at the menu which I knew by heart.

"I'm good with anything except anchovies, I can't stand those things." Tom said as he made a funny face. He was kind of cute when he let himself relax.

"My favorite is a Hawaiian pizza. Is that okay with you?" I asked as I put the menu down to see his reaction.

"Sure that sounds great. Where do you want to sit?" Tom asked as he handed my Mom a $50-dollar bill. Which Mom handed back to him.

"Your money is no good here Tom. And I have a private booth reserved in the back with a dog bed next to it for you guys to have some privacy." Mom was feeling proud of herself right about now.

"Thank you Janet." Tom said and then he took me by the elbow to lead me back to the table. Do I look like I can't walk alone? Or do I look like a girl that needs a man to show her where to go? Calm down now, just calm down. Mongo bumped my leg to get my attention from staring at Tom's hand on my elbow. I looked up to see that he was realizing that he had done something wrong and let loose of my elbow. I was calmer and I put a smile back on my face because I know I was probably scowling.

"Mongo go ahead." Was all I said and Mongo started in the direction or our table with the reserved sign on it and the dog bed right next to it. You really couldn't miss it, the restaurant wasn't that big. Feeling like I might have over reacted I wrapped my arm though Tom's and we both started walking to the table. I was relaxing more and Tom was relaxing now as well. He had been tense when I first put my arm through his but it was probably because he realized I am not one of those City girls that like to be led places. I am not only a country girl but I am an independent woman with a mind of her own.

When we got to the table he led me to the side next to Mongo's bed where he was currently sitting. I sat down and then he went to the other side so that we were facing each other for a better conversation. Mongo then laid down knowing I was okay now.

"Sorry about that, I am used to being the one in charge of all situations. I haven't dated in a long time." Tom was being honest about his mess up and I guess I can't really be mad at him, he doesn't really know me yet.

"Sorry, I'm a country girl who is used to doing things on my own with Mongo. I don't really date either but I always thought it was because I was really picky about the guys. I don't date guys on vacation because I don't ever plan on leaving Oakridge, it is my home." I think I was sharing way too fast because Tom's face fell when I said that.

"I'm sorry; it's been a long time since I really dated too." I said in way of an apology.

"But I thought you were dating that other Were-Squatch who was staying with you?" Tom asked me. I just knew this was going to come up at some point on this date.

"Okay let me explain about my relationship with Harry before we go any further. I met Harry when his crew of Bigfoot Getters came here to film a show. I helped them to set up at Waldo lake and took them out on the hunts, where we wound up meeting you and your brothers. Then the chase and then you bit me which sent me to the hospital for a week." I don't know why but I showed Tom my hand where there is a small scar from his bite, it has been going away a lot faster than any other scar I have ever had. And then I continue my rant.

"That was my first week with Harry. The second week with Harry consisted of me and Harry staying home and watching movies because we had you and your brothers stocking me and my two friends because of this mating frenzy thing. The couple of times we did get to go out on a date the crew was with us for safety sake and you and your brothers still showed up and ruined that as well. So my dating history with Harry has basically been him cooking for me and watching movies at my house." I know I was getting louder when explaining what his impact on my life had been since meeting him and his brothers but I couldn't help it. My Mom and the council were fighting for Tom to have a fair chance to date me when Harry and I hadn't really gotten a fair chance either. By the time I was done I was breathing heavy and my body was starting to get warm again which meant I was starting to change.

"Carrie, I am so very sorry about all that I was just trying to get your attention the best way I knew how. Please calm down before you change in front of strangers." Tom's voice was calm and he started to get up and that's when I felt Mongo at my side. He started to climb up into my lap and lick my face. I started petting him and trying to keep my face away from his tongue.

"Mongo, no more kisses. I rubbed his ears with both my hands and then I rubbed my forehead against his. I was starting to calm down now. I was feeling cooler and breathing better now.

"I'm sorry I have upset you Carrie. I will take you home and let the council know that we are not compatible. I will go and cancel our order." Tom said as he turned with the saddest expression on his face I had ever seen, I could almost feel his sadness.

"Tom wait!" Mongo got down off of my lap and sat on the floor close to me.

"I'm sorry I had to rant. Let's start over again, okay?" Tom nodded his head and then he came over to stand in front of me again.

"You are a wonderful woman Carrie. Do you really wonder how I see that you are a beautiful, intelligent, exciting, passionate woman? My Squatch was attracted to you right away and that for me meant you were someone worth getting to know. I would love to start over and do this the right way with you." Tom leaned in and kissed my forehead. Nothing sexual or inappropriate, but sweet.

When Tom leaned back I could see my mom at the counter watching us. I smiled up at Tom and gave him a wink.

"At least we are both in human form this time." I said with a laugh. He smiled up at me and then he leaned down and whispered into my ear.

"And I must warn you, I bite." And when he leaned back I made sure to have a wide eyed expression on my face and then I said, "Yes I know! But this time I can bite back." Then I smiled and turned out of his arms to sit back down in our booth. It only took Tom a second then then he was sitting in his seat again smiling like someone who had just won something. I think I won this round, not him.

We sat and talked about our families until our pizzas came. Dad brought them both out to us so that he could meet Tom of course. He placed them on the table and Mongo was right there waiting for his slice of his pizza.

"Mongo you know you have to wait for it to cool." I was saying as Dad set them down smiling at me and then at Tom.

"Dad this is Tom Johnson." I said and they shook hands.

"Nice to finally meet you Tom. I hope you like my pizza as much as you liked biting my daughter." Dad said laughing at his own joke. It made me laugh too but Tom wasn't sure how to take it though.

"It's okay Tom you can laugh too. It's funny." I said and he then laughed a little, at least his smile was genuine.

"Sorry Tom I had to say it. At least we can laugh about it now, right buddy?" Dad was talking to Tom trying to convince him that it was funny.

"Sorry Dad that may have been too soon." I said with a smile.

"I will go now and let you too eat in peace. I hope you enjoy it Tom. Hope to see you again." Dad gave me a side hug and then he was off back to the kitchen to make pizzas for others. The place was starting to fill up fast, I hadn't really noticed until now.

As always Dad made a great pizza and Mongo is always happy with his. I gave Mongo his whole pizza just so he wouldn't keep bugging me so I could eat in peace as well and listen to Tom talk. He really did have a nice voice, it wasn't Scottish but it was nice none the less.

I learned that Tom's parents were born and raised in California and that his Grandma Carol was the Sasquatch that was the famous Patterson-Gimlin footage of bigfoot, take in October 20th, 1967 at Bluff Creek, California. I guess it was two days after the full moon and his Grandma Ester was looking for her husband who she had feared was going through a mating frenzy. Pretty funny huh? His Parents Norm and Nancy still lived in Willow Creek and they visited every year to see all of their boys here in Oregon.

I also learned that Tom is 30 years old and that each of his brothers are separated by two years. So Tom being 30 years old then that means that Frank is 28 years old, Gary would be 26 years old, Abel is 24 years old, Zeek is 22 years old, Kelly is 20 years old and Jeffery being the baby of the brothers would be 18 years old. Wow his parents had to have been super busy.

I told him about our families' heritage being the first Native Americans to make Oakridge our home all the way back to great-great Grandpa Henry Hunter. And all about the family that has dispersed and made homes within other tribes and became other kinds of Were's.

"Before we came here we had no idea there were other Were-Squatch's let alone other kinds of Were's. Our family has always stayed away from others and figured out things on our own. My Grandpa Calvin and Grandma Ester Johnson were the first of our Were-Squatch bloodline that we know of. They never talked about their lives before the family. We never got to know any cousins or relatives anywhere else. The council is going to look back in the records to see if they can find anyone of our family. I called my parents this morning and they were very excited to hear there were more of us and want to come to visit your family as well as to meet you of course." Tom was very excited and was way past the whole thing with my Dad, which means he doesn't hold a grudge; I guess he really is a nice guy.

We talked and talked for hours we talked so long that at some point my mom came and got Mongo to take him potty in the dog park across the parking lot in the corner. Dad had put it in especially for people traveling with dogs that way they would stop to eat somewhere that they could also let their dog go potty too. He really is a smart man, my Dad.

When my Mom brought Mongo back and took our empty pizza pans away I looked at my watch to see that it was after 6 o'clock. I was so shocked that Tom and I had been talking for more than 6 hours. Tom saw me look at my watch and then he looked at his in surprise as well.

"Wow I have never had a lunch date that lasted until dinner before." He said rather shocked.

"Me either. Do you want to go somewhere else to have dinner or are you hungry?" I asked him as Mongo got up and walked over to put his head in my lap.

"Can we please go home I need some outside running time please?" Mongo said in my head. I looked up at Tom and he was checking his phone, something I hadn't done at all while I was here. But I guess if anyone was trying to get ahold of me then I would have heard it, right?

"I don't know if you have noticed but being a Were, anything makes you hungry a lot more and we have to consume more calories than most people do. So my brothers and I always have protein bars and things with us at all times, plus we eat at least 4 times a day." Tom was saying but he hadn't answered my question yet. Was he trying to find an excuse to not be with me anymore today or was I just being paranoid? And do I care? Yes, I think I do, I think I like Tom. I'm not sure how I like Tom but I do like him so far.

"It's okay you can just take me home if you have something else going on." I said as I looked around the restaurant to see there were still quite a few people here, but I guess there would be since it is now dinner time.

"No, that's not it. I was just reading a text from my Mom, the council got ahold of them and they exchanged as much information as Grandma and Grandpa would give them. It seems that we also may be descendants of the Molalla Tribe but we are part of the seasonal workers that went to California and didn't return. So Your Grandfather the Chief is trying to make sure that we aren't related before you and I go any further with the Full moon coming?" He said as he looked at his phone and then set it down with a look of utter defeat on his face.

"Listen Tom, we can still get to know each other okay. If we are related, then we can look at it two ways. One we may be so far separated that it doesn't matter and two if it matters to either of us then at least we have gotten to know each other which is what family does anyway, right?" I was saying this but was I not sure that what I was saying was true for me? If I truly want Harry, then this could be my out? Now Tom was looking at me kind of funny.

"Carrie, it's just weird to think that the woman I have been having shall we say un-family like thoughts about could be related to me is really freaking me out. I think I will take you home but I would like to come and get you tomorrow night. I want to take you into Springfield to go and watch a movie and have dinner, like a real date. Hopefully my parents and the council can find out what they need to before then?" Tom was trying to be hopeful.

"I was thinking that we should do something different but close to that. How about you come over for dinner and watch a movie at my house? I will cook or I can have some of the guys that work for the food truck bring us in something for dinner? They love me!" I was going to have some research done by Amanda when I got home tonight. I needed to know for myself if this could be the loophole I was hoping for. Was I hoping for it after spending this time getting to know him? My head was spinning right now, I just needed to get home with my Mongo and relax.

"Okay but on one condition. I will bring you dinner and then we can watch a movie. Would you like me to bring a movie or do you have one in mind?" Tom was trying to take more control of the situation; being the oldest son he was probably more the Alpha of the group, which I fear that I too am an Alpha as well.

"Harry and the Henderson's?" I asked jokingly and Tom actually laughed too. He really was a nice guy.

"Let's not do that one. Do you enjoy action movies or spy movies?" Tom was trying to see what kind of movies we had in common I see.

"How about an action hero movie? I would love to see that Aquaman movie!" I said knowing that most women in American wanted to see that movie just to see Jason Momoa, and I am definitely one of them. Tom kind of smiled; he knew what I was doing too.

"So I am guessing you like Jason Momoa?" Tom asked me with a grin on his face.

"Yes I do. He was awesome in the Game of Thrones but I think his best work was in Stargate Atlantis. I loved that show, my Dad bought the whole series on DVD and I used to steal them to watch them so much that my Dad bought me my own copies." I said giggling as I remembered the good old days when life was easier.

"I remember that series, I forgot he was in it. Okay I will bring over Aquaman if we can watch some of the Stargate Atlantis DVD's too. Deal?" Tom reached across the table to get me to shake his hand to seal the deal. I reached my hand out to meet his and when our hands touched there was an electric shock but not the kind that hurt it was a little tingly and kind of gave me goose bumps.

"Wow that was weird. You got a deal Tom." I said as I took my hand back, it still tingled.

"Okay so I better get you home then. Did you want to stop and getting anything to take home for dinner being so late or are you good to go?" Tom was asking as we both slid out of the booth. Mongo was up and ready to go.

"No, I'm good to go. I have things at home to make and the food truck basically is in my backyard, so I'm good." I was starting to ramble now. Why did I feel like I didn't want the date to end now? Was it because he may be unattainable if we are related? What the hell is wrong with me?

Tom, Mongo and I started heading for the door when we saw my Mom coming our around the counter to say good bye to us. She gave me a hug.

"I hope you guys had fun, you seemed to be." She said looking from me to him and then back again.

"Yes we have a great time! Thank you Janet." Tom said as he held out his hand for her to shake but alas my Mom is a hugger, so she pushed his hand aside and went in for a hug. Tom froze for a second then he hugged her back. Mom finally let him go and then she turned around and went back behind the counter again.

"You kids have a good night and be good!" Then she went into the kitchen and we couldn't see her anymore.

"Is your Mom always like that?" Tom asked as he put his hand on my lower back to lead me out the door with Mongo leading the way.

"Yup, pretty much." I said and giggled a little to myself.

"Okay then, subject change. How do you think this date was in a scale of 1 to 10?" Tom was asking as he opened my door and then the door for Mongo. I climbed up inside and turned to see him waiting for an answer. Mongo hopped up on the seat and laid down and Tom closed the back door, still waiting for my answer.

"I will tell you once you get me home safely." I said with a very mischievous smile.

"I'm not sure what that smile means but I'm liking it!" He said as he closed my door and hurried around to climb in behind the wheel.

It didn't take long to get back home. We made small talk until we pulled into the driveway and he parked the SUV and jumped out to let Mongo and I out. I let him get my door this time, it didn't hurt to let a guy do things for me every once in a while and if he was raised with good manners then who am I to discount him for them.

He opened my door and held out his hand for me to take to get out. Then he opened mongo's door and he pretty much bolted out of there and ran into his front yard potty area. He never even said he had to go. Tom walked me up to the door and waited as I unlocked it. One it was open I turned around to find Mongo running straight for us. Tom grabbed me and turned me out of the way as Mongo ran into the house.

"I have no clue what has gotten into him!" I said as we both turned our heads to see where he went in the house.

"POOP!" Mongo said very loudly in my head. He almost slammed into the back sliding glass door, now I know he had to poop and he didn't want to do it in the front yard.

"I need to let him out the back yard door. Do you want to come in for a minute?" I asked even though I knew he was in a hurry to get somewhere else, I just didn't know where and I kind of wanted to know.

"I'll wait right here while you go and let him out." Tom said as he opened the door a little more for me to go in.

"Okay." I walked in and went straight to the door and opened it for Mongo. I left it open so that he could come back in after he was done. I walked back to the front porch where I left Tom. He was looking at his phone again and seemed to be a little nervous.

"Well, I had a good time tonight and I look forward to seeing you tomorrow. Do you know what time you will be here?" I said as I stood just outside the door. Tom put his phone back in his pocket and then walked right up to stand I front of me not leaving very much space in between us. I barely had time to think.

"I would like to be here at 5 o'clock if that's okay? Do you need me to bring you anything else?" He asked looking me in the eyes and then he looked at my lips which made me lick them to see if there was something on them. Tom let out a groan then looked me in the eyes again.

"Nothing I can think of." Was all I managed to get out before Tom did what I didn't think he would after the information the council had found out so far. If we were related, then was this his saying he didn't care? He kissed me thoroughly, it started a little soft but then I think I made a noise because he then increased the pressure and then his arms went around me and somehow mine went around him. It was like I was in high school again, kissing on the porch knowing that someone could catch us at any time.

There was a spark, I won't lie. The same one that had happened when he touched my hand after dinner but this time in was in my lips and I know he felt it too. The goose bumps were traveling up and down my whole body. It felt so good but it also felt so much different than when Harry kissed me. And that's when it stopped affecting me, I thought of Harry and the toe curling lust inducing kisses he and I shared. It was like a bucket of cold water hit me and I stopped the kiss. We parted a little and he and I just stared into each other's eyes.

"Wow, did you feel that spark too?" Tom asked breathing hard as he put a little more distance between us.

"Yes, I have never felt that before. Have you?" I was breathing hard; I hadn't noticed until now and I usually knew what my body was doing.

"Are you guys done yet?" Mongo asked in my head which made me jump out of Tom's arms all the way.

"Mongo talks to you, doesn't he?" Tom asked as he looked down at Mongo and then back to me.

"Yes, do you have any animals that talk to you too?" I asked as he pulled out his phone and looked at it again.

"Only once I've transformed into my sasquatch form in the woods. The animals that aren't afraid of us will talk to us but I didn't know that a pet could do that too." Tom said putting his phone back into this pocket again.

"Tom, is everything okay? Are you waiting on a call or something?" I was kind of irritated that he kept looking at his phone but if it was something important them maybe I could help?

"My brother's didn't listen to me today. While I was with you they left me a message that they were going into the woods to change and relax. But after your Uncle Jared said to be careful because the SMM Bigfoot Hunters are running around out there then I am worried about them, I don't know what to do." Tom was seriously nervous and you could tell that he was not used to asking for help or his brother's not listening to him either.

"Hang on and let me call my Uncle Jared to see if he knows where the SMM Bigfoot Hunters are right now. I have a feeling that the Deputies are keeping an eye on them." I said as I pulled my phone out of my pocket and dialed Uncle Jared. He answered on the second ring.

"Hello Babygirl! Everything okay with you?" Uncle Jared sounded a little worried; I guess I don't call him as often as I should.

"I hope not Uncle. Do you happen to know where the SMM Bigfoot Hunters are right now? Tom's brothers went out into the woods to change and relax and he's worried about them." I said as quickly as I could.

"Yes I know where they all are right now. The SMM Bigfoot Hunters just tried to get onto your Grandpa's land again so they are all sitting in squad cars. As for Tom's brothers they are also on your Grandpa's land and they are safe. They will be heading back to the hotel to meet up with Tom in a few minutes. Your Grandpa gave them permission to change here but apparently they go to close to the Forest service land that butts up against your Grandpa's land in the back and the SMM Bigfoot Hunters saw them rough housing and tried to shoo them. Everyone is fine and the SMM Bigfoot Hunters are going to jail for trespassing and for trying to shoot the brothers while they were playing in monkey suits on private land. That way it's not up to your Grandpa and they will be sent to the courthouse in Eugene for their trial and all that. No more worries about them now." Tom heard everything you just said sorry Uncle had to put you on speaker phone because that was just too much to repeat.

"Thanks Sheriff for all your help. Let my brother's know I will be waiting for them when they get back." Tom said as he hugged me really quick.

"I will see you tomorrow. Bye!" And then headed to his SUV obviously preoccupied with his brothers and the trouble they almost had gotten into.

"Hey Tom!" I yelled while covering the phone so that my Uncle couldn't hear me.

"I'd say it was a 9 but the ending needs improvement!" I yelled and smiled at him, his face lit up and he smiled too. Then he waved and jumped into his SUV and was gone with a wave. I uncovered the phone and put it back to regular mode and up to my ear.

"Thanks Uncle Jared.  Love you."  I said as I started walking into the house.

"Welcome, Babygirl.  Love you too. Bye!"  Then Uncle Jared hung up as I closed my front door to a very lonely house.

# **Chapter 28**

Mongo and I curled up on the couch to watch a little TV when there was a knock on the Glass sliding door.  Mongo didn't bark or run to the door but got off of me and walked slowly into the kitchen so I knew it was probably one of the girls.  When I got to the door and moved the curtain aside I found both Amanda and Trina standing at the door waiting.  I unlocked the door and opened it for them to come in.   Both girls had smiles on their faces that disappeared when they saw Mongo and I looking so glum.  We watched Mongo sniff each of the girls then headed back to the living room and crawled into his bed next to the fireplace and went to sleep.  Then they looked at me.

"What's wrong with him?  And what's wrong with you?"  Amanda asked as she headed for the kitchen.

"Do you have something to drink or do you need a glass of tea?" Amanda asked as she went to the cupboard and grabbed three glasses when I shook my head.

"So answer the questions, please!"  Trina said as she took me by the arm and pulled me back into the living room and sat me on the couch.

"I really can't explain what is wrong with me right now. As for Mongo I think the poor guy is having Harry withdrawals. Either that or he is sensing what I am feeling that is majorly confused." I was saying when Amanda handed me a glass of iced tea and then she gave Trina one as she sat down on the coffee table facing Trina and I.

"Okay that really doesn't explain anything. So what happened on the lunch date?" Trina asked as she set her glass on the coffee table next to Amanda.

"Well, the date went pretty good I thought. We ate pizza and talked for hours, we hadn't even noticed the time until it was after 6 o'clock. We learned so much about each other's families and then he had to look at his phone, which he had on silent for the whole time we were at the Pizzeria. Which I thought said something about how he was willing to focus just on me, right?" I know I was starting to ramble and they did ask me what happened, didn't they?

"Yes, shutting off his phone was showing you he was taking you seriously." Trina said. She and Amanda seemed to be on the edge of their seats listening to me so I went on.

"Then he looks at his phone and there are texts from the council. It's not bad enough that they were making me date him but then they do this background check into his family and they tell him that he may or may not be to me. What the hell!" I wasn't very happy and I was starting to get a little more stressed out.

"Which if you wanted an out this would be a perfect excuse, right?" Trina asked me.

"That is something that I have already asked myself and now that it is a possibility I am upset that it is yet another thing that may be out of my control and not my choice!" I was getting louder I know but I was actually stressed about this. Mongo got out of his bed and walked over to me and put his head in my lap. He knew I was stressed too, poor guy. I rubbed his ears.

"I'm okay Mongo, go back and lay down. I am fine." Mongo went back to his bed and laid down again.

"Okay so what happened after he told you that you might be related? Did he bale or try to get past it?" Amanda asked scooting toward me a little bit more and taking my hand to keep me calm.

"Well we talked about the options if they do find that we are related." I said as then took a deep breath and exhaled.

"Okay and they would be what exactly?" Trina asked as she took my other hand.

"Well, if Tom's family and my family are related then it would be so far back that the blood lines would be different, which is option one. Option two is at least we found family and we can still get to know each other just not in a romantic way. Which I am fine with either way, shouldn't I be?" I was so confused right now.

"Sure you should be. But how did he react to what you said?" Amanda asked me.

"That's even more confusing. We agreed to get to know each other and then we shook hands. Which there was this weird spark between us that wasn't electricity but it sort of was electricity. It's hard to explain other than it gave me this warm feeling and then goose bumps." I was getting goose bumps now just thinking about it and the girls saw them too.

"So, then what?" Trina asked breathlessly.

"Then we decided to end the date because his brothers did something stupid. So he brought me home, but once we left the Pizzeria he acted interested in me again, being all flirty and stuff and even set up another date with me for tomorrow night. A movie and dinner here at my house." I was still rather confused about it still.

"Then when he brought me home he told me he was worried about his brothers they were out in the woods running as Squatch's and the SMM Bigfoot Hunters were still in the area, which made him really worried. So I called Uncle Jared and found out that his brothers were here on Grandpa's land because Grandpa thought it would be safer for them but then the SMM Bigfoot Hunters were also caught here on the land trying to shoot the brothers who were roughhousing in the back of the property next to the Forest Service land." I was stressing about that all over again.

"Well as the oldest brother I bet Tom was really stressed out about finding that out. What happened then?" Amanda asked.

"Well Uncle Jared arrested the SMM Bigfoot Hunters and they are being sent to Eugene to go to court and be held in their jail because they actually shot at the brothers this time. Uncle Jared convinced them that the brothers were roughhousing in monkey suits or something like that. And that they had almost killed real people. So we will see how that plays out." I wasn't sure what Tom was going to do to his brothers either since they disobeyed him either but I wasn't going to say that out loud.

"Okay and then what happened with Tom?" Amanda was really on the edge of her seat wanting to know everything that happened. You would think that I lived in a soap opera or something.

"Well, did I mention that Tom kissed me?" I asked feeling a little embarrassed.

"NO!" Trina and Amanda both exclaimed.

"Well when he dropped me off after we made plans to see each other again, we were saying good bye and well he went to hug me and then he kissed me. You know that spark of warmth and goose bumps that this handshake gave me?" I was starting to feel a tingle again.

"Yah." Both Amanda and Trina responded breathlessly.

"Well I got it again when he kissed me. That warm, electrical, sparky, goose bumpy feeling all though my body. Is that weird?" I asked them both but hey seemed to be in a daze.

"Then I was thinking how I was enjoying this kiss and then I started comparing that kiss to Harry's kiss. Then I realized that Harry's kisses made my toes curl and lust run though me and then all of a sudden Tom's kiss wasn't goose bumpy anymore. Which made my brain go all haywire and I stopped the kiss right there. Do you think I should have done anything differently?" I asked Trina and Amanda both. They looked at each other and then at me and where we were all still holding hands.

"Um, Carrie? I don't know about Trina but I was actually feeling the sensations you were just describing through your hand. I mean I actually felt the goose bumps and then the toe curling, everything!" Amanda was getting a little overly excited telling us. The whole time Trina was nodding her head.

"I felt it all too. Wow girl you are really not only emotionally sensitive but you can transfer it to others through touch too?" Trina had this amazed look on her face.

"I had no clue I could do that." I looked at both of them blinking my eyes and trying to focus.

"Wow, you were feeling all of that? No wonder you are drained right now. Yes, I can feel that too." Amanda was saying as she stared at our hands.

"So, what do I do now? I'm confused, he didn't actually say he wasn't going to pay attention to what the council found out and he also didn't say that we were going to be just friends right now either. Because I know friends do not kiss like that, at least not any of my friends." I was trying to make a joke of it but Trina and Amanda just looked at each other.

"Carrie honey, we have been friends for a long time and this feeling your emotions through holding your hands is definitely a new thing. That being said we can also feel how confused and upset you are right now too." Amanda said just as Mongo made his way over and put his head back into my lap. I looked down at him and let go of the girl's hands to rub his ears.

"I can feel it from across the room." Mongo said in my head.

"I'm sorry guys. I know you didn't come over here to see me in such a wreck." Rubbing Mongo's ears actual made me feel better though. But just touching Mongo always seemed to do that.

"That is what I am here for. Protect and help you." Mongo said in my head. Then I looked at my friends again.

"So, how about we forget your day and get some food and watch some movies just us girls and Mongo? We are staying the night again by the way." Amanda said in her no nonsense tone.

"All righty then. Oh, wait I almost forgot. Amanda do you think you can do some digging and see if you can find out whether or not Tom is related to me. I know the council is checking into it but I would feel better if you looked into it too? Okay, now who is making dinner I am starved and so is Mongo." I said and Mongo woofed and backed up a little so that I could stand up.

"I can do that first thing tomorrow. For now, we are getting dinner." Amanda and Trina both stood before I did and held out their hands to help me up off that couch and out of my pity frame of mind. These were my friends and they were always here for me no matter what.

"I will take orders and go out to the food truck and get our dinner. Mongo, do you want to go with me?" Trina was saying as she headed to the small desk at the far end of the living room and got out paper and a pen to write down what we wanted for dinner. Mongo gave her a woof and then stood beside me, basically telling her he wasn't leaving my side.

"Okay then but I am sure Harry is out there getting dinner as we speak." Trina said looking between Mongo and I.

"You can go and see him if you want to go and see him Mongo." I told Mongo as I took the pen and paper and wrote what I wanted to eat.

"Will you be okay without me? I will not say anything about your date with Tom." Mongo said in my head and I smiled.

"I know Mongo. Go and say hi to Harry. Tell him I said hi too." I gave Amanda the paper so she could write down what she wanted and then I got down on my knees and hugged Mongo. He was my fur baby, my little boy and he wanted to see the guy that had somehow become like a father figure to him. Life is funny sometimes.

"Okay I got the order; Mongo are you ready to go?" Trina slid the door open and Mongo took one more look at me then he ran out the door not waiting for Trina to follow him. It made me smile.

Amanda and I got out the TV trays and set them up in front of the couch and then we looked through the movies and picked, "Big trouble in little china" for while we were eating and then so that we could all have a good cry Amanda chose, "P.S. I love you" with Gerard Butler in it. All of us love that movie and cry pretty much all the way through it. Crying is a good stress reliever isn't it?

Trina brought the food back within a few minutes and Mongo was definitely in a better mood.

"Harry says hi back." Mongo said in my head as he ran into the house and sat by his food dish waiting for his dinner as well.

"That was fast." Amanda said as she walked into the kitchen to help Trina get some plates down so that we could eat. Trina got our glasses out of the living room and refilled them with new ice and tea while Amanda told her what movies we picked.

"Perfect!" Was all she said and then we took our food into the living room after I gave Mongo his.

"Well, you may have had a weird date today but at least you are ending the evening with us! We love you Carrie!" Amanda said and we all clinked glasses before we started the movie and ate or wonderful dinner thanks to the great cooks from the Bigfoot Getters crew.

"To the Bigfoot Getters, without them we would have had a very boring life right now." I said and we clinked our glasses again. I pushed play on the remote. At least this evening will still be fun and I am with people I love. This made me think about Harry for a minute, which also made me smile.

"There she goes again. Watch the movie and lose yourself in it girl. Quit thinking!" Amanda said and then she took a bite of her dinner which I soon followed. Let tomorrow be tomorrow while I am in today. Kurt Russell and Gerard Butler here I come!

## **Chapter 29**

The next morning, I woke up refreshed and ready to start my day, even though it was a Monday. Once again I woke up to find Mongo alone in bed because the girls got up early and headed to the trailers to do whatever they do during the day to help with the show. I do know that the Bigfoot Getters had to have their episode done and ready to air in 2 weeks, so just after the full moon, but other than that I have been out of the loop.

I jumped into the shower and left Mongo to sleep on the bed. I never take very long in the shower anyway. When I was done I dried off and brushed my hair then put it up in a ponytail so it was out of my way. Then I went into the bedroom and put on some comfy jeans and a green t-shirt. Then I put on my comfy socks and sneakers before I went into the bathroom and put on a light amount of makeup. I never go overboard with makeup, just not my thing.

When I was done putting myself together for the day I woke Mongo and we headed into the kitchen. Mongo went out to go potty while I made us breakfast and we ate quietly. I checked my phone but had no messages and feeling bad about not being at work I decided to give Johnny a call. His cell rang only twice and then he answered.

"Hey, what's up?" Johnny asked and he sounded like he was worried or something.

"Not much, is everything okay with you and the office?" I asked him as I sat down on the couch to talk.

"Everything is good. We found out that it was Monica that contacted the SMM Bigfoot Hunters and told them about the Bigfoot Getters being out on a hunt that night. She was dating Jed Monroe. She is now fired and I heard is currently in jail with the whole bunch of the SMM Bigfoot Hunters because they were shooting at your friend Tom's brothers up on your Grandpa Hunter's property. I'm glad you weren't out there this time. How are you feeling?" Johnny could talk forever; he hardly took a breath while telling me the latest.

"I'm doing okay. At least we know now that the SMM Bigfoot Hunters are out of commission and can't hurt anyone else for a while." I said as I was trying to think of a way to ask what exactly my Mom had told him.

"That's good to hear. So obviously your Mom told you that she talked to me about you needing this week off as well." Johnny was always on point when it came to reading people.

"Yes she did. What exactly did she tell you?" I wanted to be cautious with what I told him, I still wasn't sure who knew what and how much about what has happened to me and about my family.

"Well, it doesn't sound like she told you everything that she and I talked about you." Johnny was stalling.

"No not really, Mom has left a lot of things out of conversations that we have had lately." I know I was being cryptic but he also knew my mom.

"Okay Carrie, let me tell you right now that I know everything that your Mom knows. Does that help?" Johnny was trying to be blunt but he wasn't quite there.

"Nope you need to be more specific because I have had a lot of revelations lately about me and my family and I really need to know what Mom told you." I was starting to get upset and I really didn't need that right now.

"Okay Carrie, you know that I have known your Mom for a long time, right?" Johnny asked me.

"Yes." What else was I to say?

"Then I am going to tell you something that I have known since I was a teenager. I know all about your family and your heritage as Were-Squatch's as well as your Native American heritage. I found out when your Mom changed in front of me and your Grandpa Hunter took me into your family and shared the secrets with me. That is also part of why I am your boss as well as your friend. We all knew you were very much into the woods even though you were not a Were-Squatch at birth but now that you are it's an even better job for you. Please don't hate me Carrie." I could hear what he was saying and it was slowly sinking in. Johnny knew about me before I knew about me. I guess the best way to explain it would be to say I was in shock.

"Wait, what? You don't mean to say that the only reason I got my job was because of my Were-Squatch family history do you? Because I went to school and I got good grades to be able to do this job. This is a job that I have always wanted this is my dream job Johnny!" I know I was freaking out but maybe I was misunderstanding what he was saying.

"No I am not telling you that is why you got the job! You were the best candidate for this job, grades and all. I am just saying that this was the perfect job for you and that is just a bonus to why you have the job. I am not only a friend of your family but I am your friend too. And I always will be. You are my best employee and then I trust you more than I do a lot of people. I guess what I am really saying is that your job is yours; you will never have to worry about it. Do what you need to this week and I hope to see you at the full moon ceremony, yes I have been invited. It is pretty much a Were-wedding isn't it? I have to go before I get you anymore upset and your Mom kicks my butt. Talk to you later!" Johnny was trying to get off the phone as quickly as possible. I was seeing meanings in this conversation that weren't truly there. Have I lost it?

"Wait! Were-wedding? What are you talking about Johnny?" I was really confused.

"I thought you understood what the choice was that you were making? You have to choose between Harry and Tom at the full moon ceremony Carrie. Either Harry to mate with for life or with Tom because he is the one that bit you. You are choosing your mate for life either way. I have to go Carrie. Call your Mom if you have more questions or your Grandpa Hunter. Bye." And Johnny hung up, what the hell was going on that I didn't understand what my deciding was all about?

"Holy Shit! I am choosing a husband!" I yelled out loud to no one in particular. It just fricking hit me.

"I thought you were taking this a little too lightly!" Mongo said in my head. I jumped off the couch and spun around to see him sitting next to the sliding glass door.

"You scared me mongo! I thought I was alone." I sat back down with my thoughts.

"I know that's the way it used to be when we couldn't talk. But you were never alone, I was always here for you." Mongo said in my head and then he came over and jumped up on the couch and laid his head in my lap. Wow, my decision just took on a whole nother level!


The rest of the day I worked on cleaning the house. It was only Mongo and I and we didn't really make that much of a mess. I did notice that the girls took their clothes bags with them this time so I'm not sure if they were coming back her to sleep again or not. I did the dishes, the laundry, vacuuming and finally the dusting. It just felt good to be doing things even if it was cleaning.

After all that was finished Mongo and I had a quick lunch and then I started folding all the clothes. My day went rather fast and I kept my head clear of thinking anything too deep while I was doing it. I watched some old episodes of CSI and I loved trying to figure things out while they did. I left the sliding door cracked open for Mongo to be able to run in and out so he could play in the yard. It was a warm day; spring was defiantly in the air today.

I decided to take another shower after all the cleaning I did today so at 3:30pm I went into the bathroom and did just that. I stood under the water and just enjoyed myself for a little while. When I was done I stepped out into the bathroom and brushed my hair but left it down. I did my makeup just the usual amount and then I headed into my bedroom to dress. Mongo came running into the bedroom and jumped up on the bed.

"Are you having fun?" I asked him when he turned in a circle on the top of the comforter 5 times before settling down.

"Yes, Harry played with me. He tossed my favorite ball and a stick for me too. Then he went back to his trailer. I think he was trying to see you through the door but you never came out." Mongo said in my head and it made me want to cry. He was following the rules of not seeing me and I was too without even thinking about it. I could have looked out the window a time or two but I was just so focused on not thinking about either one of them that I missed my chance to see him.

"Well, I guess I will try to be by a window more often. I got all the housework done and I have showered and am getting ready for my date with Tom." I said to Mongo as I went to my dresser to figure out what to wear. I never had to think about what to wear when I was with Harry, it was more natural.

I grabbed another pair of jeans out of my drawer; they were still warm from the dryer too. I put them on over my matching bra and panties set, not that Tom was going to see them. Then I pulled out my gray t-shirt with the green shamrock on the front that said 'You pinch, I punch' written on the front. That always made me smile. Then I put my socks and sneakers on. This may be a date but we are having a home date and this is the same kind of clothes that Harry saw me in; Tom was not getting any special treatment from me. And with that I went through the living room and into the kitchen to see what I was going to do about dinner.

I refilled my iced tea and then I decided to call Amanda and see if she had any updates for me and also to see if she would bring Mongo, Tom and I dinner. She answered on the 3$^{rd}$ ring.

"Hey lady I thought you would be calling me earlier than now?" Amanda said in her way of a greeting.

"I was cleaning my house all day. Did you find anything out for me?" I asked her as I sat down in the chair at the kitchen island.

"I actually haven't found much, which is weird to say the least. I could only track his family back to his Grandparents that he talked to you about, but I can't find anyone after that without more information from Tom. Maybe his family changed their last names at some point?" Amanda was saying and then it sounded like she covered her phone and was talking to someone.

"I know you're not supposed to have any contact with Harry right now but he wanted me to tell you that he is still here. And he hopes you aren't too upset that he was playing with Mongo earlier and that he wasn't doing it just to get your attention." Amanda was repeating Harry; I could hear him in the background.

"Tell Harry that I know he is and that Mongo already told me. He can play with him anytime and that Mongo had fun." I wanted to talk to him but I wasn't sure what would happen if we broke the rules.

"Does Harry know what you are doing for me?" I asked her not sure if I wanted to know or not.

"Yes, he wanted to help." She said and she sounded like she was moving.

"Okay. So I also wanted to get your help on something else as well if you can spare a few minutes?" I said as I heard the sound of a door closing. Then there was a tap on the sliding glass door.

"Can I come in so we can talk face to face please?" Amanda said just before she hung up the phone and walked in the door.

"Hey, that was fast." I said as she came in and sat down beside me.

"I had to get out of the trailer. Harry was right there trying to hear everything we said. I know he's going through a lot and so are you but he is really depressed. Terry said it's hard to get him to pay attention to anything that they need to get done for the show." Amanda was saying, she needed to vent too I guess.

"So what's going on with the show stuff?" I asked to keep the conversation going while I got up the nerve to ask her to get dinner from the food truck for Mongo, Tom and I.

"So, Terry, Harry and Jerry plus the crew and Trina and I are going out to the back of your Grandpa's property tonight to get some more sound bites and a little more nighttime filming done for the show. So they won't be around until late night. Terry said he really needs Harry to focus on his job right now. And it's also good because that way he isn't sitting around here watching and listening to you having a date here either." Amanda was right about that.

"I hadn't even thought about what Harry would be doing during the time that Tom is here in my house with me on a date." It was definitely and OMG moment on my part.

"I know you have a lot to think about right now." Amanda said as she took a drink from my glass.

"So all you did was cleaning today?" Amanda asked me as she looked around.

"Wow pretty clean in here!" She said with a whistle.

"I also called Johnny and found out some more information that my Mom failed to make sure that I understood." I said as I started to explain everything that Johnny had said to me as well as the fact that I was making the decision of a lifetime, a Were-wedding basically. Amanda was so awe struck that her mouth literally fell open and she was speechless.

"I know right?" I said as she just sputtered to think and talk at the same time.

"Oh and I need to ask a favor of you too. Do you think that you could bring me dinner so that I don't have to cook? I will need enough for Mongo, Tom and I. What do you say old buddy old pal?" I asked her giving her s light punch in the shoulder.

"Yes, I can do that for you. Do you know what you want?" Amanda asked as she slid out of her chair.

"No, just get whatever their special is for Tom and I and Mongo gets a burger patty and a bowl of fruit. Do you want me to write it down?" I asked as she stopped at the sliding glass door.

"Nope I got it; I'll be back in a few minutes. Do you need anything else?" She asked as she slid out the door.

"No that's all. Thank you Amanda!" I went to the kitchen cupboard and pulled out two plates and set them on the counter then I pulled down one glass and set it next to the plates. I gathered silverware and napkins and set them on the counter as well. I know I was just doing things to keep myself busy but what else was I to do? Now that I know that Harry won't be around tonight kind of felt weird. We were going to be unsupervised tonight and I wasn't sure I was ready for that.

About 20 minutes later at almost 5 o'clock, the time that Tom said he would be here Amanda came back and knocked on the sliding glass door. I opened it and took one of the boxes that she had been carrying.

"Wow this is a lot of food!" I said as I took it into the kitchen following Amanda.

"I know, when Mike and Stephen heard the food was for you and a guest they made you something special and made me promise to tell you that they would like you to tell them how they did tomorrow over breakfast. They miss you is what Mike said." Amanda said with a smile and a little giggle.

"So what did they make?" I asked as I opened up the first box to find perfectly steamed broccoli cauliflower and carrots with a light butter and garlic. The second box had perfectly grilled teriyaki chicken breasts with a small container of extra sauce and the last box held the sweet pineapple rice that Mike's Mom makes at her Hawaiian BBQ restaurant in Springfield. And there was Mongo's fruit salad bowl with two hamburger patties in the last box. My mouth was watering now and my tummy was starting to rumble too. That's when mongo came running into the kitchen from where he had been sleeping on the bed. He could smell the food too.

"Wow they really went all out for me. Did you tell them thank you for me?" I asked Amanda as I set the boxes in the oven with her help so that they would stay warm.

"Yes I did and they said you have to come for breakfast to repay them. Period!" Amanda said as she started heading to the door again to leave me.

"Let them know I will be there in the morning. And thank you Amanda I really appreciate this." I said as I gave her a hug and she hugged me back. Then she slipped through the sliding glass doorway and was gone.

## Chapter 30

With Amanda gone, I was left standing in my kitchen smelling some really yummy food.

"Tom should be here soon Mongo, do you want to wait and eat when we do or do you want dinner now?" I asked him as he sat next to his food dish. Then he looked toward the front door and took off.

"So, Tom is here now? I'm coming too!" I said following Mongo through the living room to answer the front door before Tom even knocked. He was walking up with a plastic bag in one hand and a bouquet of pink roses in the other and a huge smile on his face. He was wearing a green U of O polo shirt with what looked like brand new jeans. His boots were the same cowboy boot but they seemed to have a nice thick sole instead of the regular slick bottom. Probably, so that he could run in them if he had to. He was a handsome man but he was a different handsome than Harry, it's hard to explain how. And then he gives me this look with a twinkle in his eye.

I know how this looked; I had the door open before he got to it to knock so it looked like I was so excited he was here that I couldn't wait to open the door for him. I'm not sure that I feel that way at all though, but do I correct what he may be thinking or let it go? If I say something then it might upset him plus, I really don't want any drama tonight either.

Mongo sat next to me in the doorway and didn't move until I stepped aside for Tom to come in the house.

"Well, hello!" Tom said in a very good mood and he even leaned over to kiss my cheek as he walked in the door, and yes the kiss sparked on my cheek. I felt it and I know he did too because he leaned back a little pretty quickly after the spark. Then he handed me the roses and winked at me.

"Hello and Thank you. I haven't gotten flowers let alone roses in a very long time, if you don't count the hospital, which I don't." I said and laughed a little which made Tom laugh as well.

"Nice place, mmmm something smells good." Tom said as he followed me through the living room and into the kitchen.

"Thanks. Yah my friend Amanda brought us food from the food truck. They guys made it special for me. I hope you like Hawaiian BBQ?" I said as he set the bag on the kitchen island. I could tell there was a movie in the bag but it also looked like there was candy too. Tom saw me looking at the bag and smiled.

"I brought the movie and I also grabbed some junior mints and some red vines for the movie. I figured you probably already had the popcorn." He said with a wink.

"I do have the popcorn. How did you know?" I asked as I grabbed the two glasses and started filling them with ice for the tea.

"I just figured if you loved watching movies then you would also have the popcorn for watching said movies. I am a smart cookie sometimes." Tom said as he sat in one of the chairs at the island.

"So, I have a question." I said as I poured the tea and handed him a glass.

"Okay, shoot." Tom said and then took a sip.

"Do you want to eat first and then watch the movie or watch the movie while we eat? I have TV trays that we can set up in the living room." I said as I went to start pulling the food out of the oven where I was keeping in warm.

"I haven't eaten and watched a movie in a long time. Let's do that, sounds like fun!" Tom smiled and then he got out of the chair and came to help me with the food.

It didn't take us but a few minutes to make our plates and I also gave Mongo his dinner before we headed to the living room. I set mine on the coffee table and went to grab the TV trays but when I turned around Tom was there to take them from me. He just smiled.

"I'll take them and set them up." Tom tried to take both but I only let go of one.

"It's okay, I can set mine up." So Tom let go of mine and we walked to the couch together. We set up the trays and then I got up to put the movie into the DVD player after he had unwrapped it. He bought a brand new copy and it looked like he got it from the store here in town.

Once I got the player set up and made sure the surround sound was set and then we were in business. Tom took a bite of the pineapple rice.

"This stuff is really good. And this is Hawaiian BBQ huh? Can I get this anywhere else besides the food truck?" Tom asked and I paused the beginning of the movie so that I could respond without having to yell.

"Yah, there is a restaurant in Springfield that is Hawaiian BBQ. It belongs to one of the cooks Mom's own it. Yes they are from the island so it is totally authentic food. They don't serve the mixed steamed veggies though that was just because they know how much I love them, they do well with the rest of the meal though don't they?" I asked as I forked some more of the veggies and put them into my mouth. They tasted so good.

"Yes they do. I think I will have to take my brothers to this place when we get back into the valley." Tom was saying as he put more food into his mouth. It seemed to be the end of the conversation so I started the movie again.

We didn't really talk at all through the movie itself when we finished the food on our plates we just set the trays aside to deal with later. After I moved my tray that's when Mongo came over and laid at my feet for the rest of the movie. It was definitely a very action packed movie that I wouldn't mind watching again. I couldn't get enough of Jason Momoa, Aquaman!

We never even got to the candy because we were so stuffed from dinner. This was fine with me. Once the movie was done and I took it out of the DVD player and handed it back to him we moved into the kitchen. Tom sat at the island while I took the leftover food out of the oven and placed it into the refrigerator, it was cool enough now. I filled his glass with more iced tea and started to rinse the dishes so I could put them into the dishwasher when he got up and took them from me to place in the dishwasher after I rinsed them.

"Here is the part where we talk again." Tom said as he placed the silverware into the washer and put his hands under the still running faucet to rinse his hands off.

"So, what do you want to talk about?" I asked as I went to get a drink from my glass.

"I think that I should fill you in on a few things that I found out today." Tom said as he grabbed his glass too.

"Sure, do you want to go and sit on the couch while we talk?" I asked pointing in the living room direction.

"Okay, I will follow you." Tom said as I started walking back into the living room and sat back down on the couch were I had been sitting before. I set my glass on the coffee table after he passed by me to sit down right next to me, as in no space for, well space! Okay here we go.

"So what did you find out today?" I asked hoping that my breath wasn't too bad right now.

"Okay well I talked to my parents today. Come to find out my Grandfather had changed his last name when he left home. He didn't have the best home life and when he left it was before he knew he was a Were-Squatch. So the council had a hard time trying to find my family heritage. So, Grandpa got ahold of them and told them what his last name used to be. Bad news is that we are somewhat related but it is pretty far back. I mean it's like your Grandpa's great Uncle's part of the Molalla that were migrant workers that moved from Oregon to California and back every year. But my part of the family stayed in California." Tom was explaining to me and he was actually excited about this.

"Wow, really?" I was interested too.

"Wait that many greats back that would mean that he was great-great Grandpa Henry Hunter's brother, right? That is so cool that they can track that far back and find people." I was excited to know the history almost as much as Tom was.

"So we are related but not enough for it to be a problem between us, if you are still interested in dating? I mean I know we were kind of worried about if but…." Tom left it hanging, he was giving me an out and I wasn't sure what to say about that, it was kind of a shock.

"Well, I said I would give us a try and dating isn't the same as you know doing anything that can't be taken back. But I'm glad we know something more now." I wasn't sure what to say right now and I think that Tom was just seeing the silver lining in this situation.

"Okay then. So there is something else you need to know. My parents will be here for the full moon ceremony and they want to meet you. I know it's kind of weird to do it that way but if you do decide that I am the one that you want to spend the rest of your life with then they wanted to meet you before we do anything as well." Tom was talking about meeting his parents before the ceremony to help me make a decision? What if I decide that I don't like his parents and say no just because of that or what if they don't like me?  And what if I choose Harry does that mean they are going to be pissed?

"Okay, I guess that is fair since you have met my parents already." I said with a smile that I didn't really feel.

"And you still have to meet my brothers.  A couple of them think they can steal you away from me before you choose too.  They just don't get the bond that we have since I'm the one that bit you.  I truly am sorry for biting you and yet not sorry at the same time.  Does that make sense?" Tom was rambling now, was it because I wasn't saying much?

"No I understand.  If you hadn't bit me I would never have known about the other side of my family's heritage.  Thank you Tom for biting me!" I was being sarcastic at the end and was trying to be funny but I think Tom thought I was being super serious about it.

"You're welcome.  Maybe I could bite you again sometime?" Tom said as he started leaning toward me and I think he was going in for a kiss but I kind of freaked a little and moved to grab my glass to take a drink.  He didn't seem effected by it.  He just smiled and grabbed his drink.

"So, I noticed that the Bigfoot Hunting crew was gone from out back.  Are they out to dinner or something?"  Tom was making small talk now.  I hadn't heard the crew leave; I wonder how soon after Amanda left that they loaded up and left?

"They had some more sounds bites and some hunting to do for the show to finish.  They are at the back of the property." I said as I leaned back again on the couch.  I was feeling a little stressed about being too close to Tom and what would I do if he tried to kiss me again?  I needed to go to the bathroom.

"Will you excuse me I have to go to the restroom?  If you need to its right here at the beginning of the hall, I will use the one in my room.  I'll be right back and then we can talk some more."  I know I was being a little too cheerful as I headed for my bedroom Mongo fell in step with me and I closed my bedroom door, then went into the bathroom and closed that door as well. I really did have to go potty but I left Mongo sitting in my bedroom so I could have some privacy at least for a few minutes.

As I was washing my hands my cell phone started ringing in my pocket. I dried my hands and pulled it out to answer it, it was my Mom.

"Hi Mom, what's up?" I asked not really putting too much effort into talking.

"I just wanted to know if Tom had told you the news about what the council found out about his family and ours?" Mom asked sounding rather happy.

"Yes, he and I were just talking about that. I guess that his Great-great grandpa was great-great grandpa Henry Hunter's brother. And he thinks that it's far back enough that it doesn't matter if we get together. Mom what do you think about this?" I know I was whining, but I was confused about all of this.

"Well, it is pretty far back in the line that we are related but the fact that his Grandfather changed his last name to Johnson and was able to find a Were-Squatch female as well as his son doing the same thing just doesn't add up for me or your Grandpa. So the council is going to do some more digging so you still have time before you have to make a decision." Mom said and it actually gave me a little bit of peace to know that they were still looking into it.

"Thanks Mom. Oh, can I ask you a question?" I was still trying to figure out the spark thing.

"Sure Babygirl? What's wrong?" Mom was still my Mom even though she kind of left a few things out of my life for a while. But she may know why the spark happens.

"Well, don't read too much into this but there is this weird thing that happened when I shook Tom's hand at the restaurant and then when he kissed me goodnight last night." I said as I sat down on the lid of the closed toilet.

"Oh, I know what that is! So I am just going by what your Grandpa told me when I was younger but there is this thing that happens when a Were-Squatch bites his mate. You know we have these mental telepathy powers, right? Well when we are bitten or we bite someone then we are connected to them mentally as well. The full moon ceremony will finish the connection. So if you choose Tom then you and Tom will be connected mentally from there on, but it is also the same with Harry if you decide to choose Harry then during the mating he would bite you and thus making a connection. So when you and Tom touch you are felling that connection wanting to be completed. Under no circumstances are you to allow him to bite you again unless you are mating him and after the full moon ceremony! Do you understand?" Mom was explaining this rather well I thought but the idea of Tom accidently biting me and then it becoming permanent made my stomach turn.

"Please tell me he knows he can't bite me again to make me mate him?" I wasn't sure Mom knew or not but I had to ask.

"Your Grandpa and the council told him just that. No biting!" Mom made sure to emphasize.

"No problem! I am not feeling very good right now though. My tummy is doing summersaults right now." I really was getting light headed and queasy too.

"You will be fine; you just have to remember that you are the one in control here. You have a very serious choice to make but the choice is still yours. Just calm down and go back to your date before he thinks you fell in the toilet and are never coming back." Mom just had to be funny.

"How did you know I was in the bathroom?" I asked her, I didn't remember telling her.

"I have really good hearing remember? Just like you do, now. Go back to your date and just be you. Have a good time. Good night Babygirl! Love you!" And Mom hung up before I could say anything else.

"Yup, I love you too." I said out loud to no one. I put my phone back into my pocket and headed out the bathroom door. When I was halfway to my bedroom door there was knock on it. Then I heard Tom.

"Are you okay in there?" He asked as I opened the door.

"Yes, sorry about that my Mom called me while I was on the potty." I said with a sheepish grin. Mongo bolted out of the bedroom past us on his way to the front door. Then there was a knock on the door, then another and then another. I looked at Tom and he looked at me.

"Were you expecting anyone?" Tom asked as I headed past him to the front door where Mongo waited patiently.

"No I wasn't." I said as I opened the door to find Mike Stone and Stephen Jefferson standing on the porch with smiles on their faces and each holding a small food box with the lid closed.

"Hey guys, what's going on?" I asked as I opened the door more so that they could come inside. Then they saw Tom and then looked at me. They still smiled but you could tell that they weren't sure about Tom being there.

"We knocked on the glass door but when you didn't answer we came around the front. We brought you dessert." Mike said as he handed me his box and then Stephen handed me his. I smiled because they were just too sweet.

"Thank you guys! What are they?" I asked as I tried to balance the two boxes. Mike leaned over and opened his box.

"I have made the most decadent chocolate mousse, I was told that you love Heavenly chocolates so I called your Mom and she took me to get some to make this mousse with. It turned out to be the most perfect mousse I have ever made." Mike was smiling from ear to ear.

"Oh my, Mike I can't wait to try it! I love Heavenly chocolates!" I was saying as Stephen stepped closer and opened his box.

"I made you a chocolate covered strawberry cheesecake also using the Heavenly chocolates that I stole from Mike." Stephen said as he winked at me and elbowed Mike.

"You guys are going to make me fat! But I love it. Do you think there is enough for all of us?" I asked the guys as I closed the front door with my foot and we headed to the kitchen. My tummy was no longer upset, once I smelled the chocolate I was all good again.

All three of the guys follow me and Mongo headed to the living room knowing if it's chocolate he wasn't getting any anyway so he went to his bed instead. And let me tell you what was in these boxes were the size of a small pie would feed us all four of us but by the time I got to the kitchen Tom didn't look to happy.

"I think there is but Mike and I have already had some. Those are for you and your guest." Stephen said as he and Mike both got the not happy vibe from Tom. This made me look at them all before I pulled out plates and forks.

"Nonsense! You guys are welcome to have some too. Tom which would you like or would you like both?" I was being polite to Tom but I was also getting a little upset that he wasn't being very nice to my friends in my house. I know he hadn't said anything but it was the way he was acting.

"No thanks. I think I better head back to check on my brothers anyway. I will give you a call tomorrow and set up out next date. Keep the movie and I will talk to you tomorrow." Tom was saying as he waved at me and the guys and actually headed for the door. That was a total turnabout from the last date we had. I was surprised he didn't ask me to walk him out. Was I supposed to volunteer to walk him out? Then the door closed and he was gone. I just stood there and looked at Mike and Stephen.

"I don't know what to say about that?" I said as the guys each took a seat at the kitchen island.

"I hope we weren't interrupting anything Carrie." Mike said as he looked around.

"I kind of hope we were." Stephen was saying as he sat down.

"No you weren't interrupting anything. I mean we were technically on a date but the movie was over and I was trying to figure out what to do next. With Harry dating was easy with Tom I hate trying to figure out what to say and what to do, do you know what I mean?" I know I was rambling on and all I wanted to do was hug these two guys that were so nice to me.

"Well that has to tell you something in its self, yah know? Dating shouldn't be hard." Mike said as he got up and started serving the dessert for all three of us. I took a bite of the chocolate mousse first. It was so good it made my toes curl and gave me the little tingles in my jaw.

"Oh Mike, that is soooo good! Almost, better than sex!" I said without thinking. I was so embarrassed then we all started laughing.

"Good to know!" Mike said as he took a plate from Stephen. Then I took a bite of the Chocolate covered strawberry cheesecake and that was so amazing too.

"Oh Stephen, that is sooo amazing too!" I said almost purring as I chewed.

"But not better than sex?" Stephen asked playing like his feelings were hurt, what a ham.

"Yes, almost better than sex too! You guys are too talented, why don't you have some fancy restaurant somewhere?" I was truly amazed by their food.

"We tired and that just wasn't enough for us. We like seeing the people enjoy our food and we can't do that in a fancy restaurant, plus we get to have adventures with the crew and meet cool people like you and your family." Mike said as he actually blushed.

"Well I think you guys are amazing and I am really going to hate it when you leave." I said getting a little sad.

"Well, who knows where the future will take us?" Stephen said on a positive note. When I looked down to take another bite I found that I had eaten it all already.

"Well, we better go and let you get some sleep. I think I heard the trucks come back." Stephen was saying as he moved out of the kitchen and came to give me a hug. Then Mike gave me a hug too.

"Thank you guys for the dessert and the advice. You are welcome to bring me food anytime. See you in the morning for breakfast!" I said as they slipped out the sliding glass door and headed back to the food truck. I could see the lights on in some of the trailers and the truckers were back. I wonder why I didn't hear them return?

I closed the sliding glass door and then I thought I better see if Mongo had to go potty first.

"Mongo! Do you need to potty before we go to bed?" I yelled into the living room and Mongo shot out of there and almost ran into the glass door. I opened it for him and let him out and then I decided to walk out onto the back patio to breath in some fresh air.

"Hey lady! Do you want company again tonight? Amanda yelled over the fence. I thought about it for only a second.

"Yes Ma'am I do! You and Trina coming back?" I asked as I walked toward the gate where she was standing.

"Yah, we will be over in a few minutes. Tom is gone then?" She asked nonchalantly.

"Yes, he left a little while ago when Mike and Stephen brought me desserts. They were so good! They actually made them using Heavenly Chocolates; did you have anything to do with that?" I asked knowing there were only a few people who knew of my addiction to Heavenly Chocolates.

"That was me!" I heard Harry's voice as he walked out of the darkness heading straight toward us.

"Hello there. I think I need to thank you then." I said not sure what else to say. We knew we weren't supposed to be seeing each other but I don't think we could really help it.

"I'm going to go and get my stuff and grab Trina too. Be back in a few!" Amanda said as she took off leaving Harry and I standing on the opposite sides of the fence from each other.

"You're welcome. Everything okay?" He asked and moved a little closer to the gate.

"As well as can be expected. I'm still finding new things out from my Mom. She still doesn't seem to like to give the whole information at once." I was saying as I took a step closer to the gate.

"Anything that I can help with?" He stepped closer to the gate.

"No, Grandpa and the council are working on it." I stepped closer to the gate.

"If you need to talk I am sure we could call each other on the phone that wouldn't break the rules, would it?" He took the last step and was up against the gate.

"I could ask if it's against the rules." I said as I too was now up against the gate. If I leaned forward just a little bit, we could kiss. And I think that Harry knew what I was thinking because he took the last few inches and the top half of his body came over that gate and he grabbed me and kissed me like there was no tomorrow. It felt so good to be in his arms again. I wasn't thinking only feeling, this is where I was meant to be. My toes curled my body was on fire and it wasn't the chocolate mousse this time.

I don't know how long we stood there kissing but it was the clearing of throats that made us stop. Neither one of us wanted to stop but we knew we had to. We both stepped back from the gate at the same time. Harry moved aside for Amanda and Trina to walk past him and through the gate. They each grabbed one of my hands and led me away from the gate and away from Harry.

"Night!" Harry said as he closed and latched the gate behind the girls. I was in a daze but I still managed to respond.

"Night!" Was all I could manage and both girls were giggling like they were school girls again. They drug me into the house where Mongo was sitting on the couch and I swear he was smiling too.

We then went straight to bed and I wasn't talking about anything no matter how many times the girls tried to get me to spill.

## **Chapter 31**

When I awoke the next lovely Tuesday morning, I found the girls gone yet again. Mongo was still here but if the other mornings are the same as this morning then the girls have already taken Mongo out to potty so I was going to do all the things that I would normally do in the morning. I went potty and took a quick shower. I dressed in my jeans and my comfy green t-shirt with Lucky written on the front. Then I through on my socks and tennis shoes and headed for the kitchen with Mongo on my heals. It was just after 9 am by the clock on the microwave, I opened the sliding glass door and let Mongo out and left it open a crack. Then I went to the refrigerator to pour me fresh tea. When I opened the fridge I found a note from Trina on the tea pitcher.

'Carrie,

*We were up early so I made you some Dragon fruit & Melon green tea. I hope it makes you day a little better with some yummy fruit in it. We will meet you for breakfast at 9am if we don't hear from you text us later so we know if we are staying the night again.*

*Love you,*

*Trina'*

I sure do love those two! I poured myself a glass and took a quick drink. It was so yummy! I headed out the sliding glass door just as Mongo was coming in.

"It's time for us to go and have breakfast. The girls and Mike are waiting for us!" I slid the door closed and Mongo lead the way to the gate. We were over by the food truck just as I got a text from Trina telling me they had us a seat. I went to the food truck and Mike was ready at the window.

"Good morning pretty lady! What would you like for breakfast?" He smiled at me.

"I would love some Biscuits and gravy with sausage and scrambled eggs please. And Mongo will have the same." I said as I leaned up to the window so he could hear me. Mongo sat at my feet and gave me a woof; I knew what he wanted to eat.

"I will bring those out to you. The girls have the table at the back in the shade already. See you in a few minutes." Mike said as he ducked inside to make our orders. I grabbed 2 water bottles and a small bowl that they leave out for Mongo and headed to the table in the back where the girls were waiting for me. They started waving right as I came around the corner. I smiled and waved back as well as I could with stuff in my hands that is.

I looked at all the other tables and there were a few of the crew members and they all smiled and waved at me but I didn't see Harry anywhere. I guess I was hoping to see him this morning, especially after last night's kiss.

"He's not here right now." Amanda said as I sat down across from her smiling.

"I can see that. Is he inside still?" I asked her as I poured Mongo's water in his bowl.

"Nope, Terry had him go with him James and Brad from the food truck to get some more food supplies from the place down in Eugene not far from Heavenly Chocolates." Amanda said as she took a drink of her water bottle.

"Oh, so I guess they will be gone for a while then, huh?" I asked as I too took a drink of my water bottle trying to hide my disappointment.

"Yah, they just left a few minutes ago. I think he drug his feet about going so that he could at least see you when you came to have breakfast with us, Mike and Stephen." Trina said with a little bit of a giggle.

"I guess I should have gotten up earlier. I don't know why I'm sleeping so much more lately. It must be the change or something?" I said as Trina nodded her head in the direction of the food truck. Mike must be on his way over here with the food.

"Okay Ladies. Trina you have scrambled eggs and bacon. Amanda had the pancakes. Carrie and Mongo had the biscuits and gravy with scrambled eggs and sausage, just like Stephen and I." Mike said as he and Stephen passed out the food and then the guys sat down with us to eat their breakfast.

"We have someone inside the truck taking care of things for a while so we could eat with you lovely ladies." Stephen said reading my mind. I cut up the biscuits and the sausage for Mongo and then set his plate on the ground for him to eat next to me. Then I dug into my own all the while trying to keep up with the conversation.

"So Carrie, have you made a decision on which guy you like more yet?" Stephen asked as I almost choked on my mouth full of food. I finished chewing and swallowing as everyone at the table stared at me.

"Yes and No. I don't really want to talk about that right now." I said as I looked between him and Mike.

"It's okay we understand. We don't know Tom but he seems to be an okay guy." Mike said as he patted me on the back. I grabbed my water bottle to take a drink to wash my breakfast down. When I was done everyone had moved on to another topic. The end of the episode taping and the inevitable moving on of the Bigfoot Getters, the whole crew.

I just sat and listened to them all talk trying not to read too much into it. Because if I did then I would have to ask myself would Harry still leave with the Bigfoot Getters and the crew to tape the next episode or would he be happy to stay with just me? And what would he do for a job if he stayed to be with me? These are things that I also need to consider in my decision as well. But I think I will just set that on the back burner until I have my week to choose. I will make my pro's and con's lists for both men when I have more time to sit and think.

I know my mind was off in space because it was Mike telling me that my phone was ringing in my pants that brought me back to earth. I pulled out my phone and the caller ID said it was my mom calling. I thought about not answering but in the end I did.

"Hello Mom! What's up?" I asked in my cheery voice trying not to be too loud while everyone else was still talking at the table.

"Hi Babygirl! I am heading down to Eugene to see your Aunt Nova and have lunch. I was wondering if you weren't too busy today if you would like to go with me? We can stop by Heavenly Chocolates and you can bring Mongo. I already have his car seat in the car too." Mom was pretty excited and she knows if she says Eugene then I am there, but I am wondering why?

"It sounds good to me. I have to be home by the evening, Tom and I are doing something tonight and he will call me this afternoon to talk about it." I said as I started to gather my stuff from the table. Everyone stopped talking and looked at me.

"Mom, I need to clean up and get Mongo's service dog stuff together. How long before you get here?" I asked and then I heard a car in the driveway.

"Oh, well I'm already here but I need to go up to the house and see you Grandma first. Text or call me when you're ready or I will just wait in the driveway when I come back this way after talking to your Grandma, that is. See you in a few!" Then mom hung up the phone, I knew she was on her hands free but it was always weird to talk to her as she drives by on her way to see Grandma and Grandpa. I stood up to watch her drive by and wave from her little Subaru Forester in what else but forest green.

I turned to see everyone else at the table had also stood and waved at my Mom as she drove by with a smile on her face.

"So, you are going to town with your Mom huh? Do you really think you will be back in time for a date with Tom?" Amanda was asking as she grabbed her empty plate with mine and I picked up Mongo's from the ground before anyone stepped on it.

"We should be. It's not like it will take all day to have lunch with Aunt Nova and go to Eugene. Besides if it did Tom would understand, I think?" I said as I was absent mindedly throwing the garbage away and putting the water bottle in the recycle bin.

"Yah, right. The guy didn't like the fact that Stephen and I showed up with dessert let alone crashing your date!" Mike said as he too was throwing away his empty plate.

"You should call him before your Mom gets back here and let him know ahead of time at least." Trina was saying as we all started walking in the direction of my house.

"Yah, I guess I should at least do that. Thanks for breakfast guys it was great as usual! Ladies I will see you tonight. If I'm not back by the time you guys want to go to bed go ahead and go, you each have a key to my house anyway, make your selves at home." I said as Trina and Amanda each gave me a hug and a smile.

"We hope to see you for breakfast tomorrow to Carrie." Stephen was saying as he and Mike headed back to work.

"Yah, we like spending time with you girls." Mike said as he tossed his water bottle into the recycle bin and then the two guys were gone back inside the food truck to make others happy with their food today.

"Bye guys, I will try." Was all I got out before they closed the door with a wave.

"Okay, go and get ready and don't forget to talk to Tom." Trina said as she and Amanda started heading for the trailer where they had been working.

"Okay, Okay, I will. Talk to you guys later!" I said with a wave and with Mongo by my side we headed back into the house so that I could gather his service dog harness so he could go anywhere with me as well as my purse and the paperwork I had to go with his service stuff. I also had to grab my badge just in case I needed it and place it in my purse too.

Since it didn't take me that long to gather everything I pulled out my phone and dialed Tom's number. He answered on the second ring.

"Hey Beautiful, I was just about to call you." Tom said as a greeting.

"Wow, okay. I was just calling to let you know my Mom was coming to pick Mongo and I up to take us to Eugene to have lunch with my Aunt Nova and we were stopping at my favorite chocolate store and I wanted to give you a heads up since we are supposed to do something tonight. What did you want to talk about?" I asked as I sat down for a minute and took a sip of the tea that I had left on the counter earlier, yup still cold.

"Well, that works out better than I hoped then. My brothers and I had to come back to Eugene for business reasons. So I was going to call you and ask if you wanted to meet me in Eugene instead of me coming back to Oakridge tonight? Since you will already be here then I can pick you up from wherever or your Mom can drop you off? Either way I will get to show you my apartment and my office here." Tom was actually sounding excited about showing me his stuff and I guess it wouldn't hurt. I mean if he gets out of hand I can take care of myself.

"Okay that sounds good. I will talk to my Mom and see if she would like to drop me off. Do you want to text me your address so I have it and what time do you want me to show up?" I was actually looking forward to it; it might be fun to get out and about in Eugene again.

"Sure I can do that. What about 5 o'clock? Does that sound good? We can go to either sushi or there is a bar right around the corner from my apartment. We can decide when you get here." Then Tom put his hand over the phone and was talking to someone.

"Okay." Was all I got out before he talked again?

"I'm sorry Carrie, I have to go and deal with something really important. I will text you the information and we can talk when you get here." Tom was in a hurry but he did truly sound like he would rather talk to me, but that could all be in my head too.

"Okay. See you at 5. Bye Tom!" I couldn't think of anything else to say.

"Bye Carrie see you then." And then Tom hung up. I swear 2 seconds later I got the text from him with his address on Park Avenue. I'm pretty sure I have been in that area before when I was in college. I'm sure it will come back to me when I see it though.

Then I heard the horn honking in the front of the house Mom was here, which meant I had no time to change for my date later. Maybe Mom and Aunt Nov would like to take a trip to the mall with me? I haven't done that in years, I could use a few new shirts too. Mongo had his service harness on and was sitting at the door waiting to go outside. I opened the door and he ran to go potty before we got into my Mom's Subaru. Mongo loved to travel and he loved that my Mom always had organic chicken dog treats for him too. So Mongo loaded up and I climbed into the passenger seat ready to update my mom on what I needed from her today, besides chocolate.

After updating my mom no more than I got in her car on everything that Tom and I had talked about she got on the phone with Aunt Nova who was now going to meet us at the Valley River Mall in Eugene so that we could find me something new for my date tonight. I was thinking that a new pair of boots or sandals would be good too. Plus, my chocolates from Heavenly Chocolates, we couldn't forget those too.

It never took us long to get into Eugene when Mom was driving compared to when I was driving, she had the lead foot in the family. We made great time and were waiting for Aunt Nova by the main entrance. When she got there she was in a really good mood.

"This is going to be so much fun! I haven't been shopping for clothes with girls in such a long time. Where to first ladies?" Aunt Nova was ready to have some fun shopping, which in case you were wondering being a tomboy growing up, I hate clothes shopping. That's why I stick to jeans and t-shirts whenever I can. But this being a special occasion and getting to spend time with not only my Mom but Aunt Nova too was the best part.

"Well, I was thinking sundress maybe? Do you know which shop we can get something like that? And we can't forget to stop at the fun t-shirt shop too, I need some more funny t-shirts, mine are getting old." I was saying as the three of us linked arms and started off to find the perfect sundress. I felt like singing, "We're off to see the wizard, the wonderful wizard of Oz!" But I was too afraid there might actually be wizards around so I didn't. It did make me smile though.

First stop and I have tried on six dresses and I really like the very first one I tried on. It was a beautiful turquoise blue with a marble white running through it. Nice thick shoulder straps that covered my bra straps and it was a twirling dress, I loved wearing those ones. I will also need to grab a pair of white leggings to go underneath too. I think there was a display of them over by the dress rack as well. I went back into the dressing room after the sixth dress to change back into my clothes when I heard Aunt Nova and Mom talking, Were-hearing and all.

"I just love the smile and new found excitement in her face right now. She just looks so happy and so do you for that matter. You finally got your Were-girl you were always hoping she would grow into Janet." Aunt Nova said in a quiet voice.

"I know she has had to come to terms with everything new lately and still nothing gets her down. I am so proud of her, I always have been. But, I just wish she didn't have to go through this choosing thing. But since there are two men interested in her and they are both Were's and there are so few of us Squatch's left that the council is putting all this pressure on Dad and I to make sure that she does the right thing and gives both men a chance to court her." Mom was saying and her voice was not like I had ever heard before, there was so much emotion in it that she usually hides.

"Your daughter is a smart capable woman and even though she wasn't born a Were she has come to terms with it very quickly and she has made the best of it. She now has a bigger part in the family destiny and I think on some level she knows that. She also knows that she is loved even when she wasn't a Were we all loved her but now there are so many more doors open to her in our community of Were's! Carrie is amazing and no matter whom she chooses they are the lucky ones and we will be too." Aunt Nova said with strength and positivity toward me!

When I finished getting dressed I came out of the dressing room and hugged them both.

"You heard all that, didn't you?" My mom asked as she saw the tear roll down my cheek.

"Yes I did. You do know that there are a lot of things I still need to know about this stuff, right?" I asked as I set the other dresses that I didn't choose on the rack next to the dressing room door. Mongo was waiting patiently at the door I had just come out of. Then I handed Mom the blue dress.

"I know dear and we will talk more at lunch. This one is perfect!" She held it out and then laid it over her arm.

"Okay. Yes, that is my favorite too." Aunt Nova said as she gave me a hug.

"Okay then. Now I need some white leggings and then we can go and find shoes, maybe boots or sandals then off to get my t-shirts to." I said as I started walking with Mongo by my side to go and grab the leggings. Then I saw a small blue half sweater that was the same color as the dress and I had to grab that too, it would be cooler in the evening and it went perfectly with the dress.

Mom brought my dress up to the counter where I had put the leggings and sweater. Once I paid for them and got our bag we headed to another store just a few doors down and I looked at boots, sandals and even some cute little tennis shoes. I wound up getting all three pairs. The cute little black sandals that had the wrap around ties that made my feet look like something out of Roman times were to chilly to wear yet during the evenings so the cute little light brown and turquoise suede ankle boots for this evening plus the cute little blue light blue tennis shoes for running around in. Then my Mom and Aunt Nova took me over to the t-shirt store where I bought six shirts. Each funnier than the last, except for my Aquaman shirt with Jason Momoa in it, that one is just plain sexy.

With shopping done for now we headed to the nice restaurant on the second floor for lunch. Mom liked to be spoiled every once in a while. We were seated right away; there was no waiting at all. The place was very nice and the tables had bouquets of fresh flowers that smelled wonderful. There was very nice waiter that gave us menus and then walked away to get out waters.

"This is one fancy place; I don't think I've ever been in here before." Aunt Nova was saying as she looked at the menu.

"I've been in here a few times with James but never for lunch. Everything sounds so good too." Mom was saying as she perused the menu with hungry eyes. I think I was hungrier than usual too, because we had breakfast why was I so hungry now? Then I looked at my watch, it was almost 3:30pm. Then I looked down at poor Mongo who hadn't said a word the whole time we had been out and never complained about anything, which I am sure he had to go potty by now. He just laid at my feet, the waiter and the hostess neither one even gave him a second glance after seeing his harness. But when the waiter came back with our ice waters he had a bowl of water just for Mongo, how nice.

"Have you decided on what you would like ladies?" The Waiter asked very nicely.

"I will have your steak, rare and baked potato with sour cream and the garden salad, ranch." My Mom said as she set her menu back on the table.

"That sounds wonderful, I will have the same. Plus, if you have a fruit bowl I will take that as well as 1 hamburger patty nothing on it for my service dog, please." I said and then laid my menu on top of Mom's

"And for you, Ma'am?" The waiter asked Aunt Nova who was still flipping back and forth between two pages.

"I will have everything they had except can you change the steak for a nice salmon filet?" Aunt Nova being a Were- Eagle it seems prefers fish to beef, good to know. I had to smile to myself about that one.

"Very good ladies. I will return with your meals shortly." Then he took all the menus and headed to the kitchen.

"Did you guys notice what time it was? We have been shopping for hours and it's not too far from the time I'm supposed to be dropped off at Tom's place." I said with a little worry in my voice. I still had to change.

"Don't worry it's not that far away, you gave me the address already and I programmed it into my phone so after here we will stop at Heavenly Chocolates and then I will drop you off. Did you want me to take your chocolates and drop them off at your house when I head home?" Mom was very confident about her time management but I was starting to freak out a little bit.

"Sure, that would be great Mom thanks. I guess I could change in the restroom after we eat." I was saying as I smelled them cooking the steaks in the back. Then the waiter came out with our salads. Which were a little bigger than I thought they would be, but they were delicious. I slipped Mongo a few pieces of the harder lettuce that he loved to crunch.

"Are you doing okay Mongo?" I asked him just to check.

"I am doing fine; this has been fun for you. I can wait to go potty until we are done here. I am hungry though." Mongo said in my head.

"I know Mongo, foods on the way. You are being such a good boy." I said while rubbing his ears when he sat up to eat the lettuce pieces.

"Carrie dear, you do know that you can talk to Mongo in his mind as well, don't you?" Aunt Nova asked me as because she noticed people watching Mongo and I. The restaurant wasn't full or anything but they were a different class of people, you could tell by their clothes and the way they looked down on how I was dressed in my jeans and t-shirt. Mom and Aunt Nova though were always dressed like they were going to have high tea with the Queen, so to speak. They were dressed in nice cream colored slacks and where Mom wore a cute little pheasant blouse in a light pink Aunt Nova had a flowery tank top with a see through white cover shirt. Both wearing strappy sandals with beautifully painted toenails. Mom didn't usually dress this nice for the woods but whenever she was in public she was picture perfect.

"Actually No I didn't know that. Mom hasn't told me all the fun things that I need to know yet. But Mongo told me a few things as well as my Cousins filling me in too. Harry didn't even know some of this stuff either because of his, um, person leaving him clueless about a lot of stuff." I told Aunt Nova who looked a little shocked about it. Then she looked at my Mom who was kind of sinking into her chair a little.

"Janet, you should have at least told her the basic's by now. I know you didn't have a chance to teach her from birth but once you knew she was changing you should have said something to the girl." Aunt Nova was starting to raise her voice and then caught herself.

"Sorry about that. Janet?" Aunt Nova wasn't letting this go.

"I was going to tell her then this whole thing with Harry started and I wanted to make sure she was changing and then the council got involved with this whole "you must choose thing" and then I thought she wouldn't want to speak to me since she thought that I was in on the decision to make her choose between Tom and Harry.  Well I guess I was just keeping the surface part of everything going without letting her see too deeply." Mom was flustered and rambling and it wasn't a pretty sight.  I don't think I have ever seen her this way before.

"Okay Mom, we need to have this talk but not here and not right now, okay?  Here comes our food."  I was trying to calm her down before the waiter reached the table.  This was going to be a quiet lunch now.

## **Chapter 32**

I was right about lunch going by quickly with barely any conversation.  Mom and Aunt Nova talking about the next ceremony and how the whole family was going to be there as well.  Then I left them to go and change.  Mom kept Mongo so I didn't have to take him into the restroom with me.  This was downstairs not far from the elevator if they used it to leave the restaurant.

I changed quickly and made sure all my tags were off and placed my other clothes inside the bags.  I put on the boots and they looked good, they also gave me a few extra inches so I wouldn't feel so short when I went out with Tom.  Then I met Mom and Aunt Nova at the main entrance where we met coming in and Mom had already let Mongo go pee on the grass next to a bush where he was out of the way, Mongo was very good about that.

We gave hugs and said our goodbyes to Aunt Nova and Mom and I headed to Heavenly Chocolates before she was going to drop me off. We didn't have the kind of time that I usually give to the chocolate shop but I did my best not to go overboard though either. I got my truffles and my dipped salted caramel drops, blueberry drops and the cherry drops, then I grabbed a few milk chocolate pecan chortles and then I added a bag of the milk chocolate buttons to make some chocolate covered strawberries for later in the summer. I was buzzing around so fast trying to make sure that I got everything and then I made it back to the car before Mom did. It was a good thing Mongo waited in the car; I can't take him in there not just because the place sells food but because of the chocolate itself. I know he's a good boy and all but even I can't resist the free samples.

Once Mom was back in the car we headed to Tom's apartment. This felt so weird; my Mom was dropping me off at a guy's apartment. I let that sink into my brain a little. I was very nervous, I didn't know what to expect. Did all the brothers live in one apartment? We never talked about that or about boundaries for his brothers while we are dating because I was not planning not dating any of them, Tom was the only one and that's only because he bit me.

It didn't take too long to get there at all. Mom found a parking spot right in front of the building Tom was standing out in front of the building waiting for me. How nice was that? He was dressed in what looked to be brand new wrangler jeans and a nice blue button up western shirt that was pretty close to the color of my dress. He was wearing a Stetson cowboy hat and cowboy boots. He really did make a good looking guy in western wear but was he really a country boy? Or was he dressing this way to make me notice him thinking that this is what I wanted in a man?

"Isn't that sweet? He's been waiting for you." Mom said as she put the car in park.

"Yes it is and I am so nervous my stomach is doing back flips." I said as I reached across and hugged my mom goodbye.

"Thanks for lunch and all the fun of shopping." I said as I leaned over the backseat and unfastened Mongo.

"You're welcome and we will have a talk about the things that I haven't talked to you about yet. We will have to make some time during your thinking week, okay?" Mom was asking before I climbed out of her car. Tom was waiting next to me to help me out of the car.

"Okay, sounds good to me. Love you and say hi to Dad for me!" I said as I got all the way out of the car. I took my bag that had the clothes and shoes I was wearing earlier in it and left the rest for Mom to take to my house when she dropped off my chocolates. Mongo was out the backdoor no more than I opened it and he was sitting by my side looking around. Then since I wouldn't give him my bag Tom went around to say hi to my Mom, she rolled down her window to talk to him.

"Mrs. Randolph thanks for bringing her here." He was saying very politely.

"It's no problem Tom. I hope you guys have a good time tonight." Mom was saying as Tom stood up and smiled at her. Then he said, "I have a fun time planned for us."

"All righty then. Have fun you three." Mom said as she started to back out since I had my stuff and Mongo and I were standing on the sidewalk waiting for Tom.

"Right this way you two." Tom said as he put his hand on the small of my back to guild me into the very nice, very tall building that his apartment was in. We passed by a doorman and went straight to the elevator. Climbed on in when the doors opened for us and then Tom punched the button for the top floor. There were 4 floors and they lived on the top?

"So I never asked do you and your brothers live together?" I was asking before we got to there so I knew what to expect.

"No we have the whole top floor though. I have my own apartment and so does Frank and Gary but Zeek and Abel share one apartment and

Jeffery and Kelly share one as well.  There are only 5 apartments on the top floor but we have them all.  The landlord that owns this building also owns the building two doors down that we run the Emerald City Security out of so we have a great commute to work."  Tom laughed as his own joke; it made me laughed a little too.

"So the office is two doors down but most of your work is done off sight doing bodyguard work and such for famous people, right?"  I was asking to clarify what I had heard from him so far but I think some of my facts came from Amanda when she was doing research on them for me too.

"Yes, that's right."  He seemed happy that I was remembering our conversations, or at least retaining the information.  Then the door dinged and opened to all the other Johnson brothers waiting in the hallway to see us.  Each one of them had flowers for me.  And each one of them had a huge smile on their faces.  I was shocked to say the least.

"Guy's, we talked about this!  You are going to scare the girl off!  I'm sorry Carrie; they are just really excited to see you again.  It's been hard to keep them away from you since they think they may have a shot at your heart too."  I know Tom was just saying the last part to make me smile but honestly I was a little more freaked out than I thought I would be.  The brothers started coming forward and handing me their flowers one by one.

"It's good to see you again."  Abel said as he handed me a bouquet of carnations which I loved in grade school.

"We just wanted to welcome you."  Frank said as he handed me a bouquet of daisies.

"And we wanted to make sure you were dating the right brother!"  Zeek said as he handed me a dozen red roses, then he took my free hand and kissed it before he took a step back.

"Don't scare her Zeek.  We just wanted to say hi."  Gary said as he handed me a bouquet of wild flowers and stepped back quickly.

"And we went in on this one together!"  Kelly said as he and Jeffery handed me a huge bouquet of pink, white, red and yellow roses.

"Yah, but I picked out the colors for what they mean to a lady." Jeffery said as he bowed in front of me and then the two of them stepped back together.

My arms were full of flowers and my bag hanging off my arm as well; I was very overloaded and could barely see over the flowers.

"Thank you guys, all of you. The flowers are wonderful and I can honestly say I have never gotten so many flowers all at once." I smiled and was trying to be as nice as possible. Mongo bumped my leg telling me he was a little uncomfortable with the closeness of everyone in the hallway. So I turned to Tom and smiled.

"Oh, yah! Let's take you into my apartment so you can sit down. I would take your flowers from you and carry them for you but I think my brothers might take that the wrong way and it just might cause a fight." He put his hand on my lower back and steered me toward the first door on the left. He unlocked it quickly and then escorted me inside and closing the door behind us so that his brothers were left in the hall. Mongo was glued to my leg so I knew he wasn't going anywhere.

"Were you serious about your brothers fighting over me?" I asked him and I know my eyes were probably the size of saucers.

"Yes and no. I think that if I wasn't the one in charge of this family then they would have fought me for the right to have you for themselves. But you would still have the right of choice so don't worry." Then he winked and smiled at me. I set everything on the kitchen counter which was the first flat spot as I walked in the door. The apartment had an open concept to it. Kitchen on the right as you walk in the door then you are walking into the living room with big picture windows that looked down on the street below where we just came from. The to the left is the bathroom and then the bedroom, which instead of having a wooden door it had a sliding frosted glass door that recessed into the wall when not closed. It was defiantly fancy and his furniture was defiantly manly. Leather couch and matching chair, huge TV with satellite dish and a computer set up right in front of the main picture window facing the front of the building.

"You can really tell a man lives here." Was all I said as I walked around. Mongo sat next to the couch and waited for me to walk around. He knew I would return to there to sit down.

"Sorry, guilty as charged. I do say I don't really spend that much time here. We are usually working and when we aren't we are all together at either Franks or sometimes Zeek's apartments. Frank is a great cook and Zeek has all the video games and a bigger TV than I have." Tom said as he walked up behind me while I looked out the picture window at the side of the building facing where their office building.

"It is a rather nice view of the city and you even have a small park down there too." I said as I noticed people in the small park with their dogs.

"Yes, the park is nice and the view is okay but I do have to say what I am looking at right now is even better than any of that." Tom was saying as he got super close to me and touched my hair then when I turned my head he looked into my eyes. Then he touched my bottom lip with his finger and I felt the shock, the tingling shock that I always get when he touched my bare skin. He was going to start leaning forward and I kind of wanted to kiss him but I also didn't.

"May I kiss you Carrie?" Tom asked me in a whisper. I didn't know what to say. I didn't know what I wanted to happen between us either, I was so confused. I blinked my eyes and then I nodded my head ever so slightly. Then I closed my eyes and waited for him to kiss me.

The pressure from his lips was so light that I wasn't completely sure he had started to kiss me until the shock zapped my lips. Then he put even more pressure into the kiss and I turned my body to face his and he pulled me into his arms. On a scale of 1 to 10 it was definitely at least an 8 or 9 but it wasn't quite there to a 10. The 10 makes your toes curl and your body hum. But I tell you what he did give it a really good go and it was definitely a great effort. Then I felt Mongo bump my legs and I knew that this was getting to hot too fast and Mongo was helping me pull out of this hypnotic state I was going into with this kiss.

I pulled back a little from the kiss and Tom tried to follow my lips to keep kissing. Then he opened his eyes and looked at me.

"I'm sorry if I was getting carried away. I just love kissing you. I have to ask you, do you feel the spark like I do whenever we touch?" Tom asked breathing heavily, he being so sweet and gentle and I could tell he really wanted to take this to another level but he knew there was no way we were doing that until my decision was made and we still had a few dates to go for me to get to know him, the real him and not just the hormone driven Were him.

"Yes." I said kind of breathlessly. Then I looked back down to Mongo.

"We should probably go and start our date. What do you have planned for us this evening?" I asked as I pulled a little further out of his embrace. He took the cue and let me go, he looked a little sad but he knew this was not going to be a date like dating others. If we slept together then we would be mated and then that was it. No more choices, No more Harry. So I had to be careful.

He put a smile on his face and then he led me over to the couch so I could sit down. He stood for a couple minutes and it looked like he was a little uncomfortable in the crotch area to me. I hadn't meant to lead him on and make things happen, it was a mutual thing. Tom cleared his throat and then he took a seat next to me.

"So there is a sushi place the next block over or we can go to this other place called 'The Barn Light' if you would like to try that?" Tom was saying and I knew about the Barn Light from my Eugene days, I thought I knew this neighborhood.

"I've actually been to the Barn Light. I would love to go there; I haven't been there in years!" I was excited; I knew where I was without a problem.

"Wow, really? Well let's go then!" Tom said as he almost jumped up from the couch to take me out. Mongo stood up and stepped back out of the way and then he was right there at my leg again.

"Oh, can I leave my bag here while we are out?" I asked as we started toward the door.

"Yah, and you can leave all your flowers from all your admirer's too." Tom said as he opened the door to find all of his brothers still in the hall.

"We were just wondering if we could all go with you to dinner. We know it's supposed to be a date and all but she has to get to know the family anyway and we want our time with her before Mom, Dad, Grandma and Grandpa get here to meet her." Frank was saying, trying to convince his brother that this was a good idea. All the brothers were dressed in nice new jeans with nice western button up shirts in different colors like Tom was. They were all wearing cowboy boots and hats as well as belt buckles that were quite large. But it made you look down there, didn't it?

Tom looked at me to see what my reaction was and I have to tell you I was a little taken aback because Tom hadn't told me the rest of his family was coming to meet me this week.

"So, your whole family wants to meet me?" I was in shock, I was never a really popular girl in school but I managed to have a few close friends. I did not ever have a lot of men basically fighting over the chance to spend time with me or to have their family meet me a.s.a.p. since apparently Were-weddings happened fast.

"I was going to tell you tonight at dinner so that you wouldn't freak out. My brothers and I have met all the family members that were at the ceremony the other night. So I just figured that if you choose me then you would probably like to meet my family first and since once you choose who you want to mate or marry in a since then you would like to meet my parents before the ceremony." Tom was talking so fast that my head was spinning. Mongo bumped my leg which helped me to focus.

"Okay! Now that I know we can move on with the evening. No, I don't mind the brothers coming along and Yes, I will meet your parents when they get here. Can I use your restroom before we go?" With that I turned and went to the bathroom with Mongo right next to me. Before I closed the bathroom door I heard one of the brothers make a comment, "Does she take her dog to the bathroom with her too? How weird is that?" I don't know which one said it but Tom did reply.

"Mongo is her companion; he helps her to stay calm and makes her feel safe. You got a problem with that then you can stay home!" Tom was putting that brother in his place. Then I finished closing the door. Tom stood up for not only me but for Mongo too.

While I was going to the potty Mongo faced the door and waited. I texted Amanda what had just happened and about Tom's family coming to meet me this week.

She texted back, "That she didn't think that was fair to Harry."

Then I replied, "I know, and I am freaking out about his brothers. I will fill you in on everything when I get home tonight. I just needed to vent."

She texted back, "Girl you put up with a hell of a lot more than I would. See you tonight. LOL"

Then I texted, "Thanks! See you tonight not sure what time."

She texted, "We will keep the bed warm for you."

Then I put the phone back in my pocket, washed my hands and went back out into the kitchen where Tom and his brothers were waiting for me. Yay, group date anyone?


When we got to the Barn Light they had a very large table that we all fit at and I had the feeling that if Tom didn't go to this place often at least some of his brothers did because the waitresses knew them by name. But who wouldn't remember 7 handsome guys that happened to be brothers?

The guys all ordered beer except for Tom; he ordered an iced tea for himself as me. Since he still had to take me home tonight, drinking would not be a good idea.

"You know we can't get drunk don't you?" Frank leaned over and asked me.

"No I didn't. I just don't really like alcohol, I love drinking tea." I said as he listened to me very closely on my left side. Tom was seated on my right side and all the rest of the brothers were sitting in a circle around this huge table all watching me and not all the girls wandering around trying to get their attentions.

"It's our metabolism, breaks the alcohol down very quickly. Which is a good thing but also a bad thing because we can't truly experience being without inhibitions." Zeek said leaning over his brother Frank to talk to me. Once he was done talking Frank pushed him back into his seat.

"Chalk that up to something else I didn't know. Any other pearls of Were wisdom, I'm all ears?" I said as my tea was set in front of me and the waitress gave me a really unhappy face. I guess this is not going to be a good night.

"What else do you want to know?" Tom asked me as he took my hand in his to hold. Making all of his brothers a little antsy in their seats.

"I don't know, that's the problem. My Mom wasn't prepared to tell me anything because they never thought I would go through the change." I said as I used my left hand to bring my drink down so I could take a sip from it since Tom had my other hand.

"There are a lot of things that you should know, but this is not the place to talk about them." Tom said as a group of 4 women came up to the table and tried to get the 4 brothers on that side to go to the dance floor with them. They looked at me and without thinking I nodded my head for them to go. All 4 popped out of their chairs and grabbed the closest girl to them and headed to the dance floor.

"Wow, they are already excepting you as their Alpha, my mate in leadership!" Tom said into my ear. I didn't even think before doing what I did, I guess it must come naturally to me.

"Would you like to dance?" Tom asked me as he stood still holding my hand.

"Yes, I believe I would." Then I stood and let him lead me to the dance floor, Mongo stayed under the table where my feet had been. And wouldn't you know it once we got out to the dance floor, that's when they throw a slow dance in. Tom took me in his arms and at first we were the proper distance between us but as we danced we got closer to each other. After a few minutes we were one person and I had my head on his shoulder. He smelled good, it was a mix of his cologne which was just a hint of Stetson and then the woodsy smell that I know was the Were-Squatch in him. I rather liked the smell and my Were-Squatch side did too.

We danced the whole song and I had my eyes closed the whole time. I think at least two of his brothers tried to cut in because Tom growled twice and I could almost sense them when they got close. I was happy to be just with Tom for this dance. Just before the song ended though my tummy decided to make itself known by rumbling very loudly. I don't think any of the regular people would have heard it but I know Tom did. He laughed a little and leaned into my ear.

"I'm guessing you are as hungry as I am?" He said it in a very husky voice which vibrated through my body making me more aware of the fact that he was turned on by me, just from dancing! I was a little as well if I was being honest with myself at least.

"Yes, I am. I am sure poor Mongo probably needs to go potty too." We had been there at the bar for a little over two hours and I know that Mongo can hold it for a long time but I was also feeling a little guilty that he had to hide under a table to be in here with me.

"Why don't we order our dinner here and take it to go. We can walk through the park so Mongo can go potty and then we will take dinner back to my place to eat by ourselves?" Tom suggested just as the beat of the next song started to get louder and we walked back to the table. Poor Mongo was ready to go, but he stayed under that table until I sat down and petted him.

"Potty please, soon? Hungry too. Very loud in here and lots of people." Mongo said in my head as he laid his head in my lap.

"We are going to order dinner and then take it to go. We will take you to the park just around the corner to go potty and then we'll go to Tom's apartment to eat. Can you wait that long buddy?" I asked trying the whole talking in his head this time.

"Yes! I like this better talking. I can wait a few minutes more." Mongo said in my head and licked my hands as he got very excited that we were sharing a conversation for the first time without anyone else hearing us which made me smile.

"What has made you smile Carrie?" Frank asked as he leaned toward me.

"I have just held a whole conversation with Mongo and no one heard it but the two of us. I am pretty proud of myself." I said without thinking of how that would make him feel that I had left the brothers out of the conversation. This was an afterthought when I saw his facial expression change all of a sudden. Then he lowered his eyes from looking into mine when he talked to me. Great I have offended him now.

"I'm sorry did I say something wrong?" I asked Frank over the music.

"No, Ma'am I just forgot you were an Alpha is all." Frank said as he sat back in his chair. I had to think about that for a second. I leaned over to him and he leaned back to me.

"What is that supposed to mean?" I asked him and he wouldn't meet my eyes.

"It means that most of us cannot talk to the animals in human form, only a true Alpha can do that. When we are Were-Squatch we can communicate with them but only then." Frank said and then took a quick look at my face again.

"I knew I should have been the one to bite you! Then I would be Alpha with you by my side! I need some air, I will see you later." Frank got up very quickly and walked over to Tom and talked in his ear really quick and then he left the bar.  What am I supposed to do with that information?  Fudge!

A few minutes later when the waitress finally came back to check up on us again Tom asked for 2 menus which she returned very quickly with.  Most of Tom's brothers were still out dancing with the regular girls that had asked them.  When Zeek noticed that Frank had left and was not coming back he scooted over into Frank's empty seat.

"I was wondering do you have any sisters?"  Zeek asked me as he leaned in a little too close.  Mongo growled a little from under the table.  Zeek sat back in his seat a little more.

"No Zeek I'm sorry I don't.  But I do have a lot of cousin's though.  I'm not sure which ones are Were's already but I am sure that most of them will be at the full moon ceremony.  Or you can talk to my Mom and see if she can put you in touch with any that have the recessive gene to be turned if you guys hit it off that is."  I said thinking that maybe I could help all the Johnson brothers find mates if Mom would help me.  Which made me smile; I could be the Were-matchmaker.  That could be fun.

I looked at the menu and decided that chicken strips and fries would be great for both Mongo and I.  They didn't have any fruit for Mongo and I but I guess we could always get more at the food truck in the morning.  I leaned over to tell Tom what I wanted to find him staring at me with these intense eyes, like he was undressing me right here in the bar.  Then he sort of snapped out of it and smiled.

"I think Mongo and I would like the chicken strips and fries please.  Can you wait for the order while I take Mongo out to the park?  He really has to go and I know the food is going to take a few minutes to cook."  I said as loud as I thought was necessary in his ear with all the noise going on.

"No, I will order and Zeek can wait for it while I take you two to the park.  Zeek, you will wait for our food and then bring it to me at the apartment, we will wait out front and then you can come back if you want too.  Frank went home already."  Tom said over me to Zeek as Zeek kind of leaned over me as well. I guess large families don't really have boundaries that much from what I have heard or it could be another Were thing too?

"Okay Tom, no problem!" Zeek said as he sat back in his chair and looked a little happy. Tom looked at me and then leaned over.

"What did you tell him a minute ago?" Tom asked me over the music.

"I will tell you when we go to the park!" I yelled back the current song was so loud my head was starting to bump along with the drum. Tom got up and went to the bar to order our food and pay for it. Then he pointed back at Zeek who waved at the pretty bartender and then he came back to me.

"All set, let's go." Tom said as he helped me out of my chair. He set a number on the table next to Zeek for the food order. Patted Zeek on the back and then we headed for the door. Tom's other brothers who had been dancing came running over before we made it out the door.

"Where are you guys going?" Abel yelled.

"Taking Mongo to the park and then Zeek is bringing us our dinner which we will be eating at my place alone. You guys stay and have fun, Frank went home already. We can all talk in the morning!" Tom said to all of his brothers except for Zeek who stayed at the table. All Tom's brothers looked at me and without thinking yet again I nodded at them. They all rushed me and hugged me at the same time and then they took off back to the dance floor and to the ladies waiting for them to return. Tom just looked at me with a huge smile on my face. Just before we walked out the door I heard Tom say to himself, "I got me a True Alpha!" and he shook his head. He didn't know I was watching him or that I heard what he had said. I am guessing my stock value has increased in this family?

## Chapter 33

Once we got outside we started walking back toward the park, that's when I noticed that McStud's Doughnuts was still open. My tummy rumbled again and I talked to Mongo in his head.

"Hey buddy, do you think I can stop and get some doughnuts before we get to the park?" I was getting the hang of this talk in his head thing.

"Only if, you get two doughnuts for just me!" Mongo said in my head and I smiled. Tom saw me smile and then he stopped walking and looked at me. Mongo and I stopped walking when he did.

"What's the matter? Did I do something wrong?" I looked up and down the sidewalk, there weren't that many people around right now. Tom shook his head.

"I just realized why Frank left; you were talking to Mongo in his head too weren't you? And you told Frank what you were doing or he figured it out, right?" Tom asked me in a very excited manner.

"Pretty much, he said that only a True Alpha can do that and that you guys couldn't do that. Only when you were changed could you talk to them." I was being careful of my wording in case anyone else was listening to us.

"You and I are the only ones that I have ever heard of that could do it." Tom said as he smiled even bigger.

"Really, my Mom and Grandpa can do it as well as Harry. I just figured it was a Were-Squatch thing." I was excited to hear that I was special but when I said Harry's name Tom kind of lost a little of his happy.

"Well, that is a lot of True Alpha's. I am not surprised about you Grandfather though, it is probably a part of why he is special. But you being a True Alpha is really good, it means when we have kids they will all be True Alpha's." Tom started to smile again; I will let that one go for now.

"Hey, can we stop at the McStud's Doughnuts and grab some for dessert later? Mongo said he can hold it for a few more minutes if he gets two doughnuts for himself also." I said laughing which made Tom laugh too.

"Sure, we can run in there really quick. They always have great doughnuts ready and waiting." Tom said as he opened the door for Mongo and I to go inside. We chose a dozen doughnuts and were back out and heading for the park in record time. Tom carried the box and I could smell them the whole walk to the park. The park was really nice and Mongo found the perfect spot to go potty and was back to me within minutes. By the time we walked to the Park Avenue Apartments Zeek was standing outside waiting for us.

"Your dinner, my lady!" Zeek handed me the food bag instead of Tom, which was weird. Tom took it from me and all the while Zeek just stood there staring at me with a dumb look on his face.

"You can go back and have fun now!" Tom said in a louder voice than he needed, scaring both Zeek and I and making us jump. Mongo sat at my feet and gave him a dirty look. Then Zeek took off like a shot headed back to his brothers at the bar.

Tom, Mongo and I went upstairs to his apartment so that we could eat our dinner. Tom seemed to still be in a good mood but we didn't really talk until we got inside his apartment.

"Are you okay with me letting Mongo loose from his leash?" I asked out of respect for his place.

"Sure, go ahead. The only thing I ask is that he doesn't get on the couch or chair please." Tom asked and then looked at Mongo, who nodded his head once, then I took off the leash and Mongo went into the living room area and laid down next to the couch.

"Okay, can I help with anything?" I asked as I walked into the kitchen where Tom was pulling down some plates to put our food on. He even had a plate for Mongo's food, which he set on the floor in the kitchen.

"Nope I got it. Hey, Mongo dinner!" Tom hollered for Mongo to come and get his dinner in the kitchen. Mongo came trotting right in to eat. Then Tom took his plate and mine to his small kitchen table at the end of the kitchen before it turned into the living room. Then he went back and got two glasses of ice tea that he had made ahead of time for me. I smiled that he thought to make some for me.

"I see that smile. Yes, you have gotten me on drinking iced tea too. I made it for you but I really enjoy drinking it." He said as he set our glasses down when he sat down in his chair.

Our food was still warm; Zeek must have ran it over when it came out. We ate in silence for a little while and then Tom decided to talk.

"So, I think that I should update you on my family since they are coming to meet you. And I know that the council has been asking them for more details about Grandma and my mom's families." Tom was saying in between bites. I just smiled because my mouth was full so I just nodded.

"Well, my Grandma says she was from another Were-Squatch tribe in the Redwood Forest. She didn't know much about her heritage past that though. Her parents didn't like the fact that she was mated to another Were-Squatch from somewhere else because my Grandpa was disowned from his tribe because his chosen profession was being a logger. My Grandma left her tribe to be with Grandpa and they had three sons. My Dad is the oldest and his brothers left home at an early age to see the world." Tom took another bite and I was almost done eating mine. Mongo must have finished his too because he was now lying at my feet under the table.

"Did his brothers leave before they went through the change? Did they know what they were?" I had to ask.

"Yes, they knew from an early age what they were and they left after puberty and their first couple of changes. They didn't want to be loggers; my Dad did though so he stayed. Then one day he saw my Mom in the woods where he and Grandpa were doing some logging. She was just walking through the woods with some red wolves by her side." Tom stopped for a second to take a drink.

"Were there really red wolves in California?" I asked, I didn't know that much about red wolves but I had never heard of any in California before.

"Well they weren't really wolves; they were my Mom's family. You see her Dad was a Red Were-wolf and her Mom was human, at least until after Mom and her sisters were born. My Mom was the only one out of the three children they had that were not a Were-anything. Mom wasn't sure she even wanted to be a Were-wolf but when she met my Dad they fell in love almost instantly." Tom was looking off into the distance, like he was seeing his parents fall in love. Then he took his last bite of chicken and smiled at me. My food had been delicious but now I was thinking about McStud's Doughnuts when Tom started talking again.

"So, where was I? Oh, yah. My parents fell in love but my Mom's family didn't like her being with a Were-Squatch. Her Dad even tried to run him off. But then my Mom went looking for him on the full moon while her family was busy doing their Were-wolf thing. And she ran into my Dad while he was in a mating frenzy after meeting her and well, Dad bit Mom and they were married at the next full moon. They have been happy ever since." Tom was finished saying and then he stood up taking his and my plates to the kitchen to place them into the sink. Then he picked up Mongo's and placed it on the counter. He opened the box and put the two doughnuts that I chose for Mongo on his plate and set it on the floor again.

"Mongo here are your doughnuts buddy." Tom said while watching for Mongo who shot out from under the table no more than he saw Tom place the plate on the floor. Then Tom got down two small plates and placed a doughnut on each one and brought mine over to me. I took a drink of my tea.

"Thank you Tom." I said as he looked at me when he sat back down in his chair.

"I want to be totally honest about everything with you Carrie. I feel that when a person is hoping for a real relationship you should be totally honest." Tom was saying as he took my left hand in his and then he pulled it to his lips and kissed the back of my hand.

"Thank you Tom. I know you what you mean. Is there anything about me and my family that my Grandpa or Mom hasn't already told you that you would like to know?" I asked when he released my hand. I picked up my doughnut and took a bite. I chose the chocolate éclair with the nice smooth vanilla pudding inside, I know I played it safe compared to Tom's white chocolate icing with cocoa puffs cereal on top.

"Well they did try to fill me in on everything and they are pretty proud of your family heritage. But they didn't fill me in too much about you personally. They thought those were things that you and I should learn about each other. Like your favorite color?" Tom was asking simple questions, this I could handle.

"Blue is my favorite but sometimes I like black too. But it really depends on if its clothes or just a color of something other than clothes." I was saying as I took another bite of my doughnut. Tom smiled at me and then took his napkin and wiped my mouth. I'm not sure how I feel about that, I have always been independent and I have never had a man do that before.

"I might have guessed that by your dress, which is beautiful on you by the way. I didn't even get a chance to let you know that I find you breathtaking this evening." He smiled and got all goo-goo eyed at me. Which I found to be a little creepy.

"Thank you. We didn't get much time to ourselves before your brothers got involved in our date, did we?" I asked him knowing the answer all ready.

"Yah, we are kind of a package deal, my brothers and I." Tom said and he took a bite of his doughnut.

"Wait, what? I am not marrying you and your brothers, no way! I am a one-man woman Tom!" I was starting to freak out, there was no way I was having more than one husband at a time and from what I was told mating was for life, literally death do part stuff. Tom dropped his doughnut back on his plate so that he could take hold of my hands before I bolted.

"No, no Carrie that's not what I meant. Good to know that you are a one-man woman though. I meant was that if you choose me you are getting six little brothers that will be looking to you and I for guidance. But that's all; they are not to touch you in a husband wife kind of way, ever!" Tom was on his feet and calming me down. I could seriously see myself running out there.

"Okay, sorry I miss understood. I am all new to this Were-thing and I still don't know all the rules. I was pretty sure it was mate for life and truly death till you part but I wasn't sure if being an Alpha meant you had to take on more than one mate, which I am against by the way." I said calming down and Mongo was at my side with his head in my lap now. Tom let go of my hands so I could pet Mongo to calm down.

"All right now that I have scared the hell out of you, what is your favorite food? Oh wait it is Heavenly Chocolates, right?" Tom was answering his own question because he actually knew the answer.

"Every good, yes it is. I also love McStud's doughnuts too by the way." I said with a smile, I was calm again and back into a better mood. Mongo and I's connection was definitely very deep.

"Okay good to know. Um, not to change the subject but what were you and Zeek talking about that made his so excited earlier?" Tom asked me taking the last bite of his doughnut now.

"Oh, yah I almost forgot about that. He was telling me that he and your brothers were having a hard time finding Were-Squatch girls. Which Grandpa said Were-Squatch's period are hard to find. Anyway, I told him that I would talk to my mom and Grandpa and see if we couldn't come up with some Were recessive gene girls either in my family or friends of the family in the various tribes that would be willing to date a Were-Squatch and if there is a love connection then be willing to change into a Were-Squatch. He freaked a little about that, sorry." I said as Tom got up and walked into the kitchen to get us another doughnut. Yummy!

"So do you think your Mom and Grandpa would actually help you do that?" Tom asked when he came back to sit down.

"Yes I do. They are the ones saying there are not enough Were-Squatch's and that our species is the only Were's that have to have a recessive gene to be able to change. Well you Mom got the choice and I am sure there are other girls out there that would do the same for love." I was saying getting more and more excited about it.

"Wow you would really do that for my brothers?" Tom asked in wonder.

"Yes, why not? They are nice guys and they are very handsome men." I said and then took a bite of my doughnut. Tom smiled again and started to get his napkin to clean the chocolate off of my mouth again but then he thought better of it and leaned in and licked my lips then he kissed me. It was a gentle kiss that sent a spark when he touched me. Between the doughnut and his lips, I made a very content sound that he took as encouragement to deepen the kiss. With my doughnut forgotten as well as his. He stood taking me with him and our bodies were close together yet again. He really was a good kisser but in the back of my mind I was adding, but he's not Harry.

We both jumped at the sound of someone knocking at his door. I don't know how long we had been kissing but I know I was blushing to say the least. My body was starting to react to Tom and I know his was to mine, it was rather obvious.

"Hold that thought." Tom said as he went to the door.

"What do you need guys?" Tom said to I am assuming his brothers.

"We just wanted to say goodnight to Carrie before we turned in. Is she staying the night cause it's super late you know." I think it was Gary talking, he didn't usually say much. Tom turned and looked at me. I smoothed my dress back into place, I'm not quite sure how it shifted like it did, and then I nodded that it was okay. Tom opened the door more and let his brothers in. They were all there even Frank.

"Hey guys, no I'm not staying the night, Tom is taking me home my girlfriends are waiting up for me." I said as they all came in and crowded around me.

"Well we just wanted to give you a hug good night before we turned in." Jeffery said as he came up to me first, him being the youngest of the brothers is probably why. I nodded my head and he came into my arms, it wasn't a weird hug but like I was hugging a child. He was by no means a child in physical form but I think he was kind of on a mental level somehow. Or it could just be this whole Alpha thing, I just don't know but it felt natural to me.

The guys each hugged me after I let go of Jeffery and I think they went in order of age, the youngest to the oldest ending with Frank. After each of them hugged me they the hugged Tom and headed to their apartments with a "Bye!" over their shoulder. They were a good bunch of kids? Guys or are they just men? Frank being the last was also the one to hug me the longest, and the comment he made was still stuck in my head, "I knew I should have been the one to bite you! Then I would be Alpha with you by my side!" Tom tapped Frank on the shoulder and Frank let me go. He did stand there looking into my eyes for a few minutes before he left without saying another word. He looked so sad.

Tom closed the door and then he looked at the clock to see what time it was. It was a little past midnight and now he was the one who looked very sad.

"I think I better get you home before it gets any later." Tom went into the kitchen and closed the box of doughnuts and placed it next to all of my flowers. Then he went into the living room and picked up a small bag that was sitting by his bedroom door. When he saw me looking at his bag he stopped and looked at me.

"It's my overnight bag. I will go to the hotel the guys and I have been staying at instead of driving home tonight." He simply said.

"Do you already have a room reserved?" I asked as I picked up the dishes from the table and picked up Mongo's plates from the floor.

"No, but I am sure they will have a room for at least one night for me." Tom said confidently.

"You could sleep on my couch for one night. Amanda and Trina are in my bed with mongo and I but the couch is free if you would like to stay." I offered because I felt so bad about him having to take me home even thought it was late.

"Are you sure you are okay with that?" Tom asked as he dropped his bag next to the counter and came toward me to take the dished from my hands.

"Yes, as long as you understand that there will still not be any hanky-panky." I said in my joking voice but also it was a serious thing. He knew what I was talking about.

"Yes Ma'am, I wouldn't do such a thing. Besides, this means we can start our next date sooner. I will already be there." Tom said as he wagged his eyebrows up and down at me to make me laugh.

"Sure Tom we can do that." I did laugh and it felt good.

"Oh, don't forget we have to let Mongo into the park again before we go." I said as I grabbed my bag of clothes and tried to put some of the flowers in it.

"No problem. I need to run next door and let Frank know where I will be overnight and tomorrow. All the guys are staying home the rest of this week. They will be at the full moon ceremony though. My parents will be in on Friday which is our last date so it will be a family date. Is that okay with you?" Tom asked just as he opened his door to go next door.

"Hold that thought!" He yelled as he ran out to the door. I heard the knocking and then he was talking and then Frank was talking and then Frank closed his door a little harder than I would have thought would be respectful then Tom came walking back inside to me.

"Is everything okay with Frank?" I asked him knowing it probably had something to do with what Frank had said to me.

"Yah, he's just acting weird is all. I don't understand why?" Tom looked upset and confused. So beings that he wanted honesty I went to him and closed the door then led him to the table by the arm.

"Sit, I need to tell you what happened earlier with Frank." Tom sat down and so did I. I took a deep breath and told him what Frank had said to me word for word that I could remember. Tom didn't look happy at all.

"Thank you for telling me. His behavior makes more sense now. He wanted you for himself and he thinks he could lead this family if he had you and not me. He is also an Alpha which is why I think he is going to cut out on his own someday. Well, all I can say is I hope you can get this Were matchmaker thing going quickly, cause I have a feeling he's going to be a jerk for a while." Tom said with a smile and then he jumped up from his chair and pulled me up too. Kissed me quickly on the lips giving me another shock and then he smiled.

"Well, let's get this show on the road." Tom said as he grabbed his bag as well as the doughnuts box, handed me my bag and then he collected the rest of my flowers and nodded for me to head out the door with Mongo. I had Mongo's leash on him and walking out the door. I could get used to him carrying things for me at least.

I took Mongo potty while Tom loaded everything into his SUV then we were headed back to my place in Oakridge and Tom was staying the night on my couch. I hope I hadn't bitten off more than I could chew with this. We hadn't even discussed what we were doing for our date tomorrow yet. Well we will have time on the trip home. I wasn't tired yet but I am sure I will be by the time we get home.

We were about halfway home when Tom finally spoke. I was beginning to wonder what he was thinking so hard about but I guess being in charge of six brothers and a business would be more time consuming than I had ever thought of.

"So what do you want to do tomorrow, just the two of us?" Tom asked me.

"You mean the three of us; I have to have Mongo with me." I reminded him.

"Sorry slip of the lip, the three of us tomorrow?" Tom was taking this very well.

"How about we take a hike in the back of the property? There is a creek and a waterfall back there that I would love to show you and Mongo knows every inch of the property." I said getting excited.

"Sure, we can make it a picnic too. Have you taken anyone else out there?" Tom asked and I knew he was fishing to see if Harry and I had been back there together. We hadn't but I had thought about taking him there.

"Nope, just Mongo and my two girlfriend's, Amanda and Trina. We have been over every inch of Oakridge when we were teenagers. We loved exploring everywhere; it was a little boring in a small town." I said as he smiled at me.

"I can imagine, at least I had my brothers with me at all times." Tom said as he came into Oakridge.

"Well Amanda and Trina are like sisters to me, so I kind of know what it's like to have siblings. Plus, during the summers a lot of my cousins that were my age would come and stay with my grandparents so we had them to hang out with as well. Did you know that my Uncle Jared isn't that much older than me? He was a lot of fun as a kid, before he joined the military and became a man." I was really filling Tom in on me and my family. I guess he would see them all at some point and since I will be meeting his in two days I guess he should know.

"Wow, you sound like you had a lot of fun as a teenager and I am sure you got into plenty of high adventures too. Did you ever see any of your cousin's change into whatever Were they were?" Tom was asking.

"Nope, by the time my cousin's hit puberty which is when there Were gene activates we were all doing separate things. I think my grandparent's house was probably where they were educated on their Were-stuff. I can only guess because I still haven't been fully informed on everything yet." I said as we pulled into my driveway.

"The house is dark; I bet the girls went to bed without me since it's so late." I said as I got out of the SUV and opened the backdoor to let Mongo out. He went straight into the yard to go potty. He was happy to be home.

"I'm sorry we took so long, I just wanted to spend as much time with you as possible and then my brothers butting in didn't help." Tom said as he got everything out of the back and came up behind me as I unlocked the door. He had everything but my purse this time.

We went in very quietly and Tom followed me to the kitchen where I tuned on the light. I pulled out a couple of vases and added the flowers to them and then added sugar and water. I managed to get them all into three vases in total. I left them on the kitchen island. Then I grabbed my bag and my purse and headed into the living room turning off the kitchen light as we left. I grabbed the blanket and pillow out of the hall closet next to the bathroom and took them back into the living room where Tom was putting his bag into the chair.

"So, here is the blanket and pillow. You know where the bathroom is and the kitchen help yourself if you get hungry or thirsty. The girls get up really early so I will try to tell them you are here before I go to bed. And I will see you in the morning." I said as I started to turn to go to my room where Mongo had already gone. He was in a hurry to go to bed and he wasn't waiting for me either.

"So, I guess this is good night then?" Tom asked as he walked around the couch and took me into his arms and kissed me. I got the shock when his lips touched mine. I had to say it felt weird having him stay in my house and I was kissing him. I was better with it when we were at his place and now in mine it just wasn't right. Good thing it was only a quick kiss and then he let me go. He smiled at me and I smiled back.

"Good night Tom." I said as I started walking to my room.

"Good Night Carrie. See you in the morning." He was said and then I was gone into my room and closed the door.

I did my evening things and changed into my night clothes in the bathroom. When I came out to sneak into bed I found both girls and Mongo sitting up in bed.

"Sorry I was trying to be quiet." I said as I came to the edge of the bed.

"We were awake when you got home. So, Tom is staying on the couch?" Amanda asked me in a whisper, knowing he was.

"Yes, it was too late for him to drive home and the hotel would be booked for the night. Besides we are going on a hike in the morning for our next date." I said trying to defend my decision.

"I wasn't saying anything bad about it, calm down. What happened this evening?" Amanda asked, she knew me so well.

"Spill it all sister or we are keeping you up all night." Trina said in her loudest whisper.

"Okay, okay!" I said just before I recapped my whole evening to them both. It only took me a half an hour but by the time I was done they were both shocked and awed about the twist my life had taken.

"So, that's my evening. Are you guys ready for bed now?" I asked climbing into bed because I was exhausted.

"We will be exploring this more later but yes, sleep is good." Amanda whispered and she laid down.

"Night ladies." Amanda said with a yawn and then she closed her eyes. Then Trina laid back down as well.

"Night." And she closed her eyes too. That just left Mongo sitting there. I pulled the covers over me and Mongo cuddled up to me.

"Good night girls, Night Mongo." Then I closed my eyes but then I heard in my head.

"Night, we will hike in the morning." Then Mongo closed his eyes too. I reached up and turned off the lamp by my bed and the house was now silent. I fell asleep very quickly.

## **Chapter 34**

With the new morning, comes new things to freak out about, right? Well it was that way for me at least. I guess the girls forgot that Tom was here because they both came shrieking and running back into the bedroom after finding him awake on the couch. They were in their night clothes and they went in to the kitchen to start the coffee that they love to drink and Tom only said 'Good Morning" to them. Then I get woken up with the shrieking, why me? It's only Wednesday for goodness sake!

"Okay girls, it's not like you are wearing Lingerie or something. For God's sake Amanda you are wearing your Dad's old night pants and t-shirt, and Trina you are wearing sweatpants and a t-shirt!" I know I was cranky first thing in the morning after not getting much sleep. I was having nightmares about someone stealing me in my sleep.

"Right, we kind of over reacted didn't we?" Amanda was saying as a way of apologizing.

"Sorry we woke you." Trina was saying while ringing her hands. Then the pounding on the front door started. Mongo was out of bed and running to the door. I put on my robe as I walked to the front door. I glanced in the living room to see Tom sitting on the couch fully dressed and smiling at me. He mouthed "Sorry". I opened the door to find Terry, Jerry and Harry standing on the porch huffing and puffing like they had ran a mile or something.

"We heard screaming!" Harry said as he started to walk in the door. Terry stopped him before he could walk in.

"Sorry buddy you have to stay put. Are the girls alright?" Terry said as he looked behind me.

"Yes we are fine, just being stupid girls." Trina said as she walked around me and into Terry's arms.

"Where is Amanda?" Jerry asked just before she also walked around me and into his arms.

"What scared you guys?" Harry asked looking from me to the girls and back at me again.

"I wasn't scared they were the ones who screamed. They got up to make coffee and found Tom on the couch, he said good morning to them and they freaked." I said in the way of explaining everything and then I saw Harry's face. He was first shocked and then mad and then he was just sad. I saw all these emotions pass across his face in seconds.

"Well as long as you're okay I will head back to my trailer." Harry said and then he was gone, he moved very quickly.

"So, you girls are okay then?" Jerry asked as he kissed Amanda's forehead.

"Yes, we are fine. Like I said, just being stupid girls." Trina answered for both of them. Amanda just nodded her head.

"Okay then are you two coming out for breakfast soon?" Terry asked both Trina and Amanda but he didn't look at me.

"Yah, just let us get dressed really quick and meet us at the back gate." Amanda said and then she kissed Jerry really quick and ran into the house followed by Trina who kissed Terry and ran. I was left holding the door.

"Will you and Tom be joining us this morning Carrie?" Terry asked but I could sense that he was only being nice.

"No, not this morning Terry. Thanks anyway." I said as I was getting antsy to close the door.

"Okay then. See you later." Terry said as he turned to walk away.

"Yah, bye." Was all Jerry had to say as he too turned and followed Terry around the house and back to the trailers. I closed the front door and went into the living room.

"Sorry about that, in my defense I did tell them you were here last night." I said as I stood in the doorway.

"That's okay; I think I scared them a little." Tom said as he stood up.

"Do you want me to leave? I can always come back later for the hike." Tom was being so sweet about all of this.

"No, you stay right here. I'm going to go and get dressed since I'm totally awake now and we can make some breakfast. Then we can go on our hike. Sound good?" I asked as I started to turn to go and get dressed.

"Okay, sounds good. I will wait right here and try not to scare anybody else." Tom said as he sat back down on the couch.

"The remote is on the coffee table if you want to watch TV while you wait." I said as I was halfway down the hall.

"Okay, thank you!" Tom yelled up the hall to me.


The girls were already getting dressed when I came into the room.

"We will be out of your hair in just a minute. Make sure you take you cell with you hiking along with a walkie in your backpack please." Amanda said as she kissed me on the cheek and hugged me really quick on her way to the bedroom door.

"Yah, we will have ours on our channel in case you need any help. Love you!" Trina said as she did the same to me.

"We'll let Mongo out into the backyard to go potty while you get dressed!" Amanda yelled, she was halfway down the hall already.

"Okay, Thanks!" I yelled back. Then I noticed that the girls hadn't taken their bags with them this time, I guess they figured they would be sleeping with me again tonight. They knew what I was going through and they also knew that I can't and won't be having sex any time soon.

I got dressed in record time, just a light grey t-shirt and my khaki shorts with my hiking boots that were very worn in. Then I put on a little makeup and put my hair in a ponytail. Grabbed my backpack that has all my emergency hiking supplies as well as the walkie talkie that the girls and I always use when hiking and headed for the living room.

"Hey I just need to grab a bag for the food and get that together and we can head out after breakfast. How does that sound?" I asked out loud when I starting walking down the hall thinking that Tom was still in the living room. But when I stopped in the living room Tom was gone and everything was back in order. You couldn't even tell that anyone had stayed the night.

"I'm in the kitchen! I hope you don't mind I started to get breakfast ready for us. I was just going to make breakfast burritos really quick, I'm almost done." Tom was saying as I walked into the kitchen.

"Wow, Okay that sounds good! I was actually going to do the same thing." I set my bag by the sliding glass door and then let Mongo back inside.

"Great minds think alike." Tom said with a smile. Mongo went straight to his water bowl and I went to the cupboard where I kept his dog food and filled his bowl. Then I got a plastic gallon sized bag and put some of his dog food in it and placed it in my backpack as well.

"Okay then I will grab out picnic lunch stuff while you are doing breakfast then." I said as I grabbed my insulated cooler bag for our food.

"Sounds good to me." Tom said while cooking the scrambled eggs and they looked like they had ham and onions in them, yum!

First I went to the fridge and grabbed the peppered chicken deli lunch meat, cheese slices, a small mayo bottle and then I asked Tom, "We are having peppered turkey deli lunch meat sandwiches, do you want anything other than mayo for it?"

"Nope I'm good with that." Tom smiled at me when he turned off the heat to the skillet and then he came over to the fridge and grabbed the burrito shells from the bottom shelf while I went to the set the food in the cooler bag.

"Do you have a preference on chips? I have plain potato or Dorito chips?" I asked when I went to the chip and cracker cupboard.

"Either one is fine with me." Tom was now placing the eggs into the shells and he looked like an expert when he started rolling them up. He saw me watching him do this and smiled.

"Being the oldest I learned really quick how to make breakfast for all of us boys. We had a lot of breakfast burritos before going to school every day." He was smiling and you could tell he had happy memories of his childhood. That was nice to see on his face.

"We had extra kids mostly during the summer; otherwise it was just me until the girls came around. But their Mom's usually made sure they ate before leaving the house to come to mine, but lunch was a different story." I was saying as I grabbed the plain potato chips and placed them into two sandwich bags. Then I grabbed the bread and placed six pieces into a gallon storage bag, wrapping them in a kitchen town from the drawer so they didn't collect moisture from the cold things in the bag and put them and the chips into the bag. Then I went to the cup cupboard and grabbed my two reusable water bottles and filled them with ice and tea and grabbed four bottles of water from the fridge and placed them in the cooler bag as well. Once I was done I saw that Tom was too. We had our plates on the kitchen island so that we could eat together before we took off hiking.  He was a thoughtful man.

We ate quickly and were out the door with Mongo in no time.  Tom insisted on carrying the food cooler bag since it was heavier than the emergency bag. We headed out the front door and jumped into the 4 runner and I drove us to the back of the property. We parked and started our hike through the woods I used to run and play in, and that was before I became a Were-Squatch.

We had been hiking a little while just walking slow and taking our time looking at everything there was to look at in nature.  We came to salmon creek which runs through the whole property and eventually goes out to the river.

"Hey let's stop and sit for a few minutes to watch the water move by.  It's too bad we don't have fishing poles." Tom said as he helped me down to the water's edge and we sat together on a large bolder next to the water as Mongo ran around in the water splashing and drinking the water.

"Yah I usually have them with me.  I have two collapsible poles that are in the back of the 4 runner but I didn't think to grab them." I said sitting with my legs dangling down the side of the boulder.

"It's so peaceful here.  Not like the city, always moving always changing. I almost wish I could stay here." Tom said as he slid back down the boulder and walked to the water and squatted down to look.

"So that leads me to a question about the future.  If I choose you then how are we doing the whole living arrangement and the jobs issue? I have my dream job working in the woods with Mongo; I can't just give that up!  And living in the city was tough on me when I was going to school but now being a Were-Squatch as well as having Mongo, city life just makes my skin crawl, do you know what I mean?"  I know I was being honest about my feelings and decisions but Tom wasn't looking at me when I was talking he was looking in the water and then across the creek.

"I know how you feel. When my brothers and I first came to Eugene it was rough but we came to love living in there. With our line of work, well you don't see very many famous people needing a body guard in the woods do you?" Tom was saying as he walked back to the boulder to sit on it again, carefully navigating the smaller stones he was walking on so he didn't twist an ankle, which I have done before.

"That doesn't quite answer my questions though, Tom." I said as he climbed back onto the boulder right next to me to were our legs were touching then he placed his right hand on my left thigh and looked into my eyes.

"If you and I are meant to be then we will find a way to compromise." He said then he leaned over and kissed the end of my nose, giving me an electric shock again. This one made my teeth tingle and made me have to pee.

"I have to go potty!" I said as I jumped down from the boulder and headed over to the wooded area behind us. I always had a napkin in my pockets for just such an occasion.

"Okay, Mongo and I will be right here. And I won't look, I swear!" Tom hollered at me as I went around a tree with a few bushes around the bottom. Looked like a good place to me. I turned to face the creek and Tom's direction and started to unfasten my pants when I heard something rustle the bushes behind me. I stood straight up and turned to face that direction. I know that there is the possibility of running into bears out here, so I always have. My pistol was in my backpack over by the boulder though so I didn't have that on me. I squatted down and made myself small enough to see under the bushes and I listened. A few minutes went by and then the rustling of the bushes came again. Then a pair of boots came into view. And I got pissed off; there shouldn't be anyone in these woods. Then it came to me, I can talk to Mongo even if he wasn't right here.

"Mongo, there is a man here in the woods behind me. Grab the gun holster out of my backpack and bring it to me, quickly but carefully!" I think I yelled in Mongo's head.

"I'm on it!" Mongo yelled back in my head which made me wince a little bit. The guy was still standing there in the bushes, I could see past his ankles but he was wearing a pair of hiking boots that had seen better days. A few seconds later Mongo was at my side with my gun holster which also had my badge on it as well. I pulled my gun and stood up. Mongo and I slinked around the backside of the bush coming up behind that man.

"Mister you are on private property and I suggest you put your hands up!" I said in my most authoritative voice, I sounded pissed even to my ears. The man set a rifle down on the ground and then put his hands in the air. He was wearing dirty jeans that had seen better days along with a red checkered flannel shirt over his long johns' top that you could see through the holes at his elbows along with his hiking boots that I saw with his socks over the bottoms of his jeans.

"Now slowly turn around and face me. And no funny business or my dog will bite your balls off!" That's when mongo started with the growling and snarling, hell if I didn't know the dog I would have wet my pants. The guy turned around and smiled at me, smiled! He was scruffy and had unkempt hair sticking out of his nasty, greasy baseball cap and he stunk too.

"Sorry Ma'am. I know we aren't supposed to be here but we know there are Bigfoot here and we have to kill one to get on TV." The man was saying as I recognized who he was. It was Billy Bob Brockman, the weapons specialist for the SMM Bigfoot Hunters.

"I thought you fella's were told to not come back here. Aren't you supposed to be in jail in Eugene right now?" I asked as I heard and felt Tom come up behind me. Billy Bob lost his smile then. Sure the woman with a gun makes you smile and never mind the snarling dog that will eat your balls but you lose you smile when a man comes into the picture, idiot!

"We got out on bail." Billy Bob shrugged his shoulders.

"And you thought what; you wouldn't get caught again being on private land?" I asked him knowing he wasn't the smarted tool in the shed, obviously.

"Well, not really. We thought that your people wouldn't even see any of us since the land is so big." He really was an idiot, and he was the weapon specialist?

"When did you guys get here? And where are the rest of you?" I asked him and he just stood there for a second.

"Mongo, sick balls!" I growled out. Mongo started to lunge, which gave me an automatic reaction from Billy Bob who then screamed and covered his crotch.

"No please god! No!" Billy Bob was close to tears at this point.

"All the guys are here and we are all over the property!" Billy Bob said while crying and shrinking down into a small ball trying to cover his privates as much as possible. Tom went up to where he was and took his rifle.

"Do you have any more weapons on you?" Tom asked the Billy Bob. Billy Bob just shook his head and then he seemed to have a second thought and pulled a knife out from under the front of his flannel shirt and tossed it on the ground still in the sheath.

"Carrie dear, would you like me to call the sheriff? Or is this a shoot them and bury them situation since they obviously don't follow the law either?" Tom was asking in a serious voice but I could see the smile on his face, he was having a little fun with this guy.

"I'm not really into have to dig a hole today; can you call my Uncle the Sheriff for me please?" I was still talking when Tom pulled out his cell phone. I wonder what he would have done if I had said yes let's just shoot him and leave him for the animals? Tom got Uncle Jared on the phone right away and they were already at Grandpa George's house warning him that the SMM Bigfoot Hunters had been seen in Oakridge this morning.

"Well Darling you take me on such fun adventures! Your Uncle will be here in about 15 minutes. He knows exactly where we are; apparently this is your favorite thinking spot?" Tom was saying when he was putting his phone back into his pocket.

"Well, so far you haven't been bored with me, right?" I asked with a smile.

"No, I can honestly say I am never bored with you around." Tom was smiling too.

When we started walking Billy Bob out to where we had parked the 4 runner, it went quicker this time because we weren't stopping to smell the roses per say Tom leaned over to me as we walked.

"I love that movie too by the way." Tom smiled.

"Oh yah and I don't know what you are referring too." I said coyly

"Stand by me, the movie. The part when the junk man telling his dog to 'sick balls' and the dog is supposed to attach the kids balls. That is what you were referencing, weren't you?" Tom started out strong but then at the end he was second guessing me because I managed to keep a straight face. Then I couldn't hold it any longer so I smiled too. But I knew that Billy Bob was listening to us so I had to say otherwise.

"No, not really. I just taught Mongo to 'sick balls' whenever a man pisses me off!" Then I winked at him and looked forward toward Billy Bob again and Tom got what I was saying.

"Remind me <u>NEVER</u> to piss you off!" Tom said loudly.

We could hear the sirens coming long before we saw my Uncle pull up. We had Billy Bob sitting on the ground waiting for Uncle Jared when he got to us. He was in no hurry once he saw I had everything under control.

"Mr. Brockman, I would say nice to see you again but it's not. You are trespassing yet again on private property. Can you tell me where your friends are Sir?" Uncle Jared asked as he stood over Billy Bob with his hand on his gun.

362

"They are all in the woods Sir. Can you please take me to jail so that I can get away from the Lady with a gun and her dog that eats balls, Sir!" Billy Bob said as he looked over at Mongo and I. Mongo gave a lunge with a growl and snarl just to give his performance a little oomph.

"I can do that Mr. Brockman. Do you want to call you friends from the car and tell them to turn themselves in as well?" Uncle Jared asked as he helped Billy Bob off the ground, winking at me and escorted him to the back of his squad vehicle. Then Uncle Jared had Billy Bob make his phone call to his friends who also agreed to meet Uncle Jared at the police station. Then Uncle Jared took his phone and put hand cuffs on him and placed him into the back. Then he came over to talk to us.

"So, I am guessing he was a date crasher? Did he see anything that I need to know about?" Uncle Jared was very protective of me and especially of what we were.

"He only saw us on a date nothing else Uncle Jared." I said and Tom chose that moment to put his arm around my shoulder. This did not escape Uncle Jared's notice.

"Okay then. I will be taking the whole lot back into custody and the Eugene police will be contacted to pick them up yet again. I told your Grandfather that he should have let me do this the first time but he wanted to give them a chance and that's why they saw all the Bigfoot that night they came out here." Uncle Jared said and was watching Tom for his input on the subject since it was him and his brothers that almost got shot that night.

"Sorry about that Sheriff." Tom said and you could tell he was.

"While I appreciate you saying that and all, I still have to deal with the aftermath. I just hope that we can convince them to not return again." Uncle Jared was referring to the full moon ceremony that was basically my wedding any way you looked at it.

"It would be too dangerous for them all to be here and the council will not allow it if there is too much danger. So I hope these guys get the drift and stay away. I will be monitoring the situation. I'm going to take the prisoner in now." Uncle Jared had just dropped a bomb on our heads.

"I will talk to you later Babygirl! Bye Mongo, good boy!" Uncle Jared kissed my cheek and then leaned down to love on Mongo for a minute. And then he climbed into his SUV and left. Leaving us, to finish our picnic date.

## **Chapter 35**

So we went back to the creek with me stopping on the way back to finally pee and then we had our picnic lunch. Tom wasn't in a very talkative mood now and I guess I wasn't either. He was still blaming himself for coming to the property that night to kidnap me and leading the SMM Bigfoot Hunters right to us.

"So what do you want to do after this?" I asked as I took the last bite of my sandwich.

"I don't know what do you want to do?" Tom asked starting to get back in his playful mood again.

"Well we had to have lunch late because of that yahoo, so if you want we can continue to the falls or we can head back and watch a movie at my place?" I said and that's when Tom pulled out his phone to check the time.

"Actually, we should probably head back to your place. I still have to get home to attend to some work stuff so that you and I can go out tomorrow. It will be our last date alone since my parents will be here on Friday for the family date." Tom said as he took the last bite of his sandwich. Mongo had been laying in the sun enjoying nature and the quiet since he wolfed down his lunch already.

"Oh, okay. Do we know what we are doing then?" I asked with interest.

"No, not yet, but I will come up with something just for the two of us." Tom winked at me and he was back to being a happy guy again. I wonder what had him in such a funk, could he really be that sorry about his and his brother's actions that night to bring the SMM Bigfoot Hunters into our lives.

"Okay, just remember that it has to include Mongo. Just think on Mongo as my child, that's what my parents and grandparents do." I said with a shrug of my shoulders.

"Yah, I guess that is a good way of thinking about it. But what happens when you do have children?" I noticed that he said when and not if there. I had to smile.

"Then I guess he will be the oldest child then." And with that I started cleaning up our picnic lunch with a smug smile on my face. Mongo got up out of the sun and came over to me. Then he put his forehead against mine and then laid himself down on me knocking me over and onto the blanket we were sitting on to eat.

"He really is you big kid, isn't he?" Tom asked while joining me in laughing at Mongo's actions.

"Yup, he's my boy." I said and hugged my oldest kid. Tom started cleaning up where I left off, smiling the whole time.

Once we got back to my house I gave Tom a quick peck on the cheek and he took off for home to deal with company business so he could spend more time with me. But was he going to be able to do that if we got married? Would I have to give up my job or would he commute from here in Oakridge? So many questions to answer and I never even got to think too much about those questions with Harry since we weren't thinking long term at the time.

I was stuck in my head as I unloaded the 4 runner and took everything inside. Tom had taken his stuff to his truck before we even left this morning so he didn't even have to go into the house. I unlocked the door and Mongo went inside before me.

"We have company!" Mongo said in my head. I was just thinking it was Amanda and Trina at the back sliding glass door but it wasn't it was Mike from the food truck.

"Hey Mike!" I said as I slid the door open after putting everything I had in my hands on the kitchen island.

"Hey I was just checking on you since I didn't see you for breakfast or lunch. Is everything okay?" Mike was a good guy and I have a sneaking suspicion that it was Harry sending him in to check on me.

"I'm good Mike; you can let Harry know I am all in one piece too." Mike smiled and blushed a little.

"Am I really that easy to read?" Mike said looking at all the flowers on the kitchen island and raising an eyebrow as if to ask who they were from.

"Yup, and the flowers are from Tom's brother's by the way." I said as I stepped into the kitchen and started putting stuff away as well as throwing away our garbage from the picnic. You take it in the woods you take it out again.

"Cool, well I was just wondering if you were going to be coming out for dinner from the truck tonight since Tom left." Mike said and then winced at how that sounded. I caught it too and smiled.

"Yes I will be and you can let Harry know too. I'm not supposed to see him but if he happens to be having dinner at the same table as the girls and I then I don't think that it's technically breaking the rules." I said as I folded up the cooler bag and put it in the bottom of the pantry.

"Okay then I will see you out there. Bye!" Mike was assaying as he slipped back out the sliding glass door and I was left in the kitchen alone.

I figured I better give my mom a call and update her on what Tom told me about his family history when my phone starting ringing and it was her.

"Hi Mom I was just about to call you!" I was actually shocked.

"Oh, well I guess it's a good thing I called you then. I just wanted to update you on Tom's family." Mom said as I sat down on the couch to talk.

"Seriously? That's why I was calling you. Tom told me all about his family, what he knew anyway. His parents and grandparents are coming into town on Friday for a family date." I said with a little sarcasm.

"Well, I just spoke with his Grandmother Ester and his Mom Nancy and they already filled me in. Can you believe his Grandmother's family disowned her for marrying a logger, of all things?" My Mom was very pro tree I think that has to do more with being a Were-Squatch than anything but she also lives in a logging community too. So those kinds of things were normal for us.

"I know right? And his Mom's family was Red Were-wolves? I mean seriously she was the only one to not get the Were-gene?" Mom and I were gossiping like old times now and it made me smile.

"I know right? Well at least she found her husband Norman and they are happily married." Mom was saying about Tom's Mom.

"So, I am guessing you guys are friendly now?" I asked just to see what her opinion of them was.

"Oh, yes they are very nice ladies. And his Grandma Ester also gave me the names of her family so that the council can contact them. One to let them know there is a council and two to let them know that their family has been accepted into it and to see if they would be interested in knowing any of us. We are hoping to expand the Were-Squatch presents. Plus, Amanda has done wonders with the information that Harry gave her about the guy who bit him also!" Mom was getting super excited.

"Really? What did she find out? And why didn't she tell me yet?" I was asking rather fast but Mom was there with the answers for me.

"Well you have been busy dear. Anyway, the guy is not from our family that bit him! There is yet another Were-Squatch tribe and they are in Montana! Your Grandpa wanted to be the one to contact them personally and he will let me know how that went later tonight. And he will be contacting the Redwoods Were-Squatch tribe that Tom's grandmother came from as well. By the way your Dad and I are having dinner with your grandparents tonight, so I better go." Mom was really getting excited and I was too. Things seemed to be coming together and in a good way too.

"Oh, okay Mom, say hi to Dad for me and tell him I love him. I love you, bye!" We always said we loved each other when we got off the phone.

"Okay Babygirl, Love you too. Bye!" And with that my Mom hung up. Mongo bumped my legs I hadn't even noticed him come into the living room.

"Are you hungry buddy? Do you want to go out and have dinner at the food truck tonight?" I said while rubbing his chest and then his ears which he loves, I think all pit-bulls do.

"Yes, I could eat." Was all Mongo said in my head and then he got up and started walking to the sliding glass door so we could go out through the back gate. I just followed him as he led me to what was becoming one of my favorite places to eat, I can't wait to see what the guys had for dinner options tonight. I also couldn't wait to see Harry either; I hope that Amanda has passed on all the information to him before I get there.

Mongo and I sat at a table with Amanda, Trina, Terry, Jerry and Harry. Harry sat across from me and Trina and Amanda sat on either side of me. Mongo and I had Stephen's fully loaded famous pizza and we both loved it. Harry didn't talk much to me but the looks I got were a mix of him almost adoring me and then he would look like he was in pain. He knew that I had to do what the council had asked of me but he also now knew that there were other options for Were-Squatch's. Our friends left by two's from the table. First it was Amanda and Jerry and then it was Trina and Terry which left Harry and I by ourselves at the table.

"I was hoping to get a chance to talk to you alone. I know the council doesn't want us to spend any more time together until you have mad your choice, but I was just wondering if your Mom was going to let Tom and his brother's know about the tribe that Amanda found in Montana? You know in case they wanted to go and introduce themselves and see if they could also find mates?" Harry sounded so hopeful that Tom would give up his claim and move on, which I kind of did too.

"Mom was going to let my Grandpa call them after he talked to the leader of the Were-Squatch's in Montana. We don't know if they even want outsiders there and or the tribe in the Redwoods. I just hope that my Grandpa George can be his usual persuasive self when he talks to them." I said as harry started reaching across the table toward my hand. I looked around and no one was looking in our direction so I reached mine hand to him as well.

"I have missed touching you." Harry simply said and then he smiled.

"Me too." I smiled so much it made my cheeks hurt.

"So how long before someone sees us you think?" Harry asked as we heard someone coming.

"Carrie!" Amanda yelled which made both Harry and I jump and part our hands.

"You scared the hell out of us Amanda!" I yelled back at her as she walked to the table next to me.

"I'm just trying to help you not break any more rules from the council. It's getting late, Trina and I are ready for bed and we wanted to know if you were ready to go now?" Amanda said as she bumped my shoulder when she grabbed her water bottle she had forgotten.

"That sounds good to me." I said reluctantly as I stood and turned to go with Amanda and Mongo back to the house.

"Carrie, wait! I will walk you guys back to the gate at least." Harry said as he jogged around the table to walk next to me to the gate that wasn't that far away. It made me smile.

"Sure, why not?" I said and he held out his arm for me to take. It only took me a second and then I let him lead me to the gate, really slowly. Amanda, Trina and Mongo got tired of waiting for us to catch up and went on in the gate. Amanda and Trina walked inside leaving the gate open along with the sliding glass door when they went through it. Mongo went off to go potty before bed, leaving Harry and I at the gate to say goodbye.

"So, I got you safely to the gate." Harry said taking my hand from his arm and pulling it to his lips.

"So, I hate to ask but I need to know something." I said rather hesitantly.

"Shoot, I will answer you honestly." Harry said still holding my hand.

"Knowing that there are more Were-Squatch females out there, are you tempted to go and see what your options are?" I asked but in the back of my mind I wished that I hadn't, I don't think I really wanted to know after all but I couldn't take it back now. Harry put a finger under my chin and raised my face so that he could look me in the eye.

"You are the only one that I want Lass. If you choose Tom know that I will not choose another. I will be available for you if he were to die, and no I won't kill him either. I will just wait for you because you are worth waiting for. I love you Carrie, for now and forever." Harry was so honest with me that it actually made a tear roll down my cheek which he wiped away.

"I did not say these things to make you cry or to put extra pressure on you. I just needed you to know how I feel." Harry leaned forward and kissed me lightly on the lips. Then someone cleared their throat.

"Carrie! It's time to say good night to Harry and come in!" Amanda was right there yet again to remind me that I was doing something that I shouldn't be doing. Harry let my hand go and he took a step back.

"Good night Lass. Sweet dreams." Harry said as he turned to leave.

"Good night, my love." I said as I turned him back around and kissed him quickly on the lips and then I ran to the sliding glass door where Amanda and Mongo both were waiting for me. I stopped and turned to face Harry again. He had closed the gate and was waving at me with a dumbfounded look on his face. And then I ducked in the door followed by Amanda and Mongo. I felt like a kid again, giggly and full of joy. Just like I usually feel around Harry. Harry loves me and I love him.

## Chapter 36

    I fell asleep quickly last night and had wonderful dreams about Harry and I being together.  With him I know his was a career with the show but he was willing to make changes to his schedule for me anytime.  Harry loves me and I love Harry, all 6' 4" of that Scottish stud!  Now I just had to figure out how to tell Tom without telling him that I have made a decision before I'm supposed to be making my decision.  Which is harder than you would think.

    The next day, waking up early when the girls woke up anyway, without screaming.  We all did our morning routines without too much of a hassle.  We all took showers which wasn't that difficult, one would climb out while the next went in we never even had to turn off the water and we had plenty of hot water to do it.

    Then the four of us counting Mongo all went out to have breakfast at the food truck together.  Amanda had talked to Jerry already this morning and he let her know that they had a video conference with the

Animal Channel's producers about their show and wouldn't be out to breakfast. So we had breakfast with Mike and Stephen. The conversation was nice and easy going and it was a great beautiful Thursday morning. A few minutes after we finished eating I got a phone call from Tom, I was expecting it to be him calling to plan our date this evening.

"Good Morning Tom!" I said answering the phone.

"Good Morning Carrie. I know I was supposed to call so we could set up our date for this evening but my parent's and grandparent's came in early and we are planning a family meeting. Then we are supposed to go out to your grandparent's this evening for dinner. So I have to cancel our date for this evening, but we are still on for the family date tomorrow. Is that oaky with you Carrie?" Tom was talking so fast it was hard for me to keep up and when what he said finally registered what could I say, no?"

"Well, that's okay. I understand, let me know tomorrow what you planned for the family date." I said as I sat there listening to Tom with people in the background. It almost sounded like they were at the airport or something.

"Well we kind of have that planned already. My family and all of your family are having dinner tomorrow night at your Grandparent's again. Apparently your Grandma May and your Mom are fast friends with my Grandma Ester and my Mom. We will just have to wait and see how our Dad's and Grandpa's do in the same space. Both my Grandpa Calvin and my Dad are Alpha's but they respect that your Grandpa George is not only an Alpha but also the Council Chief of the many Were-kind Indian Nations. Which is pretty impressive to them as well." Tom was going on and on I thought he was in a hurry to get off the phone and see his family but I guess not.

"Wow okay that sounds good to me. But I wonder why I'm not invited for tonight?" I asked him even though I was sure he didn't know anyway.

"I think it's because it's their first meeting I guess. Oh, here they come now. I have to go and I will see you tomorrow evening. Bye!" And Tom hung up the phone before I could even say goodbye.

"Okay that sounded like a long conversation you had in mere seconds!" Amanda made the observation out loud.

"Yah, apparently Tom is cancelling our date tonight because his grandparents and parents came in today instead of tomorrow. And they are all having dinner at my grandparent's tonight without me. Should I call my Mom and ask why I wasn't invited or leave it alone?" I was asking Amanda and Trina but my heart wasn't really in it.

"Well didn't he say you were doing a dinner with all of you tomorrow night though?" Trina asked.

"Sorry, he talked loud." Trina said as an apology for knowing something already that was in a private conversation.

"I would just let it go and enjoy and evening with us girls. Why don't the four of us counting Mongo here go to Springfield and have lunch and then go and see a movie.  Then depending on what time it is we can go out to dinner somewhere and then come home and veg out?" Amanda was suggesting. It did sound like fun and it had been forever since us girls went out together.

"Yah that sounds good to me! Let's do it!"  I was excited now. A girl's day out and we got to take Mongo with us too. I love having a service dog, they can go almost everywhere.

"Where are you ladies going?"  Terry asked from behind me. I spun around on the seat to see Terry, Jerry and Harry standing there. Their meeting must be over and they looked happy so it must have been good. Harry just looked like he was happy to see me again anyway.

"We are having a girl's day out since Tom cancelled his date with Carrie. We are going to Springfield to have lunch, watch a movie and then go out to dinner before coming home to veg out on her couch." Amanda said as a matter of fact as she stood up and went to Jerry to tell him what we planned. I'm not so sure it was just for Jerry's benefit though.

"So you ladies are going out for the day without us?" Terry said as Trina came around the table to be with him. Mike and Stephen went back to the food truck to get out of the way. I'm not sure if it was because they didn't want to know what was going on or they wanted out of there in case there was an argument.

"So what are we men supposed to do today then?" Jerry asked all of us ladies but especially Amanda.

"Maybe you guys could have a guy's day? Go into town and do something too, just not with us." Amanda kissed Jerry's nose and he smiled. Harry just stood back listening but not saying anything at the moment.

"Can we at least meet you ladies somewhere for dinner?" Terry asked looking at Amanda and I as well as Trina. Amanda and Trina looked at each other and then at me and I nodded. Why shouldn't I go out to dinner with the group?

"Sure why not?" I said as I looked at all of them.

"It's not a date it's a group thing and Harry and I just so happen to be in that same group so it's not breaking the rules." I said as I stood up and turned around to face everyone including Harry. Then I saw my mom walking toward us and I know she heard what I said. She smiled at me and then at everyone else in our little group.

"No it is not breaking any rules. You guys all go and have fun in a group; I give my okay for that. Carrie, can I speak to you for a moment." My Mom was being so cool right now which made me wonder what was happening now. Mom took me by the arm and we walked to the gate by my house and Mongo was right at my side.

"Everything okay Mom?" I asked her, she was in a good mood but it seemed like she had something serious to say.

"I wanted to let you know that Tom's Grandparent's and Parents are here and they are all coming out to meet with your Grandparent's, your Dad and I tonight." She was acting as if this was a surprise, but then she didn't know that I had already talked to Tom.

"Mom, it's okay.  That's why the girl's and I were going out today. He cancelled our date to go see you guys but I was just wondering why I hadn't been invited?" I wasn't sure I wanted to know now.

"Well, you already know that you're Grandma and I have become friends with Tom's Grandma and Mom. We have exchanged information about the other two Were-Squatch tribes with them and they have contacted the tribes themselves as well. We are having a talk tonight about viable mates for Tom's brothers but Ester and Nancy also wanted to talk about a viable mate for Tom if you choose Harry. Which I can see you already have, Honey. And I think you know you have also, even though you were supposed to be neutral until the ceremony." Mom gave me that Mom look. She was trying to see if I was upset about Tom's family looking for him a replacement for me as well as the look on my face when she stated the obvious about my decision already. I think she saw what she needed to see.

"I also wanted to talk to you about maybe putting together a database of women in the many tribes that have the recessive gene and may be interested in changing to another Were tribe? You know like a Were-dating site that anyone with a Were recessive gene can find someone to love even though there are another Were type other than the Were tribe they were born into. Like in this case if a Were-Sasquatch is looking for a mate he could court not only girls that have the Were-Sasquatch recessive gene but could be a Were-wolf or Were-Cougar recessive and willing to make a change to have a great guy? Would you help me Mom and maybe Grandma too? Plus, help me with the whole Tom situation?" I asked not knowing if this was something even she would feel comfortable doing.

"Yes, and I think you Grandma May would also be interested in helping make a database of women and maybe some men too?  Being connected to these new tribes is really going to open up the dating possibilities for the younger generation, and maybe a few of the older as well. You never know who might be looking for a mate. I will also help Tom's parents and grandparents go toward a viable mate for Tom if you want me to. I won't push them or Tom but I will make sure that he sees his options. Okay, give me a hug and you go and have fun with your friends. I love you Babygirl." Mom saw as she hugged me very tightly and I hugged her back. I was very happy that it seemed my mom was finally on my side for a change in this situation. Let's just hope that Tom takes it okay as well. He may even back out of the ceremony if he finds someone else who doesn't have to choose between him and the man she loves.

Mom left shortly after talking with me. And I could tell by the look on Harry's face that he must have heard everything we had talked about. And I am sure he shared the information with the group because everyone was smiling at me. Even Mongo had a smile on his face sitting next to me when I stopped to talk to the group.

"Yup, we know! Harry has big ears and a big mouth, are you sure he's not he big bad wolf?" Amanda asked in joking. She and Trina both came forward and hugged me. Then she turned to the guys.

"Well let's get this show on the road and have some fun today guys. Whose truck are we loading up in?" Amanda said as she looked at everyone standing around.

"I'm riding with the Lass if you guys want to take the SUV. I know Mongo prefers his car seat." Harry suggested as he came up behind me.

"Hey, this may be a group thing but it's kind of like your first date! You know since you guys couldn't really go out because there were Sasquatch's and guy's stocking you Carrie!" Trina was saying as we all started heading for my house where the girls and my purses were.

"Yah, I guess it is. Thanks for bringing that up Trina!" Amanda said as he bumped her.

"What did I say?" Trina asked dumbfounded. She didn't understand she was talking about Tom and his brother's ruining our dating before but that Harry couldn't interfere in Tom and I dating. Well the tables have turned and I hope that we are going to have fun today and tonight. Harry won't be sleeping at my place the girls will be but still I can enjoy my time with Harry instead of feeling guilty, I think today was a win, win. We were going to have fun!

## **Chapter 37**

  We left for Springfield shortly after we had made the decision on where to meet for lunch first.  We chose to meet up at the Buffalo Wild Wings for lunch, the whole drive down to Springfield from Oakridge Harry and I had a great conversation about everything and nothing at the same time.  He told me about how the meeting went with the Animal Channel's guys and how they are very excited about the show.  There is a possibility of having the Bigfoot Getters film a series of more hunts here in the area. Everything was so natural and easy when I was with him.

  Once we got to the restaurant we ate and laughed and had a great time, so much so that the time just flew by and we had to go to a later movie than we had originally planned.  We drove around to the theater side of the mall and went inside.  For a Thursday night it wasn't so bad we got in threw the ticket line quickly and the refreshment line was super-fast only two other people in line besides us.  Harry paid for my lunch and

Mongo's when we ate at BBQ Wingville. Then he paid for my ticket for the movie so I felt it only fair if I bought the refreshments. We got one large buttered popcorn to share. I got my red vines and he got his junior mints plus our two bottles of water. Neither of us was really into soda much. Mongo was right there with us the whole time being such a good boy too.

When the movie was over and we all met out by the vehicles that we had parked in the outer part of the lot so that Mongo could go to the restroom easier we decided to go to dinner at the IHOP down the road from the mall. We were seated right away they never have a problem with service dogs and I was really in the mood for some strawberry pancakes with strawberry syrup. And of course Mongo had his plain pancakes with peanut butter on them; he is a peanut butter freak. We all had such a great time just hanging out together and talking, about everything and nothing all at once. Harry and I fit together like two pieces of a puzzle and our puzzles pieces fit well with Amanda and Jerry's and Trina and Terry's. We were three best friends who just so happened to be dating 3 best friends and it was amazing! And again Harry paid for Mongo and I's dinner.

After dinner went late from all the fun we were having we decided to get headed home. This time the guys rode together and the girls rode home with me. So as we separated into the two different vehicles we paired off to say good night. Trina and Harry were on the other side of the 4 runner, the doors were unlocked and Mongo was safe inside already. Trina had her backdoor open and about to get in when Terry turned her around for a very passionate kiss goodnight.

Jerry and Amanda were by her open door as the front passenger and Harry and I were by the driver's door but I hadn't gotten a chance to open my door yet. I had put Mongo in his seat in the back so when I closed his door was when Harry took the opportunity to grab me and kiss me until I was so light headed I couldn't think straight. When our lips finally parted I swear I was crossed eyed.

"I have missed you so much Lass. I will miss you again once you get into this truck. When will I be able to see you again?" Harry almost seemed desperate to know.

"I'm not sure, I still have to go through the family date tomorrow night with Tom and then I am supposed to use the next week to think about my decision. Which I need you to know that I have already made, but!" I had to put my hand on his chest to keep him from kissing me again until I could finish what I needed to say.

"But, I cannot make this decision known until the full moon ceremony. They only way out is either my decision or Tom giving up his claim on me. So for the next few days I have to stay away from you again." Harry's facial expressions went from looking so happy and then he went to sad and then back to hopeful all in a matter of seconds.

"But, if you choose me Lass then we can just see each other carefully can't we? No one needs to know, do they?" Harry wanted to see me even though we couldn't I know he was going through a rough time with everything going on but I was too.

"No, we can't chance it. I don't know what the council will do if we are caught breaking rules." I said honestly.

"But we are breaking rules right now aren't we?" He asked.

"No we went out as a group this was not a one on one date and we have my Mother's permission just this one time. She is trying to help us be together we just have to give it a few days and then we can be together. And Harry, it will be together forever! Mates for life, death do we part! Are you ready for that?" I really needed to know that he was ready for the forever.

"I've been ready for forever! I guess if we have to wait a few days it won't matter in the long run. Just know that I will be thinking about you every minute of every day my love." Harry said as he gave me a hug and put his face into my hair at my neck and lightly kissed my neck that in turn gave me goose bumps like you wouldn't believe. Then he pulled back and smiled at me, he knew what he had done to me. So I gave him payback, I pulled him back down for another hug and this time I kissed his neck slowly and gave it a little lick before I pulled away. I could feel him physically shiver in my arms before I pulled back far enough to see his face.

"That is so not fair Lass." Harry was very affected by that and now I smiled.

"All is fair in love and war, my Love!" Then we had to separate so that I could open my car door. Terry and Jerry came around this side of the truck to get Harry so they could go to their SUV. Plus, I think they knew he needed help to walk away from me; can I help it if I excite him as much as he excites me?

"Let's go Harry, it's almost midnight." Terry said as he took Harry by the arm.

"Good night Ladies!" Terry and Jerry both said as the same time while they waved at us. I jumped into the 4 runner and turned it on.

As the guys went to their SUV I became sad and I think the girls knew it too. This was the last time I was going to see Harry for the next week. Next Friday is the full moon ceremony and I have my family date with Tom and his family tomorrow night and then I have a week to think. I have already made my choice but there are still things that must be done. We will see where this coming week takes me. One way or the other I will be getting a mate for life a week from tomorrow. Now it's time to head home with the girls and get to bed, I am still pretty awake but I know that will all change on the ride home.

When I got home and went to put my cell phone on the charger I noticed a text from my Mom.

"Everything went great! I love Tom's family everyone is really interested in making the database for finding mates and your Grandpa said to let you know that we are all going to work on it. I will call you in the morning, not too early because I can see that you are not home yet. I hope you and the group had fun. Love you!" I know she will still call me pretty early in the morning. I had to share this with the girls before we all got into bed, so I read it out loud to them.

"Well that's good news right? I mean this way you won't feel so guilty when you choose Harry, right?" Trina asked me.

"Yes this is good, and it will give me something to work on as well. I knew Mom and Grandma would love this idea too, being matchmakers for Were's." I said as I sat on the edge of the bed.

"So, that means that Tom won't be too upset that you don't choose him though, right? I mean his parents are already trying to find him options even before the full moon ceremony so that he has the option of rejecting you before you do it to him so that he can save face, right? A dominance thing, maybe?" Trina was saying while Amanda came out of the bathroom from brushing her teeth.

"I would think as much." Amanda said when she walked around the bed.

"This is fine with me. I may be an Alpha but I don't think that I am too much of an Alpha to need to show dominance yet. Maybe I will later but not right now." I said more to myself than to the girls, I think Trina would understand being a primate expert but I still liked to hear feedback too.

"I think that everything will work out in the end. So you have the family date tomorrow so let's get some sleep. Besides maybe he will dump you tomorrow and you won't have to take the week to think after all?" Amanda said as she rolled over and then Trina climbed into bed next to her. I laid down and turned off the light and then Mongo jumped up to cuddle with me on the outer edge of the bed. Sleep came fast; I had a great day out.

Friday morning came fast, I had dreams about Sasquatches having a party and dancing around and there were a lot of them too. Maybe I was seeing the future with all the Were-Squatch tribes coming together one day soon, maybe even on the full moon if they all come. And just as I predicted,

Mom called bright and early, it was a good thing that I had already gotten up and dressed and was taking Mongo out to potty when she called.

"Hello Mom, good morning." I said as I answered the phone.

"Well, good morning to you too. I'm guessing you had a nice time with your group last night?" She said in a very good mood.

"Yes, I sure did. How was your evening?" I knew she was calling to update me on what she found out. I walked into the house to sit on the couch while I was talking on the phone with Mom.

"Well, I have good news and bad news. I am assuming you got my text last night and it was too late for you to text back when you and the girls got back home?" Mom was just clarifying what I already knew before she began the big reveal.

"Yes I got your text Mom and it was super late but the lunch at Buffalo Wild Wings was great and then we saw a movie and then we ate at the IHOP which I haven't done in a few years at least and then we had long conversations and it was great!" I was in a good mood this morning and I think it had a lot to do with the group fun.

"Okay so your Grandma May and I had a long talk with Tom's family and your Grandpa George had already talked to the two tribes not only about joining the council, which they will as well as them sending all information on anyone that is wanting to seek mates outside their tribes. I already have a list going after I called the tribes that are already in the council after talking to you yesterday. So I had more than a few options for Tom and his brother's to see when they got to your Grandparent's for the meeting slash dinner last night. They each found a couple to take a look at and Tom's Mom pushed him to look as well." Mom was so excited she just kept on talking. I got a few okay's and and's in there as she kept right on talking.

"I tell you what Tom did find one he liked but he said he wasn't giving up on you yet. He said he was taking this to the end even if you didn't choose him because he wanted to make sure that if Harry backed out that you would still have him. He is just too sweet you know?" Mom finished talking but I was a little in shock to find out that he really was willing to stick it through until the end even if I didn't choose him.

"That is really something don't you think?" Mom asked again breaking me out of being stuck in my head.

"That that is something all right. I mean it's great that he might have found someone else but for him to hold off just in case Harry backs out? Does he really think Harry will, back out on me I mean?" Was I being paranoid now? Harry loved me and he said so again last night, he said he wanted me forever, mating is for life he knows this. Now what do I do, ask Harry about this or leave it alone?

"Mom, you don't think Harry will back out on me at the last minute do you?" I asked knowing this was telling her just what was stuck in my brain now.

"He has stuck in there this long dear. I really don't think he is going anywhere. Don't take what Tom said to heart, he was just covering his pride in being an Alpha. He wouldn't let you go now unless you make him because he was the one that bit you, remember?" Mom was right, that was probably what it was.

"Okay, well then. Are we still on for the family date tonight then at Grandma and Grandpa's house? Should I just show up by myself or wait for Tom? Is he supposed to call me or is he thinking I will already be there?" I was all over the place now.

"You're rambling again dear. You really shouldn't show that you're insecure right now. You need to show that you are the Alpha in charge of your life, because you are. Now you come up here at 5 o'clock on the dot. They will be here at 6 o'clock and this will give us a little bit to talk about the lists that we have and the options for how to connect some of these Were's with each other. Your Grandma May is very excited about this too by the way. She is very proud of the fact that you came up with this idea." Mom was making sure that I knew I had done something good without overly congratulating me for it.

"Okay then I will see you guys at 5o'clock on the dot. Love you!" I was ready to get off the phone now.

"Okay dear. Love you, Bye!" And with that Mom hung up the phone. Now I just needed some help from my friends to pick out what I was going to wear this evening.

For the rest of the morning and afternoon Mongo and I were just being lazy and watching movies on the couch. At lunchtime Trina and Amanda came in the house with lunch for Mongo and I from Mike and Stephen, which was a wonderful chicken salad for me and a nice juicy burger patty and fruit bowl for Mongo. Then while we ate lunch I filled them in on everything about my conversation with my Mom.

## Chapter 38

    I texted the girls so they could help with what to wear for the evening. It was at around 3 o'clock. They came into the house right away and they were all too happy to come back and help me find out what to wear for the dinner date with Tom's family, all I had to do was text them when I was done taking my shower and wanted them to help with my hair and makeup as well as what clothes to wear.

    Both women went straight for my closet; they both pretty much knew what I had for clothes. They got out the little black dress that I had worn under my graduation gown when I graduated from the U of O. It was a slinky little number that barely came to the middle of my thighs and the top was very wide open for cleavage to be in full view, did I tell you they were the ones that picked it out for me in the first place? The shoulder straps were large enough to hide my bra straps so I didn't have to go without or use a strapless bra because these D sized girls needed support.

    Trina went to my dresser and grabbed the matching bra and panties that I had also warn that time because they were black lace and they made me feel a little sexy.

    "Wait, why do I want to feel sexy for tonight again?" I asked as I slipped them under things on.

"Because when you feel sexy you feel confident and you are an Alpha who should feel confident at all times, remember?" Amanda said with her hands on her hips.

"Yah, my Mom said something like that too." I said not really feeling it right now.

"Yes, you told us and that it why you are being a full Alpha tonight." Trina said as she dragged me into the bathroom to start on my makeup. Poor Mongo just laid on the bed watching and sleeping, sleeping and watching. I think I saw him smile a time or two.

"I'll start on the preliminary work for the hair while you do her makeup." Amanda said as she walked into the bathroom and plugged in the curling iron she brought with her. I just sat back in the chair and relaxed while my best friends made me look glamorous; I knew I was in good hands with them.

After an hour in the bathroom, which I am glad I texted them early, I was finally finished. I actually didn't even look like myself, I thought anyway.

"You look so fricking hot!" Amanda was saying as she left the bathroom.

"Hell yah she does!" Trina was saying as we walked into the bedroom so that I could put on my dress which they had to help me get into because it was so form fitting, and this girl has curves I am no stick figure.

"Okay now where are those cute little black sandals with the wrap around ties that you bought when you went shopping with your Mom and Aunt Nova? The Roman looking sandals?" Amanda asked as she went to my closet looking through the shoe boxes.

"Top beige box on the left." I said just as she grabbed that box to pull out.

"These are so cute and they make your feet look great as well as your ankles." Trina was saying as she sat me down on the bed and both girls were putting the sandals on me. Man was I being pampered or what?

Once they were done that's when I got to look at myself in the full length mirror in the back of the bathroom door.

"DAMN!" Was all I had to say about myself? The hair, makeup and the clothes with the sandals I was a total babe!

"So, now you just have to be able to get into your 4 runner and drive up to your grandparents without smudging or ripping anything. Would you rather take my car since I won't be going anywhere?" Amanda offered me her little red Honda Civic; she loves her car and never lets anyone drive it if she can help it. This was an honor!

"Wow, that would be great and it's an automatic so I won't have to worry about shifting either. Thanks Amanda!" I said as I hugged her, then I grabbed for Trina to join us in this hug which she did.

"Thank you both for helping me. This is so amazing!" I was about to start crying when Amanda pulled back from me.

"I know you are not going to start crying and ruin our awesome work on you. And you might want to grab your jacket because it is time for you to head to your grandparent's house." Amanda was saying as she went to my closet and grabbed the light black sweater that went great with this dress.

Mongo jumped down off the couch and came up to me, wagging his tail and smiling at me.

"Do I look that good Mongo?" I had to ask.

"Yes, yes, yes you do. Let's go see Grandma's!" Mongo said in my head, he loved going to see Grandma May as well as my Mom; they both spoiled him like crazy. All I could do was smile.

"Alrighty then. We should go potty before we go though, right Mongo?" I went into the bathroom and did my thing then I came out and found Amanda and Trina had taken Mongo out the front door so he could go potty as well while I was busy.

Amanda and Trina walked me to Amanda's car which was parked next to the 4 runner and helped me get Mongo inside and then I sat down in the driver's seat. It felt so good to be sitting in here with this dress on and knowing that I was looking really good.

"All right we will be waiting up for you to get home because we want the entire details Alpha girl." Trina said as she stood back.

"You have fun and remember that you are hot and you are an Alpha!" With that Amanda closed the car door and I started the engine and drove to my grandparent's house for a night of fun, hopefully.

Grandma May and Mom met me at the door with ooh's and awe's at how I looked and that made Grandpa George and Dad come to the door of course which led to whistles and smiles.

"Babygirl, you don't look like a baby anymore." Dad said as he gave me a side hug.

"That is a good thing isn't it?" I asked as I came into the house with Mongo by my side.

"Well yes and no. I didn't think you were interested in Tom, this is going to not only drive him nuts but his brother's too." Dad was saying as Mom took me from him and hugged me too.

"James she is just showing Alpha self. She feels sexy and when a girl feels sexy she feels power and therefore her Alpha comes out." My Mom knew exactly what the girls had done to me, which makes me wonder if she didn't have a talk with them about what I should wear tonight before I did? Mom was wearing her usual flowery tie dye sundress in light blues and pinks and Grandma May was wearing one just like it except she liked throwing purple in hers too. They both had their hair up in a bun with fancy white chop sticks and their white strappy sandals. Where my Dad and Grandpa George were wearing their usual jeans with a button up well-worn western shirt, Dad in light blue and Grandpa's was a tan beige color which I think used to be brown.

"Okay then, she is defiantly an Alpha!" My Dad said with confidence.

With that being said my parent's and grandparent's took me into the sitting room and we all sat down to discuss what was going to happen this evening. Grandpa was the first to start.

"So, Carrie I know that the council and I have put some demands on you because we thought that the Were-Squatch population was dwindling, which we have now seen has not been the case. The tribe in the Redwoods, along with the Montana tribe are bursting at the seams with Were-Squatch, granted they are in California and Montana and not her in Oregon but there are some that are willing to relocate. That being said, No I will not force you to court any other Were-Squatch males." My grandfather said with a little bit of mirth in his eyes.

"That's good to know at least. But what about the ones I already have? I have made my choice and even after letting Tom court me I still have not changed my mind and neither had Harry for that matter." I was definitely feeling my Alpha-ness, because I had never stood up to my grandfather like this before.

"Your Mother has told us as much. I still wanted you to get to know Tom before we even gave the possibility of another mate for Tom. That being said I know that your Mother has told you that his parents have chosen a mate for him but he is waiting for the full moon ceremony just in case he is needed. As your escape hatch if you will." My grandfather was trying to be so nice about what he was saying but he didn't need to.

"Mom explained everything to me already Grandpa. I know that Tom doesn't want to commit to another if there is a chance that Harry will back out on me. Harry has stuck around this long and even with me having to date another man. He loves me and I love him!" I really needed to calm myself down before I said something that was really bad and might get myself into trouble with Grandpa or the Council; I have to think of him as a Chief as well as my Grandpa.

"I just wanted to make sure you were aware. I should have just asked your Mother." Grandpa was being a little grumpy now. I guess I might have gone a little too far.

"I'm sorry Grandpa; all this is so new to me that I forget myself sometimes. I am an Alpha and therefore I get these strong feelings and have to make them known. Is there anything that we need to talk about before they get here?" I asked trying to get this conversation back on something positive.

"It's okay Babygirl; we know what it feels like to be a new Alpha. Do you have any questions before the Johnson's arrive?" Grandpa was in a better mood now. It never took him long to get over something that makes him upset; I would think that would be a good trait to have in a Chief.

"No I can't think of anything. I have had most of everything explained to me so far." I said as we heard someone knocking at the front door.

"Well then let the evening begin!" My Grandpa said as he stood and so did the rest of us as My Mom went to answer the door and let the Johnson's in for a nice dinner at home. I could smell Grandma May famous elk roast from here, yum.

Tom was the first through the door and I swear his jaw dropped when he saw me. He was greeting my Mom when he came in and then he saw me standing with my Dad and Grandpa. He totally ignored them both then he headed straight for me. The smile on his face could light up a room, that's when I realized he thought I was dressing this way for him. I guess this look was a double edged sword for me. Yes, it made me more confident but it also sent the wrong message to Tom that I was still interested. Shit! Tom came straight to me and took me in his arms for a hug. He was looking good though too in his black suit and dark blue tie.

"You look amazing Carrie! I can't wait for you to meet my parents!" Then he turned around to face them as they too came in through the door. His Mom was a very lovely woman. She was at least 5' 8" tall and she was wearing a beautiful dress that looked like it came from a very expensive store and not from anywhere around here either. It was a simple black with a slit up the side to just below her hip and the black velvety fabric was covered in a black lace that made it all look like one material, which it probably was. She was wearing very high heels in black as well and her hair was piled on top of her head in a very well-crafted bun beehive creation, it made my curls draped down my face and held back with a silver clip look frumpy and her makeup looked like it was done by an artist.

"Mom this is Carrie!" Tom introduced me to her and she just looked at me like I was a new species of monster or something.

"Carrie this is my Mom, Nancy!" Tom was saying and pushing me toward his Mom.

"It's good to finally meet you Carrie!" His Mom shocked me by taking me into a big hug and smiling like she thought I was a star or something.

"I have heard so much about you from Tom and his brother's." She held me at arm's length to look at me.

"You are as pretty as the boys said you are. And your Mom and Grandma are so proud of you and your accomplishments with the Forest Service too." Then she hugged me again. Then she pulled away again and turned to get her husband's attention who was the next to come in through the door.

"Norm come and meet Carrie, she is so beautiful!!" She was yelling at her husband who came over to us very quickly. Norm was a very handsome man and looked like an older version of Tom exact height and weight but with salt and pepper hair and a few wrinkles around the eyes.

He was wearing a suit and tie, the suit in a dark blue almost black and his tie matched. He was also wearing black shoes that probably cost more than I have in the bank.

"I know you are new to being a Were but we are very touchy feely people and we give lots of hugs and affection, I hope you don't mind?" Nancy was saying as her husband, Tom's Dad also gave me a huge hug and then held me at arm's length to look at me. Then Tom's Grandparents came in the door and came straight down to join in the hug. Grandma Ester was a tall woman at over 6 feet tall and she was dressed in a nice summer dress that had beautiful flowers on it and white sweater over the top. Her hair and makeup were impeccably done with her hair also up in a bun. Tom's Grandpa Calvin was also dressed in a suit and tie but his tie had flowers on it in the same material that was on Grandma Ester's dress and his hair was whiter than salt and pepper. And then Tom's Grandparents started hugging me as well, while Tom's Dad still was.

"I am getting used to it." I said not thinking about what I had just said. That of course was the worst thing I could say because then Tom's brother's all piled into the house and made a group hug with me no more than they saw me. Every last one of them had to grab ahold a hug with their Dad still hugging me and I swear they were all wearing the same suit and tie combo as Tom and his Dad but they were in varying shades of blues and black and Frank even had on a dark charcoal grey suit which they all looked very handsome in. I'm surprised I noticed what with everyone hugging me so tight and then their Mom started hugging me with the group. It was like I was the new chew toy and all the dogs wanted me, weird huh?

"Okay everyone please let Carrie breath!" Tom yelled over the top of everyone in the hugging pile. Then you could hear the growling and I wasn't sure where it was coming from. Everyone hugging me sort of stiffened and then one by one they let me go and took a step back from me. That's when I noticed it was Mongo at my feet, he had been trying to get everyone to let me go and growling was what he went with to get them to let me go. He must have felt my unease with everyone one me like that. I looked down at Mongo who was still only growling but everyone was a little way away from me now but he was looking at them all one by one. I leaned down and touched his head and he stopped.

"It's okay Mongo. They are friends, I am fine and so are you." Mongo relaxed and looked up at me.

"I thought they were hurting you. They will stay back now or I will bite!" Mongo said in my head and then he smiled and stuck his tongue out panting.

"Everyone is fine Mongo, no one is hurting me. Besides we are Grandpa's house do you think they would hurt me here?" I said in his head and then I said out loud, "it's okay Mongo. They are friends." And then I smiled as I pet his head.

"Remarkable, she is a true Alpha! I know she was talking to the dog in their heads and yet she is not in her Squatch form! And this is the famous Mongo!" Nancy seemed amazed by this, something I have been able to do since I was bitten but I wasn't going to say that out loud.

"Yes, a true Alpha! Extraordinary!" Norm was saying as he too was amazed by me. He walked to his wife and they held each other's hands just looking at me.

"I'm sorry. Yes, this is Mongo; he is my best friend, my partner and my fur baby. We are inseparable!" I said as they looked back and forth from me to Mongo. Tom's brothers were still in a circle around me and Frank was at my right elbow when I felt him touch me and it made me jump a bit. I turned to look at him and he had a very big smile on his face and leaned down to whisper in my ear.

"You are the most beautiful woman I have ever met!" And then he cleared his throat, "Can I talk to you for a moment alone?" Frank asked me and I know my eyes must have bugged out when he asked because Tom was right in front of me within seconds looking from his brother to me.

"Carrie, is there an issue here?" Tom asked me but was looking at his brother.

"No, Frank has asked to speak to me alone for a second. I think we can go into the next room for a moment to speak, I will be right back." I said with more confidence than I was feeling. Tom took a step back and let Frank, holding my elbow, led me into the next room to talk. Mongo was at bumping my leg as we walked because he was not leaving me alone. Once in the next room Frank was looking at me strange.

"I just wanted to let you know I was sorry for what I said the other night to you. I may have felt that way about being the first to bite you but I never should have said it and I just wanted your forgiveness." Frank was very sincere in what he was saying and I was happy it was that and not a declaration of love or something; I don't think I could handle that tonight.

"I understand that hormones get the best of us all sometimes, consider it forgiven and forgotten. Friends?" I asked putting out my hand to shake.

"Yah, friends!" And then Frank hugged me again laughing. He really was a nice guy, just not the guy for me.

"So, may I have her back now?" Tom asked from behind me. Frank let go of me and started heading back into the other room but then stopped and turned to me again.

"So, does this mean you will still help me find a mate, since we are friends?" Tom smiled so big he was really like a big kid.

"Of course I will and my mom and Grandma are helping me too. I heard you were looking at some photos last night, did you find one you liked?" I asked seeing Tom wince a little since he probably thinks that I know he was looking as well.

"Yes, I did and she is one of your cousin's. Very cute and smart too, just like you!" With that Frank left the room bumping hi brother Tom on the way out, not sure if that was a friendly bump or a "it's you turn" kind of thing.

"Are you ready to go back and visit with everyone?" Tom asked me as he took my hand and turned for us to reenter the sitting room where everyone else was.

"Sure, I hope we get a chance to talk privately later though." I said as we started walking, then Tom stopped and turned me toward him.

"Your Mom told you about my Family having me look to see if any of the viable females were of interest to me, didn't she? She tells you everything except what you needed to know about Were-Squatch's!" Tom seemed to be a little angry but was that because he was truly interested in someone he saw or was it because of my Mom not telling me what things I really needed to know and not having family and others tell me instead of her?

"Yes Tom, she told me. And she also told me that you weren't going to do anything until I made my choice at the full moon ceremony." I said as I looked him in the eyes.

"I just want to make sure that you are taken care of Carrie! If I back out and then Harry backs out because he no longer has to fight for your affection, then you would be left without a mate and I just can't do that to you! I bit you, I chose you, or rather my Were-Squatch chose you but in the end it was a great choice! I am not mad or upset about choosing you but I just wish I was sure that Harry was the right choice for you if he is the one you choose!" Tom as getting loud and I know that our Were hearing was really great now and all but sometimes I wish others didn't hear everything that was being said to me around here because it seemed like everyone came running around the corner to see what was going on between Tom and I at this moment.

Tom was standing in front of me and my Grandpa, Dad and Mom were all by my side within seconds. And poor Mongo was growling again and he hadn't growled at Tom since he was a Were-Squatch for goodness sake. I know my face was turning red and I know Tom's was as well.

"Is everything alright in here Babygirl?" My Grandpa asked as he almost got in-between Tom and me.

"Everything is fine Grandpa; we are just having a heated discussion, that's all." I said patting him on the arm.

"Heated discussions can go one of two ways with a Were, Babygirl. One leads to changing and hitting the other is usually changing and mating and we don't want either of those things here tonight. So if we could all just go into the sitting room and have a seat and talk I would feel a whole lot better." Grandpa was talking as a matter of fact but I really didn't think that the way we were talking was going to lead to either of those things happening but to save face and because I know I was as red as a tomato right about now we all started walking into the sitting room.

Tom put his hand on my lower back to lead me through to the love seat on the far end of the sitting room to sit with him. All eyes were on us and I thought that was a little overkill, really!

"So, I just wanted to make sure that you know it has nothing to do with you Carrie, but I and Tom's Grandma Ester are the ones pushing Tom here to choose another mate, just in case you don't choose him in the full moon ceremony. We know that you and the other man, Harry have a connection and the only reason that Tom bit you was because of the mating frenzy! And well, it is nothing against you because you are a lovely girl and are amazing and a natural Alpha and would be a great addition to the family if you so choose to be! But well we still want all of our boys happily mated and that includes Tom as well since he is an Alpha also." Tom's Mom Nancy was a talker, just like my Mom when she gets on a roll. I can see why they are going to be such great friends.

"No, I truly understand and that is what Tom and I were talking about." I said and Tom took my hand in his and smiled because we both felt the shock run through us.

"I saw that! Ester did you see that?" Nancy stood up and walked over to Tom and me. We were both very confused and were looking at each other when not only Tom's Mom Nancy but his Grandma Ester and my Mom came to stand in front of us. This was freaking the hell out of me now!

"What's going on?" Tom asked them all as they stared at us smiling.

"Do you too feel a shock every time you touch?" Nancy asked us. Tom and I looked at each other and let go of our hands. Then we looked at them staring at us and nodded our heads as the same time.

"Look at that! The mate shock, or at least that's what we called it when your Dad bit me!" Nancy was saying to Tom. Then Tom looked at me and shrugged his shoulders. Nancy and Ester looked at me and then at my Mom.

"Doesn't she know about the mating shock? Haven't you told her about it?" Nancy was kind of confused and mad at the same time.

"I don't even know what a mating shock is! I've never bit anyone and I am a pure blood Alpha." Mom was defending herself for not informing me about something I am guessing she also had never heard of.

"Wow, okay then! Sorry!" Nancy shrugged her shoulders then looked at Tom and me.

"The mating shock is the connection between the one who did the biting and the one who got bitten when it comes to a Were-mating. You see if you change someone they have some of your changing magic so to speak running through them. Case in point here, Tom bit Carrie and so there is a mating bond between them so the shock is there every time they touch. No when and if they mate the shock will go away, for now. It comes back each and every time you are pregnant because you are making a Were-Squatch yourself. Do you understand?" Nancy was pretty good at explaining to us but my head was a little fuzzy about this and it seemed that Tom understood though.

"But what if she doesn't choose me, will she still get the shock when she is pregnant?" Tom asked in a very straight forward question.

"Yes, I got it with every pregnancy I had and your Grandpa Norm didn't change me I was already a Were-Squatch. We just didn't share the mate shock between us." Tom's Grandma Ester said as she smiled at Tom and I both.

"So, if she chooses Harry they won't share the mating shock but if they have children she will be shocked by him then?" Tom was asking these questions but I was thinking them.

"Yes, Tommy boy! She will." Tom's Grandma Ester said.

"Tommy boy? Your Grandma calls you Tommy boy?" I couldn't help but laugh at that. Everyone around us laughed except for Tom.

"I don't understand why that's funny? Both my Grandparents and Parents called me that since I was little." Tom was looking at everyone trying to figure out the joke.

"Well, for one thing we call Carrie "Babygirl" and you are "Tommy boy" that in itself is funny!" My Mom explained.

"And the movie Tommy boy was hilarious too!" My Dad said laughing because Tom looked nothing like Chris Farley.

"That is funny!" Tom finally got the joke and we all had a good laugh.

## **Chapter 39**

    A little while after we all had our good laugh and I was made aware of the mating shock and why it happens then we all sort of relaxed and just talked about things.  We mostly talked about the database for the mating options but I think we need a good name for it too.  We tossed around some options and finally decided that we should call it the "Poly-Were database or PWD".  Then it was time for dinner.

    Grandma May made her famous elk roast with all the veggies that go with it.  She also made gravy from the trimmings, which is so good poured over the meat and the potatoes.   There was light conversation while we all ate at the very large table that is used for some of the council meetings I have no doubt.  I always wondered why they had just a huge table when there weren't that many of us here for the holidays but I guess there will be more of us now that I know the family secret.

    I sat next to my Dad and Tom sat on the other side of me. The conversations that were going on everyone had a chance to voice an opinion on. But what caught everyone off guard was what Nancy asked my Dad.

"James, why haven't you become a Were-Squatch yet?" Nancy asked from across the table. Everyone stopped eating and talking to hear what his response was.

"Actually Nancy, I never really thought about it. Janet never brought it up and I never thought to ask her to bite me." Dad said as he shrugged his shoulders. Mom put her hand on his arm.

"Is that something you would like to think about?" Mom asked him with a very serious smile on her face.

"I don't see why not. Our daughter became a Were-Squatch like you so why shouldn't I. Is there any drawbacks to doing it?" Dad asked the table but of course there were only two of us that could answer that. Tom's Mom who was bitten and me.

"I haven't found any Dad. I know I was born to be a Were-Squatch now, it was only a matter of time for me." I said and Tom reached over and gave me a side hug.

"Glad I could help with that." Tom said as he smiled at me.

"I haven't really found any either, and from what my parents described when they were going through the change into their Were-wolf selves they have pain and discomfort when they first start changing. But when I became a Were-Squatch it's like a warming sensation all over my body and then I changed." Nancy was telling my Dad and then she looked at me.

"Is that what you experience Carrie?" Nancy asked me.

"Yes that is exactly what I feel, warmth that starts in my face and then it moves over my whole body. It's amazing really." I said as I talked to my Dad. Wow, my Dad may be changing also, that is so cool.

"Plus, the life expectancy is longer being a Were but you also can't get drunk, I don't know if that is a thing for you or not? But the health benefits alone, you don't get sick you heal quickly too!" Nancy was saying to my Dad. There were a few things that I had found out from my family,

Harry and Tom of course. Most of which Harry found out from trial and error, where Tom's family taught him everything he needed to know.

"Well, Honey we can talk about it more later if you like." My Mom was telling my Dad, he then leaned over and kissed her. My parents were still very much in love.

The conversations went back to everyone talking and Tom leaned over to talk to me quietly.

"So, starting tomorrow you have a week without my brother's and I have you decided what you are doing without guys around yet?" Tom was fishing to see if I planned on spending any time doing something he can crash I was thinking in the back of my head.

"Actually, I thought I would go back to work for a few days, other than that not really." I said honestly.

"Oh, okay that sounds like fun." But it didn't sound like Tom thought it would be fun.

"What are you doing this week?" I asked him just to be polite.

"I'm working, same as you. I would tell you who we were working for but it's confidential. I could tell you but then I would have to kill or marry you so that you couldn't testify against me." Tom was saying as he winked at me. He thought he was being funny, I didn't really think he was funny.

The evening ended shortly after dinner, Tom and his family had a long drive to get back down to Eugene. His parents and grandparents were staying at the Hilton, being from the country they sure do prefer the high life that is for sure. You would think being a logger was just an okay profession but they seemed to have a lot of many, which makes me wonder how they got that money. But really it was none of my business and I really don't feel like I fit in with their family anyway. The boys are all country but his parents and even Tom was a little more on the richer side of things were I am a simple country girl with simple country girl taste.

402

Once Tom and his family left Mom and Grandpa wanted to talk to me. I followed them into the sitting room again and sat down on the couch. I was pretty sure this was going to be bad news.

"It's not bad news!" Mom said as she sat down next to me on the couch. I looked at her with a question on my face.

"How did you know that was what I was thinking?" I had to ask.

"I'm your Mother and it was written all over your face and to be honest we have been giving you a lot of bad news lately." Mom said as she leaned over to hug me. Grandpa George sat down on the coffee table across from Mom and me.

"Babygirl I just wanted to let you know that I am sorry that we forced you into courting Tom but at least you make some new friends if nothing else. Your Mom tells me that you have pretty much made up your mind and will be choosing Harry on Friday night at the full moon ceremony." I just nodded my head and Grandpa continued.

"I just want you to know that I have spent a lot of time with Harry and his friends and I find Harry to be a great choice. He may not know everything there is to know about being a Were-Squatch but he at least is willing to learn and it has been great spending time with him." The look on my face must have been one of surprise because Grandpa sat back and smiled with a little laugh.

"Where do you think he has been spending his time while you were out with Tom?" Grandpa said as he took my hands in his.

"Harry is a great choice and he too is an Alpha, he's had to be to survive after his change and then being left to figure things out on his own." Grandpa said seriously.

"And I am sorry I wasn't there to fill you in on more of the things that being a Were-Squatch will change in your life. I was still in shock that you are now a Were-Squatch like me; I never thought you would be because you didn't change at puberty like you should have. But you showed so many signs when you were younger especially with Mongo that it all kind of threw me off when you did change. And I really didn't know about the mating shock thing either, really!" Mom said as she leaned over and kissed me on the temple.

"Okay so this week you were supposed to be deciding on which man you are going to choose but since you have made your choice you can resume your regular duties with the Forest Service which I hear you were planning on doing anyway. Since you have chosen but Tom will still be there in case your Harry changes his mind I need to know if you would choose Tom if Harry does leave?" I know that Grandpa was only looking out for me and I had thought about that scenario but I wasn't sure if I could.

"Well in the beginning of this all you told me that I HAD to choose one or the other, is that still the case?" I asked not knowing if the rules were written in stone somewhere.

"It is the custom that once bitten you have to take the man who bit you as your mate unless you were already betrothed or married. But that was more for the people that were not in a Tribe of their own kind already. I will talk to the council but I think I can speak for them and say that you can choose not to take Tom for a mate if it is okay with him as well. From what your Mother and I have seen it appears that Tom does truly have deep feelings for you which may be love but we cannot say for sure. That is between you and him." Grandpa was beating around the bush again. I kind of took that as I still had an option which is more than what I had before. But I still didn't think that Harry was going anywhere either, he loves me and I love him.

"Okay Grandpa I get it. So what do I need to do for the ceremony on Friday?" I needed to know ahead of time if I needed to get anything to wear and what I needed to do.

"Your Mother and I will be taking care of most of the preparations. This is a wedding of sorts but you can still choose to have a real wedding later, maybe this summer. There will be a lot of people at this ceremony. All the Were's from around Oregon will be here as well as the new Tribes from Montana and California. So we will be able to make a few love connections while they are here as well. Your Mother has already started calling and e-mailing all those that the Johnson boys were asking about so they are all coming to the Full Moon Ceremony too. Even the young lady that Tom was checking into." Grandpa said with a wink at my Mom.

"Yes, they have all agreed to be here. This is going to be the biggest gathering we have ever had here. Which reminds me Dad have you talked to Jared yet? He said that the Jed Monroe, his brother Cletus and the rest of the SMM Bigfoot Hunters all have ankle monitors put on them and they are on house arrest for the next month until their trial. So we won't have to worry about them. The rest of the Bigfoot Hunters have left town as well. All except for your Bigfoot Getters friends, that is." Mom was relaying the good news about that, this way we don't have to worry about party crashers at least.

"Okay so big party, lots of people, everyone will be safe, got it!" I said as I was getting antsy to get home and update the girls before bed.

"But, let me remind you that you still need to be safe and watch out for hunters!" Grandpa just wanted me to be safe, that was all.

"I got it Grandpa! Okay I want to get home so I can fill in the girls and get to bed. Oh, one last question! Do I have to stay away from Harry during this week still since it is supposed to be my thinking week?" I asked just before I stood up off the couch.

"You don't have to but I would like you to have your life go back to normal and see how he fits in it Babygirl. You need to make sure that he is the one and he also needs to be sure you are the one for him as well. Do you understand what I am saying?" Grandpa gave me a big hug that my Mom joined in on as well.

"Yes, I understand. I love you guys!" I said getting a little teary eyed. Mongo bumped my legs reminding me he was there for me too. Well at least I have love in my life from my family.

I left my grandparents' house after saying good night and giving hugs to Grandma May and Dad. Mongo and I drove Amanda's car back to the house and the girl's met me at the front door. I couldn't wait to recap the night to them and let them know all the new things that I had discovered.

## **Chapter 40**

Saturday morning brought with it a few changes to my life. Mongo and I were up and out of the house in record time to go out to the trailer that Harry was staying in. But it wasn't Harry that met me at the door when I knocked. Terry was happy to see me at first but then his face dropped when I told him I was there to see Harry.

"I'm sorry Carrie I thought Harry would have called you or at least texted you to let you know what was going on." Terry said as he stood back and invited me into the trailer.

"He didn't do either of those things. Why? What's going on?" I asked with fear in my voice I know it because my stomach dropped thinking the worst right off the bat, Harry had changed his mind about me.

"He got a call last night and he threw clothes in a bag and said he would be back in a few days. He didn't even tell me to say anything to you that's why I thought he had or would call and talk to you or texted you." Terry said with a shrug of his shoulders. He sat down at the bend of the table and I kind of fell down on the other bench. My heart was breaking at least that is what I thought the pain in my chest right now. I just wanted to sit and cry.

"Okay, well would you have him call me or something when he calls you? Or I guess I will just wait to hear from him." I said in my sad voice.

"It's going to be okay Carrie! He didn't leave you; he just had an emergency, that's all!" Terry touched my hand on the table trying to comfort me. But I wasn't feeling it, not right now. I got up and Mongo lead me to the door.

"Thanks Terry, I'll see you around." I said as I opened the door and walked out. I was back in my house in seconds it seemed and I barely made it to my bathroom before I started crying. And I didn't stop crying for a while, not until Amanda threatened to break down the door did I hear her yelling for me on the other side of the bathroom door. I hadn't even brought Mongo in here with me. Was Tom right in the fact that Harry wasn't sure he wanted me for a lifetime mate? I'm so lost and confused right now.

Once the bathroom door was open I managed to cry out everything that Terry told me about Harry leaving last night but I don't know what else was said I was really out of it. Was this grief and a broken heart? What the hell do I do now? And how did this man mean so much to me to basically paralyze me from being me because he is gone?

"I'm going to text that S.O.B right now!" Amanda was yelling as she went back into the bedroom and grabbed her cell phone off the night stand where it was charging.

"No, don't if he had wanted to talk to me and let me know what was happening then he would have. I am never without my phone and besides, if he wanted to leave me I guess now is the best time before we are mated for life and that only makes my choice easier when I only have 1 choice, right?" I know I wasn't all there in the conversation but I think I said that.

"Wait your Grandpa said just last night that if you choose no mate at all then he was good with that or something to that nature didn't he?" Trina asked holding me on the bathroom floor where they found me.

"He said if it was okay with the council and with Tom and his family then I could go without a mate. But that would mean talking to them about how Harry just left me after all the things I said good about the man and how he loved me because that is what he said! He said he would wait around for me even if I chose Tom and then if Tom were to die and not form his hand then he would still take me as his mate! That is what the said!" I know I was ranting now and I hadn't noticed that Amanda was texting anyway.

"Done and sent!" Amanda said as she came back over to sit on the floor with me and Trina.

"What did you say?" Trina asked her.

"Basically that at least a phone call or a text would be nice to send to someone if you intend to break up with them and run away like a coward! Plus, I put a couple of the flipping off finger emoji and the poop emoji too." Amanda said with a giggle.

"But you don't know why he left yet; maybe it was an emergency with his Mom! Did you stop to think of that before you got on the F*ck off train? And why didn't you just call him, never mind you would have left a very mean message wouldn't you?" Trina answered her own question when Amanda smiled again.

"Carrie, why don't you send him a message asking him if he is okay and what is going on?" Trina was always the voice of reason, when I go off the deep end she is the friend that jumps off with me. It's good to have them both on my side and in my life. Trina got up and got my phone off the bathroom counter where I set it when I came in here. Then she handed it to me. I sat there and stared at it for a few seconds and then Trina took it back from me and started texting.

"Harry, I heard you left last night after your Mother called. I hope everything is okay, please text me or call me with details. Smiley emoji. There that is now sent." Trina said and then handed me my phone. We all sat there looking at my phone for a long time and nothing happened. Then I started crying again and so the girls got me up and washed my face and took me out to the living room and sat me on the couch.

"I'm going to see Stephen about breakfast for us all and I will be right back!" Amanda said as she headed for the sliding glass door and out she went. Trina curled up beside me and Mongo crawled into my lap. I was crying and exhausted all at once. I know I fell asleep with the warmth of the two of them on me.

I awoke a few hours later with just Mongo on my lap keeping me warm. The girls were talking in the kitchen and I didn't even bother trying to listen to what they were saying. My phone was beside me on the end table and I looked at it to see if I had any calls or texts, there was nothing. I fell back to sleep, I know it was because I was depressed but I didn't know what else to do.

Sometime later I was woken up by my Mom and she held me for a little while and I fell back to sleep, I don't even remember anything she said to me. Then I was getting a little cold and I reached for the blanket that used to be on the back of the couch to wrap myself in. When I put it up to my chin I could smell Harry's natural sent on it and then I started crying again. What had I done to deserve being left like this? No word at all, what the hell! Then I heard Mom talking in the kitchen on her phone.

"Yes, she is so depressed that all she is doing is sleeping and crying. He hasn't contacted anyone and it's been two days! I'm worried Dad, she may have not mated with Harry but she is showing the signs of losing a mate. This could kill her if she doesn't snap out of it!" Then there was a pause where the other person was talking to her.

"Do you think that is the best option here?" Mom asked but I didn't know what the option was.

"Okay, call me when you get there and let me know what you find out. Okay and then we will move on with plan B after you find out. Love you! Bye!" Then I heard Mom walk into the living room but I was too tired to even open my eyes. How could it be Monday already was the last thought I had before I was out again?

Over the next few days my Mom and my friends never left my side. I knew they were worried about me but I just had a hard time staying awake without crying and the crying made me tired. They made sure that I ate but I couldn't tell you what I ate, nothing tasted like anything to me. Mom made sure that I showered and went to the potty every few hours and they all took care of me and Mongo too. Poor Mongo couldn't even get through to me. He tried talking to me in my head but I just couldn't answer him. He was worried and stayed by my side except to go potty and eat of course. My Mom kept trying to tell me something but I couldn't understand her either.

Whenever I was awake enough to comprehend what was going on around me I was checking my phone without finding anything from Harry at all. And I know Amanda had said something about Terry and Jerry leaving for a while but I don't know what happened with that either. Then my Mom came into the bedroom where I had pretty much gone into a self-induced coma of sorts from the depression. She pulled the covers off of me and starting yelling as loud as she could. Amanda and Trina came in and started doing it too.

"It is Friday and you are done with this crap! Young lady you will snap out of this and bring yourself back into this world where you are needed and wanted, DO YOU HEAR ME!" My Mom was so loud but something was happening with me too. I was actually starting to come awake again and not with the groggy just waking feeling either.

"Carrie you have to get up and we have to get you ready! It's Friday for goodness sake!" Trina's yelling wasn't really yelling so much as a raised voice. But I was hearing her!

"Carrie you have to get up now! It's been a frigging week since Harry left and you need to snap out of this!" Amanda was beside the bed with a hot cup of coffee, something I never drink because of the caffeine. She put the warm liquid to my lips after my Mom pulled me up into a sitting position. It smelled good and I took a sip and boy did it have a kick.

"Is there alcohol in that coffee?" I asked as I pulled it back to me.

"Hallelujah she speaks and she is ALIVE!" My Mom yelled to the sky as she raised her arms over her head.

"Well I'm not dead yet." I said as I drank more of the coffee and little by little I was feeling more alive. I was starting to feel like me again.

"Did you say it's Friday as in the day Harry left or is this Friday as in full moon ceremony day?" I wasn't sure how many days had passed but a whole week? So much for going in to work and keeping busy.

"Is what happened to me normal?" I asked my Mom out of the blue.

"No, not really. What it seems you just went through was what all Were's go through when they lose a mate, but you and Harry haven't mated yet as far as I know anyway?" Mom was saying while staring at me. I was drinking more of the coffee and had to swallow before I could speak again.

"No Mom, we never mated. I don't know what happened to me, I have always been an independent woman but when I heard that Harry left me I just shut down. I couldn't think or feel anything besides sadness and hopelessness. I wasn't sure I was going to survive, I probably wouldn't have without you guys." I was speaking from the heart; they all really pulled me though.

"Are you better now?" Mongo said in my head and I actually heard him too. I leaned over and hugged and kissed his head.

"Yes, Mongo I think I am better now." I told him. Then I looked at my Mom.

"So, why did I act that way if we weren't mated Mom?" I asked as I decided to try to take a step out of bed because I really had to go potty now.  Once my feet hit the floor I was on my way to the bathroom with everyone following me.  My bathroom is a nice sized bathroom with a double sink counter top and a walk in shower as well as a garden tub that is separate from the shower plus a nice toilet but with everyone in there with me it made it a little smaller to be in.

"Well you are awake and you are peeing on your own without me having to drag you to the potty so those are all good signs."  My Mom was saying to me and the girls.

"So, what was going on with me, Mom?"  I asked her again since they were all in here with me we might as well continue the conversation.

"Well, I talked to your Grandpa and he conferred with the council that you were actually going through the loss of a mate and they believe that in fact if the two of you have not mated physically but you are still going through this then you are soulmates as well as Were mates.  It doesn't happen often in the Were-Community but it does happen."  My Mom was explaining to me and the girls.  But that led me to my next question.

"If I was going through this does that mean that Harry was also?"  I asked her on my way to wash my hands.

"No one has heard from Harry since he left.  We don't know what happened to him and your Grandpa is very worried.  He contacted Terry and he and Jerry couldn't get ahold of Harry or his Mom on the phone so they went to Veneta to find out what happened.  And that was this morning.  But your Grandpa said that we have a ceremony to go through and you have to attend it.  He will explain to the gathering that you have a soulmate bond and that you will not be choosing a mate tonight.  But the other Tribes are all here to socialize anyway so they will be happy to have more time to visit and possibly find their mates tonight or at least possible mates.  But you must attend this with the family."  Mom was saying as we walked back into the bedroom.  Amanda went to my closet and started pulling clothes out and Trina was getting my under things from my dresser drawers.

"Wow, I kind of feel like sleeping beauty here, except it was my mom that woke me out of my coma." I said trying to joke. All three of them stopped what they were doing and walked over to me and they all gave me a hug at the same time.

"We are always here for you Carrie, no matter what." Amanda said as they separated from me again and returned to getting my clothes out. That's when I noticed that they all had pretty sundresses on, Mom in a white with lavender, Amanda's was white with pink swirls and Trina's was white with yellow swirls and they had their makeup and hair done too. I looked at the dress on the bed and it was a sundress like theirs but it was white with light blue splashes on it.

"Your Grandma May needed something to do while we waited to see how you were going to make it through his, so she made tie dye sundresses for each of us and she is wearing one that has all the colors leftover from ours in it, they really turned out great!" Mom was saying as she twirled in hers.

"My phone is ringing and it's Terry!" Trina said as a way to get us to quiet down so we could hear.

"Hi Sweetie! What did you find out?" Trina asked in her normal voice. Then she looked at me and continued talking.

"Yes, she just woke up a few minutes ago and she seems herself. Why? What?" She sat down and then she listened for a second.

"Wait let me put this on speaker phone so that everyone can hear you!" Trina was saying very fast as then she pushed the button on her phone.

"Okay Terry you are on speaker now and we are all hear you." And then we heard Terry.

"So the good news is we found him and he is safe. The bad news is he was called home by his Mom but when he got there he had an altercation with a Were-Bear who was harassing his Mom which is why she called him in the first place. He only had a few cuts and bruises from that but his phone was broken during the fight and then the next morning his Mom couldn't wake him. She called the Were Doc that they have for the Were-Bears here in Veneta and they didn't know what it was so they checked him into the Were-hospital here on Tribal land. His Mom had no way of contacting us because his phone was broken." My head was spinning and I was either going to start crying again or throw up. Mom saw me and came to my side.

"The good news gets better because he just woke up a few minutes ago and is freaking out that it is Friday and he thinks that Carrie is going to think he left her and take Tom as her mate so he has been screaming at me to call ever since I got here which was like 15 minutes ago! The Doc here is totally confused on what happened because he is fully healed from the fight." Terry sounded like he was running out of breath.

"Tell the Doctor that the council thinks he and Carrie where both going through what would have happened when their mate would die. The council also thinks that since they have not physically mated yet that it is because they are true soulmates!" My Mom was yelling to the phone so that Terry could hear her.

"Shit, really? I didn't think that was a real thing!" Terry turned and repeated what my Mom said I am guessing to the Doctor who was there in the room with them.

"Okay then. The Doc is totally amazed too and he wants to know if he and a few of his Clan can come to the full moon ceremony tonight as well?" Terry was relaying the message.

"Yes, all are welcome. Make sure that you don't leave without bringing Harry back with you and tell him to bring his Mom too!" My Mom yelled back to Terry.

"Okay, will do. We will see you guys in about an hour or so! Bye Everyone! Love you Babe I will see you soon." Terry said as he was about to hang up the phone.

"Love you too!" Trina said and just before they could hang up I had to yell too.

"Wait! Tell Harry I choose him and I love him!" I yelled just in time before Terry hung up.

"Already done! See you guys soon!" And with that Terry hung up the phone.

Once Terry hung up the phone Mom looked at me and then she sat there for a few seconds before she finally talked.

"You do realize what you and Harry have is super special. You thought he had left you so you felt the death in your heart and then he being soulmates to you felt the same death and therefore you both were stuck with mate death sickness that all Were's go through when a mate dies. Some do not survive it; I think that is why I never offered it to your father before now. Somewhere deep down inside me I don't think I would survive if he were to die before me. And now you know what it will be like if Harry dies before you and he knows if you die before him." My Mom was so sad and yet she was also amazed. Harry and I had a love that would surpass all others and a love to pure that it went all the way to our souls, hence soulmates.

"Well, let's get this girl ready for her soulmate and have a mating ceremony like no other!" Amanda was saying as she pulled me off the bed and Trina showed me the cute little blue lace bra and panties to match that were going underneath my sundress for this evening. I guess tonight will be one for the record books.

"And by the way ladies you will have to return to your trailers with your men or take them to your homes maybe? When the ceremony is over, Carrie and her new mate will need some much deserved alone time. And Mongo honey you are staying with Grandma May and Grandpa George tonight as well." I looked at my Mom funny because whenever the girls didn't take Mongo, she and Dad took him to their place.

"Oh, I see that look Mongo and from you too girls. I have decided I am biting your Dad tonight. I don't want to live another day without him by my side forever, or as much time as we can get that is." And Mom smiled and kissed my cheek. Then Amanda and Trina took me into the bathroom and started on my hair and makeup. It didn't take them long since I think I had showered last night but I'm not totally sure on that.

"But wait, if Harry is bringing his Mom then where will she stay?" I asked as the girl helped put my dress over my head.

"She will be staying in the guest house at your Grandma and Grandpa's house and I have a feeling that Mongo will want to spend some time getting to know Daisy as well." Mom was saying as she set her phone down that I hadn't realized she was texting on.

"Yah, I just updated your Grandparent's and they had already been called by Terry. So everything is all set. Now we just need to get you to the ceremony on time. Are you hungry?" Mom was just on the ball; it truly felt like no time had passed for me. And yet a whole week is now gone. Well mated bliss and forever await me. Full moon ceremony and Harry here I come!

## Chapter 41

    It is Friday night and the full moon ceremony is about to begin. I still haven't seen Harry or Terry and Jerry yet. Mom and the girls dragged me into the golf cart that Grandpa used on rare occasions to shuttle people around, and they used that to bring me up to the main party area where everyone seemed to be gathering. My Mom suggested that I find Tom and let him know my decision now before anything got started and to tell him what happened this last week, she was sure he would understand soulmates. I was getting nervous but Mom had a point I should talk to Tom and get it over with so that he wasn't waiting around for me. I found him and his Dad talking with a few of the council members.

    "Sorry to interrupt, can I steal Tom for a few minutes please?" I asked no one in particular but his Dad responded for them all.

    "Sure, take him away." Tom's Dad was a very nice man. Tom smiled at me and he left with me to walk over by the garden in the side yard, yes the same garden that Grandpa George gave Harry and me the talk in.

    "So, you look better. I heard you were under the weather this last week. I'm sorry I didn't find out until tonight or I would have checked in on you. I just knew that Harry and I were to stay away from you until you made your decision tonight so I wanted to respect that." Tom was saying as he offered me a seat in one of the chairs.

    "So, you don't know what I was sick from then?" I asked him kind of hoping that I wouldn't have to spell it out.

"Yes, the council members were just updating my Dad and I on what happened with you and Harry. I'm guessing this is you letting me know ahead of time that you are choosing Harry huh?" He looked down at the drink in his hand and then back at me.

"I understand the whole soulmate thing and I wouldn't give that up either. I had really hoped that you were picking me but I understand. So I am guessing that congratulations are in order, may I give you a hug at least before you make it official?" Tom was always polite and he was a very nice guy. I sure hope that we are able to help him and his brother's find their mates using the PWD.

"I don't see why not." I said as I stood and so did Tom. He came around the table and he hugged me. Yes I felt the shock where our skin touched yet again and I know he felt it too. We were just pulling away from each other when we heard a commotion in the outer part area so we headed in that direction. When we came around the corner of the house where everyone else was Harry was walking around looking for me I would assume. Then he saw me and he looked at Tom and Tom took a step back and lowered his head giving Harry the respect of an Alpha. Harry came running up to me and took me in his arms, dipped me to the side and kissed the hell out of me right here in front of everyone. That's when we heard the clapping start and we kind of stopped kissing to look into each other's eyes. Harry stood me back up and we faced everyone together, everyone was clapping for us.

My Mom came running up to us and she was smiling like she had just won an award or something.

"Save it for the ceremony guys! Harry your Mom and Daisy are waiting at the side over there and as soon as your Grandpa George can get the council together we are heading to the ceremony site. Are the two of you ready for this?" My Mom was straight and to the point. But there were a lot of people waiting on us that was for sure. Then Mom took off and grabbed Dad by the arm and headed to Grandpa George. They talked for a couple of minutes while Harry and I watched and then Grandpa George hollered and hugged them both. Harry turned me to him.

"What's going on with your parents?" Harry asked me.

"Oh, Mom is biting him tonight to make him a Were-Squatch. She said after seeing what I went through when I thought I had lost you she wasn't giving Dad another day of being mortal. This way they will age at the same rate and Dad will have a harder time dying and leaving her behind. Or something like that. I have missed you so much, I thought you had left me and didn't want me as your mate." I was saying to him with my heart on my sleeve.

"I never even thought you would think that. We weren't supposed to see each other for this whole last week so I didn't think you would miss me." Harry said as he put his hand on the side of my face looking into my eyes.

"After the family date we had my Grandpa gave me his and the council's blessing to be with you this last week to see how you would fit in my life here so that I could be sure of my choosing you before my waiting week." I said rushing to tell him everything I could. Our hands were all over each other while we spoke. I had my hand on his face and his on mine while we were slowly getting closer and closer to each other.

"I felt the loss of you like you died the morning after I got to my Mom's. I had a fight with a Were-Bear and I was recovering from that when I felt it. I shut down and didn't know why." He said as he kissed my forehead.

"And I thought you left me and felt the pain go straight through my heart and I just shut down." I said as I kissed his cheek.

"I felt it the moment that you felt it. We are true soulmates and after tonight we will be mated. We can have a wedding whenever you like. I will never leave you again my Love." Harry was saying as we moved even closer together. Then we heard someone clear their throat. We both turned to find my Grandpa George standing right next to us. I know we both turned red and we separated a little and faced him.

"Everyone is waiting for the ceremony to begin and you two are not jumping to the end without the beginning. Now if you two will follow me we can get this thing on the road. We looked at each other and smiled then Harry took my hand and we followed Grandpa George to the ceremonial area where I was first awakened as a Were-Squatch. And now I will be officially mated to this man that I have chosen who it seems was chosen for me a long time ago if you believe the story of soulmates that is.

From all the hype you would have thought that the full moon ceremony would have been longer and maybe a little more drawn out. I guess I was expecting more of a wedding ceremony and it wasn't. My grandpa George took me into the ceremonial circle and walked around the circle while holding my hand like he was showing me off. Then he stopped in the center of the circle and yelled so that all could hear him.

"Carrie of the Were-Squatch clan who was bitten who do you choose as your mate? Will it be the man who bit you Tom or will it be your soulmate Harry? Men who are wanting this woman to be their mate come to the center of this circle!" My Grandpa turned in the circle as he spoke again. Then he stopped when Harry entered the circle. He spoke to Harry but yelled so that everyone could hear him.

"Harry of the Were-Squatch Clan, do you accept Carrie not only as your soulmate but as your mate for life?" Grandpa George asked him but he never hesitated he was staring at me the whole time. I was glad that I had talked to Tom ahead of time so that he didn't enter the circle also.

"Yes, I am here to claim my soulmate and mate for life, if she will have me!" Harry always being himself, I know he added the last part for me. My Grandpa turned in the circle and then asked me the question.

"Carrie of the Were-Squatch clan do you accept Harry as your soulmate and mate for life?" Grandpa already knew what I was going to say but a ceremony has its rules so I yelled for everyone to hear me.

"Yes, I choose Harry! My soulmate and mate for life, whom I wouldn't survive without!" I had to add that it just felt right. Both Grandpa and Harry smiled and there were a few chuckles from the crowd.

"They you Carrie and you Harry are given the permission of the Council Chief of the many Were-kind Indian Nations as well as the council itself. You are now blessed to come as one again in true soulmate fashion. You may take your mate!" Once Grandpa said that I had never seen a man run to fast as Harry did to come to me and he claimed his first kiss as my future mate. He picked me up and carried me out of the circle. Then he set me down right next to my parents who were waiting at the entrance to the circle and kissed me again.

Then we heard my Grandpa address the people again.

"While I have your attention good people of many Were-kinds we have a treat for this evening. My daughter being a Were-Squatch pureblood and happily married to a human would like to have a biting ceremony here and now. We have not had one in many, many years because of the dangers of the bite, but she is biting him so we should have a problem. Now I need four strong braves from any clan willing to help out. It should only take a few moments and then we will be having a wondrous party for our new additions." As Grandpa was speaking four men came out of the crowd, Cousin Dan was one of them and he waved at me so I waved back. The other three were not guys I knew personally but I knew at least one of them was a Were-Bear; he came with the Doc from Veneta.

"Okay my darling daughter Janet please bring James out here to the center of the circle!" Which my Mom did and then as they stood there before everyone Grandpa had the two men take Dad by the arms and the other two took his legs.

"Dad doesn't even seem nervous at all. Mom must have told him what to look forward to." I whispered to Harry. Then as everyone watched my Mom went up to my Dad and kissed him on the lips. Then he nodded to her and she leaned in and bit him on the neck, it only took a second. Dad looked at her when she pulled back and then Dad kind of went limp and then he stood straight up like he was the Scarecrow from the Wizard of Oz! Then the men let go of his legs when Grandpa tapped them on the shoulders and they stood back. After a few more minutes Grandpa tapped the other two men and they let go of Dad's shoulders and Dad was left standing there.

"It is done! James is now a Were-Squatch like his wife and daughter!" Grandpa gave Dad a hug and then Mom leaned in and kissed Dad. Within a few seconds of them kissing Dad started changing into his Were-Squatch form and so did Mom. Everyone cheered! My Dad was a dark reddish-auburn haired Sasquatch and he was a lot taller than Mom! This was an amazing evening and it wasn't over yet not until my man and I mate for life back at my house! I am sure everyone won't mind when Harry and I disappear a.s.a.p.!

Being that it was celebration as well as the ceremony that we went though we had to stick around an at least say hello to people. I still needed to meet Harry's Mom, who I assumed was the red haired lady that had a very pretty pitbull sitting with Grandma May and Mongo. Harry took me by the hand and led me to where they were now sitting. His Mom was a very beautiful woman, she was around 5'6" with fire red hair and a she had her hair down with curls that looked to be natural. She was wearing very little makeup and she seemed to be about my Mom's age. She was dressed a lot like me, my Mom, Grandma and my friends except her sundress was white, black and then had purple swirled and splashed on it, I really liked her dress.

Harry's Mom Karen was a very nice lady and was all smiles when Harry brought me to her for an introduction.

"Ma, this is Carrie! Carrie this is my Ma!" Harry was so happy that I was finally meeting his Mom. She stood and gave me a huge hug.

"Just call me Mom; I know there is a wedding to be planned so why wait in calling me anything other than Mom. And this is Daisy." Karen turned and introduced me to Daisy, Harry's fur baby. She was so excited and very pretty. I lowered myself to say hello to her, she was so excited she was dancing around trying to get as much affection from me as she could which made Mongo a little jealous. I petted them both on the head until they almost knocked me over.

"You belong to my Harry now too?" Daisy said in my head and my eyes went super wide and I looked at Harry who was just standing there hugging his Mom to his side and watching us.

"Yes, Daisy I belong to your Harry too. So does Mongo if you really want to get technical." I said with a laugh and a smile. Harry looked from Daisy to me.

"Did she just talk to you?" Harry asked with astonishment on his face.

"Yup, that would be a yes." I said as I rubbed the top of her head.

"You are still mine too! But I like Daisy too!" Mongo said in my head and so I started rubbing his head again also.

"And Mongo just talked to you also because I just saw the look on your face." Harry said as he took a step forward and crouched down to give the dogs some of his attention as well. I stood and was hugging my Grandma May when Tom and his brother's came over to talk to us.

"We are going to go and talk to people since there are so many people from not around here to talk to." Grandma May said as she and Karen walked the dogs a little bit away from us so that we could talk with the Johnson brothers.

"We just wanted to congratulate you guys and give you a hug goodbye for now." Tom said as he leaned forward and hugged me really quick. Then all of his brother's piled in on the hug, pulling Harry in on it as well. We were all laughing when we separated.

"We just wanted to thank you. We have each met with a few of the ladies that are interested in courting and we owe it all to you and your family Carrie. I just wanted to let you know that my brother's and I are very grateful and happy that we met you." Tom was saying as his youngest brother Jeffery came forward.

"Yah we are all grateful he bit you!" Jeffery pretty much yelled getting a laugh out of all of us, how else can you take that.

"We are going to go and collect out lady friends and introduce them to our parents. Like I said we are super happy for you both. See you guys around!" Tom said as he and his brothers shuffled off to find their lady friends, how cute.

Harry was holding me in a side hug when he nodded in the direction of my cousin Dan who was heading our way.

"I just wanted to say congrats to you guys too and that I am taking your advice Carrie. I'm planning on asking out the lady that I have had a longtime crush on when she moves to Lincoln City. I have taken the position to work with her and her Orca's that she is bringing with her from OceanWorld, San Diego. I will update you when I can, we will see where this goes." Dan said as he leaned in and kissed my cheek and then shook Harry's hand.

"I'm glad you are my new cousin Harry, welcome to the family! I can't wait for the wedding; hopefully I will have a date. See you guys around." With that Dan headed off to stand and talk with his Dad and the council members he was talking too.

After a few minutes Harry and I headed over to the Bigfoot Getters crew table to see all of our friends. Everyone was in attendance and this time Mike, Stephen, James and Brad were here not tending to food things but enjoying themselves. My cousin Koda had his band "Right Around the Cornerstone" playing and there were people talking, dancing and eating all over the area. The special lights that were strung up everywhere made it look like a super starry evening and added a little magic to the place as well.

My Aunts and Uncles were all here and mingling with all the new members here tonight. Grandpa George had some tents and tepee's set up in the field out back for all those who decide to stay the night and who haven't already gotten rooms at the Oakridge Lodge & Guest House. Everyone was getting along and my parents looked very happy too. We decided to walk over and see who the new comers where that they were talking to, when my Mom waved us over with a smile.

"Everyone I would like you to meet my daughter Carrie and her mate Harry." My Mom introduced us to three men and two women. It was defiantly a husband, wife and three children. The husband and wife were about my Parent's age. They were both over 6' tall and everyone one of them had a dark reddish almost brown hair.

"Carrie and Harry these are the Jones from the Redwoods clan in California. This is Tad and Miranda and their three children, Sara is 20 years old, Tommy and Timmy are both 18 years old. Sara is here to meet with Abel Johnson and Tommy and Timmy are just here window shopping they said." My Mom said with a smile as we shook hands with each of them when Mom introduced us. Tommy and Timmy both turned red and smiled both a little on the shy side it seemed.

"Nice to meet you all. Sara, Abel is a very nice guy and he loves to dance just so you know." I winked at her and she smiled.

"I know he said there is a night club not far from his apartment in Eugene. How do you know him?" She asked me rather quizzically.

"Well, his oldest brother Tom is the man that bit me actually. I have spent time with all the brothers and I have to say they are a very nice group of gentlemen." I said and that's when I saw Abel headed this way.

"And speak of the devil, here he comes." I said as Abel came over and stood next to me.

"Abel I hear you are here to meet with Sara here. Sara this is Abel Johnson." They shook hands and this was the first time that I have ever seen Abel be speechless. My mom noticed the uncomfortable silence and jumped in.

"Abel these are the Jones from your Grandmothers Tribe in The Redwoods of California. Tad and Miranda this is Abel Johnson." My Mom was being a little on the formal side but meeting the parents for the first time can be nerve-racking to say the least.

"It's nice to meet you!" Abel took each of their hands in a very nice strong handshake and looked them straight in the eye showing respect. Sara's brothers were talking and then they stepped forward to shake hands with Abel and to introduce themselves as well. They had smiles all around that it for sure. Then my mom jumped in yet again.

"If you guys haven't eaten yet there is a lot of food over there next to the small building." Mom said as she pointed them in the right direction. All four of them looked at their parents and they then nodded so they took off to go and get food. Eating together is always a good ice breaker when meeting new people. At least that is what I have found anyway.

As I was looking around I noticed that Grandpa George was trying to wave me over so Harry and I said our good-byes and headed in his direction. When we got to his side he hugged me to him and then he hugged Harry too. My Grandpa was so happy right now. And that's when I noticed the people he was talking to.

"Carrie and Harry this is Jameson Gupp and his Sister Maryland and her three daughters who are all Were-recessive gene girls that are looking for possible mates. The girls are triples; let me see if I remember your names. Sarina, Page and Angel, did I get that right girls?" My Grandpa was asking as he pointed to each of them and they nodded as he said their name they looked to be in there early to mid-20's.

"Very good, Mr. Hunter." Maryland nodded her respect. Jameson and Maryland looked like they might have been twins as well. They were both over 6' tall and their hair was a dark shade of blonde and the 3 girls had differing shades of light blondes. They looked like they had some

Nordic blood in their heritage along with their Native American blood. All of the girls were wearing jeans and tank tops and they had the cutest leather boots that had a Native American design on them with fringe.

"Call me George please, Maryland. We are all very happy that you drove so far to join us in the celebration. We haven't had a turn out like this since I was a child and I won't be telling you what year that was either." Grandpa said with a smile.

"Well welcome all of you. I hope that we can find you a few nice guys from our PWD so that you can start your courting as soon as you would like girls. Are you already on the PWD? My mom and Grandma have kind of taken over the list and have been matching people already." I was saying as Page started nodding her head.

"Yes, we are already on the PWD and we have had several men interested in us? We are to meet with Zeek, Kelly and Jeffery Johnson. And our Mom is wanted to also join the PWD as well since she is a widow." Page said as she spoke to me and then checked to make sure that her Mom was still going to go through with it.

"She has an appointment to go over some PWD with your Mom Janet later. Janet said it wouldn't take long. Our Dad was a human but Mom is a full Were-Squatch though." Angel said as she stepped closer to Page. You could tell that Page was the Alpha of these girls; I think she and Zeek would hit it off very well. Angel was more of a Jeffery girl and Sarina being so quiet was more like Kelley.

"You know I would say that Page and Zeek would hit it off very well. Angel and Jeffery, then Sarina would be a perfect fit for Kelley." I said out loud not thinking before I spoke.

"Wow, you are good. That's exactly what I was thinking." My Mom said from behind me as she and my Dad came walking up with Grandma May and Harry's Mom Karen plus, Mongo and Daisy. Mom looked at the girls and then she looked at their Mom.

"Maryland, you and I have a date to make a profile for you and I have some men for you to take a look at as well. Pardon us but we are going window shopping." My Mom smiled as she and Maryland walked away chatting like they were old friends. That's when I heard a whistle off in the distance. I turned to Harry and he looked at me.

"Did you hear a lonely whistle just now?" I asked Harry.

"Yes, I did. I wondered where it came from?" He asked as his Mom gave him a big hug and stood there with us all talking for a while, she seemed to fit right in with all of us with no problem. And it seems that Daisy and Mongo are pretty inseparable as well. The two of them have been running and playing with each other between staying close to Karen and Grandma May of course.

There were so many people here and I as so many new faces that were form the Redwoods Clan and the Montana Clan plus all the other Were's that came including the Doctor and his family from the Veneta Were-Bear's. Harry and I just sort of wandered off on our own to get something to eat and have a seat next to our friends. Right Around the Cornerstone was playing and there were a lot of young people dancing and having fun. My family, my friends and my Were-Community were all getting along and everyone was mingling and it just made my heart feel so good to see it all. I think after Harry and I finished eating our very late dinner that we are going to disappear and make our mating official.

## Chapter 42

We snuck off from the celebration with only letting our parents and my grandparents know that we were leaving. I saw Amanda and sent her and Trina a text letting them know not to bother coming to my house tonight, which they already knew anyway. They had planned on taking the guys home to their houses since there was no reason not to anymore. I got a thumbs up emoji and a smiley face tongue hanging out emoji from them. I know that Harry had sent Terry and Jerry a text as well and we said our good night's to Mongo and Daisy, which Mongo had decided that he should keep watch over Daisy and Karen tonight just in case, which I thought was super cute. We took the golf cart home that Mom had borrowed from Grandpa, he wouldn't miss it and he had several others anyway.

We parked the golf cart by the side of the house and once we had climbed out of the cart. I met Harry at the front of the cart and he took my hand as we walked to the door. We were alone finally and no one was going to stop us from doing what we were meant to do from the beginning. I unlocked the front door and we walked in still holding hands. I led the way into the house and Harry closed the door with his foot and spun me around and into his arms. He picked me up and walked us into the bedroom where the girls had not only cleaned my room but had at some point changed the sheets and made my bed. Then they even placed rose petals all over my bed and on the floor making a trail to the bathroom. Harry and I smiled as each other and he wiggled his eyebrows at me with a very big smile on his face.

"Why do you suppose they made a trail to the bathroom Lass? Should we take a look?" He asked me as he sat me down on my feet.

"I'm intrigued myself, let's go and take a look." I said as I started for the bathroom.

"They have to have snuck away while we were busy talking to people and set all this up." I said as we walked into the bathroom and the garden tub had been filled with warm water and rose petals. The petals were on the floor on the counter and in the tub. Harry and I looked at each other and smiled while we started to take off our clothes.

"Wait, do we really want to take off our own clothes for the first time with each other or do we want to prolong this and take each other's clothes off?" I asked as I stopped to taking off my clothes to watch Harry take off his shoes. Harry got his second shoe off and stopped to look at me. My sandals were going to take me a few minutes to get off because of the lacing but I was willing to watch him take off his clothes while I still had mine on.

"Well we are going to have a rather long life together and this may be our first time together but it will not be our last." Harry was saying as he dropped to his knees and started to untie the laces of my sandals as I sat on the side of the tub looking down at him.

"True." I said as I ran my hands through his hair as he was unwrapping the lace and then he switched to the second sandal. Then I leaned forward as he almost finished with the second lace and kissed the back of his neck.

"That is going to get you into trouble sooner than we are going to make it into the tub, My Love." Harry said as he raised his head and dropped the second sandal on the floor with his shoes. Then he stood and started to take off his shirt, as he walked closer to where I sat on the edge of the tub. I couldn't help myself I leaned forward and had to touch his chest and move my hands slowly down from his very strong, muscular chest and down to his very chiseled abs. This man could give Michelangelo's

Adonis a run for his money, talk about perfection and he had just the smallest amount of light red hair on his chest and his love trait that lead into his pants.

"You are so perfect, I just can't stop myself." I said as I stood just enough so that I could place kisses on his chest and make my way down to his love trail making him moan and make noises that I haven't really heard from a man before. I didn't really have very much experience with men and it was mostly in college where it was a wham bam thank you, Ma'am. Harry grabbed the tops of my upper arms and brought me to a standing position with a smile on his face.

"Oh no you don't, I get to see you now My Love." He pushed the shoulder straps of my sundress to the side and let it try to drop to the floor. Have I mentioned how curvy I am with rather large breasts? Dresses do not just drop off of this girl but that was okay because it made if far enough for Harry to reach the back of my bra and unhook it then he helped me to take it off and push my dress down, then he just stood there for a moment staring at my breasts. Which made me a little self-conscious and I tried to cover my breasts with my arms which made Harry blink and then he pushed my arms back down and smiled at me.

"Those are too perfect to cover up Lass." Harry said as he leaned down and took one of my rosy nipples in his mouth and gently suckled and rolled the tip in his mouth on his tongue. This sent a shockwave of pleasure through my whole body starting at the nipple and shooting to my vagina making me feel the wetness starting to flow from the level of excitement I was feeling. My god if he could do that just from suckling my nipple then I was in for a world of pleasure!

My body shook and my legs gave out as Harry caught me before I fell he looked into my eyes and smiled.

"And that is just the beginning Lass." From that moment Harry and I took out time taking each other's clothes off, next I slowly unbuttoned his pants and slowly pulled them and his underwear down his legs. Once they passed his very ridged staff it bounced when it was set free from the underwear. It was huge! Seriously I just don't know if it is even possible that it is going to fit inside of me. I must have gasped when it popped out.

"It's okay Lass, it won't hurt you." Harry said as I finished pushing his pants to the floor and he stepped out of them. He then stood in front of me again, feeling bold I took his very swollen staff in my hand. Now I have given a blowjob before so I knew what to do with a penis in my mouth but what I didn't have experience with was one this large.

"You don't have to do anything you are not comfortable with Lass. I would love to move on to taking the rest of that dress off of you along with your panties. You know our senses are heightened, I can smell you are excited Love." Harry was saying as I leaned forward and took just the tip into my mouth. I did the same thing that he had done to my nipple to the tip of his penis. Harry gasped and started to shake just standing there. So I got bolder and put more into my mouth to get the sides of it wet I licked it a little as well. He placed his hands on my shoulders and begged me to stop. I pulled my mouth away and looked up his very ripped torso at him.

"If you keep that up we will never make it to the best part." He said as he took me by the shoulders and lifted me to a standing position again and as he did so I let go of his staff to see what was next. Harry took my sundress and pulled it along with my panties down to the floor for me to step out of. Then as I stepped out he stopped my left leg and made me set my foot on the side of the tub.

This was something that I had never experienced before. He got down on his knees before me and leaned forward kissing my inner thigh and then he kissed closer to my womanly folds and then he took his hand and widened the folds that protected my womanhood and took my lady bud into his mouth and he suckled it and flicked it like he did my nipple and I almost lost my balance because my whole body went limp but he kept me up. The tingles and the electricity that ran though me made my vagina buzz and I could feel the wetness that was now dripping from my and even I could smell my arousal. I had just had my first orgasm that was not of my own making with my battery operated boyfriend.

I could no longer stand and Harry knew that it was time to move on to the tub if we were ever going to get into it while it was warm. So Harry picked me up and slipped into the tub with me in his arms. I was weak as a lamb I swear I had never felt like this before. We just sat in the tub for a few minutes and then Harry moved me to sit between his legs facing away from him and I laid there in his arms for a little while longer then Harry started putting water on my hair to make it wet.

"I am guessing that was a new experience for you Lass?" Harry was saying as he put more water on my hair. Then he lifted my head and wet it some more.

"That was the most amazing thing that I have every experienced without doing it for myself." I said honestly and with a very large smile on my face.

Harry grabbed the shampoo by the side of the tub and started to wash my hair being ever so gentle. I must have dozed off for a few minutes because I woke when he was rinsing my hair and then he put the conditioner in my hair and rinsed again. I was so relaxed this was the most amazing thing to happen to my body.

Harry then took a wash cloth and started to put my body wash on it and lather it up. He then slowly started washing my breasts slow and lovingly as he went. He missed the parts that were touching with was okay because he then moved on to my lady folds that he had paid so much attention to before and washed me very slowly and rubbed my lady bud that made little shocks shoot through me yet again. This time I knew what was happening I could feel the orgasm building yet again. Then he stopped and started to rinse me bringing a whining to my ears, it was coming from me.

"We aren't done Lass, not by a long shot. But you are so relaxed right now I think that we are going to get out of this tub and I'm taking you to bed so that we can recharge for round two." Harry said as he again lifted me into his arms and climbed out of the tub together. He set me on my feet and I had to touch the counter so that I could stand there while he dried me off before he dried himself off. Then he picked me up again and took me to the bed. He pulled back the covers and laid me down and climbed in with me. I don't remember much after that because I was out in no time I was so far beyond relaxed.

It was few hours later that I woke up and found myself wrapped in Harry's arms. I turned and kissed him awake and with that we moved on to round two that lasted for at least an hour. Once he and I both had a mutual orgasm something that I thought only happened in romance novels, boy was I wrong! We woke each other up three more times before it was morning outside. My body was so sore that Harry and I took another bath that he drew for us. It helped a little bit but it was our stomach's that needed attention now. With a sore body and an empty tummy Harry and I managed to get dressed and into the kitchen in search of food. We were officially a mated pair and we were starting a life together now. Is that amazing or what?

# Epilogue

Exactly one month after becoming a mated pair, Harry and I have been having a blast melding our lives together. Harry has started work for the Oakridge Forest Service along with Daisy. The four of us get to work together most of the time, but he still does his 'Bigfoot Getters' show just not as often.   Harry and I have spent a lot of time with my parents and Grandpa George out in our back property doing our Were-Squatch thing as often as we can, we don't even need a full moon...

Terry and Trina are still together as well as Amanda and Jerry, which leads to the fact that we are planning a wedding and not just any wedding but a triple wedding with them.   Harry's Mom is moving to Oakridge and is helping Grandma May and my Mom with the PWD and we have brought more than a few couples together, mainly the Johnson brothers but a few others too.

Harry and I are just sitting down with my Mom and his Mom to talk about some of the wedding things that we wanted to make sure to incorporate in the big wedding that had to do with just us. Harry is sitting on my right and my Mom on my left as I sat at the head of the table drinking iced tea and thinking that I had thought my life couldn't have gotten better but now I sit here knowing that it had gotten a lot better and not only for me but for Mongo too.  I'm still not sure if Mongo thinks of Daisy as a mate or as a sister, I will have to ask him at some point.

Harry's Mom leaned over him to pat my hand because I wasn't paying attention to what was going on again.

"Are you felling okay dear?" Karen asked as she looked at me. I had been feeling a little run down lately but with the working again as well as the massive sex-a-thon that my man and I have every night, well I've been tired.

"I'm just a little tired Karen, I will be fine." I said as I set my glass down. My tummy was doing flip flops right now so I placed my hand on my tummy and thought maybe I was just hungry. Harry saw me doing this and leaned over to talk to me.

"Do you need something to eat Lass? I can go and make you something." He said as he started getting up.

"No, we need to decide on our part of the ceremony for the wedding." I said as I touched his hand before he got up and I got a little static shock, we both felt it because he looked at me funny as he sat back down.

"Okay Lass. But you let me know if you need something to eat." He said and looked at my hand while he rubbed his. No one else had seen the shock happen apparently.

"So, your Grandpa George is ecstatic that you all want to have the wedding in the ceremonial place. And that you all want to include the whole Were-Community and mingle with everyone." Mom was so excited that everything was coming together.

"Okay so what else do we need to decide on before we can go and have some lunch because my tummy is putting up a fit that we haven't had lunch yet." I said as I put my hand back on my tummy and looked at my Mom.

"The last decision that you two need to make is where you are going to honeymoon? Everyone wants to put in on that so that you won't have to worry about anything." Mom said as she stood and touched my shoulder as she walked by on her way to the kitchen.

"Well, we have a little time to decide that one so Harry and I will talk about it and get back to you guys." I said starting to stand up and wobbling a little as I stood. Harry stood and took ahold of my arms when he did and we both got another shock which really snapped this time. But this time I felt it not only in the place where we touched skin to skin but also a little snap in my tummy too.

My Mom walked back into the room and saw Harry looking at me and me looking at my tummy.

"Is everything okay?" She asked but she had a strange look on her face. Karen walked around Harry and touched my tummy which made my Mom do the same. They both got a shocked look on their faces.

"Carrie, Lass touch me again." Harry said as he too touched my tummy as I stood there with them all three touching my tummy I reached up and touched his cheek and we both got the electric shock again but this time they all three must have felt it because they all pulled their hands off my tummy at the same time. Mom looked at Harry and asked him.

"You do know what this means don't you?" My Mom asked Harry who then looked at me and smiled the biggest smile I had even seen on his face outside the bedroom that is. My Mom may have been asking Harry if he knows what it means when you feel the mate shock when you are not a bitten mate. According to Tom's Mom it meant you were pregnant and with as much wonderful sex as Harry and I have been enjoying, I can believe it.

"I think the Lass just figured it out as well. We are expecting aren't we Love?" Harry asked me to make sure that I had come to the same conclusion as I just had.

So many things were going through my brain right now. I am getting married to my soulmate, who is also my Were-Squatch mate and my best friend who has brought such love and joy into my life. And now I am going to have a baby? This is so amazing and I am sure that everyone can see every emotion passing across my face right now as well.

Harry picked me up and twirled me around with laughter and excitement. My Mom and my future Mother-in-law were holding each other and laughing.

"We are going to be Grandmother's!" My Mom yelled as she and Karen hugged each other like they had something to do with it, while I am being swung around like crazy making me super dizzy. But I am happy and laughing too. Harry loosened his grip on me and let me slide down the front of him until I was on my feet again.

"Lass you have made me the happiest Scot in the entire World!" And then he gave me one of those soul sizzling kisses that make us both breathless after we got passed the mate shock that is. I had heard happily ever after was for fairy tales well I got my beast and he says I am his beauty! So I guess this fairy tale has a very happy new beginning because it sure isn't an ending, we have a long life together ahead of us and we are going to love every minute of it!

## **<u>Not</u> The End**

## **The Beginning!**

Made in the USA
Thornton, CO
05/07/22 22:56:55

8a5f6fa3-fd68-40bf-957f-83400f87c3b1R01